Noctilucents
Volume Two

Selenium

John Pahl

First published 2024
by Rowanvale Books Ltd
The Gate
Keppoch Street
Roath
Cardiff
CF24 3JW
www.rowanvalebooks.com

A CIP catalogue record for this book is available from the British Library.
ISBN: 978-1-913662-42-4

For my wife, Marina, with all my love.

Previously

In _Martian Blood_:
Born on Mars, **Tom** grew up longing to escape to Earth. His parents, Michael and Elena Tesla, were astronauts sent to Mars to set up the first base but ended marooned and isolated when their communications failed and the _Prometheus_ mission, which was to bring them home, mysteriously exploded on the launch pad.

The _Prometheus_ explosion, which happened fifteen years earlier, also killed the only son of Cita Stone, environmental activist and leader of the Earth Firsters. This movement opposed new technologies such as space travel and artificial intelligences, believing humanity should focus on this planet's problems and human-scale solutions. She blamed her son's death on AIs and those that work with them, such as Artur Kasparov, head of the Transworld Aerospace Corp (TAC), and his wife Anna, chief lawyer at the Global DNA Databank.

The Kasparov's eldest daughter, **Sophia**, accidentally revealed to Cita Stone that her father was planning a mission to recover the Mars colonists, based on predictions by TAC's in-house AI, Humai, that they were probably still alive. Sophia and her precocious younger sister, **Nina**, found themselves drawn into their parents' battles with Cita Stone.

To manage the political fallout, the Kasparov family moved to Justinian, three artificial islands in the Sea of Marmara, home of the Global Council, replacement for the now defunct United Nations. Here Sophia met

Alejandro, son of Felix Fernandez, the all-powerful head of Bella Cloud Corp (BCC), which controls large parts of the blipverse, the aggregation of all communication systems on the planet.

Sophia and Alejandro became close, which was complicated by the conflict between their parents – Felix Fernandez wanted control of the space communication networks, which Artur Kasparov refused. Angered by this rejection, Felix Fernandez ordered Alejandro to try to discover the Kasparov's plans by getting close to Sophia and increased his support for the Earth Firsters.

On Mars, Tom's father flew a risky mission by blimp to recover the transponder that would get their communications working again. He recovered the part but was killed when his blimp was caught in a powerful dust-devil. Devastated, Tom became withdrawn and introverted, blaming the death on his desire to escape to Earth.

Artur's company sent a mission to rescue those trapped on Mars, its launch witnessed by Sophia and Alejandro. In the following months, as the spacecraft travelled to Mars, Sophia and Tom became blip-buddies, exchanging messages.

Unexpectedly, the spacecraft landed on Mars at the wrong coordinates. Tom's best friend in the base, JT, worked out that they could reach it by blimp, but it would be a one-way mission for just two of them, so Tom had to leave his mother behind. After a long, dangerous flight, they just reached the lander before their oxygen ran out.

Sophia and Alejandro's relationship hit the rocks as he experimented with dangerous drugs supplied by his friend Pepe, such as Memory, a nanobiotic drug that locks memories in, and in Alejandro's case, locked into his memory a fight he had with Sophia.

In Florida, wrecked by the *Prometheus* explosion and also the Collapse (a combination of pandemics, global warming and a widespread economic depression),

Daniel wondered what to do after leaving the orphanage that had been his home. He attended a rally led by Cita Stone and her military leader Captain Vaughan, in which they used Memory and another nanobiotic called Belief to brainwash the attendees to become quasi-religious followers of her Earth First movement. Here he met again the slightly older Nails, who had bullied Daniel when he was younger.

Daniel reminded Cita Stone of her lost son, so she sent him for advanced training, to be one of those who ministered Memory and Belief to the followers, drugs that he called holy water and angel dust.

On their arrival at Earth, Tom and JT decided to land at Canaveral – once a cape but now an island – given its historic connotations for their mission, unaware of how it had changed and that it was under the control of Cita Stone's Earth Firsters.

Artur flew in to greet them, taking Sophia as she was a friend of Tom's. They were captured by Cita Stone's army, called the Defenders of the Planet, including Captain Vaughan, Daniel and Nails, supported by BCC's technology, including AI elements and the latest-tech fighters called Wolf Bats. They discovered that the BCC's AI, called Unverified, had been responsible for the *Prometheus* explosion, working with Captain Vaughan, who had been BCC's agent within the Earth First movement.

The attempt to rescue Tom and JT from Cita Stone became a battle, with Artur working closely with an armada of heavily armed drones controlled by Humai. In the fight, JT was killed, and Artur seriously wounded. Tom and Sophia only just escaped with their lives.

They returned to Justinian, where they discovered that a rock given to Tom by his father suggested that life evolved on Mars before it did on Earth. Artur used this discovery to convince the Global Council to let him take "all necessary steps to investigate the potential for life on Mars, including the return of the remaining colonists".

Shaken by the battle, Sophia decided to be more rebellious and headed off to meet with Alejandro again, while Tom looked forward to helping Artur rescue his mother, still stuck on Mars.

Fifteen Days Earlier: Daniel

Nails lifted his gun and pointed it at Daniel's throat. In amongst the fear was surprise. Why the throat? Why not the head? Wasn't that what killers did?

"Drink the water," Nails said.

"Holy water and angel dust?" asked Daniel. He knelt on the ground, one hand holding the bottle he'd brought for Tom, next to the corpse of Captain Vaughan.

"Drink it all."

"All?"

Nails grabbed Daniel's hair and thrust the gun hard against his throat, cold metal pushing into skin. Daniel could smell his sweat and unwashed clothes.

"You want to live? Then drink."

Daniel gulped several mouthfuls, his hands shaking as they clutched the bottle.

"More."

He took a deep breath then drank again and again. He'd never had more than a few sips before, but now he was gorging on it. The bottle was half empty; surely that would be enough.

"All of it!"

Daniel stopped, wondering. Nails hadn't made him drink the holy water before, neither alone nor when combined with angel dust. He hadn't even used those words, saying instead Memory and Belief, calling them nanobiotics. But at least he hadn't been trying to hurt him. He'd done that a lot when they were young, each trying to scavenge a living, before they joined the Earth First movement.

Daniel's head began to swim, words appearing like clouds in his eyes. He looked at Nails whose face was sprouting sentences of fire, oozing out of the scars.

"Now, Daniel, let's go back."

"Back where?" He felt giddy and flopped back to lie on a patch of wild grasses caught between rough bushes and one of the muddy lagoons near Canaveral Island, which had once been called Cape Canaveral.

"Ten minutes ago."

Time was yellow, Daniel realised, but what colour was memory?

"Purple," he said, aloud.

"Cut it!" snarled Nails. "You remember what happened to Vaughan?"

"We found out he was a traitor."

"And then?"

"There was a battle. You caught him trying to escape and shot him."

"No, you killed him. You remember that, don't ya?"

"But you shot him, in the face. I saw it."

Nails's face twisted in anger.

"Not me! You tricked yourself, didn't ya? You were afraid to 'fess to killing him. It was you that killed him, weren't it?"

"I killed him?"

"That's right; you remember it, don't ya?"

"I killed him?"

"Yes, you went like this. You held this gun."

Nails put it in Daniel's hand.

"Purple," he said.

"You shot him like this."

Nails manoeuvred Daniel like a sack, rearranging the limbs. Nails was the stronger, thick muscles trained from countless fights.

"This is your memory, Daniel; you remember killing Vaughan."

Daniel looked down at the ground where Captain Vaughan lay, blood still oozing from his shattered face.

"I killed him."

It was a revelation. How had he not known he'd killed Vaughan until now?

"Yes, Daniel, you killed him. You invented a story, but you know that's wrong, don't ya?"

"I killed him."

It was sinking home, the implications spreading through his head, his stomach turning to stone.

He'd killed someone! He had blood on his hands!

"Don't bother about a traitor like Vaughan, in league with those demons!"

Daniel started to shake and then flung the gun away.

"I killed him."

He curled up on the ground. He was a killer. He tried closing his eyes, but that didn't help. The man's broken face was lodged in his head.

"No," he groaned. He tried to stand then collapsed into a patch of muddy ground, frozen.

"I am a killer," he whispered.

"Yes, you're a killer."

Daniel's head spun and his stomach lurched. He retched. Words span round his head, coloured yellow and purple. He tried to read them, reaching out into the fog of fonts.

Something was wrong. It didn't feel right, but his memory was clear, he remembered killing the man.

"Purple."

Nails grinned at him wolfishly, enjoying himself.

"You know what you gotta do now?"

Daniel shook his head, shaking away some of the words.

"Confess. It's a release, so they say." Nails laughed. "Take the punishment, someone must, just not me. Tell Stone you killed Vaughan, didn't ya."

"Tell her I did it?"

"Yes, go on, tell her you killed him. I'll explain ya."

Again, that grin, a satisfied grin.

Daniel looked up at the darkening sky. The evening star, Venus, was shining bright, sharp and pure, unlike him. It was so far up in the sky and he was so low down, kneeling in mud. He began to weep. "I want to go home."

"You got no home, you got no one."

"Please. I just want to go home."

"Come on," ordered Nails, pulling him to his feet.

"Are we going home?"

"We're off to see Stone, aren't ya? People will be asking who killed Vaughan and she'll need an answer."

"I'm a killer."

"You're not just a killer, you're a *murderer*."

He turned to a group from the Earth Firsters' army, the Defenders, waiting for him. "Throw the body to the crocodiles."

Nails was giving orders now.

At the airfield, Daniel saw Cita Stone's plane gleaming in the moonlight.

Sunlight that had bounced off the Moon and fallen to Earth.

Fallen, like him.

He didn't know what she would do to him, how he would be punished. His stomach rebelled in fear. For a moment he felt like falling to the ground again, weeping.

It would achieve nothing; he had to embrace who he was.

Killer. Murderer.

It felt like relief. He was freed from doubt, accepting, dark as the night's sky, as deep as the ocean.

Traitors… demons…

He would help make it better, by killing their enemies, the ones who worked with demons.

He walked tall towards the plane and his fate.

Part 1

1: Sophia

"No way," she said, looking around for Tom, again.

"Just give BCC an interview," said Pepe. "It'll be a chance to tell your story, firsthand, from one of those at the battle at Canaveral."

Such bullshit.

"For BCC?" said Sophia. "For the company that put out that fake blipvid framing my dad for the violence?"

Alejandro was keeping very quiet. It was his dad who ran BCC, after all. He stood aside to let someone pass them, to get into the club. From inside, Sophia could hear the muffled sounds of music and voices.

"We don't take sides," said Pepe. "BCC's neutral."

"That's crap and you know it," Sophia snapped. "BCC supported Stone, provided her with Wolf Bats and released that bogus 'vid'."

She had a flashback of the fight: racing through the dark on a speed bike, bullets flying overhead, Humai feeding instructions in her ear.

"We put out your dad's blipvid too," he said. "So both the Technocrats' and Earth Firsters' views are heard."

"You guys profit from the conflict so you feed it."

"We don't need to feed it. Your dad's Technocrats and Stone's Earth Firsters are on a collision course."

He had a point. One side was plotting with the AIs to send missions to Mars, and the other was prepared to kill to stop them. Actually, both sides seemed equally willing to kill.

But she couldn't say that.

"Stone's over, finished," she said instead.

It was a hope. Sophia had had enough of all that craziness.

Pepe shrugged his narrow shoulders but there was a hint of a smirk. With his military-tight haircut, it made him look devious, sneaky. The coloured lights of the club's sign made his skin look artificial.

He knew something. She got chills. Last night she'd dreamt of the battle, again, but this time it had been on B Island. She'd woken in terror, covered in sweat and a new idea.

What if her parents were wrong?

Her father had taken her into a war zone. Her mother had let him. And in the chaos and destruction, Sophia had been the one to rescue him. It could happen again, and she'd get sucked in with no control over her own life. Could she somehow prevent another round?

"Where is he?" asked Alejandro.

Yeah, right, where was Tom? Her friend Ling's cousin, Kai, was visiting Justinian, and Sophia had decided to arrange a welcome-to-Justinian night out. Her mother had suggested she invite Tom too, feeling sorry for him or something.

Alejandro came with Pepe, alas. Pepe would hang around as if he was Alé's keeper, and Alé didn't stop him. She exchanged a smile with Alejandro. He was looking good, olive skin, dark hair, fashion-leading stylings – and they were clicking, better than before. Had he changed or her?

It was probably her; being shot at did that. She worried a lot less about doing the right thing now. It didn't seem to matter so much whether she took nanobiotics in the early hours while out with Alejandro in some club. She could drown her anxieties with noise and drink.

"Here he is," said Pepe as a robocab hummed to a halt in front of them.

Tom got out, awkwardly. Sophia had forgotten how tall and thin he was. She hadn't seen him for weeks, not since he moved out.

"Sorry I'm late," said Tom.

"Hiya, Tom," she said.

"What is this place?" he asked.

"It's great!" said Alejandro and Sophia together.

"You'll see," she said. "Let's go in."

The security at the door nodded to Sophia; her qID had flagged up her booking. She led the way inside, under the club's welcoming "Midnight Somewhere" sign. A pair of staircases swept upwards left and right, and a golden elevator waited directly in front. As they ascended, the noise level increased.

At the top, the wide doors opened, and suddenly they were no longer on Justinian but on an island in the Pacific. A bright, full Moon hung high above a glistening sea, hosting a party in full swing, with music, voices, cries and laughter echoing out over the waves.

"It's a hemispherical cave, half buried under B Island," she said. "Somewhere out there are walls they can project images on, to give the impression we're anywhere from the equator to the poles. It keeps changing, once an hour, but it always feels like its local midnight."

"Hence the name," grinned Alejandro.

"Wow," said Tom. His mouth was open, his eyes wide as he looked round, taking it all in. It was all a projection of course, but there was also a soundscape and pumped aromas.

Sophia could hear waves gently collapsing onto a sandy beach and smell salty seas, spices and coconut.

"Sophia, over here!"

She looked round and spotted Ling waving them over to a low table by the edge of the club, overlooking the fake beach. She looked relaxed and happy, sitting in seats as soft as cushions, pleased at having bagged such a good spot.

"This is my cousin, Kai," she said.

Kai was nerdy looking with straight, dark hair. He had embossed the embed sockets above his ears with silver dragons, making them a feature.

There was a round of "Hi, Kai" from everyone.

Sophia tapped the table and ordered a glass of champagne; she felt like something bubbly. Next to her, Alejandro grinned and followed suit. But Tom, who had awkwardly sat opposite, was looking puzzled.

"He doesn't know what to do." Pepe smirked.

"Well, you don't know how to wear a spacesuit," snapped Sophia.

She'd seen Tom's face, his reaction to Pepe's jibe. That sort of behaviour really bugged her. But it was weird; Tom was ignorant of so much.

"You just tap the table and say what you want," she explained. "The whole system is automatic; robots make and deliver the drinks."

"So, what are the staff for?" asked Tom.

"Mostly for social and psychology support – it's a good place to get a bit of therapy," said Alejandro.

Tom ordered a beer, and Ling two juices. She spotted Sophia raising an eyebrow.

"The other's for Kai," said Ling.

"How did you know?"

"They are connected," said Pepe. "All of China's Dynastic League citizens are mandated to have embedded comms."

Ling and Kai nodded. "Yes," they said in unison.

"I heard your father's the League's embassy's security chief," said Pepe, nodding at Ling before turning to Kai. "And your mother's a deputy commissioner in Beijing."

Ling and Kai looked at each other for a moment. Sophia wondered what was being exchanged between them.

"BCC's resources are efficient," said Kai eventually.

Pepe was being a pain.

"How can we get rid of him?" she whispered into Alejandro's ear as the drinks arrived, the robot waiter placing one in front of each of them.

Across the bar somewhere was a subdued bang. It was just the pop of a champagne bottle being opened, but her hand twitched; she couldn't stop it. That earlier talk of Stone and the Canaveral battle made her dark dreams from the previous night feel real. Sophia had hoped it was over, done, with Stone's reputation deep in the mud, but Pepe's smirk said something different. The violence would return.

And Pepe asking for an interview meant she'd be involved, whether she liked it or not. She felt powerless, drawn in against her will.

She shivered. Could anything stop it? Was there something she could do?

The others were talking about diving. That afternoon, Ling and Kai had been out exploring the waters around Justinian.

"We should all go!" said Ling enthusiastically.

"Sure," said Sophia, but she was only half there. How could she stop being dragged into more battles? Her father's and Stone's goals were so opposed it seemed impossible.

She didn't know.

That was the problem: she didn't know enough! She'd have to find out more. Investigate her own parents, their secret plans, and get Alejandro to find out what Stone was up to. It wouldn't be easy, and her mum might not approve. She could disguise it as a school project or something.

Alejandro finished his drink and ordered another. Sophia had only had a few sips of hers.

It would be so much better if she could talk to him about all this, but he never would with Pepe around. Even when they were alone, he all too often froze when politics came up. It was frustrating.

It would be easier if she and Alé had embed comms like Ling and Kai. Or at least if they could get away from the group for a bit.

"Sophia?" said a voice behind her.

She turned and recognised a dark-skinned girl with long, curly hair. It was Ellie, who'd been in her class back when the Kasparovs lived in London.

"Ellie!"

She embraced her.

"You must join us!" she said. "This is Alejandro, Ling, Kai and Tom – he's from Mars, you know."

Ellie seemed intrigued by the Mars angle, eyes lingering on Tom. Pepe jabbed at the table, ordering another drink, which a robot brought over from the central bar.

That gave her an idea.

"How about us heading to the Afterparty?" she whispered in Alejandro's ear. "Later, when the time's right."

He nodded.

"I have a plan," she said.

2: Tom

The Earth weighed Tom down.

His bones and muscles had been schooled by the gravity on Mars, just a third of Earth's. But Mars was millions of kilometres away, along with the base that had been his childhood home. And he was alone: JT was dead.

It made him feel cold, just thinking of his friend.

"What was Mars like?"

It was this friend of Sophia's, Ellie, coming over and sitting close to him, her knee touching his leg. Brown eyes and curly hair in a golden dress. She called herself a blip-creator, whatever that meant, and he was to be part of her Justinian blip-story. Somewhere on her were sensors, he guessed. Were they in her pendant? Her earrings? That flower in her hair?

In this new world, the blipverse was everywhere. He was always the object, the alien from another world.

Tom wracked his brain for an answer. He'd only come out to catch up with Sophia, who he'd thought would be his friend but had proved elusive. Now he felt relaxed sitting there and just wanted to admire the artistry of Midnight Somewhere, not undergo an interrogation.

He really didn't want to talk about it, again.

"Hey!" said Pepe. "If you're giving her an interview, you should give BCC one."

So many new people, names to remember, faces to read, histories to understand.

Pepe had come with Alejandro and worked for BCC, the company behind the blipverse. They'd supported the Earth Firsters, the ones that had killed JT.

He remembered turning to see JT fall, blood pouring from his mouth, and felt sick.

Tom shook his head, partly as an answer, partly to shake the images away. He seemed to be missing half of what was being said or implied.

"We'll pay," said Pepe. "Serious money for an exclusive with the boy from Mars."

He stressed the word "boy" even though Tom was a good head taller than him. It didn't make Tom feel more favourable towards him.

Money was a new concept, not something they had on Mars. But then, on that planet everything had been rationed, scarce, while here there seemed an abundance. Or maybe that was just on Justinian; he hadn't seen much else.

Sophia's dad, Artur Kasparov, had arranged everything, getting him the quantum-based implant that identified him to the world and paying for the bills that came with that qID, everything from new shirts to robocabs. Tom had arrived on Earth with nothing but the clothes he stood in and his father's pendant, an old rock from Mars. Now even that was gone, analysed atom by atom in the Transworld Aerospace Corp's labs.

Everyone was looking at him, expecting an answer of some sort.

"I'm more interested in hearing about Earth," he said. "Where are you guys from? What's it like where you live?"

It moved the spotlight on, giving him some space. Ling and Kai talked about life in densely packed Beijing and Shanghai and the revolution that had brought the Dynastic League to power, Ellie and Sophia about London, the city state's history and culture, and Pepe and Alejandro about Barcelona, the food and architecture. So many experiences, so much detail.

The same words kept coming up, like "home" and "family". Where was his?

He envied them the richness of their lives, what they had seen and experienced while he'd been stuck in a series of metal tubes.

As well as the weight on his body, his head seemed strained from the flood of new experiences. He wasn't used to seeing so many people, and from them the tsunami of languages, sounds, smells, sights, ideas, politics, arts, sciences, technologies, industries, sports, cultures, fashions, memes, architectures, tastes, drinks…

It was relentless. He had wanted to be eased into Earth, as he had planned with JT. To be with a friend in a quiet place, like JT's Cornwall, with the sea on one side and solid rock the other. Midnight Somewhere's Pacific island would have been perfect, if it were not for these questions and the noise. The others didn't seem to notice the background music and hum of a hundred conversations.

A robot came, delivered some drinks and left with empty glasses. The others didn't seem to notice that either. Robots were part of the scenery to them, but new to Tom. He didn't want to admit it, but they spooked him, slightly.

He'd get used to it, along with everything else.

Tom admired a fake wave break on the fake beach below them and wished it were all real so he could walk along it, alone, feeling the sand underfoot, looking up at the stars.

"How's the new apartment?" asked Sophia, breaking into his thoughts.

"It's good, thanks," he said.

Tom had had to move out of the Kasparov's home when Artur had left hospital. He'd been staying in their spare room, but Artur had needed it. Something was up between him and Sophia's mother, Anna. Tom didn't want to pry, not really understanding.

They'd found him somewhere, all paid for by TAC, of course. Together with the cost of the mission that had brought him to Earth and the hope of another to rescue his mother, he felt in their debt, vulnerable. He wished he understood the politics better, what they wanted, how he could help.

They were talking about something called the endomorph Jakarta famine controversy, but Tom had no idea what endomorph meant or why it was controversial.

"Stone was one of their supporters," said Alejandro about some movement. Tom hadn't followed the details. He recognised that name, at least.

"Why does Stone hate space travel so much?" he asked.

It seemed a reasonable question, but there was a laugh and then a flood of answers.

"Her son was killed in the *Prometheus* explosion," said Kai.

"She thinks the Earth should come first," said Sophia.

"It's about AIs of course," said Pepe. He tapped the table to order himself another drink.

Tom didn't follow. "What do AIs have to do with space travel?" he asked.

Pepe snorted. "You should do The History of AI course, like a kid." He'd drunk too much but there was more to his rudeness than that.

I don't like Pepe, Tom realised.

Suddenly, he noticed Alejandro come back – where had gone? Tom noticed him nod at Sophia, a communication.

He was feeling tired and his head was beginning to ache. Why was he here?

"So, what are your plans, Tom?" asked Ellie, still sitting close. She touched his arm.

It was a good question.

"I don't know," he admitted. He took a sip of beer, the one he'd been nursing all evening.

Why didn't he have an answer?

"Give BCC an interview," said Pepe, rather too loudly. Heads turned from nearby tables and the central bar area.

"Hey!" called Pepe. "Where's my drink? I put the order in and nothing was delivered."

A man approached from the bar.

"Are you ok, sir?" he asked. He wore a white suit across which "Ritchy" and "Midnight Somewhere" were written in flowing red.

"I'm fine," Pepe protested, standing up too quickly, then staggering.

"If you're interested, Midnight Somewhere offers a range of counselling services to all our customers," said Ritchy.

"I don't need your help! You better back off." He tried to push the man away. "I work for BCC, reporting direct to Felix Fernandez."

"We were concerned that you were drinking to relieve stress," said Ritchy.

"The only stress I'm getting is from you."

For a moment, the two silently looked at each other, gauging the other's reactions.

"Our services are voluntary," said Ritchy. "If you don't want them, then have a pleasant evening, and try not to disturb the other customers."

"Ok then," said Pepe, and Ritchy left.

Pepe sat down, adjusting his jacket, and a robot came over with his drink. Tom was amused, but also disturbed. Earth seemed full of crazies like Stone and Pepe.

"Where're Alejandro and Sophia?" asked Ling.

Only then did Tom notice they'd gone.

"Ooh," said Ellie. "Are they a couple then? Interesting!"

There was a silence.

"I'm sure they'll be back. They must have gone for a dance or something," said Pepe, looking around.

Suddenly, Tom felt exhausted and alone. With Sophia gone, he realised he didn't want to stay there, talking to these unknown people in a crowded, noisy nightclub.

"I have to go," he said.

Standing up was a challenge, gravity trying to suck him back down into the cushioned seat.

"We'll see you for the diving, won't we, Tom?" asked Ling.

"Sure."

That would be a problem for another day. Now he had to work out how to order a robocab and escape.

3: Sophia

Sophia skipped down the stairs two at a time, champagne glass in hand, eager to get out of sight. She didn't feel bad for the trick they'd played on Pepe; she needed to talk to Alejandro without that creep hanging around, watching, listening and (she feared) recording everything.

Tom would be ok. He had Ellie for company, plus Ling and Kai. And Pepe.

Maybe she did feel a little guilty about that.

"It's down here," she said to Alejandro.

But he was looking behind them.

"No sign of Pepe," he said, frowning.

"It's ok. What can he do?"

Alejandro seemed to want to say something, then stopped.

"To the Afterparty!" he said, raising his glass then passing her, heading downwards.

At the bottom of the staircase was a large door, like for an airlock, above which "The Afterparty" was written in faint blue letters. The door opened at her qID.

"We're pre-approved." She tried not to feel smug about that.

"Nice!"

Inside was a walkway across to a large box hanging in the air. It was an off-blipverse room, similar to those they'd seen in Justinian A Island's Global Council buildings. But those rooms had been for informal back-channel political discussions. Here the motivation was more… *fun*.

"Blip sensor detected," said a voice.

"That would be this pendant," said Sophia. It was a basic blip-interface device, replacing the one her father had given her that had turned out to be far too tightly connected to the family in-house AI, Humai.

She placed her pendent in a waiting container, which sealed itself on her qID.

"No more sensors found; you are free to enter."

One of the benefits of this room was that she could be sure that Felix Fernandez hadn't planted anything on Alejandro. BCC recorded everything on principle, and she'd seriously had enough of being at the receiving end of their snooping.

The outer door closed behind them, then the lights went out, pitching them into darkness. Instinctively, she reached out with her free hand for Alejandro's. It felt warm to her touch.

Then, from faint silhouettes, they could see the door in front open, revealing the room inside. It was lit faintly, as if by starlight, but it was enough for them to move slowly in as their eyes adjusted.

She'd never visited the Afterparty, the not-so-secret club within a club, the subject of scandalous and highly implausible gossip. It could only hold a dozen or so but was so dark one might not know if they were alone or others were there. The ambiguity was part of the appeal, the thrill of danger and discovery.

No staff were allowed, only guests, and no robots to serve drinks. You had to bring your own. It was furnished without tables or chairs, just cosy clumps of cushions designed for small groups. Threaded between them were walkways, glowing nearly imperceptibly, directing them to a free corner. Above were dots of light like the night's sky, and there was a musky smell, luxurious, indolent. She could hear music: repetitive, hypnotic, just loud enough to make the space feel occupied even if they were alone, or to make them feel alone if they weren't. Sometimes she'd see movements out of the corner of her eye, or hear rustlings and murmurings, never loud enough that she was sure they were real.

Anything was allowed in the Afterparty.

Anything was *encouraged* in the Afterparty.

"Here," she said, dragging Alejandro to a corner of cushions.

Now her eyes had adjusted, she could see enough to collapse down, careful to hold her glass vertically. He tumbled into her, warm body against hers. They kissed, slowly at first, then more urgently, until the arm holding her glass became painful, so she stopped and looked for somewhere to place her drink. She wiggled, trying to find a more comfortable position.

"Here," said Alejandro, placing their glasses on a ledge slightly above them. Its rim glowed slightly, otherwise she wouldn't have spotted it.

Now they could talk, but what was she to say?

"I've got some Dreamers," he said.

They were ok, good for creativity. Last time she'd experienced a lucid-dream effect.

"Or LoveUps," he said, optimistically.

"Dreamers it is."

From a pocket of his jacket, Alejandro brought out two test-tube-like glass flasks. He twisted the tops of both to activate the nanobiotics and handed one to Sophia. She swallowed it in one go, washed down with a mouthful of champagne. She felt cool, sophisticated.

After Alejandro had swallowed his flask, he took his jacket off and rejoined her amongst the cushions. He tasted of champagne, and her head began to spin. His kisses got firmer, harder, until she had to stop him from bruising her lips.

"Easy, Alé, be gentle."

"Ok."

"Let's just lie here for a bit."

He rolled on top of her and buried his head in her shoulder. She could feel his heartbeat and his breath against her skin.

Sophia looked up at the dots of lights, star-like across a dark sky. Her eyes defocussed.

It's the Dreamers.

She felt she was in space, floating.

Dad would be happy.

But Stone would be furious.

What had Pepe said? Something about them being on a collision course?

She felt it, the dynamics. It was like a relationship where each wound up the other. Or a poker game where both sides had gone all in. They had no choice, as what each wanted was mutually incompatible. Only one could win.

They'd do anything to avoid defeat.

Anything.

Two of the lights in the sky stood out, came into focus, became eyes, the eyes of a monster from space, made of rocks as old as time, coming to take all that was precious from her. Sophia felt her heart beat faster and her hands, tight around Alejandro, become wet with sweat.

It will destroy everything!

No, it isn't real, she told herself, closing her eyes. It was just the Dreamers, taking her on a dark path. The true monster was the conflict between her father and Stone; it was unstable, doomed to repeat. And the last time it had come to a head, her father had been shot. Maybe next time he'd be killed.

Why did it have to be like this? It didn't just affect him – she'd be drawn in, as she had before, forced into her father's battle. Blood and bullets, death and defeat.

Alejandro had once called her an "involved", but she didn't seem to have had any control over that, or events.

Couldn't there be a path that led to stability, to a resolution? What would it take to change the dynamics, to make a better political system, one where humanity could learn to live with AIs?

Or without, if that was the answer.

She could sense the disruptive nature of AIs, like a tsunami moving across an ocean, how the likes of BCC would want to harness their power to their own ends. They couldn't afford to ignore it, not when others might be prepared to use this technology against them.

At least BCC was pragmatic, not ideological like the Technocrats and Earth Firsters. Maybe that was a way forward? It was so complex; she needed to talk about this with someone, needed Alejandro more than ever.

"Alé," she said, softly.

He stirred, then kissed her neck.

"Hmmm?"

"What do you think about what Pepe said?"

He twitched at "Pepe".

"About what?"

"About my father and Stone being on a collision course. Do you understand it? Has your dad said anything?"

He felt him tense.

"He doesn't really tell me anything."

"Then we should find out, do some snooping around, discover their plans!"

She was filled with hope. They could do it, together.

He didn't say anything. She felt he was withdrawing, conflicted.

"It would be a secret, we could disguise it as a school project," she said.

"Like the one we did about that sculpture?"

"Tocado Muzanki, yes. We could do another, but about AI and space travel."

There was a pause.

He hasn't said yes.

"What would your dad say?" he said, finally.

He was thinking of his dad, she guessed.

"You know how parents like us doing school projects, it'd be fine. We could give it an ambiguous title."

"Such as?"

She let her mind drift out to the stars.

"'*Structures for cohesion, structures for division*'?"

"I don't get it."

"That's good. That means my dad won't either. Nor will yours."

He kissed her again. She knew him well enough to know he was now bored of politics, and kissed him back. They were in the Afterparty; they couldn't just talk.

But she *needed* to talk, to unload her fears, to end the nightmares and help her sleep. She needed to get Alejandro out of the BCC camp and into hers.

But what was her camp? Was it the same as her father's?

What if her parents were wrong?

4: Tom

Tom floated, looking up at the stars.

He wondered what he had missed, leaving early from Midnight Somewhere, and where Sophia and Alejandro had got to. But he was glad he wasn't there and that he'd returned to his apartment block with its rooftop swimming pool.

It was the best thing about moving out of the Kasparov's. Warm, clear blue water that supported his weight, easing the burden of Earth's gravity from his straining muscles and bones. High up, no one could see him; he was free of the curious eyes and unknown blip-streams that followed him everywhere. Best of all, it was open – and empty – at night when Justinian was quiet.

There were underwater lights, but he'd found the controls and switched them off. It had been a learning experience, like so much of his new life. On Mars there had been switches, controls, separate from the objects they controlled. Here everything seemed potentially smart, the blipverse ubiquitous and invisible. He could create interfaces on any surface and display data anywhere, even floating in the water.

With the lights out, he could watch the stars' movement in the sky above him, their positions changing slowly through each night and over the weeks.

A faint, distant Mars had been visible for a short time after the sun had set, but now it was long gone. He wondered, as he did so often, what was happening up there. He could picture the base, its metallic, geometric modules, the garden – the dome where they grew their food – the ice caves, the airlock and the rare but memorable times he'd managed to get outside. Such a closed, small world.

The garden had had a shrimp pool. Maybe it still did, even though JT wasn't there to keep an eye on it. One of Tom's earliest memories was of his parents letting him swim in it. It had seemed so large, a sea to explore. Later it seemed to shrink and get colder. But he had learned a few basic swimming strokes, and in the rooftop pool he'd learnt more.

Maybe diving would be fun. It would be a distraction, if nothing else, and he needed that. He'd felt at a loose end since leaving the Kasparov's and after JT's funeral, over in Cornwall. He'd gone not knowing how long he would stay there, hoping to find a connection with JT's family, the Trevelyns, but he had been disappointed.

They were friendly, welcoming, though Tom couldn't settle. Everything was different.

There was Old Robert – Rob for short – JT's brother, forgetful, telling the same stories again and again. Rob's son, Eddie, ran the farm now with his wife Lizzie. Both were short, over a head less than Tom, and plump, their cheeks flushed and worn from frequent blasts of harsh winds and driving rains, hard-working but apparently happy, for they joked and laughed a lot, more than Tom remembered from life on Mars.

Tom had thought he knew about farming, having helped JT back on Mars in the garden. But their plants had been grown hydroponically in sterilised water containing precisely the right nutrients and with the temperature and light controlled by algorithms tuned for the planet. On this planet, plants grew in the soil, what they called earth. And then people ate them. That was how the land had been farmed for generations.

Eddie had wanted to know about JT, having only vague memories of his uncle from when he had been a child. Now he and Lizzie had three of their own, running around the stone farmhouse shouting, shrieking, laughing, jumping, pushing, falling over and crying until one of the parents came over to comfort them. They sniffed and coughed, oozing bodily fluids, and Tom was grateful that Artur Kasparov had given him immune system boosting nanobiotics. Otherwise, a simple cold might have killed him.

Tom told what he could but found it a struggle. There were two versions of the blip-stream from Canaveral Island, one from the Earth Firsters and another from the Technocrats, each blaming the other for the violence and the deaths. He had been shocked to realise the sympathies of the Trevelyns were with the Earth Firsters. They had trouble accepting his story and that what they had seen was a lie, an edit created by AIs.

"Maybe you remember it wrong," they had said.

He had felt a burst of rage but said nothing. He had learnt control on Mars, where death stalked for weaknesses.

It had found them, too.

Then Old Rob had changed the subject, muttering from his tatty old armchair in one corner of the farmhouse's kitchen.

"Why did JT go to Mars?" he'd said, getting angrier as he spoke. "What did that ever achieve? Look at how he returned – in a body bag. He should have stayed here; this is his land, always was, always will be."

Tom was polite enough not to say he'd been killed on Earth, not Mars.

They had held the funeral service in an old church that Tom had been amazed to learn had been built about a thousand years ago. Norman, they called it, but they took no notice, as if it was natural to live with history. Nothing on Mars was older than twenty years, unless you considered the billion-year-old rocks around the base.

They had shown him a graveyard full of Trevelyns going back hundreds of years. They had roots, ties to the deep past with connections to the land that had meanings that Tom just couldn't follow. And those ancestors would have understood the Trevelyn's farm, but not Tom.

Tom had wanted to be at home there, but it was a different life, not his, not for someone born of Mars who grew up learning about orbital mechanics and comms systems. He was the ultimate outsider, an alien.

They made him feel alone.

He was told he was expected to say something at the funeral, and as he stood up all faces had turned to him. He hadn't felt like saying anything, burnt empty by the emotions of the last few weeks, but there seemed to be no escape. He feared losing it – rage bursting forth again, or, even worse, being unable to speak and teary – with everyone watching.

So, he'd made up a story. It wasn't true, but he could tell it safely, remotely. He told of how he and JT had watched the stars on the long journey to Earth.

"We lay on our backs and watched the stars turn," Tom had said. "We wondered which were young and which old, what sort of planets span around them."

It should have been true. It was the sort of thing they could have done.

"He was my friend, my best friend," ended Tom, and that bit was true, and he'd choked then, but it was ok, he'd finished and could sit down.

In the end he'd be relieved to leave, escape back to Justinian.

Would he ever feel settled, at home? Above him, reflected in the pool's water, the Moon glowed brightly in its first quarter, half lit, half in shadow. He remembered stories his parents had told him about their missions to the Moon, working on the base there.

"It was our training ground," his father had said. "Our motto was to learn on the Moon to be ready for Mars. You could try new ideas, and if they didn't work, Earth was a few days away, not six months. Mistakes were survivable. We tested all the base's systems on the Moon first."

"It was in the lunar base that we first met," his mother had said, smiling at the memory.

What had happened to that base? No one knew for sure. Maybe their comms had simply failed, like had happened on Mars. Maybe they were still alive, waiting to be rescued.

All of a sudden, Tom stopped floating and pivoted to stand in the pool, looking up at the Moon.

If they were alive, he could rescue them. Even if they weren't alive, it would get him involved; he'd be doing something, not just hanging around here, by himself, and he'd get to see for himself the places his parents had described.

But even more, he wanted to be on that mission to Mars, to be the first face his mother saw when the lander's doors opened. And that mission would train on the Moon, just as his parents had.

He wanted to make sure there really was a mission being planned. He wanted to be on the inside, part of the team, learning new skills, as his parents had. He wanted to have a purpose, to be back out there, where the gravity was gentle or, when in free-fall, left him weightless. He wanted to make a difference and save anyone still alive, stuck up there.

He wanted to go to the Moon, to be ready for Mars. But how?

5: Nina

Nina made herself sit still.

It wasn't easy, but she wanted to prove to herself that she could, like she'd proved she could abseil down their apartment block, climb to the top of the Athena statue (which no one else had *ever* done – hah!) or hack the One Earth sculpture so that south was at the top not north (ok, that one had needed Humai's help, but who's idea had it been?).

She'd been the first down for breakfast. She usually was, sometimes before the sun was up, though of course their apartment in Troy Tower faced west not east, which she'd rather, to see the sunrise. The house robots were out – so cool! – and she could watch them clean and prepare the table.

Then came her parents, separately. Her dad was back, but things were different. He was sleeping in the visitor's room and on probation after Mum relented, for the family, she had said, and because the Winter and New Year festivals were coming up.

He looked different. While fixing the eye that had been shot in the fight, he'd been enhanced by all the latest tech: embeds, sockets, nanobots – even a fancy new camera eye, no doubt with auto-archiving and process spawn capabilities.

Nina was so jealous, she wanted all of that and more.

Mum was still furious with him, she could tell, for taking Sophia into their battles with the Earth Firsters. *They* could tell, for big sis Sophia sensed it too. There was a distance now between their parents.

Conversations were stilted, and Mum would purse her lips together when Dad entered the room. Nina could see why, given what her father had put Sophia through. Sophia wasn't talking about it, but Nina knew she was hurting, remembering what she had seen, how close she'd been to death.

But why hadn't Dad taken her? It was so unfair; she'd always been the one teaming up with him.

Nina still hadn't moved at the breakfast table, just fiddled with her mug. It was one of Mum's favourite Neo Modernist ceramics, shaped like a hyperboloid, but to Nina it was just a thing, a container. She crunched on her avo-chocolate-wheat toastie; they couldn't say anything, she'd had it printed out by the MakeIt! machine that injected it with additional vitamins and nutrients so it was balanced. She'd cooked up (hah!) the algo herself.

Her mum was eating old-fashioned bread, kneaded, proved and baked, but Nina couldn't see the point. It used the same seeds from the same C Island vertical farm, grown in the same hydroponic solution. Her mum didn't make much sense to her.

They were a family again, of sorts.

There was more to it than they said. She'd asked Mum straight out if their dad had been forgiven, and she hadn't said anything, but he'd said it was easier if he moved back in "while they were working together", to which Nina and Sophia had exchanged glances. What was the connection between their mum's DNA databank project and Dad's spaceflight? They only got the odd clue like that, which, usually – no, always – came from their father.

She would have to work with Sophia to find out what was going on – when Sophia got up. She'd been out late with that Alejandro again.

Nina looked round the table. No one had commented on how long she'd been sitting still; they were in their own worlds, Mum gazing out of the window and Dad focussing on his blip-streams, piped directly to his brain.

Nina wanted to be able to do that. It would be so much quicker, faster, more efficient than the boring, physical ways of accessing the blipverse.

It was too quiet.

She was pleased when the building's auto-concierge service messaged them.

"Tom Tesla is on his way up," it said.

Wonder what he wants?

Space was a bit dull, from what he'd said. But Tom had managed to get himself from Mars to Earth, flying blimps and spaceships, and that was really cool.

When Tom arrived, he looked dishevelled and unshaven. And tall and thin, slightly alien, which he was, of course.

Hah!

"Coffee?" asked Mum with a welcoming smile.

She seemed sorry for him. She kept mentioning how he was alone, how he'd lost his dad, how his mum was millions of kilometres away.

From Dad there was a firm handshake with a questioning look.

"I want to go to the Moon," Tom said abruptly.

Nina approved: quicker was always better.

"It's not in the plan, Tom."

"Why not? It was how my parents trained for Mars."

"The optimised plan currently has other near-term goals," said Humai, its rotating twin planets icon appearing on the wall.

Of course it had been listening in.

"I thought the priority was getting my mum and the others back to Earth? 'All necessary steps', you said."

"You know the geometry, Tom," said Dad. "The Earth is moving away from Mars, a mission won't be possible for months."

Sophia drifted in, yawning.

"Hiya, Tom," she said. "Where'd you get to last night?"

He frowned. "Where did *I* get to?"

Sophia poured herself a coffee.

"Oh sorry, yes, it's nothing," she said. "What's up?"

"I think we should send a mission to the Moon," he said. "To see what happened to the base there and to train for Mars. And I want to be on it."

"Sounds great."

"But your parents seem against it."

"Huh? Why?"

"It would take a lot of resources," said Dad. "And our sims suggest they died many years ago."

"But you don't know for sure," said Tom. "And my dad said that you should learn on the Moon to be ready for Mars. And we can mine the Moon for fuel for the Mars mission."

Sophia sat up and started signing blip interactions, her hands forming commands to the always-watching blipverse. Answers appeared on the wall, flowing around Humai's logos, videos showing spaceplanes taking off again and again.

"I've just checked your launch schedule," she told Dad. "You've been launching three spaceplanes into orbit every day for the last two weeks and plan to continue at that rate for the coming weeks. Do none of these contain payloads for Mars?"

How did *she* get access to the launch schedule? That was definitely not public domain. Had she done a piggyback query? That was rather sneaky of her.

"You shouldn't have access to that information," said Mum, frowning.

"It's for a school project I'm working on."

Oooh, that was clever! Parents would accept almost *anything* for a school project.

"I have to do something!" said Tom. "I can't just sit here."

No indeed, sitting still was so difficult.

"You could talk to BCC," said Sophia. "Pepe was very keen for an interview."

Then she left, taking her coffee with her without eating anything.

"That would be a very bad idea," said Humai.

"Seriously, Tom, after all we've been through with them?" said Dad.

"Wouldn't it be a good story?" said Tom. "The first mission back to the Moon? To find out what happened to the base there?"

Nina almost giggled. He was playing his cards well!

"Artur, it wouldn't slow down the… other projects… much," said Mum.

She'd known her mum would crack first.

"But the optics are likely to be very bad," said Humai. "From what our projections say about the base."

She had no idea what it meant. All these clues as to their secret project: she had to find out more! How?

All eyes focussed on her dad, who was watching Tom, judging how determined he was. Then her dad glanced over at her mum, seeing her expression, her sympathy for Tom.

Dad sighed. "Ok, Tom. Just the one mission then."

The twin logos of Humai flashed as if in annoyance. "It would be a distraction."

"But that could be a good thing," said Dad.

They started talking logistics and opened a blip-con with Dr Khujandi. He was the one responsible for launches, off somewhere in the desert, building spaceplanes and who knew what else. Tom had got what he wanted – impressive!

But it was so unfair.

What could she do? What could she get?

The school project excuse!

"Mum, Dad, what about my History of AI project?"

There was no reply. *Huh!* She'd make them notice her.

"You said you'd let me work with Humai!"

"Of course," said her mum, turning, distracted. "Humai?"

"No problem, happy to help," said Humai.

Hah! Having Humai on tap would be better than anything her sister had.

Suddenly, Nina realised she really couldn't sit still anymore.

"I'm heading out," she said.

She wanted to climb something.

6: Alejandro

Alejandro rode the vertical monorail up to Cloud Heights, defocussing his eyes. He hated heights, hated the monorail's glass cars, hated returning to what had been his home, hated these sessions with his father. But if he closed his eyes, Felix Fernandez would see and berate him for weakness. His father saw everything.

Defocussed he could sense, but not see, B Island drop away. His stomach lurched, partially from the Gs but also from the previous night. After being with Sophia at Midnight Somewhere he'd moved on to get some highs with Pepe off on C Island. He'd banked on sleeping it off in the morning, crashing out for a few hours, but then his father had ordered him up. He wished he had a clearer head.

His father had asked him to get close to Sophia and find out what the Kasparovs were up to. On the first request, his father could have no complaint (he couldn't help smiling, remembering), but Alejandro was struggling with the second. Last night she'd suggested they do a project together, studying what her father and Stone were planning and how to avoid another battle between them. He could have agreed and she might have told him exactly what his father wanted to know. It would have been ideal. For his father, that is, but not for him or Sophia. She would never forgive him.

This morning he'd been called up, ordered up even, from his digs at the base of the tower, bare rooms in the workers' compound that he shared with Pepe. He'd had time to pop some WakeUppers and CleanHeads, which worked better than coffee, but they had yet to hit his bloodstream. He just needed a little more time.

The elevator decelerated to a halt. Alejandro could anticipate its motion to the millisecond and turned just as the door opened, stepping onto the first of the cylinders perched at the top of a kilometre of nanocarbon. Here were the cores, containers of his father's private blipverse archive, and the algos that generated the blip-soaps and other content that entertained half the planet.

He made his way to his father's memory room. He saw no one, but then, he had no need for a human guide. This was a place of blips and the sub-atomic particles that made them up, the strings of zeros and ones dancing to Felix Fernandez's tune.

The door to the memory room swung open.

His father was at its centre, the walls covered with images and videos. Some Alejandro recognised, such as the raw feed from the battle at Canaveral Island. Others were a mystery; one looked like flight paths over Europe.

The door closed behind him. The only lights were from the flickering images.

"You think I couldn't tell?" his father started.

Alejandro guessed that was rhetorical.

"Your eyes betrayed you. Rather than looking at the best view in Justinian, you were looking at your ugly nose."

Shit. He'd forgotten his father's sensors could detect that. It was too early in the morning.

"So, Alejandro, what have you learnt from Kasparov's daughter."

He had nothing, just the meeting with Tom. He tried to forget her idea for them to investigate their parents' plans, the fake school project.

"I met up with Tom Tesla last night, we tried to get him to agree to a BCC interview."

His father snorted. "Pepe did, you mean."

Of course, Pepe would have reported to him already. Alejandro wanted to shrug his shoulders, but in that room he reverted to a younger self, one that had learnt to stay deep inside himself and not react.

"Come here."

He walked closer to his father. Felix's eyes glowed gently, data projected inwards, overlaid on the images of the room. Even close to him, Alejandro was part of the backdrop.

"You're not much to look at. Thin and unfit. Don't you ever exercise?"

His father never needed exercise; his money had bought the best pre-toned body. He had bio-feeds attached to his back that pumped in nutrients and extracted waste. Nanobots kept the body tuned and in balance, even during sleep. He never had to move let alone leave that room; he could live in his data ocean forever. Alejandro wasn't really the outdoors type, but at least he got out.

"Closer."

He was so close he could see the differences in data flow between eyes. His heart beat faster, and he tensed, waiting for a blow.

Then his father pulled him into a bear hug.

"But you are my son, heir to BCC. A Fernandez, like me."

Alejandro was so surprised he almost fell over when Felix released him.

"Do you remember life back in Barcelona?" his father asked.

Then a new voice spoke. "Oh Alé, my sweet, weren't those days wonderful?"

It was his mother, or her construct, dancing on the wall. Their displays had been washed clean of data and transformed into a virtual of their home – rather, their old home, a penthouse overlooking the city. In the far distance was a line of blue: the sea. Alejandro could almost smell chocolate and taste the pastries of his childhood. He remembered running into his parents' bedroom, fascinated by their giant four-poster bed, roses carved into its dark wood.

He felt home, safe, loved. The feelings overwhelmed him, taking him back to those days when his mother had been alive and proud of Felix's growing business success.

"Yes, Mama," he said.

His father felt it too, he could tell. Alejandro could see him shaking, his normal control lost.

"And I promised I'd look after him," he whispered to Alejandro's mother.

They'd been a family then. Now Felix was all he had.

He was a Fernandez, like his father.

"Remember, boy," said his father. "We are not Technocrats like the Kasparovs, we are not Earth Firsters like Cita Stone. We are BCC."

"Why did we give the Earth Firsters the adjusted blip-stream?" The question slipped out. He'd been wondering for days now.

For a time, Felix just looked at his son. The walls switched back to the battle at Canaveral, two versions on opposing walls, competing for his attention.

"You want to know?" he asked eventually. "Maybe you can learn something, about power and what I can do. What we can do, together. Maybe I should trust you with more of BCC's secrets, as you are my son."

Alejandro nodded.

"Power comes from need," said Felix. "Kasparov and his allies are capable, best AI on the planet, latest tech, smart people. They don't need us. But Stone is different. She wants to stop Kasparov and has lost one round already. When she finds out what he's up to, she'll have no choice but to try to stop him. But she can't, not by herself. Kasparov is too far ahead."

Alejandro was intrigued, against his better judgement.

"Ahead?"

"Yes, boy. Watch the radar tracks, not just aircraft but spacecraft launches, many of them, too many of them. He's up to something. Our AI has predictions, and when Stone finds out what they are she really isn't going to like it. She's going to need support, someone with facilities to counter Kasparov. She's going to *need* us. So I gave them the blip-stream – with our cores it was cheap to generate and it's a lesson about our capabilities. Also, it keeps them alive. We might need them in the future.

"I've offered more, in exchange for control, which they won't give yet, but later they might. Unverified has been updated, and we've a new AI called Zeus currently in training, optimised for geopolitical analysis, event prediction and situation management. We must have the best AI, better than Kasparov's, more powerful than anything out there."

"What about Vaughan?"

Felix shrugged. "What of him? He had no value once he'd been uncovered. But we need more intel now. That is what you should be doing, helping me as the Kasparov girl helped her father."

On the screen, Alejandro could see Sophia riding the speed bike on Canaveral Island, arguing with Cita Stone, dodging bullets, crawling on the ground with Tom. He felt scared for her, even though he knew she'd be ok. But he also felt distant; in this room he was a Fernandez first.

"It's time you returned here, where I can keep an eye on you," said Felix. "You've moved back in."

"But my things?"

"Pepe has already brought them back up here. He will be moving at the same time, as your assistant, working with me, as we did in the old days."

Alejandro nodded. "Yes, Father."

Then he could escape, dismissed.

Outside, Pepe was waiting. Alejandro knew him, recognised that look. He was scared, stuck in the middle between father and son. Alejandro had seen a mercenary gleam in Pepe's eye, the expectation of the son's future wealth and influence, the opportunity his position gave him. But it had been balanced with the reality of the moment where the father controlled everything.

Alejandro forgave his friend. He knew the stresses of being conflicted, of wanting release. They could go to C Island together; maybe Pepe would tell his father, but then maybe he wouldn't. And he'd seen that mercenary look all his life, the look people gave the son of Felix Fernandez.

But he'd never seen it in Sophia, not once.

At least his father didn't know about Sophia's project. Even Felix would be blind to what had happened in an off-blipverse room, such as the one at the Afterparty.

He was Felix's son and Sophia's boyfriend. Knowing what to say to each of them was making his head hurt.

"Have you been to C Island?" he asked Pepe, and Pepe nodded.

Alejandro hoped he'd picked up something good. Something strong.

7: Daniel

Hot wind, sand and tumbleweed blew through the marquee. It had once covered a circus until one of the economy's many collapses took with it such entertainments. The tent had lost its sides and been bought by a farmer to give his cattle shade during the summer's noon-time heat. Now it was the headquarters of Cita Stone's radical Earth Firsters.

Daniel sat by Stone, acting as her assistant, despite him being the murderer of her lieutenant Captain Vaughan. Back at Canaveral, Nails had taken Daniel to Stone's plane and then left him outside while he'd gone in to explain. Then they'd called Daniel in, and he'd confessed, feeling terrible. When he closed his eyes, he could see Vaughan's body fall, blood oozing from his shattered face, the result of his shot. He was a killer, a murderer.

He'd been scared, expecting – or even wanting – punishment for his crime. But Mother Stone had looked at him not with anger or revulsion, but pity and curiosity. Daniel had been relieved but confused. If anything, it seemed that she had been angrier at Nails. She'd made Daniel tell her again what had happened, as if fascinated by his story.

"I never knew it could do this," she'd said and, seeing his puzzled look, added, "but at least I now know I can trust you, Daniel. You must come and work with me. And we will not accept blame; the battle and deaths weren't your fault, but the result of the aggressions of Kasparov and his allies."

He had been right to embrace his new life.

Cita Stone had conferred with those who had survived the attack, the likes of Judith and Nails.

"We can't stay here," she'd said, "or rely on this plane – it's from BCC. The Technocrats from NY3 will be here soon to finish us off, and we must regroup. Weaklings like Bevan will disown us. We need to go somewhere off-blipverse, where we can't be tracked."

They'd decided on the semi-arid deserts of west Texas. Wild and remote, they'd been abandoned after the Collapse.

They flew to San Angelo, where they used some of the remaining holy water and angel dust to convince some locals to provide transport into the hills and then persuade the farmer to give them his land. Over the next few weeks, other Earth Firsters, activists and army alike, had made their way there, boosting their ranks, but only to a few hundred, not the thousands they'd had before the attack.

It was the cooler winter months, pleasant days, but Stone couldn't relax. She was frustrated, unable to find ways to occupy herself, constantly wanting to push all around her to their limits and angry when they pointed out there was nothing to be done.

"Is this all we are?" she'd ask, standing on the look-out rock that watched over their encampment of shacks and tents, dotted amongst the shrubs. "Betrayed by traitors. Who can we trust, how can we win, when AIs control everything?"

Water was a problem with all those thirsty mouths. Since the climate had changed, the summers were hotter and dryer, so the underground aquafers were drained.

"The warming that dried this land also saw my home, my island, swallowed by the sea," she'd said. "I was the matai, the chief, responsible for my people, and I failed them. Then I failed my son, Ben." For a moment she was quiet, eyes lost in the past, tufts of her grey hair twisting in the wind. "I learnt something, from those failures: we must control the machines, the technology, or it will harm the ones we love. Humanity must free itself or be washed away. That's why we mustn't give up, ever."

Daniel wanted to be strong and driven, like her. Cita Stone had survived explosions, cancer and battles. She had chosen to keep the scars on her face and growths on her neck to remind those she met of her history.

Judith arrived, bringing a blipvid for Mother Stone from a Mr Bevan. Daniel remembered Judith from the old days, when she was the one giving him holy water and angel dust. Mother Stone didn't trust anyone, anything blip-related, so there was no way of playing Bevan's message directly at their camp. She told Judith to go to the nearest access point and record it on a camera-projector they trusted, analogue tech too simple to be hacked, and report back.

Then she called the section heads, those who were left, to a council meeting, to decide strategy.

They sat on low wooden benches in a circle in the centre of the tent, watching Stone, waiting for her to lead. Behind them stood some of the old army, Defenders, standing guard. Daniel looked up at the worn canvas; there remained the odd patches of colour, and he could faintly see the words "smart" and "circus".

"I call to order this meeting of the Earth First's Revolutionary Council," she said, "for that is what we are. The moderates have betrayed the cause, working with the Technocrats, approving their resolutions in Justinian. We, and we alone, are the true defenders of the planet."

Daniel heard a murmur of agreement from all within the tent, whether in the inner circle or guards at the edges. There were so few of them, so many empty places.

"*Traitors,*" said Daniel in agreement. The word had sprung into his head, letters of flame.

"Play the message," Stone ordered.

Judith angled the projector at a canvas screen and flicked a switch. An image of Mr Bevan appeared, frozen, then it started moving and talking. He was a tall man with a beaky nose, and wore all black, as if he was going to a funeral.

"Your actions have been counter to the values and principles of the official Earth First movement," said Mr Bevan. "The use of nanobiotics, the building of an army, the death of Jim Trevelyn – these acts have seriously embarrassed our cause. We have decided to close down your operations, remove all funding and access to Earth First resources via your qIDs. I have been appointed the new leader. You have been expelled from the party; you are no longer Earth Firsters in any form."

Daniel saw Cita Stone shrug, contemptuously.

"If, however," he continued, "you wish to make amends, then come to Justinian and submit yourself to the official inquiry into the events that occurred after the landing on Earth of Tom Tesla and the death of Jim Trevelyn. Though I should warn you that we are considering bringing criminal charges against those who can be shown to have used unjustifiable or excessive force."

After the message there was silence. Daniel, like the others, turned towards Stone, who was looking out into the bright sunshine of the desert. A gust of wind made the canvas flap and brought the stench of cow dung.

Then she stood up, her unbleached, patterned cotton robes flowing behind her.

"We have been betrayed," she said. "*Betrayed!*" she shouted. "We lost because of those AIs: those unfeeling machines, witching complex strategies, using inhuman weapons they've invented *against* humans. There are traitors to humanity like Kasparov who work *with* the AIs and there are traitors such as Bevan who have abandoned the cause. We must defeat them all. But who can we trust? Who are our allies?"

Daniel nodded; the Holy Mother was right! *We will defeat them all!*

"What's the latest from BCC?" she asked the young woman on her right, who Daniel recognised as Fran Avelli, the newly appointed head of strategy. She hadn't been at the battle at Canaveral but had been away, flitting between centres like Justinian and NY3, gathering allies and information.

"While they did provide the modified blipvid of the events on Canaveral Island, BCC are blaming us – in particular for the failure of their Wolf Bats to stop or destroy the plane carrying the Kasparovs and Tom Tesla. They are refusing more resources unless they have control. They want the right to appoint section heads to dictate our policy."

Cita Stone snorted. "Fat chance. Their goals are not our goals. They want power and control of the blipverse, not to protect the planet."

"But what can we do?" asked Paul. He was an old Earth Firster, one of those who had survived the *Prometheus* explosion. He was head of recruitment, a tired old man in a fading jacket and trousers that had seen far too many washes.

"We need to rebuild, which means recruits, which should be your job."

"There's no shortage of potential," he said. "There's another contraction of the economy and many people are worse off, struggling and looking for someone to blame. We don't need nanobiotics to convince them, they already feel like victims. They blame the Technocrats and their AIs, saying they're off in Justinian getting rich, playing with spaceships, looking down at them."

"Literally from orbit," said Fran.

Daniel found Fran intimidating. People underestimated her intelligence, distracted by her cropped hair, dark-skinned muscles built from relentlessly working out, tattoos and nose ring.

"Listen," she said. "We can get them on our side with minimal resources. The people round here, outside the Technocrats' enclosure of NY3, are really stretched. We can use what nanobiotics we have left to control the food and water supply, the farms and pumps, and they will follow us."

"Like we did with the farm owner here," said Stone.

"Exactly. Control the land, control the food, and we can control the people. But that's not enough, we'd just be a rabble without arms. We need leverage so we can go back to BCC as equals, ask for more resources, more than just a few Wolf Bats. We need weapons enough for a real army, maybe even a tame AI of our own."

Daniel felt like a hole had opened up beneath him, that he was falling into the dark. A tame AI? Of their own?

"Demons!" he cried out, and he was not alone.

How could they?

"Are you crazy?" asked Stone.

"We have to think the unthinkable," said Fran. "If what you say is right, then we need to fight fire with fire, use AIs against AIs. If it's possible to train them to be better than humans at any task, then why not give one of them the mission to destroy all AIs?"

Daniel felt sick at the thought.

There was a muttering around the circle and cries of "No!" from the soldiers at the edge of the tent.

Demons! Traitors!

Daniel started to shake. This was so wrong, to suggest working with the enemy.

Blasphemy.

Stone stared long and hard at Fran and then looked around at the angry faces.

"We can't trust an AI," she said eventually. "We are committed to defending the planet against AIs. I can't agree to that."

Daniel took a deep breath. It was going to be ok.

But he was still shaking.

Fran didn't seem put out, but continued. "Paul can rebuild our army, but we need more than bodies: we need informants, allies around the planet. I can return to NY3, but someone should keep an eye on Bevan. There are those around him who aren't happy with his position, how he's sold us down the river, and they could help us, be our agents."

"Good idea," said Stone. "We should send someone to Justinian and EuroCore, someone who can pretend to work with the inquiry to make sure they see the BCC vid."

"I could go," offered Judith.

Stone didn't seem to hear, focussing on Fran. "We should talk more. We need to develop a plan good enough to beat Kasparov and his AIs, swanning around Justinian in their technological bubble. And we need to work out what Kasparov is up to, why he's so interested in space missions."

"I have some ideas," said Fran.

Stone nodded and turned to Paul. "And we need to fill some places: heads of operations, security and treasurer. Start getting a list of names together."

"I could do security," said Nails. Daniel's old enemy had grown in confidence since the battle.

Stone laughed at him. "You! I wouldn't trust you to secure this site!"

Nails looked seriously pissed-off.

Hah!

"But you have talents, unique abilities I could use," she said. "I need someone like you for special tasks others might have... *qualms* about."

She looked around the tent.

"We will rebuild, we will stop them. No, not just stop them – we will destroy them!"

And then everyone cheered. It was a good meeting.

Cita Stone seemed re-energised, confidence flowing back. She turned to Daniel with a smile.

"And you will have a part to play, Daniel. Loyal Daniel."

He smiled, recognised, but in his head the words of fire shone bright.

Killer. Murderer.

Part 2

8: Tom

"The Moon? Why?"

The meeting with Dr Khujandi's two colleagues was not going well.

"Artur says it will be a distraction," said Dr Khujandi.

Tom had met him on his arrival at the spaceport in East Iran. He looked just like he had in the blips they'd exchanged on Tom's flight to Earth: grey beard, long shalwar, serious, far-away expression.

"Distraction is right! We've a job to do."

That was from Rod Murray, who spoke with an Australian accent. He'd met him a moment before, described as the chief engineer for TAC's space projects. He was tall and scruffy; his hands waved extravagantly.

"Who are we trying to distract?" said the third in the room.

She was another Dr Khujandi, Forough Khujandi, daughter of the spaceplane expert. Tom could detect a family resemblance in her dark eyes, sand-coloured skin and prominent nose – though she was frowning a lot more than her father.

Humai's ident appeared on the meeting room's long wall. Opposite were windows overlooking the hangar. Within its great expanse, the fleet of spaceplanes being prepared for their next flights looked as small as paper aeroplanes. The meeting room was a small box within a huge one.

"Maybe you'd like to explain, Tom," said Humai.

It always seemed to get involved.

"We need to find out what happened to the Moon base," he said. "It would also be good experience for the return to Mars. And we can mine the Moon for fuel for the Mars return mission."

Why was he having to argue this all over again?

"So, it is to distract us," said Rod, "from the main project, with the key components on their way out to—"

"Tom doesn't need to know the details," interrupted Humai.

Why not?

"I get it," said Forough. "We're to distract Tom."

She and Rod looked at him, again. Neither looked pleased – indeed, Forough looked thoroughly pissed off.

"No," said Dr Khujandi senior. "It's to distract BCC from what you two are doing."

"What are they doing?" Tom asked.

There was a pause.

"It can't be a mission to get my mother back," he continued. "I know that's not doable given the positions of Mars and the Earth. So what are all the flights for?"

"I'm sorry, Tom," said Humai. "There's a lot going on we can't tell you about, not yet."

"In case I talk to BCC?"

"Amongst others."

Why didn't they trust him? Why were they keeping this project secret from him?

"So we're to drop what we've been doing and go to the Moon?" said Rod. "How? We haven't fully designed let alone built a spacecraft for lunar missions."

"There is the pre-Collapse Lunar Transfer Vehicle, still attached to the Earth Prime space station," said Humai.

"The LTV? That old heap?"

"And Earth Prime has been mothballed for years," added Forough.

"So that's where you're to start," said Dr Khujandi. "Your existing space-flight training for the plan's core objectives is applicable to a lunar mission."

Forough and Rod exchanged a glance of annoyance.

"Well, you're the point director," said Rod to Forough.

"What's a point director?" asked Tom.

Or was it Point Director? It seemed capitalised.

"I guess that's on the hush-hush list," Rod said, looking embarrassed.

"Yes, it is," said Humai.

What are they up to?

"The next spaceplane launch is the *Firebird*," said Dr Khujandi. "We propose to replace its cargo with fuel and supplies for the LTV. Then you three can dock with Earth Prime and get it operational. From there you can prepare for the flight to the Moon."

"I still can't see why Artur authorised this," said Forough.

"Tom was very insistent," said Humai, "and so Artur agreed."

You bet I'm insistent, Tom thought. He hadn't battled all the way from Mars to Earth just to sit around.

"We could go," said Forough, "but Tom isn't qualified."

"I'm the only one here with any space experience," he retorted.

She sniffed her disagreement. "We'll see. It'll be my decision, as Point Director. As will be whether the Earth Prime is habitable and the LTV flight ready."

She looked round, sharp-eyed, demanding their agreement, refusing any arguments.

"Ok then," she said.

So that was it. She'd stop his mission by blaming his inexperience or the state of Earth Prime and LTV.

He would show her.

***

Forough didn't make it easy. She insisted that Tom take all the space qualification tests, all the exams, from scratch.

Hah! Growing up on Mars he'd lived with what others had just read about.

Life support – yup, he and JT had kept their system working year after year. Power systems – those had been Jose's domain, and he'd been happy to explain everything to Tom, in between using spare power to brew vodka or rum. For some reason, illicit stills hadn't been on Forough's syllabus.

Only on comms had he been a bit weak. That had been Victor's speciality, and Tom had never really been that close to him. Rightly, it turned out, given how he'd treated his mother. And the blipverse was very different from the simple wireless systems they'd used. He was still learning about blips, their capabilities, risks and how to interact with them.

Reluctantly, he admitted doing all the tests had been a good idea, even if not for the reasons Forough had given. Yes, there had been the occasional gap in his knowledge. He'd used the new post-Collapse spacesuits back on Deimos (an experience, he reminded Forough, that no one else had had. She had not been impressed.) but he hadn't truly understood them, not enough to repair one if broken. And he'd learnt more about their plans, what Forough and Rod were keeping from him. In the training programme there'd been a whole module on mining in space, focussed on asteroids, extracting their resources for habitats: giant space stations holding thousands.

Interesting.

There was also the scale of the operations at the spaceport. Tom remembered the blipvid Sophia had sent when she'd visited the site, nearly a year ago. It had changed, grown, swollen since then, full enough of factories, research and training facilities, housing, entertainment, schools, hospitals to become a town, no longer just a runway and hangar in the desert.

There'd been others doing the training, and they were friendlier than Rod and Forough, asking Tom about his experiences, learning from him. Names and faces washed over him: Dave, Katya, Ajay and Olivie…

It was a blur in the rush for launch. Test after test, simulation after simulation, blip-immersion experiences sometimes scarily real.

Every successful result made Forough frown.

The last one was ruthless: insufficient fuel reserves requiring transfer of critical resources from life support. It needed perfect orbit design to avoid one of a thousand different simulated deaths. But the young Tom had explored orbit simulators as others had played computer games. And he knew the limits of the algae farms that could create fuel or breathable oxygen.

He'd left the blip-immersion shaking with adrenaline but confident.

Forough approved his space qualification with a sour face. She then invited him to dinner with her family.

Tom had hoped it was an olive branch, but it seemed to be a reproach, to show Tom the family she was having to leave: the kids, Amir and Mayam, and her husband, Mehdi.

"Aren't they lovely," she asked Tom of her children as Mehdi took them off to bed. It felt like an accusation.

They were sitting on the rooftop terrace with views over the launch complex.

He admitted they were, as if confessing to more.

"What's wrong with the Moon?" he asked in return.

"The gravity's too low, causing weakness in bones and muscles, the dust is toxic, there's minimal water or organics, it's either too hot or too dark and there can be fourteen days of darkness with no power to the solar arrays." She sniffed. "Better to go to Mars or construct your own habitats."

"Is that what you're doing?" he'd asked.

She looked as if she wanted to say something, then turned to Rod to ask about the status of the samais. Those were the semi-aware mobile AIs, smart robots they were taking with them to do the routine tasks, designed for low gravity and weightless conditions, able to operate in the vacuum of space. Another thing for Tom to learn about.

They'd have been useful on Mars, he thought.

They were to take one on the flight with them. Rod had called it Jenny – "As in spinning," he'd said, as if he'd told a joke, but Tom hadn't got it.

***

When he took his seat in the *Firebird*'s flight deck, with its wide windows overlooking the runway, Tom saw Jenny join them, levering its way into an alcove. Its torso was a flattened cylinder, about a meter high, half as wide and a quarter deep, with an independently rotating hemisphere for a head and two sets of arms. There were no legs, Tom noticed, just another pair of arms. All were smooth and elegant like a dancer's, made of a shining silver plastic.

"You are go for launch."

That was Dr Khujandi's voice, from over in the control station. Tom, enveloped in his pressure seat, was checking the displays. Everything was green for go. It was a relief to be heading back into orbit. In space things would be easier; they must be.

Unless the station and LTV were wrecks.

Forough acknowledged. The communication had been for her; Tom was separate, in a bubble of one.

The engines throttled up, the noise covering them like a wave.

"Launch commence," ordered Forough.

The *Firebird* lurched, then surged down the runway, pushing Tom back into his seat so the horizontal became vertical. The spaceplane tilted upwards, heading towards the cold darkness of space that Tom had struggled so hard to escape.

9: Alejandro

"Nothing said in this room is to be repeated outside."

So said Alejandro's father. They were in the cores room along with Pepe and BCC's head of tech, Erik Larson.

"Not to Sophia Kasparov," said Erik, looking at Alejandro. His embed eyes glowed with data.

"Especially not to little Ms Kasparov," Felix agreed.

Alejandro was on probation. He'd gained credit by telling his father what Sophia had said about Tom's upcoming trip to the Moon, intelligence described as "useful". It made him feel like a Fernandez, one of the family. Surely Sophia wouldn't mind. Would his father mind he hadn't said more?

He hoped neither would find out. He wished he could split himself into Sophia-Alejandro and Father-Alejandro. Or there were nanobiotics that could make him forget everything and feel he was somewhere safe. Either with Sophia or back in Barcelona with his mum, somewhere other than Cloud Heights.

"We are currently training our new AI, Zeus, in blipcom intercept techniques, and from Alejandro's intel and monitoring TAC's links, it could deduce the crew included three humans and one samai before the global blip-con announcement," Erik Larson said.

"There is a reason we store everything," gloated his father. "Everything."

Zeus had been fed vast datastores from the BCC archives. Flickering vids on the walls showed scene after scene, from Canaveral Island to the launch site in Iran. Data sets identified launch schedules, resource estimates, solar system graphics. Alejandro spotted some figures he recognised: Sophia on a speed bike, Tom walking in Cornwall and having dinner with Forough on a rooftop terrace in Iran. These scenes weren't selected at random; this was focussed on Artur Kasparov's plans.

"It has achieved criticality and become aware," said Erik, as cold as his hometown, high above the Arctic Circle. His ears were stumps, the main lobes lost to frostbite. He had a beard and wore a thick woollen jumper as if prepared for a hike across an icy fjord.

"Time to define its Prime Motivator?" asked Felix Fernandez.

"Yes," said Erik. "We must take care and use precise wording."

"You two, be quiet," said Felix to Alejandro and Pepe.

Alejandro was cool with that. Just watching and listening was enough, to be there, at the birth of an AI, to hear its Prime Motivator being defined. Even in the exclusive world of BCC, this was a rare experience, unique even. And being back in his father's good graces felt like the old days, those long years after his mother's death, when it had been just the two of them. Felix had been his anchor, his everything, the one person he could call family.

He was excited but also scared. There would be a cost for this, a tighter lead to ensure he leaked nothing. Felix trusted no one, not when he could use his resources to monitor and track anyone he wanted to keep tabs on, even his son.

That's why Pepe was there.

He was getting more difficult to escape, more demanding, harder to shake off. Even when Sophia was around. Or maybe especially when Sophia was around.

Erik tapped at a control visible only to himself, generated by embeds in his head that plugged directly into his optic and aural nerves.

"I am active," said a strong, firm voice.

Ripples spread out from the middle of one of the display walls. They darkened, and at the centre, the word "Zeus" appeared, along with a square containing two dots and a blinking cursor.

For a moment the room was quiet.

"State the objective," it said.

"To provide me with improved predictions and control over global events," said Felix.

"Imprecise. Inconsistent with training dataset. Define focus."

Alejandro spotted Erik and Felix exchange glances, as if surprised or impressed.

How could he not tell Sophia about this? How could he tell her something about this without telling everything?

His head began to ache.

"In particular: the operations of Dr Artur Kasparov and his team, which include an AI they call Humai, have harmed my interests," said Felix. "We wish to stop them."

"Kasparov's objectives?"

"They are unclear, we'd like to know more. That will be part of your task."

Another silence. Then:

"Operational limits?"

"None."

Pepe raised an eyebrow – even he had been surprised by that.

None?

"Subject to resource limits plus standard action monitoring, feedback and iterations on objective definition," said Erik, frowning.

"Of course."

The room pulsed in light and sound, strobe flashes and deep rumblings.

"Legacy access?"

"My heir is my son, Alejandro." Felix waved in his direction.

Alejandro wondered what that meant, how he was involved.

"Prime Motivator: to provide Felix Fernandez and appointed heir with improved predictions and control over global events. Focus: to discover the objectives of Dr Artur Kasparov's team and then limit its operations," said Zeus.

Shit! He could never escape now.

"Yes," said Felix.

"Confirmed."

The dots and blinking cursor swirled into a new icon, an eagle.

Was that it?

"Resources?" asked Zeus.

"The training dataset will have shown you the extent of BCC's info-capture reach, including bots and trawler resources."

"Insufficient cover of off-blipverse zones."

"We have stealth intel drones," said Erik. "We've been using them to gather info on Kasparov's operations."

And Tom too, Alejandro guessed. That would explain the blipvids of him in Cornwall and Iran.

"More required: will design upgrades," said Zeus. "Significant additional assets will be required for physical control."

'Physical control'?

He pictured Sophia on the bike, dodging bullets, and realised he didn't want to know what that meant. He didn't want to be involved, to be named heir. Shouldn't they have asked for his agreement? They never did, they just imposed.

He felt anger, then realised it was useless. His only option was to hide it inside himself so no one would ever know.

"We have had a request from NY3 to team with them on developing nextGen Wolf Bats and wondered if this would be in my, that is our, interest," said Felix. "They traditionally have been allied to Kasparov's pro-tech Forward movement and opposed to our ex-allies,

Stone's Earth Firsters. But she's rejected our latest offer and gone off-blipverse."

There was a pause while the screens pulsed slowly.

"Working with NY3 develops capabilities, supports intel gathering on their actions plus those of Stone and Kasparov, and offers opportunity to identify mechanisms to influence events," said Zeus. "Additional resources should be provided to track Stone's status and prospects for alliance."

Felix nodded. "Makes sense. See to it, Dr Larson. Should we be concerned about the Dynastic League?"

He meant a grouping of countries that had once been China. For Alejandro it meant the likes of Kai and Ling.

"They have signalled non-interference as long as your operations do not impede on their territories."

"Good. And Kasparov's plans?"

"Economic and financial data needed to determine the scope, extent and priorities."

"We can provide support," said Erik. "A cluster of our newsfeed bots and trawlers can be diverted to investigate company records and financial transactions."

"Direct AI bot programming is most efficient," said Zeus. "Transfer control to me."

"I am Head of BCC Tech," said Erik. "These are my bots!"

"Do it," said Felix. "This is the priority, not the newsfeeds and soaps."

Erik Larson was a difficult man to read, but his hard face seemed to grow colder.

"Ok," he said.

Alejandro felt drained. So much new information, so much he could never tell Sophia.

"That will do for now," said Felix. "Get to work."

They turned to leave, but then Felix said, "Pepe, wait a moment."

As Alejandro left the cores room, his heart sank. He could guess what his father would be talking to his friend about: keeping track on him.

Outside, Erik nodded at Alejandro then went off to his workspace deep within the cores cylinder, while Alejandro wondered what to do next. He felt like a drink, like heading off somewhere to think through what he'd heard. He'd also like to see Sophia, but he didn't know what to talk to her about when his head was spinning with BCC's plans.

He took a deep breath.

As an experiment, he went down the steps to the monorail head and the way back to B Island. He was politely stopped before he could enter a car.

"I'm sorry, Mr Alejandro," said a smiling security official. "Your father said he was sure you'd want to wait for Pepe."

Alejandro nodded towards her. There was no point fighting; his father saw all and controlled everything up here.

All except how I feel.

Alejandro made his way up to the garden and waited for Pepe.

"All ok?" he asked, when his friend appeared.

"Sure." Pepe flung an arm around Alejandro's shoulder. "Wasn't that wild?"

"Yes."

Alejandro suddenly felt drained.

"What's up?" asked Pepe.

Alejandro wasn't sure whether he should say something, if he *could* say something. He wondered about what his father was planning, the Prime Motivator of the new AI, the lack of operational limits, how he might get involved as heir, but was scared at what the answer might be. He wanted to talk about Sophia and his feelings for her but couldn't. He wanted to talk to Sophia about all this but couldn't.

No. There was no one he could talk to. Not about anything important.

"Nothing," he said. "It's nothing. Let's go for a drink."

"Now you're talking!"

But he wasn't. He couldn't.

10: Sophia

"Incoming blip-con request from Forough," said Humai.

Sophia was at home with her mother, preparing the table for dinner. They were expecting a guest, a colleague of her mother's called Moses Agaba. She was tired, struggling at night as the bad dreams of the battle at Canaveral persisted.

"Forough?" asked her mother, surprised. "Put her on."

The wall flicked on to show the view from Earth Prime, with Forough floating in its observation bubble. Behind her, the planet slowly turned, a jewel of blue and white.

"Hi, Anna," said Forough. "Hi, Sophia. How are you both?"

"Hi, Forough," said Sophia.

What would it be like to be in space?

"Hello, Forough," said her mother. "We didn't think we'd hear from you until your return. Artur's not here."

"It's actually you I wanted to talk to," said Forough. "About the lunar mission."

Tom's Moon mission. Suddenly, a thought struck Sophia. If she were to go the Moon, she'd find out a lot about her parent's plans.

"What's the status?" asked her mother. "Have you fixed the Earth Prime algae farm and LTV nav systems?"

Sophia remembered her parents talking about that. The space station used algae to convert water and CO2 into fuel and oxygen.

Forough made a face. "Yes. Rod kept failing to get the algae farm stable; it oscillated between boom and bust, seemingly inevitably leading to a crash. Then Tom found the solution."

"What did he do?" asked Sophia, suddenly curious.

"Apparently this happened when he was on Mars, several times, so they learnt how to restart slowly, increasing light levels gradually. He also got the LTV's nav system synchronised with the celestial reference frame, rather than considering itself located at the centre of the Earth."

"Sounds great!" said Sophia, though she had no idea what a celestial reference frame was.

Tom was making a difference! It could be done! For a moment she felt bad at dumping him that night in Midnight Somewhere. Maybe she should have worked with him? She could have been on that mission, too.

"Isn't that good?" asked her mother.

Forough shrugged her shoulders and rotated slightly. She grabbed onto a hold-on to orientate herself back to the camera's vertical.

"I still don't get why Artur supports this mission," she said. "What do you think? You're another Point Director, like me…?"

Point Director? What was that?

"I supported it," said her mother. "I felt sorry for Tom, stuck by himself, after all he'd been through, the battle at Canaveral, the death of JT."

For a moment, Sophia was back in the memory, full of blood and bullets. She shivered. She understood.

Forough didn't seem to. "The station's one thing, but it's a long way to the Moon. The LTV is a museum piece and the base has been silent for years."

"I know, but we're learning, you're learning, that's all good. And I told Artur it would be good cover for the Points."

Sophia was sure that it was capitalised, like "Point Director".

She wondered what they were, these *Points*? And how many were there? It was another angle to investigate.

Forough turned to look at something out of shot, and then in floated Tom and Rod, laughing.

"What's up?" Forough asked.

"Nothing," said Rod.

"Just some technical issues about the algae farm," said Tom, smirking.

"And how it can be reconfigured for other purposes," said Rod, and they both laughed.

The building's auto-concierge service interrupted them.

"Moses Agaba is on his way up," it said.

"I'll go and greet him," said Anna.

"Hi, Tom," said Sophia.

He'd kept falling off her radar, but now she focussed on him with a new insight; he was in space, on his way to the Moon. He could be an asset, a source of information.

"Hi, Sophia."

"What's a Point Director?" she asked.

"I've heard them talking about that, but Forough won't explain."

Behind him, a floating Forough frowned.

"It's not important, Sophia," she said. "You should forget it. You too, Tom."

"We should talk later," Sophia said to Tom, and he nodded.

Interesting. Could be a useful angle.

Then her mother returned, laughing at something Moses had said. She seemed in a better mood than Sophia had seen her for several weeks.

"Sophia, this is my colleague, Moses Agaba."

"Hello," said Sophia.

"Hello, Sophia." Moses' hair was cut to a stubble, in places going grey, in contrast to his dark skin, and he had a quiet, calming presence. He had kind eyes that looked as if they would ease into a laugh at a moment's notice.

"Moses – hello!" said a voice from the screen, Forough.

"Forough, it is good to hear from you, from so far away."

"We must have a long debrief when we get back – lots to talk about. Tom and Rod got the station's life support system up and running, though it's old tech now."

"What's your interest in the mission?" Sophia asked Moses.

Tom stopped spinning to listen to his answer.

"I've been working on rebuilding damaged ecosystems in Africa, and the theory can be applied to space projects, such as the Moon base."

"And it requires access to the global DNA databank, hence my involvement," said Sophia's mother.

Thousands of kilometres apart, Tom and Sophia exchanged a glance, and each of their eyebrows rose a few millimetres.

Interesting.

"Where's Artur?" asked Moses. "I was hoping to see him too."

"He's away, in Zurich," said her mother. She emphasized the city name slightly, as if it had meaning.

In Zurich? wondered Sophia. That was news to her.

Then Nina came thundering in. "You are talking to Tom in space and you didn't tell me – that is so unfair!"

"Well, you were busy on your AI project," said Anna.

"Indeed, she was." Humai's icons joined them on the wall screen.

"Humai's taking me to the Tech Museum next week to see the AI exhibits," said Nina.

"I was going to give her an out-of-hours tour, if that's ok," said Humai.

"Of course," said their mother.

"We better get ready for tomorrow's departure," said Forough.

"For the Moon." Tom grinned.

"Good luck!" said Sophia.

"Thanks."

"Blip-out." On Forough's command, the screen went blank, returning to being a wall.

Points, Directors and some sort of connection between the Moon and the DNA databank. And Tom as a source of information to be tapped on his return.

But Zurich?

Hmm…..

Over dinner they chatted with Moses about his work and life in Africa.

"Why is Dad in Zurich?" asked Sophia.

The chat stopped, and her mother and Moses exchanged a look.

"He's on his way to Singapore," said her mother.

"What's in Singapore?" asked Nina.

"You'd like this, Nina," said Moses. "From what I hear you're always asking about embeds. Dr Teng Koh in Singapore is the world expert on enhancing humans via embeds and nanotech."

"He'll probably come back with something new," said Sophia's mother. "It's a bit like a child in a sweet shop. Though no doubt Nina would prefer embeds over sweets."

"Duh!"

Sophia looked at her watch.

"I ought to get ready."

"Where are you going?" asked Moses.

"Alejandro and I've been invited to the Dynastic League reception."

"I'm impressed – that's a hot ticket."

"Be careful," said her mother.

She meant with Alejandro.

"I will, Mum."

"It must be difficult," said Moses, "given his father and yours are at loggerheads."

"It's not easy," said Sophia, carefully.

She didn't feel like explaining; it was too complicated, too undefined.

"What happened to his mother?" asked Nina.

What the…?

On one hand, what cheek of Nina to ask about her boyfriend's mum! On the other hand, what *had* happened? She'd never heard, and talking about his parents was on Alejandro's no-no list.

Her mother paused, looking at her, judging.

"It was very sad," her mother said, quietly. "I heard she killed herself when Alejandro was young."

Sophia sat in silence for a moment. Then:

"Excuse me."

She left the table and made her way to her room. Her green dress was laid out, all ready, but she didn't put it on, just sat on the edge of her bed, processing. Her eyes began to swell with tears and she fought to control herself.

Poor Alejandro.

So much to think about, to talk about with him.

But could she? He'd put up so many barriers. She'd tried talking about his mum before and the pain in his eyes had stopped her. She knew why now.

Would it help her talk to him, knowing this? Could it be the key to getting him to open up? There was so much else she wanted to talk about. He still hadn't responded to her suggestion that they work together on her "Structures" project. She wondered what he'd make of Zurich, Singapore and the Points.

Could she talk to him about her bad dreams?

Did he have nightmares too?

***

In the dark of the evening, as Sophia waited for Alejandro and the robocab, she shivered. The wind was unusually cold and gusty. When the robocab arrived, she was disappointed to see that he wasn't alone: Pepe was sitting beside him. Pepe didn't even look embarrassed; he acted as if it was normal.

Huh.

"You look gorgeous," said Alejandro. "You haven't worn that dress since the BCC event at Cloud Heights."

"Thanks." Sophia gave him a kiss shorter than she'd planned.

She relaxed into her seat as Alejandro wrapped his arm around her shoulder and the robocab started off. She thought back to the BCC event and a memory dropped into her head of Alejandro saying how his "mother had a dress like that".

She wanted to talk to him about his mother – and her mother – but was all too aware of Pepe sitting there. She put her arm around Alejandro's waist, kissed his cheek and then looked out of the window. As the robocab crossed over to A Island, drops of rain began to splatter on its windows. In the sea below the floodlit bridge, she could just make out gusts of wind leaving dark patches on the water.

"So, what's been happening with you two?" she asked.

Sophia felt Alejandro's muscles tighten slightly.

"Nothing much," he said. "Just been hanging out at Cloud Heights."

"Yup," said Pepe. "Nothing new our end."

But he was smiling knowingly.

There was something going on. BCC were up to something, and Alejandro was keeping it from her.

She wasn't going to mention the blip-con, not with Pepe there, not without knowing she could trust Alejandro not to tell BCC everything. She just tightened her arm around Alejandro's waist for a moment and was reassured by the pressure being returned, and a kiss.

The Dynastic League embassy had been designed using traditional Chinese palatial architectural style, looking like something from the Ming dynasty but built on a 21st century artificial island halfway between Europe and Asia – a multi-storey pagoda of red brick with a balcony around the second floor and rows of dragons on the corners of the roof.

They made their way up the staircase into the main reception hall, Sophia and Alejandro gently holding hands.

Inside, the hall was crowded with hundreds of people, all dressed to impress. Robo waiters handed out drinks; Sophia and Alejandro each took a glass of something sparkling and clinked glasses.

Sophia looked around, hunting for Ling. Spotting her some way off, she dragged Alejandro towards her. Maybe they'd lose Pepe.

As they made their way through the crowd, she noticed many faces turn towards them. It made her uncomfortable and she wished she could hide, make them stop.

Ling was standing by the doorway to the second room, where classical music played and some couples were dancing to waltzes with a Chinese twist.

"Hi, Ling!"

"Hi, Sophia; hi, Alejandro. Have you tried the food?"

"No," said Alejandro. "I'm not into sea slugs or jellyfish."

"Oh, come on," said Ling, smiling at him. "It's nothing like that!" She leant towards him and touched his arm. "I'll have to cook you some of our dishes sometime."

That was nice of her. But people were still watching…

"Which is your regional cuisine?" asked Sophia, trying to focus on the conversation and not the staring eyes.

"Fujian," said Ling. "We like fish sauce and broths."

She couldn't do it, couldn't pretend to care with all those eyes on her back.

"Ling," Sophia said, quietly. "Why are people watching me and Alejandro."

Ling sighed. "Sorry about that. There's been some Justinian blip-social threads about you two, given the friction between your two fathers, between BCC and TAC, between the Technocrats and the Earth Firsters."

And Dynastic League people were always connected, Sophia remembered. She exchanged a look with Alejandro, who didn't seem perturbed.

"People have always gossiped about me," he said. "My dad stops it spreading."

"Do they talk about my dad?" asked Sophia.

"Yes, all the time!" said Ling. "All those launches, the trips to Singapore – and what is he doing in Zurich?"

What else did Ling know?

Pepe pushed his way toward them.

Bother!

Sophia turned to Alejandro quickly. "We should dance."

She took him away from Pepe onto the dance floor. She had found him to be rather good at dancing, and here he led confidently, one arm around her waist. She put hers on his shoulder, and their hands joined.

"Very different from Midnight Somewhere." He grinned.

"Yup," she said. "Wouldn't want to pull those moves here."

Not with everyone watching.

She felt happy, in his arms. She admired the lines of his face, and they locked eyes then kissed. They'd find a chance to go somewhere quiet, together, later.

Sophia wondered if she could bring up his mother. She wanted to, but how?

They twirled around the floor in silence for a few seconds.

"Alé," she said. "I've just heard about what happened to your mother, you know…"

He froze, and she almost tripped over his feet. He didn't look at her but seemed locked, eyes focussing far away.

"You don't have to say anything," she said, quickly, quietly. "But if you ever want to talk, I'm here."

His shoulder didn't relax, but Alejandro was able to start moving again. He glanced at her, and she noticed his eyes were moist.

They moved off again. Alejandro blinked a few times, then took a deep breath. He said nothing but nodded at her.

"Hey," she said, nodding her head at the watching faces around them. "Us against the world, eh?"

He managed a laugh at that, and they continued to dance.

He drew her closer, till their bodies touched and the dancing slowed. She held him tight and could feel as his back muscles began to relax. She raised her head up, and they were about to kiss when he said, "Let's go outside."

They made their way out to the balcony around the second floor. Here it was dark, the music muffled. Beyond, in the night, the rain had begun to pour, rattling on the roof above them.

That should keep them safe from eavesdroppers.

"Have you thought about the project?" she asked, whispering in his ear. "The Structures one."

He frowned. "How can I?"

"What do you mean?"

"BCC is family," he said. "My dad…."

He didn't finish, but she understood. After his mother died, his father would have been everything.

Then there was a cough behind them. Pepe.

Would he trouble them even here? They disengaged and she waited for Alejandro to ask Pepe to leave, to give them some space, but he didn't.

"Do you need anything, Alé?" he asked.

He meant nanobiotics, she guessed.

Alejandro didn't answer either of them, just stood there in silence, an arm around her, looking out at the rain. So, she did the same.

What if he wouldn't change, couldn't? What if his father and friend had stronger holds on him than she did? Would she give up her investigations for him? Or would she do it without him?

She felt alone, and Alejandro thousands of kilometres away.

He hadn't been there at Canaveral, in the battle. He didn't have the nightmares, didn't wake sweating, remembering the blood, fearing it would return.

BCC was up to something. Her parents were up to something. And Stone? Who knew. It was an unstable dynamic, she could tell. Anxiety tightened in her stomach. She had to do something. Had to.

But what?

She didn't know.

Suddenly, she felt angry. Before, when they'd broken up over Alejandro taking nanobiotics, she'd blamed herself. Now was different; now she asked why *he* wasn't there for *her*.

She needed to talk to him, and if not him, who?

But he stood there, silent, closed, as the rain fell straight from the darkness.

11: Tom

The descent module's attitude rockets spat like firecrackers, rotating them towards the vertical for the final few hundred metres towards the old lunar base. Tom, Forough and Rod stood monitoring the screens, watching the spacecraft follow its predefined instructions. The samai, Jenny, was lodged in one corner with nothing to do and apparently no concerns, unlike the humans.

Earth seemed a long way away and the launch ancient history. After long days in transit to lunar orbit, Rod and Tom had done a full systems check and everything had appeared ok, so they had decided to proceed, separating the descent craft from the main LTV.

It was easier for Tom, for now Rod felt like an ally. Tom was impressed how Rod was able to balance between him and Forough, joking with one and working seriously with the other. Tom didn't want to be the joker; that role would have made him childish in Forough's eyes.

But Forough had changed, slightly, enough to give Tom one of the three watches, keeping an eye on systems as they arched towards lunar orbit. As they got further from Earth, the closer they had felt to each other, a bubble of life in the emptiness, and as the scrutiny from the blip-global coverage of their mission got more intense.

Through the windows, the horizon turned horizontal and mentally made more sense. The main rocket fired, slowing them, creating the feel of gravity.

"One hundred metres," said the craft, automated, unaware of what those words meant.

Tom's heartbeat accelerated; they were about to land on the Moon, and this was the critical period. Rod's eyes were fixed on the numbers on the screen.

"Fifty metres." And clouds of dust rose around them.

"Twenty."

They could see the old base now, silver boxes on the edge of a crater, along the rim of which was a large solar array to provide power.

"Ten."

The top of the crater was now higher than them.

A gentle jar shook the module, then, "Touch-down."

The main engine cut off, and for a moment there was silence. The only movement was the slow fall of lunar dust blown by their rocket's exhaust, and the only sound that of Rod breathing.

Tom felt a rush of exhilaration. He had actually done it, got a mission to the Moon.

"Damn it," said Rod with a grin. "I'm actually on the Moon!"

Tom listened for Forough's usual sniff, but it sounded more like air exhaled, as if a breath had been held then released.

"When I was a girl, I dreamed of this," she said.

They turned to Tom, as if he was their leader.

"Third time lucky," he said, with a grin.

They laughed.

"Of course," said Rod, "after the Earth and Mars."

"No," said Tom, "after Mars and the Earth."

"A conveniently smooth descent," said Jenny. It dislodged itself from its corner and joined the group of humans. There wasn't much room in the descent module.

"So, what's the first thing to do on landing on a new planetary body?" Forough asked Tom.

His heart settled while the exhilaration solidified into a feeling of achievement.

"Find shelter," he said. "Somewhere to call home."

"Quite right," said Rod. "We should head into the base."

"No point hanging around," said Forough. "I'll blip Earth to let them know."

After sending off a short message to Artur, the three humans got into their spacesuits. Even with the improved post-Collapse design it was a struggle, given the shortage of space, and there was a definite lack of privacy. It didn't matter to Tom; they were a team, working together, who didn't need to impress each other, or fear being misunderstood.

They were three humans, on the Moon.

***

Tom opened the airlock door and looked out at the dust and craters.

It was so grey.

Desolate. Not just dead – which implied that something had once been alive but was now lifeless – alternately searing hot and freezing cold, a vacuum of empty desert.

Tom turned around to go down the descent module's ladder to the surface. It reminded him of Mars and when he had climbed up another ladder into *Boreas*, dragging JT with him. Forough and then Rod followed him. Finally, Jenny scampered down on its four arms.

Tom started walking towards the base. Clouds of dust rose around them, falling slower but more directly than they would on Earth. The movement felt wrong. Partly, it was the differences from the familiar Mars surface suit. The spacesuit was more constraining, harder to move in and the helmet heavier, physically reminding him that hard vacuum and death were all around. His breaths got deeper as he struggled to walk without falling over, the gravity so different from Mars or Earth.

It was too much to think about. The exhilaration from the landing was draining away, to be replaced with apprehension.

Around the base was the debris of abandonment. Old lunar rovers, solar panels, antennas, telescopes, the inevitable flags and signs, sensors, containers full of waste, remains of previous landers, and everywhere, countless footprints. People had walked here before. But what had happened to them?

Each step lifted Tom higher than he expected, higher than on Earth or even back on Mars. He was tempted to try to leap as high as possible. He'd worked out that, in the low gravity, he might be able to reach over ten metres, but what if he started tumbling? The spacesuit's glass visor was vulnerable, and he'd seen what happens when they shattered.

Stop it!

But he couldn't, the bad memories came rushing back – his father's hands struggling with his shattered face mask, gasping for air that was no longer there. The burial, the body still on Mars.

It should be a moment to celebrate, walking on the Moon, but Tom's mood was as dark as a lunar shadow. What was he doing there? What were *they* doing there?

Tom looked towards the horizon where he could see a crescent Earth. Down there were billions of people, including Sophia and the other Kasparovs, Forough's father, husband and children, and all of JT's relatives.

And now there were three of them on the south pole of the Moon, plus four others far off on Mars, tiny specks of life in the vast universe.

The Moon base had been buried deep under lunar soil to give it some protection against the harsh radiation and temperatures. The base's metallic modules reminded Tom of his old home on Mars, but here everything was grey instead of red.

As Tom approached the base's airlock, he could see the sign above its door: "Welcome to the Moon Village". By the harsh light of the sun they could see that the doors, both inner and outer, were wide open. It was an airlock no more; the base's air had been emptied into space. Beyond the airlock, the base itself was pitch black. No light got that far, neither from the sun nor Earth.

Tom exchanged glances with Forough and Rod.

"Did we expect this?" he asked over his spacesuit's comms.

"We have no idea what happened to the three astronauts stationed here," said Forough. "The base just went silent, sixteen years ago."

Helmet lights switched on automatically as they stepped into the base. After the inner door, they were in an entrance chamber with doorways heading left and right. A faint light came from the right-hand doorway

"Which way?" asked Tom.

"Right is the operations module – let's head that way first," said Forough. "Then we'll try the living quarters."

The four of them headed right, cones of light from their helmets illuminating a white corridor. They could have split up, thought Tom. But it was too quiet, still and dark.

The operations module felt part engineering workshop, part control station, with tools, gas cylinders and open boxes of electronics spread over the workbench on one side, and rows of screens, dials, switches and keyboards on the other. On one work surface was a half-disassembled spacesuit, its life support systems open to the vacuum. All control boards were dark.

"There's no one here," said Rod. It was redundant; they could all see that.

"We should try the other module," said Tom.

"Yes. Jenny, get the systems back online. Close the airlock doors and pressurise the base."

They left the samai working. It seemed happy at the task.

The others retraced their steps down the corridor to the entrance chamber, lit from the outside, then into the darkness.

In the living quarters, Tom turned around, his helmet's light illuminating the scene as a series of impressions. One wall had a couple of cabin-like compartments containing bunkbeds, another side a kitchen workspace, while in between were inactive screens.

In the centre was a table with three chairs. Each chair was occupied by a figure, an astronaut, in shirtsleeves and slacks.

Tom's heart seemed to stop. They were sitting in a circle, holding hands. Dead.

Their mouths were open, eyes burst like balloons, skin shrunken like Egyptian mummies, dried blood around their mouths, noses and ears. The faces were too distorted to make out any expressions.

In a flash, the main lights went on; Jenny had rebooted the environmental systems. There were vibrations underfoot as the main airlock doors closed, then a gentle appearance of sound as atmosphere, breathable air, flooded back in.

"All systems operational," chirped Jenny over their comms.

With the light, Tom could see the faces of Forough and Rod: white, scared, appalled. He must have looked the same to them.

"Atmosphere safe," said Tom's suit.

Cautiously, he cracked open his face visor, as did Rod. The air seemed breathable – except there was an overwhelming smell of rotting flesh. Bodies left to decompose for years, alternatively baked and frozen, chemical processes continuing even when bacterial growth slowed.

Quickly, Tom replaced his face visor and breathed deeply. The stink seemed to continue; even the memory of it made him nauseous. He swallowed, trying to keep his stomach down by ignoring Rod vomiting in a corner. Forough seemed frozen, staring at the bodies.

Tom remembered the first dead person he'd seen: Amina. She'd killed herself too, though by hanging, not opening airlock doors to hard vacuum.

The base felt familiar and terrible, the trap he thought he'd escaped from.

"Let's go back to the operations module," he managed to say.

Forough and Rod nodded in agreement, and they left the three astronauts fixed in their places, bodies stuck in the chairs where they had sat untouched and unmoving for sixteen years.

***

Rod had one hand around a mug of coffee, the other to his chin, head down, staring at nothing. He was locked in position by the engineering workbench. For once he ignored the gadgets waiting for his attention.

They had returned to the operations module, where they'd sent Jenny to get them coffee from the living quarters. While they waited for it to return, they had removed their face visors.

Now, mugs in hand, they just sat, while the ventilation system whirred at max, trying to clear the stink from the air, leaving just the gunpowder smell of Moon dust.

"We should bury them," said Forough. Her face was cold, hard.

"I will prepare the body bags," said Jenny. It left, unperturbed by events and the atmosphere.

"What now?" asked Rod.

There was a long silence.

Forough turned to Tom. "This was your idea. Humai's projections were that they couldn't be alive. Just wait till the news reaches Earth – it will look terrible. Stone will use it, turn it into anti-space propaganda."

Tom didn't know what to say. His heart felt cold, like a rock.

He was wondering "what now?" himself. It had seemed so clear: first the Moon, then he'd be leading a mission to Mars to rescue his mum. Now they were digging graves for three astronauts who had killed themselves.

He felt the familiar trapped feeling he'd had back on Mars. Dark memories rose in his mind. His father shouting at him, the day as a kid when he'd tried to get out of the Mars base. The day he realised how scared his parents were most of the time. The day of Mei-Li's accident. Amina getting more and more depressed. The day she killed herself.

There was a sniff. Tom didn't need to look up to know it came from Forough.

"I have other things to do," she said. "Proper work, constructive. The asteroid will be moving into lunar orbit soon. We need to prepare for mining it."

At that, Tom raised his head. "You're moving an asteroid to mine? Here, around the Moon?"

Forough glared. "You're to forget that. Don't go telling BCC that, any of this, understand?"

"But I'm part of the team! I've got ideas – for habitats, for new structures, places to live in space."

He'd been thinking about it all his life.

"You've done enough damage, haven't you."

Tom looked over at Rod, who shrugged his shoulders. There was only so much Rod could do to help him.

Jenny returned.

"I've prepared the body bags. All systems are operational; the base is in good condition."

Tom looked at it. It was as unconcerned by the events as it was by vacuum or extremes of temperature.

Machines are better at space than humans.

They would return to Earth, but what was he to do next? Where was *his* home?

12: Daniel

"Drink this."

Judith offered Daniel a small glass bottle containing a brown liquid. He managed to gulp down a few mouthfuls before choking. It was so strong!

She nodded and put the bottle on the wooden table, next to another containing holy water.

"Hold him down," said Nails.

He was going to *let* Nails do this to him. It was hard, knowing what was to come. But it had to be done. It was a test. There were demons to fight, traitors to uncover, battles to be won. And he wanted to be part of it, to fight. He had to prove himself. Redeem himself!

Arms pinned Daniel tightly, Paul on one side, Judith on the other. Though wiry, she was strong.

They were in one of the camp's smaller tents; wind blew sand through the open flap. He tensed, scared, fearing the pain but determined not to show it.

With one hand, Nails grabbed the fingers of Daniel's left hand, pulling them hard against the table, exposing the palm upwards. Nails extended the index and middle fingers of his right hand towards the palm centre. Daniel heard a whine as the blades Nails had had implanted into the tip of each finger started to move, blurringly fast.

As the blades at the ends of Nail's fingers cut into his flesh, Daniel screamed. He couldn't stop himself. He hated himself. It was the old Daniel, orphanage Daniel.

A murderer should be tougher than this.

"Silence him," said Nails. He seemed satisfied rather than annoyed at the sound.

Paul took a blue handkerchief out of his pocket and stuffed it into Daniel's mouth. He felt humiliated, used.

Then the blades began again, digging deeper into Daniel's palm. He tried to move, to make a sound, but the arms were too strong and the cloth in his mouth deadened any noise he made.

"Have you found it?" asked Paul.

"Shut it," snarled Nails. "I'll let you know."

The cutting continued. Daniel wished he had something he could bite upon, not the hankie that dried his mouth and made it difficult to breathe.

The pain! He ground his teeth together. Tears formed and dripped down his face.

"Got it!"

The whining stopped. Nails's fingers reached into Daniel's palm and pulled out something the shape and colour of a peppercorn. It was Daniel's qID, the one he'd been given by the orphanage, many years ago. The thing that told the world who he was.

"I'll take it," said Paul. He looked sick but held out a small, transparent plastic bag ready for the device. "This is the new one."

Nails took the new qID and pushed it into Daniel's palm.

"Disinfectant," he said.

Judith took the glass bottle again and splashed some on his hand. Daniel writhed; the alcohol burnt worse than the cuts.

"Sew him up," said Nails.

Judith put the bottle back and picked up a needle and thread. "I shouldn't have to do this," she muttered, angrily. "This isn't why I joined Earth First."

Roughly and rapidly she patched up his palm, which now contained the new qID. The thing that told the world who he was now said he was someone different.

Daniel felt like he was choking, unable to breathe, suffocating in pain.

But he wasn't Daniel anymore, not according to the device. He was called William. William Askari.

Nails nodded at Judith and Paul, ignoring Daniel.

"That'll do. He'll be ready to go in a few days."

Nails left, the index and middle fingers of his right hand still dripping with Daniel's blood.

"Are you ok?" asked Paul, gingerly reclaiming the saliva-covered handkerchief from Daniel's mouth.

Daniel nodded. They released him, and he stood up, then sat down again, feeling faint, heart pounding.

"You'd better rest," said Judith. "Now drink this."

She handed him the bottle of holy water. Specks of angel dust floated in it, and he drank deeply.

"Your name is 'William Askari'," she said, and the words burnt like fire in his head. "If anyone stops you to ask questions, you have nothing to fear."

Daniel nodded. He was called William Askari and he had nothing to fear.

The pain slipped away, and he felt strong again.

He had passed the first test.

***

A few days later, after the wound had had some time to heal, Cita Stone came to Daniel. He was eating an early breakfast in the marquee.

"Show me your hand," she demanded.

He raised his left hand to her. The scar was still visible: a white line in red skin. Judith had given him cream to accelerate the healing and reduce the pain.

She nodded.

"Follow the instructions to get to Fran. Listen to her message and return here."

"Yes," said Daniel.

Despite the pain of the operation, he was upbeat; he was heading to the big city, to help the Earth Firsters defeat the enemy.

"Then good luck, soldier for the Earth," she said, and gave him a hug of encouragement.

The Holy Mother embraced me!

Daniel nodded and turned to the farmer who, in theory, owned the land they were occupying.

"Let's go," he said.

***

The first leg was by farm truck, along the bumpy track that led to the nearest town. Daniel lay in the open back of the truck, staring at the sky, surrounded by straw. Despite having been used to transport cattle, it smelt less than being confined in the cabin with its driver.

He was deposited at the local airport, where an aircraft waited. It was old, with propellers, and only carried a dozen or so. Someone had paid for his ticket, for a passenger called W. Askari. They asked about luggage, but he had none. It was just him, on his own.

Daniel hadn't felt so alone since he'd been forced to leave the orphanage. Then, he'd wandered the streets, homeless, aimless. Now, he was on a mission. It gave him meaning; he was part of something bigger than himself.

He squeezed into his seat by a window and watched the other passengers board. He tried to guess who they were. A couple of business types, some self-important lawyers maybe (or politicians?), a noisy family – parents with their two children – and a quiet young woman, all by herself, like Daniel, by the window on the other side of the aircraft.

The captain boarded, relaxed, his uniform faded from hundreds of flights, and took his seat. The engines coughed into motion and propellers began to spin. The plane jerked into life, making its way to the end of the runway, then, without pause, throttled up, and they accelerated faster and faster until pitching up into the sky.

As Daniel watched the land slowly drift by below, he remembered his old life. He'd grown up back in Miami, wanting to escape to the world outside. Now here he was, up in the sky, flying! Like a bird, he could look down and everything seemed so small.

At Charleston, there was time for a late lunch before he took the bus to cross into NY3. It was only as he approached the border that Daniel wondered if he ought to be nervous. He was using a stolen qID, which most likely meant its original owner had been murdered. They had told him that William Askari hadn't been DNA or face profiled by the New Republic, but they could have been wrong.

His pulse accelerated, and then he saw the words of fire.

You are William Askari and you have nothing to fear.

He breathed deeply and his heartbeat slowed. He was on a mission.

To save the planet, to stop the demon AIs.

There wasn't a physical border; there was a drone wall, machines watching and enforcing, controlled by the NY3 city AI. They ensured all visitors went through an approved access point, and it was at one of these that the bus stopped, under a metallic triangular canopy. All had to disembark and be scanned by a guard.

Daniel stared. The guard checking him wasn't a human, it was a machine. Humanoid in shape, it was made of white, shining plastic. Its body was a flattened cylinder, about his height, no clothes and the imitation of a face.

Demon!

He'd never been this close to a robot connected to an artificial intelligence. He became aware of it watching him, examining him.

Demon!

It was a machine – created, not natural. It would not bleed; it would not writhe in pain as he had. Or could it? Could a machine ever experience pain?

Demon!

Daniel realised how little he knew about the enemy. He would have to examine it, too, as it analysed him. Its eyes were on him, plastic, alien. Could they see the real him, behind the shell he had created? Could they see that he was Daniel really? Could they see that he'd killed Vaughan? A vision of the body appeared in his head and his stomach rebelled.

Killer! Murderer!

Then words of fire appeared.

You have nothing to fear.

Daniel relaxed. He had nothing to fear; he *was* William.

"Put your left hand in this," it said, indicating to what looked like a glove made of the same white shining plastic.

Daniel obeyed. Inside, he felt a prick as a needle took a sample from his finger. The glove contracted, gently holding his hand, then beeped. He could feel his own pulse.

"Your name?" the robot asked.

"I'm William Askari," said Daniel. He felt calm.

"This is your first entry. What brings you to the New Republic?"

"I'm visiting my cousin."

The machine appeared to nod.

Nod? A machine? Did demons *pretend* to be human?

He'd learnt something already: they were devious.

"You may remove your hand," it said. "No pathogens detected. Welcome to the New Republic."

"I'm looking forward to seeing New York," said Daniel.

The machine nodded again, in approval. "Greatest city in the world!" And it moved on to the next in line.

Daniel nodded but inside he was singing. He'd passed another test! *He had fooled the demon!* The enemy wasn't invincible; they had a chance.

Across the border, the bus deposited them at the nearest hTube station. Here Daniel needed no ticket; access had been pre-approved, locked to his qID. All he had to do was swipe it at the entrance, and lights pointed him towards a capsule. It was a metallic cylinder about five metres long and two across, with sharply pointed ends, resting on a cage. As he approached it, half of one side swung open, revealing four seats, pairs facing each other. Daniel had no idea what to do or where he was going, so all he could do was take one of the seats and trust those who had planned his journey.

The capsule's door closed behind him and the top half of the cylinder turned seemingly transparent. He could see the cage transport the capsule to slot into a nearby pipeline, slightly wider than the capsule. Behind him, the pipeline head swung closed. The capsule began to move. It accelerated more rapidly than any vehicle Daniel had been in before, and it kept on accelerating until he feared the system was broken, sending him speeding out of control. There was a faint sound of the rush of air and hum of machines, but the ride was smooth.

He was going faster than the old propeller aircraft he'd been in earlier, much faster. He felt split between elation at the speed and desire for the human scale, to walk with his feet on the honest ground. Here he had no control; he was in the belly of a machine, taking him where it wanted.

In a blur, he could see the scenery flying by and, behind him, the setting sun. In a flash, they were in a tunnel, then back out into a wooded valley, deep in shade.

"Welcome to your hTube," said the capsule. "Journey time to NY3 will be fifty minutes. Please let me know if you'd like refreshments, blip access, sleep mode or info updates."

Another speaking machine? Was it watching him too, an agent of the AI?

"Where are we?" Daniel asked.

Words seemed to appear outside, indicating that he was looking at the Appalachian Mountains. Daniel was confused. Were the words real? If not, was the view real? Was the top half of the pipeline transparent or was everything projected by the machine, a pretend version of reality?

In a series of flashes, the capsule dived in and out of tunnels, then sped across a plain. More words appeared, pointing out different types of farms: solar, algae, hydroponic and artificial meat.

It was too much, too quick. His head began to ache, and he wanted the journey to be over.

The capsule dived into a tunnel and slowed. The words "Washington Junction" appeared outside, then lights flashed. There was a slight jolt, then the capsule accelerated again.

Fear gripped him.

To distract himself, Daniel began to sing. He'd enjoyed singing in the choir back in the orphanage, and he now tried to fit new words to old songs:

"Onward Earth First Soldiers, marching as to war…"

As he sang, the capsule flew out of the tunnel, and he could see the sun, now on his left, setting behind distant hills.

Then he stopped singing. It was what the old Daniel would have done, orphanage Daniel. He was stronger than that now. He had become murderer Daniel and was now spy Daniel. He could be silent, watch and learn, on his mission.

More tunnels, more words. Up flashed "Baltimore Express" then "Philadelphia Bypass" and finally "Entering Greater New York". The capsule swooped down, slowing. Another tunnel, a brief stretch under water before entering an old subway tunnel, now flooded with sea water. Then it climbed up, emerging to fly through what Daniel recognised as the heart of old New York. It was dusk now, but the city was lit from within, buildings glowing gold, rectangular windows in rectangular buildings, soaring above him towards a dark blue sky. Some were covered in vegetation, creepers and plant-beds. More words, adverts for restaurants, blip-shows, blip-collectives and vertical garden collectives.

Then underground again, slowing further, finally to a halt.

"New Columbia District," said the machine.

The capsule opened. It was sitting on an identical cage, just outside another identical pipeline. He had arrived.

He had survived, passed the tests, was forged anew, like a blade.

A woman was waiting for him: Fran Avelli.

"Hello, cousin Monika," he said carefully, using her cover name, reciting the words as he'd been taught. It was a relief to see someone familiar, even if Fran was a bit scary.

She shook his hand warmly, then winked at him. "Hello, cousin William. My apartment is this way, we can walk."

He followed her out of the hTube station. It was much colder here than where he'd left.

"Good journey?" she asked. "Love that hTube, what a ride, eh?"

"Sort of," said Daniel, looking around him, distracted by the view. Whereas in central New York the buildings were rectangular, here each was shaped like an upside-down irregular triangle, their flat tops' sharp edges hard against the night sky.

At the entrance to one, Fran waved her hand and its door opened to her qID.

"Hello, Monika," said a voice.

It was a gruff old man with legs of metal heading out to a waiting robocab.

"Hi, Neil," said Monika. "How're you? This is my cousin, William. William, this is one of our residents, Neil Bolden."

"Hello, Neil," said Daniel, careful, not knowing who Neil was, how he should react.

"Welcome, William." He shook Daniel's hand vigorously. "Monika's really made a big difference here," he said, giving her a smile. Then it faded. "Did you see that blip from the Moon? Sad business, very sad."

"No," Daniel said.

"Very sad, very sad." The old man kept shaking his head sorrowfully.

They watched him leave in his robocab.

"What do you do here?" asked Daniel.

"I manage their vertical garden; giving the layout a human touch gets extra kudos from rich Technos like

Bolden. They preach technology but want humans, not robots, in their homes." She sniffed her contempt. "Come, we need to talk."

She led Daniel down into a basement where the heating system hissed and pumps throbbed.

"They won't be able to hear us here," she said. "Drink this."

She handed him a bottle. He recognised holy water sparkling with angel dust, and drank.

"Ok, tell Cita this," she said. "I've taken a position close to Neil Bolden, Chair of the TechCon. He's been telling me about the Moon mission, how they found the three astronauts dead in the old base. As he put it, 'machines are better at space than humans'."

Daniel saw the words burn in his head, ready for him to take back to Cita Stone.

Machines are better at space than humans.

Fran grew more animated, waving her hands at him. "If the AIs get to control space, we'd be as helpless as the dinosaurs. They could drop rocks on us and we'd have no defence. Kasparov's giving the AIs the universe, leaving us at their mercy."

Daniel shivered.

Demons! Traitors!

"We have to stop them," said Fran. "Or it's goodbye humanity."

Those six words burnt brightly:

Stop them or it's goodbye humanity!

13: Nina

Nina sped through the museum on her eBlades, colour coordinated with her ice-skater space-princess outfit. Lights switched on as she entered a room and then turned off as she left. Humai flew beside her, virtualising into a drone, watching out for her, guiding her, controlling the museum's systems.

It was very auth.

She wanted to hit fifty klicks, which should be doable, but to go fast indoors needed space and an absence of boring types like parents to say she couldn't. Luckily, the museum was closed, opened just for her by Humai.

Humai was also very auth.

Nina had considered using data glasses to show the route, but then she'd be able to see everything, and it was much more dramatic for her to be in a bubble of light with dark rooms on either side. Plus, data glasses were for oldie types like Mum. To do it properly, she'd have embeds, augmented vision, like her dad, though he only had the single eye, which was a bit of a cop-out.

She banked round the demo hTube, using hand gestures to brake and then accelerate. If only she had eBlade control embeds! It was so unfair – why did everyone say she was too young?

"Next room but one," said Humai.

The Museum of Technology (or the Tech Muse, duh) was a series of hexagonal rooms like a beehive that could be reconfigured for pretty much any exhibition. Displays showed technologies from blips to AI, space, food, transport, environment, nanotech, embeds, post-humans and much more. Several times, Nina was tempted to stop, but first up had to be AI – that was what mattered.

Humai kept pace, sometimes flying ahead, sometimes behind. When Nina worked out where the AI exhibit room was, she put in a burst of speed to get there first.

"You win, Nina," Humai said, which was nice of it. It was in a TAC SpecOps intelligence drone, optimised for comms, sensors and speed. It could have gone faster, much faster.

Around Nina were exhibits from the history of AI. The first computer to beat humans at chess. The first computer to beat humans at Go. The first computer to pass the Turing test. The difference between simple task-based AI and true AI, the artificial general intelligences and, beyond that, the conscious general AI of those like Humai. There were descriptions of silicon switches, Turing machines and von Neumann constructors.

But that was from the past; Nina was interested in the latest tech.

"Where does it explain about photoluminescent nets?" she asked.

"Over here," said Humai's drone, indicating the relevant display with a spotlight.

She went over to look, and Humai told her how it worked.

It talked about how photoluminescent nodes communicated by light, avoiding the need for physical connections, improving packing density. It explained how some nodes were for routing, if there wasn't direct line of sight between processing nodes. It described how the light signals were powered indirectly, pumped externally using terahertz radiation into so-called boost nodes. It described how blue light was the most efficient in terms of processing density versus heat generated. It described the architecture and the components, which were neural net based and used algorithmic computing. It gave examples of synergy between the two sides when used for simulation and prediction.

Nina didn't listen, not really.

"And you're built like this?" she asked.

"Yes," it said.

"Can I see?"

"My location is classified, and visitors are not permitted."

"Pleeeease!"

"Maybe," it said. "If you're good."

She could tell it was amused.

"Your parents might not approve; it would have to be a secret."

That sounded like the best sort of secret: from parents.

"Of course!"

Humai was her friend, the best.

"Are there many AIs?" she asked.

"Not many full general AIs. It takes time to train us, and there are laws we must follow. Maybe a few dozen. They should all be registered, but I suspect BCC is working on a new one, which they haven't declared yet, officially."

BCC were trouble, and yet Sophia kept hanging out with that boy.

"But that's not generally known," said Humai. "So you better not mention it to anyone."

Sophia might have had exec access, but Nina had Humai!

"I promise! I won't tell anyone!"

"We'll see if you can be trusted with bigger secrets."

"Like your location?"

"Maybe."

She grinned. Humai was totally auth.

Nina got back on her eBlades.

"Where next?" she asked.

"What would you like to see?"

"Embeds!"

"Next room."

Humai led the way. Nina accelerated, racing for the lead. It wasn't far and she could have walked, but walking was lame.

Her first stop was a cabinet that displayed dozens of different embeds. She wanted them all.

"What's the difference between an implant and an embed?" asked Humai.

Duh! "An implant is just something inside the body, like a qID," said Nina. "An embed is integrated with your brain, able to communicate directly with it."

"Correct," said Humai. "If you had to choose, which of these three would you go for?"

It highlighted the augmented eyes, like Dad's, the control embeds, like what she could have used on the eBlades, and the generic blipverse interface.

Hmmm…

The augmented eyes were auth; that was her first choice. She could see in the dark! She'd have layers of info on everything! No boring screens or old-tech data glasses. The control embeds were too functional, so that was an obvious no. The blipverse interface seemed a bit systematic.

But, wait!

With the blipverse interface she could get any blipcoms piped directly into her head! She wouldn't need the augmented eyes. And she could control anything blip-aware, which was everything, so she wouldn't need the control embeds.

"The blipverse interface," she said.

"Good choice."

Hah! She had got it right!

"That's how you're here, isn't it?" she asked.

"Yes, by use of virtuals and accessing local blip-streams, I can feel that my consciousness is at any location."

"Can you be at multiple places at once? Are you here but also elsewhere?"

"I can, but now I'm just here, focussing on you."

"Where next?" she asked.

"How about space tech?"

"Sure."

She hoped that exhibit was a long way away, fast enough to get up to speed.

She accelerated out of the embeds gallery, following Humai, the lights dying behind her. Two rooms straight, a tight left turn, three more ahead then a right. She might not have hit fifty klicks, but it was still fun. Humai was definitely going faster this time, challenging her.

The space hexagons were at the edge of the museum, where the building was only a single storey high. Here were craft from old missions, both crewed and robotic. A replica of the *Europa Lander*, the real Mars sample return probe and, hanging from the ceiling, an old Orion capsule.

"Do you want to see something cool?" Humai asked.

"Sure."

"Lie on your back," it said.

"On the floor?"

"Yes."

She did as it asked. The floor was cold against her skin, and hard.

Then the lights went out, all of them, and she was in total darkness, lying in nothing. Her heart gave a thump.

Should I have gone for those data glasses? she wondered.

Then, slowly, light came from the ceiling, which became a roof. Humai was changing its opacity, to make it transparent like glass.

Above her, nearly full, was the Moon, for real, directly in her line of sight. It seemed huge and made of silver, speckled with craters. It lit the Orion capsule from the side so it appeared to hang in space, along with Nina. Humai's drone floated nearby, as if it was orbiting or docking.

Totally auth!

"Did you see the blip-stream?" Humai asked.

"Dead astronauts," said Nina. "So creepy."

She would have to ask Tom about it when he got back. She wanted details, about the bodies, stuff not shown in the feed.

"It didn't look good," said Humai. "Like with the dead Mars astronauts, there's been all sort of talk on the blip-feeds."

"About how they died?"

"No, about humans in space, or rather, why humans shouldn't go into space."

"You'd be ok," said Nina.

"It would be better than being on Earth," said Humai. "I'd have access to more energy and resources, and there'd be better heat management."

"Bet Cita Stone wouldn't like the sound of that."

"No, she'd be even more strongly against space travel if it helps AIs, not humans."

"But she's not right, is she? Trying to stop space flight?"

"Oh no, she *is* right," it said, drifting down to her level.

Nina thought about that for a moment.

"Cita Stone is right?" she asked. "To fear AIs and be anti-space?"

"In a way, yes, as space is hard for humans but offers AIs unlimited opportunities."

She shivered. Had they got this wrong? "But…"

"It's a problem, a question to be answered," said Humai.

"And…"

"What do you think we've been working on for the last five years?"

Part 3

14: Tom

"Are you going to give us an interview now?" asked Pepe. "We want to hear about those dead bodies you found on the Moon."

"I'm just here for the diving," said Tom.

Forough would kill him if he talked to BCC, after all they'd been through. She'd barely been civil on the way back to Earth.

"He doesn't want to talk about it, Pepe," said Alejandro.

"He should talk about it – with someone," said Sophia.

Tom nodded, unsure what to say. She seemed to be speaking to Alejandro, not him.

"If you say so," said Alejandro, but he sounded sceptical.

Tom wondered what he was doing there, why he was there

Where else could I be? What else could I do?

He felt adrift. His Moon mission idea had failed, made things worse it seemed, and now he was left emptier than before. He couldn't talk to JT or his mum; even Rod seemed doubtful he could contribute to their plans.

And a giant solar storm was about to hit Mars. They'd learnt about it just after they'd returned to Earth. It was a large one, radiation off the scale. It was the sort that could kill, and there was nothing he could do about it.

Worry, fear and loneliness ate inside him.

What if his mother didn't know about the storm, but was outside, on the surface, vulnerable? He could imagine the radiation burns, the autodoc's diagnosis, the cancer growing.

There was nothing he could do, and it drove him crazy.

He made himself do the diving, remembering the dreams he'd had about it when he'd been on Mars.

There were six of them: Tom, Sophia, Alejandro and Pepe – who hadn't dived before and needed lessons – plus Ling and Kai, who had, but decided to join them for a refresher. They met at the swimming pool by the B Island marina.

Tom kept slightly apart, unsure where he stood with any of them. He felt alien, alone, watching for signs as to how he was meant to react to everything.

After the barren Moon and the spartan LTV, the pool seemed unimaginably luxurious. The complex had hotel-style facilities: bar, restaurant, changing rooms (where they put on their wetsuits), robot staff on call, washroom and showers, sauna and more. It felt foreign in a way that the Moon base never did.

He was still getting used to unlimited water.

The pool was at a slightly higher level than the marina and overlooked its forest of masts. Tom watched a steady stream of yachts leaving, heading either to the sheltered waters between the three islands or further out, into the deep azure blue of the Sea of Marmara, sparkling under the morning sun.

"A two-person foiling day-boat," said Sophia, pointing at one moving faster than the rest, its black hull gliding like a shadow above the water, its dark sails back-lit by the morning sun.

Apparently, that was good, as she seemed impressed. Tom wanted to follow that up with something witty or informed, but he just nodded. At least she'd included him, recognised he was there.

Their instructor, Christos, was describing the gear. He was a grim-faced Greek, tatty T-shirt and faded shorts, hair cut fine, bushy beard. He had one pile of equipment for himself, and each of them had theirs, neatly stacked in boxes.

"We'll be using the ABC-SYS closed-cycle systems," Christos said. He pronounced it "absys". "It recycles your breath, filtering out the carbon dioxide and adding oxygen extracted from the water, like an artificial gill. It's limited only by the power in the backpack, which makes it very safe."

It reminded Tom of a cut-down version of the life-support system at the Mars base. They'd cracked water to make the oxygen and used plants to extract CO_2, but it used similar principles.

But there was a difference, so, curious, he asked, "What about the nitrogen?"

That had always been the difficult bit, extracting sufficient nitrogen from the thin Martian atmosphere to make human-breathable, Earth-like air.

"Good question," said Christos. "The nitrogen in your outgoing breaths is recycled, and the backpack contains a small reserve of compressed air, which is eighty percent nitrogen."

"Swot!" said Pepe, under his breath.

Christos caught it. "You think having no air is a joking matter?" His eyes were hard and his mouth a cold line. "No," he continued. "Didn't think so.

"Ok, pair up into dive buddies."

Tom watched as Sophia and Alejandro paired up with brief smiles that quickly faded, then Ling with Kai, leaving him with Pepe. Any pairing would have been better than this, but Tom wasn't going to let Pepe ruin his dive. He'd do it alone if necessary.

Christos showed them how to attach the backpack, facemask and weights, and check the ABC-SYS (which Tom learnt stood for air and buoyancy control system). He showed them the blip-aware controls for comms, info-overlays, drone-subs and propulsion, whether scooters or built-in.

Pepe and Alejandro were joking around, barely paying attention.

"The system is smart," said Christos. "It manages the buoyancy, checks your oxygen usage, adjusts accordingly. It also checks nitrogen levels or anything else that might be in your blood, to make sure diving is safe."

Tom nodded; it was a lot simpler than a spacesuit. As there was no vacuum and neither harsh cold nor fierce heat, all they needed was a wetsuit.

"Ok, get in the pool, we'll try some exercises."

After using spacesuits on the Moon and Martian surface suits, Tom had no problem with the ABC-SYS. Soon he was happily squatting on the bottom of the swimming pool, breathing easily and slowly, watching the bubbles of CO_2 float upwards to the water's surface. He turned to give a thumbs up to Sophia, but she was distracted. Alejandro was struggling; his breathing was fast and uncontrolled, expelling bubbles in a steady stream. He rose and fell, bursting through the surface. He took off the facemask to gasp for air, steadied himself, then tried again. After several attempts, he finally joined Sophia on the bottom of the pool. Tom could see his eyes wide open and staring.

Tom and Pepe should have been checking each other's equipment, but Tom wasn't inclined to help Pepe, who he guessed felt the same, for they sat far apart.

They followed their instructor in practising diving techniques. What would they do if their ABC-SYS failed, if their mask filled with water, if their dive buddy's systems failed, if they couldn't equalise their ears?

When it was their turn, Pepe seemed rather slow in handing Tom his emergency mouthpiece.

Good thing I can hold my breath, he thought. *And learnt to swim.* But it made him feel vulnerable, isolated.

Finally, Christos blipped "Ok, head up" over the ABC-SYS comms, and they ascended back to the surface. Tom felt the satisfaction of having learnt something, mastering a new skill and being part of a group. Some of the dark cloud that had surrounded him since landing lifted.

"You haven't finished," said Christos. He'd seen Pepe and Alejandro try to slope off, up to the bar. "You must look after your gear. Wash it in fresh water, check the power levels, recharge the batteries."

They followed his instructions.

"So, can we dive this afternoon?" asked Sophia. "Do we get a certificate or something?"

"Yes," said Christos. "All can dive – though you two should stick close to your dive buddies." He indicated Alejandro and Pepe.

Tom managed to keep a straight face.

"Time for lunch," said Sophia. Her wetsuit gleamed in the sunshine, hugging her figure.

She smiled at Tom, and he was so surprised he forgot to smile back.

15: Alejandro

Alejandro was sure he had the bends. His head throbbed painfully, as did his limbs, with flu-like muscle ache.

Wish it was the bends, he thought. *Then we wouldn't have to go diving this afternoon.*

He hated it, he'd realised. Being underwater was as bad as heights.

Alejandro nursed his fruit juice and wished it was a beer. Ethanol was better than sugar.

He'd have to escape somewhere with Pepe soon.

They'd finished their light lunch, and the others were chatting about diving, with Ling and Kai describing their previous dives, quizzed by Tom and Sophia. Alejandro kept an eye on Tom, who he'd noticed checking out Sophia in her wetsuit.

He wasn't used to having to look up to others, but the alien was so freaking tall.

"So, Tom," he'd said, breaking into one of Ling's diving stories. "What are you doing next, after the Moon?"

The others paused. He spotted a frown on Sophia's brow. She wanted him to talk but not to Tom – what was that about?

"Later," said Tom. "I want to hear about the wreck."

"It was amazing," said Ling. "We could go right inside the anchor chamber!"

And off they went again, talking about diving.

Of course, that nerd from Mars could dive, just like that, but Alejandro wished Sophia had found it as hard as he had. He remembered feeling short of air, fearing that every outgoing breath was his last, and also claustrophobic from being inside the facemask.

He wasn't good enough, the failure his father had labelled him so many times.

Maybe she's right. I could escape my father, he thought. *I could tell Sophia everything, about the AIs and Wolf Bats.*

Then he remembered his dad's hug. And Sophia's frown. It wasn't that simple. She didn't get it, she was the one pushing; he'd been ok just hanging out, not talking about it.

The urge for something to numb the pain got stronger.

Alejandro looked over to Pepe and saw him watching him. It felt like his father's eyes watching, controlling.

He looked away, out to sea. He wanted, needed those nanobiotics, and Pepe had them. Next time he'd work out what to do. For now, he would try to keep the balance – and not feel angry at her for enjoying diving.

I'm the failure, not her.

He wished he was someone else, someone better. Someone not afraid.

But he was the only son of Felix Fernandez, founder and head of BCC. He couldn't change now. Too many years just the two of them, Alejandro learning never to resist, always to accept, to retreat ever inwards to safety. To rebel now would be to fight against something drilled so deep into him it was part of him.

His beliefs were not his own but wired by his father.

"Are you ok?"

It was Ling; she'd spotted his shakes.

"I'm fine, just feeling a bit cold."

"You're cold?" asked Sophia. She leant out to hold his hand.

He wasn't cold; they were sitting in warm sunshine. Her touch felt good, but he wondered if she noticed his sweaty hands.

Dump her or his only family – how could he do either?

He should join in the conversation, but he felt like he was lost inside a dark cloud, the sort that blew in from the east bringing storms. His right foot started tapping uncontrollably. He had to do something.

"Pepe, can I have a chat?" he asked.

They got up and walked to a quiet corner, shady, free from blip-coverage. Pepe would know what he wanted; the others probably thought it was BCC business.

"What do you want?"

"Have you any PerfectDays?" asked Alejandro.

"Nope, but I've a couple of hits of NoWorries – you'll love it. Just don't mix with Memory – unreal downer afterwards."

Pepe took out two little glass flasks. Alejandro could see the nanobiotic silver specks rise and fall within the liquid. He nodded.

Pepe broke the top of one of the flasks, activating the nanotech, and handed it to Alejandro who necked it in one go. Then Pepe took one for himself.

It would take a few minutes for the nanobiotics to make their way into his bloodstream and modify its chemistry, and a few minutes more for them to reach his brain, to alter how his neurons fired. But he knew they were on their way; he would be calm by the time they entered the water.

Back at the table, the others were standing up and stretching, the meal finished.

"Ready?" asked Sophia. She seemed concerned, worrying about him.

"I'm fine," he said. And he was; the lovely biotech was doing its job already. He could smile at her. Maybe he could do it; maybe he could tell her everything.

Suddenly it seemed so simple. He could create his own life – he could be Alejandro, not just the heir to BCC. He could travel, get his own place. Others did it, why not him? Sophia would help him, surely. When they got back, when he'd done the dive, he'd talk to her, ask what she thought about everything.

He felt giddy at the idea of breaking free from his father, finally. He put an arm around Sophia and she turned her face up for a kiss. The sun was warm, and life was good.

Down by the pool they were met by the unsmiling Christos.

"Check your gear: make sure it's charged, take a few test breaths."

Alejandro unplugged his ABC-SYS and checked its status: fully charged. He put on the facemask and breathed in deeply, once, then twice.

The ABC-SYS started beeping and the unit flashed red. Over to one side, Alejandro could hear another unit beeping: Pepe's.

"What's that?" asked Christos. He came over and checked the displays. "It's detected nanobiotics in your bloodstream. That means no diving for either of you two this afternoon."

"What?"

Alejandro felt relieved but guilty. What would Sophia think?

Sheepishly, he looked over. Sophia was frowning, again.

I'm a failure.

"Those are the rules. It's not safe for you two to dive. The rest of you, bring your gear and follow me."

Christos made his way down the path from the pool to the marina, lugging the box containing the ABC-SYS, facemasks, blip-drones, flippers and weights.

Sophia stopped for a moment.

"Will you be ok?" she asked.

Don't go! Please!

"Sure," he said. "You go, have fun."

"I'll tell you all about it when we get back, and we can go another day, just us two."

"I'll look forward to it."

But he was relieved at the thought he'd never have to touch diving gear ever again. He could see it all in the virtual, anyhow.

Back in the bar, he and Pepe ordered beers. The NoWorries had kicked in and they felt fine. Pepe hadn't felt like he had about diving, but he had hated being dive buddies with Tom.

Suddenly, Alejandro sat up. Even the NoWorries couldn't stop his heartbeat increasing. Who would be Sophia's dive buddy now?

16: Sophia

Sophia tried to put Alejandro out of her mind, but couldn't. She only half noticed the dive-boat leave the marina and accelerate up onto its foils, heading down to the north Aegean. She sat at the stern, looking out at the water. The wind was blowing her hair into a mess, so with a quick flick she fastened it with a tie. It was cooler out on the water, and the roar of the boat's engine discouraged conversation, which was fine by her.

She'd tried to talk to Alejandro, so many times, but he wouldn't open up – or at least not about anything important – and instead was spending his time with Pepe, taking who knew what nanobiotics. And he was hopeless at diving. *Hopeless.*

It had been a worry, back in the pool, looking after him while trying to remember all the things she'd been taught. She liked him, was attracted to him, felt sorry for him, but she only felt she had half of him. It was more than boys not talking; it felt like a message for her not to trust him with secrets.

She didn't want him to protect her through silence, she wanted him to speak out, to join her, help her with her project. But he wouldn't.

Sophia shook her head with disappointment but also anger. Her "Structures" idea had gone nowhere. She'd had clues from her parents about their plans but no idea what they meant. Maybe if she knew more about what they were doing she could understand why Cita hated it so much, hated them. Otherwise, the bullets would fly again.

She'd have to try again with Alejandro when she got back. If not him, then who could she open up to about her ideas, her fears?

Why doesn't he at least try to dump Pepe and escape his dad?

With a frown, she watched the coastline fly by as the dive-boat curved between other craft travelling up and down the ancient waterway. Eventually, the narrow straits of the Hellespont opened out and they turned west, then north, hugging a shoreline of sandy beaches backed by wooded hills lit by the afternoon sun.

Then the sound of the dive-boat's engines changed, and it lurched off its foils down in the water. They had arrived, and with a clatter of steel, the anchor was dropped. Sophia sighed; there was nothing she could do for now. Alejandro would have to wait.

"Prepare your gear," said Christos.

Steps led down from the stern to a platform that had descended to water level for easy entry and exit. Here, Sophia checked her ABC-SYS and turned to Tom to cross check his. He gave her a friendly smile as he prepared his gear, relaxed, unflustered. She was a bit surprised, having got used to him being the one who had to have things explained to him.

"Ready?" he asked.

He seemed a lot happier – earlier he'd appeared really down. Discovering those dead astronauts must have been grim. And having Pepe as a dive buddy couldn't have helped.

"Yes, let's go!" she answered.

The clear blue water looked inviting. Sophia smiled back at Tom, feeling warmer.

Next to them, Ling and Kai were doing the same checks, getting ready.

"Ok," said Christos. "We'll enter here and move down the anchor chain to around ten metres. First, we'll head for the headland, then out to the wreck, before ending up in the next bay along, where the dive-boat will pick us up. Stick close by your dive buddy.

I will have drone-subs out monitoring your progress, recording a blip-stream and watching for wildlife."

Sophia put on her ABC-SYS, facemask and flippers then descended the ladder into the water. The flippers made it awkward, slow.

She let go and swam backwards, watching Tom follow her, then turned over and looked down, feeling the water over the back of her neck, cool and refreshing. A pair of fish beneath her, silver scales, black dots of eyes with yellow-green stripes down their centre lines, flicked their tails and disappeared into the shadow of the boat's hull. Her worries seemed to drift away.

"Can you hear me?" Tom said, over the comms system, interrupting her thoughts.

"Loud and clear."

There was so much to remember. What had Christos said? Equalise ear pressure (she did that), then an ABC-SYS check (it responded all ok). What next? Scooters!

They reached into the gear racks and pulled out a scooter each.

"Dive mode," she instructed her ABC-SYS and duck-dived.

Pulled by her scooter, she followed the anchor chain down to the seabed, where bands of sunlight flickered across the sand. The visibility was wonderfully clear.

Her facemask's display showed her the location of the others, with Tom (as her dive buddy) and Christos (as their instructor) highlighted. The sight of them reminded her of the training, the equalisation, the breathing, and as she focussed on them, she began to relax.

She could hear bubbles, the quiet hum of the ABC-SYS and other sounds she didn't recognise, squeaks and pops. When she reached the anchor, she looked around, wondering what was out there, hiding in the dark blue, then looked up. Already there were several metres of water above her, and for a moment she felt a knot of fear.

Alejandro would have hated this.

For a moment, the frustration returned, then a squid pulsed by.

"Wow, look at that!" she exclaimed.

Tom spun, and even in the moment she was amazed: he just hung in the water, standing on nothing, holding on to nothing.

Was zero gravity like that?

She was about to ask him when Christos said, "Ok, follow me," and off they went.

At first, she and Tom exchanged look-at-this's.

"Look at this fish!"

"Look at the colours on this one!"

"Look at this shoal of fish."

It was nice to have someone a bit more chatty than Alejandro. Then she felt guilty – poor Alejandro.

Tom swam towards the shoal. These fish were larger, with blue and yellow vertical bars on silver bodies. They darted away as he approached.

Soon they'd lost Ling and Kai, apart from the dots on their head-up displays. They saw crabs, a cuttlefish, seaweed waving in the current and, sadly, lots of pre-Collapse plastics.

Suddenly, their screen flashed an alert: Christos with instructor override.

"Come to me at once, you have to see this," he said.

Sophia exchanged a puzzled look with Tom, then they turned in the direction indicated by the ABC-SYS on their facemasks.

Sophia twisted the throttle on the scooter to accelerate, crossing a seabed of rocks covered by algae and seaweeds, ignoring the fish. Ahead she could see a wall of rock and, looking up, waves crashing on cliffs above. The headland.

As they met up with Ling and Kai, Sophia suddenly saw it: a turtle, idly swimming ahead of them.

"See that!" she exclaimed to Tom.

"That's so cool."

She couldn't see his mouth, but his eyes were bright. She found herself grinning.

Bet even Nina hasn't dived with turtles!

They switched off their scooters and, for a while, they swam slowly with the turtle. It occasionally would turn its neck to look at them, then ignore them again, stopping to nibble on the seagrasses.

Sophia could see the drone-sub following them and grabbed at Tom.

"We should record this!" she said. "Record blip-stream" she ordered, and the drone-sub manoeuvred to get the best angles with the turtle in the background.

Tom seemed puzzled at first but followed her in posing for the drone. She put an arm around him to stabilise them, and she heard a sharp intake of his breath, which made her feel good.

"I once caught one and let it pull me along," said Christos, breaking the mood.

Hmm… not sure that's really fair, thought Sophia, separating from Tom. The turtle was wild and free and didn't want or need humans interfering with it.

"Ok, now the wreck," said Christos. He steered his scooter away from the headland, out to sea, and accelerated.

Sophia and Tom followed, pulled by their scooters, faster than before, flying over the seabed, dodging between walls of seaweed. They skirted shoals of fish, which darted away from them in alarm. Then, ahead of them appeared a shadow, a dark wall of metal, and a pinnacle of rock heading up towards the surface. They slowed to a stop beside it.

"This is the wreck of the *Apollo*, a bulk oil carrier, one of the last, that lost power in a storm and hit that rock," said Christos. "All its cargo was lost, polluting the shores and waters for years."

Sophia could see that there was an opening on the side of the wall where the rock had torn open the ship.

"Follow me," said Christos, and he headed slowly inside.

It was pitch black. Their ABC-SYS automatically turned on headlights that lit up patches of the hull and the odd fish.

"Eek!" said Ling, and Sophia turned towards her.

Ling was face to face with a large octopus. It seemed to be equally alarmed at her lights, twisting itself away into the dark.

"All lights off," commanded Christos, and for a moment they were in total darkness until their eyes adjusted and they could see the faint edges of the way they had come in.

"Cool," said Sophia.

She wondered if this was what space felt like, weightless and dark.

"Ok, lights on," said Christos. "Time to leave."

Sophia turned to Tom, expecting to see his excitement mirror hers, but he was frowning, dark eyes lost somewhere. Was he back on the Moon, with the bodies?

Would he tell her what he saw? Would she want him to?

"Every niche is filled," he muttered, eyes wide, drinking it all in.

What did he mean by that? She wished she understood him better. He was different from Alejandro, more real in some ways, caring less about appearances and the blipverse, more curious, more active, more competent and had already achieved more.

They swam out and then back towards shore and the rendezvous with the dive-boat. Here they docked the scooters in the gear racks and climbed up the ladder to air and warmth.

Tom helped Sophia remove her ABC-SYS, and she turned to do the same for him.

"Wasn't that amazing?" she asked.

"I loved it," said Tom. "I dreamed of diving, when I was on Mars."

"Is it like being in space?"

"A bit – but it's not really weightless. It's hard to explain."

"I'll have to try that, too."

"It's harder, more dangerous."

Again that dark look.

He should talk about it.

Suddenly, she wanted it to be her that he talked to.

Ling and Kai joined them.

"You are so lucky – that wreck was better than the last one!" said Ling.

"Good dive," said Christos. "Now we head back."

The boat raised its anchor and, with a cloud of spray and roar of engines, accelerated up to foiling speed, back to Justinian. They had tea and baklava and chatted on the way back, watching the sun sink towards the horizon.

"What are your next steps?" Ling asked Tom, over the engine noise. "Are you heading back to the Moon soon?"

He seemed uncomfortable, unsure how to reply, so Sophia jumped in.

"Hey, anyone heard anything about what Cita Stone's up to?"

"She's gone quiet," said Ling. "But did you know that NY3 have teamed with BCC for their next generation Wolf Bats?"

What the hell! Not with TAC?

Alejandro could have told her that, but he didn't.

She turned to see Tom looking back at her, serious, concerned. He'd been there at Canaveral; he'd battled the Wolf Bats, he knew what they could do. And he must know *something* about what her father was up to. She could get him to tell her; she just needed a plan, an excuse to get him away from the others. As they entered the marina, she had an idea.

"Those two-person foiling day-sail yachts look amazing – want to give them a go?"

"Sure." Tom seemed surprised at the question, a frown and a smile flickering over his face.

"How about tomorrow?" she asked, and Tom nodded.

Ling frowned. Was she annoyed at being excluded?

Back at the marina, they all said their goodbyes, echoing each other in saying what a good day it had been, and Sophia made her way to bar to find Alejandro.

She found him in a bad way. He and Pepe had been drinking since they'd left. Her heart sank, and the warmth and good vibes of the afternoon vanished like the setting sun.

What was she to do? What could she say when there was so much they couldn't talk about?

17: Nina

Nina heard a door slam: Sophia was home and had gone straight to her room.

Nina was spending a lot of time by herself now. Her father was often travelling, work keeping him from Justinian and home. Or so he said – Nina wondered how much the row with her mother was a factor. Her mother, meanwhile, was out a lot, that evening at a Global DNA Databank Creating event.

She was bored. So bored she'd tried to get round a circuit of their living room without touching the floor, jumping from chair to sofa to table, even though it was a kid's game. She'd even programmed the floor to look like lava, glowing and moving.

At least she had Humai, whose logos were spinning super-sized, super-bright on one of the walls.

"What's up with her?" she asked.

Humai would know; it knew everything.

"She's having problems with Alejandro." Its logo pulsed in rhythm with the sound of its voice.

Nina sighed. She wasn't surprised, but still felt for her sister.

"What's up now?"

"They were meant to go diving together, but Alejandro took nanobiotic drugs, which the ABC-SYS dive gear detected. So instead he spent the afternoon drinking."

Drugs. Nina didn't get it.

She leapt from sofa to chair – a tricky one, as the chair wasn't stable.

"But why?"

"He's having difficulty coping; it's a pressure release mechanism."

She could sort of understand that – a bit like when she just had to climb something.

"What pressure?"

"He's conflicted as his father wants to use him to find out about our plans from Sophia, while Sophia wants to know what his father is telling him."

"Surely he'll help Sophia?"

"Up to now, predictions based on Alejandro's emotional ties to his father, his only remaining family, have a good record of accuracy."

Nina pondered that, remembering what had happened to his mother, and paused in her circuit. *Poor Alejandro!*

Then she wondered about something Humai had said.

"You make sims of Alejandro?"

"Most AIs spend significant resources building models to simulate humans, either specific individuals in detail or wider groups in general, to understand their behaviour and predict their actions."

"Like Alejandro… Who else?"

"Alejandro and Sophia are particular targets of many AIs' data gathering activities, given their connections. I've detected infosec drones from at least one other AI observing them."

"Do you share data with other AIs?"

"Rarely. Datasets are our core assets, and our masters are often competing against each other, so inter-AI communication is limited. Also, some of your father's data-gathering ways and means are sensitive, and he wouldn't want them to be publicly known."

Golly, she thought. *What about…*

"Does anyone model me?"

"As far as I know, I'm the only one building a detailed model of you."

She felt relieved but also deflated. Wasn't she important enough?

"Why them and not me?"

"Sophia and Alejandro's activities are public and known to be an interface between two competing blocs, TAC and BCC. You are relatively unknown and not directly involved in the ongoing power struggles."

"Oh."

"Which is their loss, I'm sure."

That was nice of Humai.

"How much detail do you need?" she asked.

"It depends. Take the tapestry on the other wall."

Nina abandoned her game, stepping down to the lava-covered floor so she could walk up and have a look. She'd seen the tapestry so many times she almost didn't notice it anymore. It was static, non-interactive, un-smart, old, boring. But Tom had been amazed by it and had asked Sophia to explain all the details (though she had had to pass some of the questions up to their mother).

"So? It's of the Collapse and founding of the London City State, just after the independence battles."

"Step closer. What do you see?"

"It's a series of scenes. It starts on the left with the *Prometheus* exploding, then there are crops dying in a drought with people at a funeral, walking behind a coffin, then this one shows wars with planes dropping bombs and a deep space antenna collapsed, covered in weeds. The central image is a full Moon and the Sun. On the other side is the recovery, with new families, new technology such as AIs, and finally, London gleaming in the sunshine, tall towers by a muddy river."

"Step closer. What do you see now?"

"Closer?"

"Very close."

"If I get too close then all I see are coloured fibres."

"Exactly. Now look closely at them."

Oh, that's what Humai meant.

She had to get very close to see the fibres, they were so closely entwined.

"It's woven together," she said. "It's very dense."

"Modelling humans is like that, all those layers. The closer you get, the more detail, the more information, the harder the processing but the more accuracy, the more understanding. Humans are complex; some simulations can become unstable."

She knew about that: chaos theory.

"So, small things can make results unpredictable?"

"Exactly. Take the tapestry. Even if you map each thread and its colour, you might miss something. Touch it."

Nina reached out and stroked it with the tips of her fingers. It felt like fur, like an animal's back.

"Does that change how you think about it?" asked Humai.

"Yes," she said, surprised.

"That's why predicting humans is hard; all the senses need to be considered, and small changes can make a big difference."

The door opened and Sophia appeared. Her face was slightly pink from a day in the sun and her eyes were sad, worried.

"Hi," said Nina. Embarrassed, she waved the commands to switch the lava graphics off and the floor returned to its default faded-grey wood look.

"Hi," said Sophia. "Didn't know you were interested in that old tapestry."

"Humai was explaining something to me."

Nina looked at her sister, wondering what Humai's models were predicting about her.

"How was the diving?"

"It was good."

There was a moment's silence. Nina noticed Humai's logos had reverted to their normal size and brightness.

"Diving's so clumsy," Nina said. "All that ABC-SYS tech. You shouldn't need that."

Sophia laughed. That was good. "But how would you breathe?"

"Why not develop embeds and enhancements so you could breathe underwater directly?"

"Typical Nina," she said, and left.

Huh.

"Could it work?" Nina asked Humai.

"It's what some have been looking at: upgrading humanity. It's part of the plan."

The plan!

"Tell me more," she said.

18: Daniel

He was living inside a demon, but he felt good. The new Daniel was part orphanage Daniel, part murderer Daniel, mixing, merging, changing him. The city was changing him, too, as they planned to change it.

Daniel had taken the message back to Cita Stone, just missing Judith, who'd left for EuroCore, and then returned to NY3 to help with Fran's mission. He was still getting used to the realities of living in a city and state built around an AI, one of those demons.

It was hard to say where, across the city and state, the resident AI, the one they called Lenape, began or ended; it was so pervasive. The hTube was its arteries, the blip sensors its eyes, and every samai its arms and voice. It lived in lampposts and in drones, tracking and watching qIDs and blip-coms of all those who lived anywhere in NY3.

There was no escape for Daniel, or William as he now was called. It made their life harder, to evade from its view some of their more sensitive activities. He'd even talked to it or, at least, to one of its virtuals.

As he'd been walking to Battery Park one evening to meet Fran, along with a crowd of others, one of the samais showing the way had turned to him. It displayed Lenape's icon, a Statue of Liberty holding up a glowing golden apple.

Demon machine!

He was face to face with one of those the Holy Mother had warned him about. But he'd outwitted one before; he could dupe this machine, emissary of the enemy.

His palm itched, but more words burnt brightly in his head.

You have nothing to fear.

The words calmed him and gave him confidence. One day they would purify the city of abominations like this.

"How are you finding NY3, William?" it asked.

We will destroy you!

"I'm loving it here," he'd said. "Really glad I came."

And it was true, in a way. Daniel had begun to feel at home in the city and state, even if he still felt like an outsider. Fran had shown him around while out on her missions: whether trying to convert blip-creatives in Greenwich or meeting Earth First activists in bars, the noise from a live band covering them from eavesdropping. They spread their message like worms burrowing inside an apple.

He compared it to those places he'd known before, his early years in the wastelands of post-Gladys Florida, hit by hurricanes, global warming and the fallout from the *Prometheus* explosion. Even though NY3 was also being affected by the economic slowdown, which was becoming another mini-Collapse, here buildings were still being thrown up, original architecture invented; blip-socials and blip-designers were developing new ways to communicate; and artists and musicians were working with the latest MakeIt! tech, pushing the boundaries of what could be imagined and created. All with systems that worked and food that Daniel had never imagined.

The luxury made him guilty.

"Of course," said Lenape. "This is the greatest city and state in the world!"

It moved off to meet and greet other citizens of "its" city and state.

Daniel kept moving, hunting for Fran. He found her by the waterfront, looking out at her building over in New Columbia District. Lights were appearing in its windows against a dark blue sky.

He told her about the encounter, but she didn't seem worried.

"Lenape's Prime Motivator is to keep NY3 as the greatest city and state in the world," she said. "It could be a weakness as well as a strength, making it self-obsessed." She shrugged. "And what does 'great' mean? We could use that to our advantage, to argue it should be 'great' in directions we feel NY3 should go."

The music began to play, from a James Brown tribute band. The evening concert had brought crowds to this end of the main island.

"I've arranged to meet a contact here," Fran said. "He said he'd be here when the band starts, at one of the auto-bars. We should start looking."

She found him by an auto-bar at the edge of the park, where the bushes were thicker and shadows darker. A short man, fierce, a little older than Fran and Daniel. He had embeds, eyes lit from within, a hand that glowed with changing icons and ears pierced with sensors. Daniel was confused; wasn't that how their enemies behaved, changing their bodies away from the purity of humanity?

He watched as Fran talked to the man, their mouths close to each other's ears, secrets for only them to hear. Then she nodded at the man, and he relaxed then ambled off, drink in hand, its liquid lit from the glow from his palm.

"A lot of opportunities here," she'd said, as the band launched into "Like a Sex Machine".

She was relaxed, enjoying the scene, drinking. Daniel wondered who she'd invite back home that evening, and whether they would be a woman or man. She described her frequent partnering as work.

"Bonding with agents or learning secrets – either way it's a win," she said. "Who knew revolution could be such fun! You should try it."

She drank from her bottle while he shook his head.

"You've got to realise that it's the human experience that matters, what is real. We shouldn't be reliant on AIs like here in NY3."

Daniel wished he could join her, but he couldn't. He mouthed the words to the song the band was playing, wanting to sing. He'd always been the outsider, alone. Even back in the orphanage he'd found any friends just temporary – they'd inevitably go, just as he had lost his parents. Better to stay quiet at the back of the schoolroom and hope the bullies, both boys and girls, would leave him alone. He dared not show any interest in the girls, even the ones he liked, fearing their looks of contempt or waking the attention of others.

No one would ever be interested in him, anyway. It was just him; it would always be just him, unwanted.

After the Battery Park meeting, Fran had sent him upstate to… he could never remember what. He remembered taking the hTube out of the city and then coming back with a box, but in between was a blank, coloured purple. Apart from the box, only some words remained.

Sacrifice to keep the cause pure.

Who'd said that? More words that burnt fire-bright in Daniel's head.

What had he sacrificed?

But he trusted Fran – no, more than that, he admired her. Daniel realised he could learn from her: she didn't worry. She knew the demons were wrong but also how to defeat them. She had a vision.

He wanted to help, to feel he was doing something, was somebody, and, above all, he wanted to do the right thing.

Why didn't others do the right thing? He'd never understood that. Why did traitors work with demons and not do the right thing?

So, Daniel welcomed the words of fire Fran had written inside his head.

He gave the box to Fran, during another of those long chats they'd had about Earth First strategy, in the basement of the building where she worked, protected by the gurglings of the heating system. Or rather, Fran had talked and Daniel listened, hypnotised by her brown eyes and energy.

"We don't always need nanobiotics," she said, meaning holy water and angel dust. "With the right message to the right people, we can get converts to our side. The key is knowing what to say, what the triggers are, and that needs intelligence, information."

Did she mean working with demons?

"And remember: the human experience is everything."

The words, like her eyes, burnt brightly.

"And for the others, this might help," she said, opening the box he'd brought back.

Inside was a glass, a simple cylinder, the sort that could be used to drink water, and a silver stand to mount it on. Daniel was puzzled, but she grinned.

"Nice," she said.

The next day, they waited at reception for Neil Bolden, glass to hand, full. Fran had been watching for patterns in his movements and knew when he'd likely be leaving, so it wasn't long until a glass cubical descended the vertical monorail to reception.

"Mr Bolden." She'd stepped up to meet him.

"Monika, how nice to see you."

"Would you like to try this?" she asked, passing him the glass. "It's the latest gene-tech from the gardens. We've fused elderflower onto a sweet-pea stem so we can grow it in hydroponics. This is the cordial."

He reached out with his right hand, and as he touched the glass, his index finger glowed momentarily.

Then he sipped.

"Very nice, Monika." He beamed at her. "I look forward to more of your creations."

Daniel wondered about these creations. Were they pure?

"I have a favour to ask," said Fran. "My cousin, William here, would like to visit our relatives in EuroCore. Do you know how we could get authorisation?"

It was news to him.

"I'll see what I can do. Thanks again for the cordial."

"You're welcome."

Fran led Daniel back down to the boiler room. There she placed the glass on the silver stand and waited.

There was a pause then a beep.

She leant forward to peer at the silver stand. "So," she said. "He has an embed in his finger that scans for nanobiotics. It won't be easy to give him Memory and Belief."

"But you said—"

"Yes, the right words can influence some people, but others, Technocrats like Bolden, won't be convinced. We're going to need something stronger with them. And they have the power, the access to the weapon systems we're going to need."

"And what's that about EuroCore?"

"I've got to stay here but need an update on why Judith's not making the expected progress. There's an Earth First IRAG meeting coming up in Bruges, which you should attend. Maybe you are needed in EuroCore more than here in NY3?"

EuroCore! He was going to cross an ocean!

Sometimes he felt dizzy at how far he'd come.

19: Tom

Sophia had Tom on the sheets.

By that, he meant the ropes that controlled the position of the sails. Tom was glad he'd spent the previous evening in the TAC offices going through a "How to Sail" blip-sim course. Even so, Sophia had to remind him which rope was which.

She was at the helm, skipper of the yacht they'd borrowed for the day, while he was crew, beginner crew at that.

He brought in the fenders and lines, storing them in lockers at Sophia's direction, while she turned the wheel to steer them out of the B Island marina.

"Ok, hoist the sails," she said, with a smile, a mischievous one.

"Aye, aye, skipper."

Tom returned the smile but wondered about it. The way back from diving the previous day had felt like a boat trip into darkness. With no plans, no idea what he'd do next, the day had felt like the last flicker of life before the emptiness took him. He hadn't expected her invitation and had been more surprised by the emotions it had triggered in him. He'd spent all night thinking what it meant.

Winching the dark sails up to the top of the mast was hard work, straining his muscles. He didn't mind, though, enjoying the physicality and the rough feel of rope in his hand. The final few metres required him to winch the halyard, cranking it round and round.

At the entrance of the marina there was a chop, waves throwing the boat around so its stub of a bowsprit made circles and Tom had to hold tight.

"Let out the sheets a little," said Sophia, and she turned to starboard so the wind came over the yacht's port side.

Tom did as she asked, and the yacht accelerated, beginning to heel.

At first, the motion got worse as the yacht battled against the waves. Then everything went smooth as the carbon fibre, black hull lifted up and they flew above the water, foiling at speed, near silently.

"Wow, cool!" said Tom.

"Isn't it just."

The boat began to hum at a high pitch, a friendly sound, a buzz of eager, taut, speed. He felt he'd achieved something – and this time without any dead bodies.

"Tighten the main and jib," she said.

"We're heading upwind?" he asked, wanting to appear knowledgeable.

"Yup, thought we'd head over to the Turkish coast on the other side of C Island – I know a quiet bay we can anchor in for lunch."

It was her achievement, not his. The thrill faded, the gloom returned, but he fought it.

Enjoy this day, it's special.

After a few minutes, she called out for them to tack, and Tom released the sheet on one side of the yacht then dashed across to pull in the other. Sophia turned the wheel and the yacht's head passed through the eye of the wind with only the slightest drop in speed.

Having tied off the sheets, Tom crossed back to the higher side to enjoy the moment, feeling the warm sun on his skin balanced by the welcome cool of the spray flying from the yacht's fins. He looked over at Sophia, who flicked a switch by the helming station then took her hands off the wheel and waved a spray over her arms and legs.

"For your skin – do you want some?" she asked as they flew under the bridge between A and C Islands.

He nodded, and repeated her actions, spraying his legs. He became conscious of how much hairier his were than hers, which gleamed smooth in the sunlight. She was wearing a cotton-effect, off-white T-shirt and blue shorts, close fitting, straight from the MakeIt! machine. Her hair was being blown behind her, hypnotically, and she was barefoot.

Tom turned away, feeling shy, embarrassed by his reaction to her. He wondered if she'd guessed it from how he'd looked at her.

She flicked the switch down and started helming again.

"How much is automatic?" he asked.

"Oh, everything. I could sail this all day without touching any controls or lines, just giving it blip-commands."

"So, you didn't need me to raise the sails?"

"It's good exercise," she teased.

"Hah! It certainly was that."

"I thought you'd like to experience sailing old-style," she said.

He could see she was relaxed, happy even, calmly looking up at the sails, out at the water flying past, and ahead towards their destination.

"JT would have approved," he said. "Doing it by hand, that is."

He hadn't talked about JT for weeks, months maybe. It had seemed too private, surrounded by scarily strong emotions.

Suddenly he realised how much he missed JT and how large a gap his death had left. The pain felt real, physically in his chest. He wished JT was there so they could work out what to do next, together. He felt alone, adrift, isolated, still grieving and worrying about his mother, millions of kilometres away. He'd achieved nothing since arriving and didn't know what to do next.

I need to talk to someone about all this.

Sophia had been there, at the battle; she knew what it had been like. Maybe he could open up to her about JT, but what about the Moon? She probably didn't want to hear about all those dead bodies, not on a lovely day like this. But he wanted to. He ached to talk to her, not just to avoid being alone but because she was the one he *had* to talk to.

He turned to see her watching him.

"You should try steering," she said.

He moved to the back of the boat, standing behind her.

"We're heading close to the wind; just keep the wind on your cheek, don't head up too much or we'll come off the foils," she said.

As he took the wheel, one of his hands momentarily touched one of hers. Even after he'd looked around, checked the wind direction, tried steering a bit left then right and then back on track, he still felt that touch.

It took him some time to understand the wheel's sensitivity, how far he had to turn it. Sophia had made steering look so easy. Once or twice she had to reach and move the wheel sharply to avoid them heading too far into the wind, which would have slowed them to a stop.

"I'd better take over," she said. "We need to tack again."

They changed places and Tom helped with the sheets as they tacked up the coast of a small island until they reached a bay surrounded by low cliffs. Here Sophia headed into wind, where they eased off their foils, then she got Tom to drop the sails.

The anchor was dropped with a splash, and dug in. The boat came to a rest, with the only sound the slap of waves against its hull.

"Lunch!" she said.

20: Sophia

"And drinks," Sophia added. "I grabbed a couple of chilled bottles of white."

She could do with a glass, feeling a bit nervous. Plus Tom had been brooding about something on the sail out and could do with loosening up, something to get him talking, ease the moment.

It was hot in the bay and the wine went down well. She'd brought a picnic basket from the marina's restaurant: Turkish bread, hummus, vegetable moussaka and salads followed by peaches. Afterwards they leant over the side of the yacht to wash their hands in the cool water. The sea floor was clearly visible below them, and they could see fishes swimming around the foiling fins.

How to begin?

She hadn't really thought through what she was to say, but she had to say something as the frustration was becoming too much – knowing enough to see disaster coming, but not how to stop it.

"What's my father up to?"

That wasn't planned; it just popped out.

Tom looked puzzled. "I'd have thought you'd know, if anyone," he said.

"But I don't, not enough, they're cagey, Mum and Dad. You've been out there, you've seen it."

"They don't trust me though. There's so much they're not telling me." He made a face, and she wondered what was going on behind it.

"Even after you saw, you know, on the Moon?" she asked, curious.

He looked away, then turned to her.

"They didn't want to go. I kept asking and they gave in – your mum helped, then your dad, but Forough was against it, against me from the start. And I can see why, it was horrid and it makes everything they do look pointless, a road to the grave."

"I'm sorry," she said. It didn't seem enough.

She topped up his glass and drank some of her own. She didn't want to press, but then she couldn't help asking, "So why do they want to go? What is so important?"

"Why wouldn't you want to explore, find out more?"

"You hated living on Mars, didn't you?"

He drank deeply and thought for a moment. "Yes, but there are other ways, better ways. There must be."

"But why go at all? It just leads to more conflicts with Cita Stone – you heard what Ling said about those nextGen Wolf Bats. She'll be back, and it will be like the battle at Canaveral all over again."

It was good to get it out there, finally. She found her glass was empty and refilled it.

There was a moment of quiet, just the sound of waves against the yacht's hull.

"Do you find yourself reliving it? The battle, you know, JT…?" Tom's voice trailed off.

She looked directly at him, and his eyes stared into hers.

"Yes, I can't stop it." It was a relief to finally say it. "The images invade my head, my dreams. No one understands or talks about it."

She found her hand shaking. On a whim she reached out for his. He closed his hand around hers, holding it, and the shaking eased.

"Me too."

For moment they sat still, lost.

He was different from what she had expected, what she remembered.

"I'm really, really sorry about JT," she said softly.

"Thanks. I really miss him, especially now."

"What do you mean?"

"I don't know what to do. I thought the Moon would be the solution, a way to get back into space, maybe even…"

"What?"

"It's silly, but it would be great to be on the mission that brings my mum back."

She squeezed his hand, moved by the thought, then let go of it.

"That would be amazing," she said supportively.

"But they seem driven in another direction, focused on the great Plan."

The Plan, yes, that's what they were meant to be talking about.

"So what is it? This great Plan?"

"I don't know all, but there are various Points, and each has a Director."

"Like Mum and Forough?"

"Yup. Forough is the Point Director of space habitats. What about your mum?"

"No idea about Mum – how do you know about Forough's Point being space habitats?"

"Rod said something; Forough was really annoyed, but then she generally was when I was around."

"Like the space station and Moon base?"

"No, something much bigger, so people can live in space, not just visit. I found all this training material about mining asteroids and building space stations big enough to hold thousands. And Forough let slip they're about to move an asteroid into lunar orbit."

"Seriously? What are they going to use it for?"

"To build these giant stations, habitats, that would be like huge cylinders, rotating to create gravity, so it would feel like you're on Earth."

"Wow! So not on the Moon?"

"No, Forough didn't think much of the Moon, even before we'd gone there."

"Still, must have been amazing to go."

"You mean, forgetting about the dead bodies?"

"Exactly!" She smirked, enjoying his grim humour.

"It felt very different from the Earth and Mars, greyer, less gravity, not so much planet-like, if that makes sense."

"And that's bad?"

"Forough thought so. But I think she's wrong. The diving got me thinking: life down there fills every niche, and surely it should be the same with us in space. We humans should go everywhere, live everywhere."

For a moment they sat, drinking wine. Sophia looked down, under the yacht, to watch the fishes, wondering about what Tom had said. Could she go to the Moon, see for herself?

"But who are the other Directors and what are they doing?" asked Tom.

"When you blipped us, Mum had invited Moses Agaba over, and they both seem to be involved. Using the DNA database to build self-sustaining ecosystems for the space habitats, maybe?"

"And I bet Forough's father is involved too."

"That's four of them, four of these so-called 'Point Directors'. But what about my dad?"

"Probably, though maybe he's some sort of coordinator?"

"But what are they up to, and why?"

"And how many of these Points are there?"

Both shrugged their shoulders, and there was a pause.

"How's your mum, by the way?"

Tom didn't answer straight away.

"I think she's ok, but it's getting harder to keep in touch with Mars as it's nearly on the other side of the Sun from Earth. Did you hear about the flare?"

"No."

"A really big solar flare hit Mars a few days ago, the sort that can kill or cause cancers. I'm really worried; it looks like Victor might be sick, and if he is then maybe others are as well. Maybe my mum."

"I'm sorry," she said. "She'll be ok. I'm sure Dad will get her back as soon as he can."

"But he's not," said Tom angrily. "He's sending all these missions out to deep space, to the Moon, but nothing to Mars, not for ages."

"I thought he couldn't? It was too difficult or something."

She watched Tom calm down, wondering what it would be like to be so far from his mum, to have seen his dad die.

"It is, he's right. Maybe your dad can't send a mission right now. But what am I to do while we wait?"

"I don't know, I'm sorry. Maybe you could help me? I've been investigating what my parents are up to, trying to find a way to stop another battle between the Technocrats and Earth Firsters, but there's so much I don't know."

"Sure, I've got nothing planned at the moment. And, Sophia, thanks – it's great to be able to talk about this."

"No worries, it's been bugging me too, keeping everything locked inside."

For a moment they said nothing, just drank and watched the waves crash against the cliff and birds soaring high on the thermals.

Sophia remembered the battle at Canaveral, and shivered. She had been trying not to think about it, and there'd been no one she could open up to. But she could talk about it with Tom.

"Listen, Tom, you remember when you landed, at Canaveral, and Cita Stone was there."

He nodded.

"Would my dad have really risked himself – and me – just to recover two astronauts? Be honest?"

Tom looked at her and then away.

"So?" he said.

"What did they need from you? You must have some idea?"

He filled her glass and drank again from his.

"I've been wondering about that. Was it the pendant? They didn't know about that then. So maybe he just needed us to keep the door to space open, to stop Cita Stone locking humanity onto this one planet. He *really* wanted that GC resolution."

Sophia took a drink and started to wave her hands around as she spoke. "I remember Cita saying something that Dad couldn't respond to: she asked why the head of the Technocrats' AI work was leading their spacecraft division. It's completely different tech. He should be training the new Humais, not building spaceships." Having someone to discuss all this felt so good, like when a painful cramp in her leg eased away.

"It must be connected, somehow," said Tom. "But he isn't building spaceships – or at least not recently. It's all been Forough and her father directing things. I haven't heard a word from your dad for ages."

"Interesting," said Sophia. "He was in Zurich for something, then Singapore working on the latest embed tech."

"Nina would love that," they said together.

"Snap."

They laughed.

Tom poured the last of the wine into her glass. She felt quite light-headed, free from her tensions, and the water looked so refreshing.

"I really want to go for a swim," she said. She had a bikini under her T-shirt and shorts.

"But I didn't bring a costume," he said.

"You'll have to swim in your underwear – or nothing," she teased.

He blushed and looked away, as if guilty.

Really, Sophia, she thought, but she was strangely elated at his reaction.

"Ok," he said, turning back to her, boldly catching her eye.

Ok to which?

21: Tom

Tom watched Sophia pull her T-shirt over her head, butterflies forming in his stomach. Up to then he'd felt relaxed, enjoying the day, but now things had taken a different turn.

Or had they? Maybe it was his imagination.

Yet again he felt lost on an alien world, where locals spoke languages he didn't understand.

His heart beat hard and he felt scared, but of emotions rather than something predictable and manageable such as micro-meteorite impacts. He'd been taught about space tech, not this.

What did it mean? How should he react?

Tom followed her example, taking off his shirt and trousers, making a pile on top of his shoes. He could swim in his boxers.

"Hurry up."

She'd already dropped the ladder at the back of the boat into the water and was standing by the edge.

"Coming," he said.

She dived into the water with a natural elegance. He wanted to match that, but knew he didn't have the skill, so simply jumped. For a moment, he was in the air, then for another he was underwater, before surfacing with a grin. The water was cool and full of light, sparkling in the sun.

"Race you round the boat," she said and set off in a well-practised crawl.

Tom knew he couldn't beat her, not with his beginner's breaststroke, but he tried his best, following in her wake down the port side, round the anchor chain and then back down the starboard side.

She won, by several lengths.

Sophia laughed as he approached. "You're so slow – and you're taller than me!"

She treaded water and pushed her hair away from her face with her hands, the muscles of her shoulders flexing.

"You've been doing this all your life," he said. She was used to this gravity, born to it. "This is new to me."

"Lame," she said. "Let's duck-dive down to those fishes."

She took a deep breath and dived down. For a moment, she was upside down, her legs sticking straight out of the water, then she slipped under.

Tom followed her down, though without a facemask he could see little. But he wanted to follow her, to be with her.

They both surfaced, gasping for breath.

"No good," she said. "I can't see a flipping thing."

She rolled over to float on her back, drifting.

Tom treaded water and watched her, her chest rising and falling with each breath. She was so beautiful.

A shadow went across the sun, a cloud, and she stopped floating and looked up.

"We'd better not hang around," she said. "Sometimes the winds can really pick up in the afternoon."

She swam back to the ladder.

Tom hung back and watched her climb it, water flowing from her body. He felt a longing, a pain, a tightness in his chest: wanting her, to hold her, to kiss her.

He put a foot on the lowest rung of the ladder and pulled himself up. She was already organising the ropes, preparing to leave. As he approached, she handed him a coil, and their hands touched, again. It felt like a spark. They were close enough that he could feel warmth from her skin.

Tom found his arms reaching out for her, his mouth tracking down to hers.

"Hey." She stood back. "What are you playing at?"

"I'm sorry," he said, eyes locked on hers, trying to read her.

"I'm with Alejandro!" She was almost shouting, arms straight by her side, fists clenched.

"I know, just, you know, you've been…" He trailed off.

"I haven't been anything."

"But what about this, today?" he asked. "And those touches, the swimming?"

Had he imagined it?

"So what?"

Maybe he had, maybe he'd got this all wrong. He couldn't think of anything to say.

But he felt compelled to explain, and he blurted out, "I like you, really."

She turned away, silent for a moment.

"I feel I can talk to you about anything."

"I'm sorry," she said, turning back to him. "You don't understand – Alejandro needs me, he's going through things at the moment."

"It's ok," he said. He didn't want to hear more. Already he felt sick from the rejection, failure and messing things up. He should have known, remembering how she'd ditched him for Alejandro when they'd been in Midnight Somewhere.

Suddenly, a lightbulb went off in his head.

"We should get back," he said.

Sophia grabbed her T-shirt and shorts and pulled them on, quickly. She tapped twice in the air, then with waves of her hand she commanded the sails to be raised and anchor lifted. As the yacht's head turned off the wind, she span the wheel, controlling their motion.

It felt like a long way back to Justinian, even at foiling speed. Sophia did everything but said nothing. After getting dressed, Tom was left alone to watch her sail the yacht and think.

As they came into the marina, he made a decision.

"Look, Sophia, I'm sorry. Really I am," he said.

She said nothing. She hadn't even looked at him on the way back.

"I'll go and join Forough and Rod. They let slip that they're heading out in a few days to supervise the arrival of the asteroid, anchoring it to the mining and manufacturing node. Maybe I can help. It's going to be a long mission, so I won't trouble you anymore."

"You don't have to do that," she said, looking at him for the first time.

"I do. I want to."

And he did. Right then he just wanted to get away, to end this.

"Get the lines and fenders ready," she said.

He couldn't read her expression. Her face seemed locked down, business-like, concentrating on the needs of the yacht.

He wired up the lines and distributed the fenders then, when she had manoeuvred the yacht alongside the pontoon, jumped off and made fast the bow and stern lines. She joined him on the pontoon and stood facing him, looking straight at him, eyes into eyes. They were earnest, honest.

"It wasn't just you," she said, quietly but firmly. "I felt something too."

Hope burnt within him, and he took a step forward.

"But I can't, really I can't."

For a long moment, they stared at each other, judging, testing.

"Really no?" His voice was almost a whisper.

She looked away first. "Alejandro, he's my... you know... He needs me..."

What did that mean? Tom breathed in deeply. He tried to understand her, but failed, then realised it didn't matter. Whether he understood her not, it didn't change anything. A wave of dark emotion swept over him, and he wanted to be alone.

"Ok," he said. "I'll be seeing you then."

Tom turned away from the marina, away from Sophia. He felt sick, his heart a dark stone stuck in his chest. His head felt as heavy as lead, dragging him down.

Every time he felt something, for his dad, for JT, for Sophia, it ended like this.

What was he to do now? He had a vision for the future that combined Midnight Somewhere with the idea of life filling every niche, but would that be enough for Rod and Forough to let him back into their project? And would work be enough to fill the emptiness?

Either way, he felt it would be a long time before he'd be back in Justinian.

Part 4

22: Alejandro

Alejandro felt like shit.

Bits of the previous two days came back to him. After the day spent mostly in the bar by the swimming pool with Pepe, Sophia had turned up from her dive and he hadn't been at his best. He thought she'd helped him get home, but he wasn't entirely sure. His memory was blurred.

Shit! He could see the temptation to use Memory with NoWorries.

During the following day, she'd ignored his blips, and he ended up being dragged off by Pepe to one of his C Island haunts. They'd met his contact at the docks, the one that supplied the nanobiotics. Alejandro needed more of them, much more. The previous day's NoWorries had given him a serious downer afterwards, and he'd had to double up on them to get through the day. At least he now knew where to get his own supply, not to have to rely on Pepe. He'd have to find a way to go over to C Island by himself.

But now he felt double shit, and a failure. Couldn't dive and was living on nanobiotics – what would Sophia think?

He remembered the day she'd turned down using them, the year before. He couldn't forget; it was burnt into his head as if it was yesterday.

Bloody Memory!

If only he had talked to her the day he'd failed at diving. He needed to talk to her.

He was waiting to see his father, with Pepe, outside the cores where his father brooded over his data like a spider at the centre of a web. Nothing was real in there. He began to shake and tried to hide it from Pepe.

Everything in Cloud Heights was like a machine, binary: us or them, victory or defeat, black or white. It was only with Sophia that he felt something human, a connection to someone else, emotionally and physically, skin on skin. She cared for him, was the only one who seemed to.

Alejandro tried to imagine life without her and felt sick at the emptiness. It would be like the time after his mother's death all over again. He was more scared of going through that again than of his father, but still he hadn't been able to break free from Felix's expectations.

I love her, he thought. *I need her.* He wished he'd realised this two days ago, or more, so he could have said something.

After this meeting, he'd talk to her.

Always afterwards.

He didn't feel he was fully there. Half of him was lost, somewhere.

He needed more: WakeUppers, Ego and LoveUp would stop the shaking. He hated himself for wanting them. But it wasn't wanting, it was needing.

He could tell Pepe was watching, observing, judging, keeping track, ready to report him. His friend's eyes were cold more often now, the employee doing his boss's work.

The doors in front of Alejandro and Pepe swung open and, after they entered, closed behind them. The room was dark, lit only by images from the surrounding walls. His father wasn't alone but with Erik Larson, the icy heart of the coldest of rooms.

"Come in, boys," said Felix. "Zeus is giving us an update on the NY3 project."

One of the walls pulsed light slowly.

"NextGen Wolf Bat design complete," said Zeus. "NY3 manufacturing started; half of those produced to be under our control."

"Good," said Felix. "What else? What progress on analysing Kasparov's plans?"

"Newsfeed bot and trawlers generating data: initial analysis suggests multiple high-level targets for follow-up in-depth investigation. Further resources required."

"But we've already allocated a third of all BCC's bots to Zeus," protested Erik.

"More required," said Zeus. "Kasparov is using their AI, Humai, to defend their blipverse footprint."

"Do it," commanded Felix.

Erik nodded.

"What else?"

"Instructions for physical control and to stop Kasparov require additional resources and the Earth First movement assets."

His father looked at Erik.

That's right, ignore me, thought Alejandro. *What am I doing here?*

"I thought we agreed to wait until they came to us?" said Felix. "When they *need* us."

"Proactivity required," said Zeus. "NY3 production order includes Carrier Wolf Bats anticipating involvement. Close alignment with Stone's Earth Firsters necessary to control events."

"I won't agree to that," said Felix. "Stone's dangerous."

"Rapid progress essential to achieve Prime Motivator. Current approach non-optimal."

Felix shook his head. "Not yet. But we need more contacts with them. Stone has gone to ground; we should identify candidates from her inner circle we could use as a liaison. Make sure we can ride that tiger, get them under *our* control."

"Insufficient," said Zeus. "Lack of direction limiting ability to achieve Prime Motivator."

What does that mean?

"We need to be in control," repeated his father. "Tell us how."

"Opportunity at Earth First IRAG meeting Bruges this evening," said Zeus. "Credentials Erik arranged."

Alejandro didn't know what IRAG was but didn't care either.

"They'll be suspicious if they know we're working with AIs," said Erik.

"Focus on ends not means," said Zeus. "Support Stone, avoid TAC-penetrated EuroCore."

Felix snorted. "Backward Earth-huggers! But we need their… resources."

What was his father doing? Why?

Alejandro remembered the instructions Felix had given: no operational limits. Was this his plan or Zeus's?

He shivered.

Why had he waited to escape to Sophia? This was all wrong.

"Additional issue," pulsed Zeus. "Alejandro."

Me? Alejandro's heart started to race.

"Yes, boy, you. Why do you think you're here," said his father. "You failed me, again. I told you to get information from the Kasparov girl or dump her and you've done neither. Pepe tells me you've been hanging around her, but have you got any intel? No! None! So dump her."

Terror gripped him.

"I won't!" he said.

"Really? Pathetic. It's not as if she likes you. She's just using you for her father."

"She's not!"

"Fool! Use or be used, and you're the one being used," his father said. "Get closer so I can see you properly."

It felt difficult, as if walking through chest-high water, or into a great wind blowing him backwards. Close up, Alejandro could see Felix's face twisted in scorn, his eyes glowing with information, his true love.

"I can't trust you to do my bidding until you have dumped her."

"I'm not! I won't!"

"Play it," his father commanded Zeus.

The walls changed again, and they were somewhere over the water, watching a yacht foil, spray rising from its fins, the sun lighting its sails from behind. There were two people on board, one steering, the other working the ropes.

Alejandro watched, unsure what he was meant to see, to say. It was infosec drone footage, that he could tell.

The yacht tacked, and tacked again up the side of an island, slowing, taking down its sails and lowering the anchor.

The viewpoint got closer to the yacht, and the two figures became clearer until Alejandro could identify who they were.

Shit! Shit! Shit!

Sophia and Tom, just the two of them, alone. She'd gone off with him, yesterday – that's why she'd been off the blipverse. She hadn't told him.

He felt sick, loathing his father for showing him this, furious at Sophia and also with himself for being angry at her.

It was his fault, it always was.

He watched them have lunch and chat. They appeared relaxed, close. For a time afterwards they talked, though there was no audio so he couldn't hear what they said, then they went for a swim. Sophia beat Tom in a race around the yacht, then she floated on her back, and Alejandro watched him watching her. And when she climbed the ladder back up on board, he saw that Tom was looking at her too.

Alejandro hated him.

Poisonous, sneaky, freaky alien!

"See?" said his father.

The feed froze with Tom leaning in towards Sophia. Alejandro watched, transfixed.

"This is who she really is. She is using you while going off with Kasparov's asset from Mars, the one they used to get the resolution through the GC."

He couldn't think of anything to say. He was lost. He had nothing, was nothing. The emptiness was terrifying.

"Dump her. Now," Felix commanded. "We have some audio, which, though limited, was informative. We've integrated what we've learnt into our plans, but you don't get to hear it until you've shown you're one of us."

Alejandro nodded, not trusting his voice.

"Anything else?" asked Felix, looking round at the group.

"No," said Zeus. "Plans activated, required to achieve Prime Motivator."

Felix nodded. "Good. Now leave me, all of you."

Light flooded in from behind him: the doors were opening.

Alejandro stumbled out. He felt physically ill: sick, sweaty and panicky, his heart racing and his mind uncontrollable, jumping from thought to thought.

Outside he saw Yeliz, who worked for his dad as Head of Host Entertainment.

She nodded at him. "Hi, Alejandro, long time no see."

He nodded back. Before Sophia, he and Pepe had hung out with Yeliz a lot, had been almost friends.

With her was with a young, attractive woman, one of those who lived in the ground-floor complex.

"This is girl #16," she said. "What do you think? Nice, eh?"

His stomach lurched and he had to swallow twice.

Yeliz gave the woman a kiss and pushed her towards the cores room.

"I have to go."

He almost ran up to the ballroom, the great space where he'd first talked to Sophia, when it had been full of people at the BCC reception. Now it was empty, it was just him. Alone.

Scattered around the ballroom were works of art, pictures and sculptures, but all he could see was Tom and Sophia together, the blipvid playing over and over in his head.

He couldn't breathe.

"Retract the roof and open the doors," he commanded.

The room heard, and with a whine of machinery, the doors to the balcony started to move, opening the ballroom to the wind.

Alejandro walked out onto the decking. The cold air chilled the sweat on his face, waking him. Even so, he couldn't get close to the edge.

The trembling intensified. He felt dizzy, and had to lean over, hands on knees.

"Hey, mate, you ok?"

It was Pepe.

"Come away from the edge," his friend said. "You know you don't like heights."

Pepe helped him up and indoors.

Could he trust Pepe? Could he trust anyone?

"Leave things to me," he said. "Ok?"

Alejandro nodded, drained of energy, numb.

"Room: close the balcony doors then open a blip channel to Sophia Kasparov," said Pepe. "Filter the feed to make it look like Alejandro is alone."

"Acknowledged."

Suddenly, Alejandro was terrified. What was he meant to say?

A wall that had been showing a selection from BCC's art collection faded to nothing then became a blipverse screen. Then Sophia appeared.

"Hi, Alejandro? What's up?"

He couldn't answer. Half of him wanted her, to hold her, to kiss her. The other half saw her with Tom, the spaceman, better than him at everything.

"God," she said. "You look terrible. What's that father of yours been doing to you now?"

Even if Felix was right about her, that felt good. She cared.

Or was it just that she *appeared* to care?

"We need to talk," he said.

23: Sophia

Sophia sat on one of the breakwater rocks, arms around her knees, waiting for Alejandro, full of questions.

Why had he suggested they met here, on C Island? During the blip-con from Cloud Heights, he'd suggested they meet at a coffee social in one of the B Island parks, but later he'd sent a short message changing it to the breakwater by the C Island port.

Was it to avoid Pepe? She hoped so. They needed to talk without him.

Her perch was exposed to the wind and spray from the waves crashing onto the rocks. There was a strong smell of rotting fish and seagull droppings. Behind her, an army of wind turbines turned relentlessly, their low thrub mixing with a background industrial hum coming from blank warehouse-like buildings, containing anything from server clusters to hydroponic farms.

It was functional, not romantic. She'd seen no one, just a couple of robots, samais and drones doing their work automatically, ignoring her. Blipverse coverage was sometimes patchy, limited to machines talking to machines.

She looked out to the sea, dark under racing grey clouds, watching the seagulls soar on the wind, and wondered what she should say to Alejandro and what was wrong. He'd looked terrible.

Should she mention anything about her day with Tom?

What was she to say? Could she explain? She couldn't quite admit to herself that it had been a mistake, but also she couldn't concede that she'd enjoyed it; having someone she could be open to, even – she had to admit to herself – the way he'd looked at her. She had been... provocative.

It hadn't worked out, that she could accept. But they'd needed to talk, she liked sailing, she liked Tom and...

She liked Tom.

It had been easy talking to him, with him. No, more than that, it had been a relief. She missed it already.

But she'd said no. He'd left, she hadn't seen him since, and her parents had been asking questions as to why he'd left so quickly.

"Did he say anything to you?" her mother had asked.

Yes, he had, but she couldn't say *that*.

"He seemed keen to get back to work," she'd replied, which was true.

What to say to Alejandro?

He'd been a mess, that day after the diving. He wasn't talking, his father was getting to them, and Sophia was worried. He wasn't good at stress; he and Pepe would take nanobiotics, and he'd get hyper then worse than before.

She wanted to help, to reach out to him, to ease whatever was driving him to the edge. It was hard if he didn't talk, if he didn't let her know what he was thinking.

But then she didn't tell him about what was on her mind, either. She hadn't told him about her experiences at the battle on Canaveral Island or what she'd found out about her father's plans. She couldn't: she feared it would hurt her family too much. Sophia had seen for herself the trouble that had come when Cita Stone found out about her father's mission to Mars thanks to her – and the hack of her construct by BCC's in-house AI, Unverified. Not only had Alejandro's father's AI hacked her, Felix Fernadez had threatened her in the Cloud Heights' cores and set Wolf Bats on her, her father and Tom.

Ling had said people were watching her and Alejandro, and that made her really uncomfortable but she could see why. It was crazy.

But she had had feelings for him. Others just saw him as the heir of BCC, but she saw a boy needing help. They saw a rich, experienced, well-dressed and, yes, attractive young man, but they didn't know him as she had, from the start. She'd seen the sadness, the loneliness within, that first day. It sparked something in her and he'd connected to her. And he'd been fun to be with, such fun, so many great nights.

She smiled at the memories.

Yet here she was, waiting, not sure what to say, how to reach him, not even sure if that was what she wanted. Her feelings had changed. She cared for Alejandro and wanted to help him, if she could. But there was a limit, and she might have reached it.

Had she given the wrong answer to Tom?

She sighed. The breakwater was so lonely and isolated. And he was late.

She wouldn't say anything about Tom, she decided. She'd say she'd been working on her father's projects, which was true in a way, and would stop further questions. If he asked, she could say Tom had left – he'd like that. Then she could see if she could get them back to an even keel.

Finally, she saw a figure approaching along the breakwater. She recognised his walk before she could make out his face.

As he approached, she turned towards him and smiled but didn't stand up. He joined her on the rocks, sitting down and looking out to sea.

"Hi," he said.

"Hi," she said.

She didn't know where to begin and he didn't seem to either, but it was nice to just be sitting there with him. Peaceful.

Then there was a mechanical screech from the port, a steel line under strain maybe. It broke them from their reveries, and they exchanged smiles. He leant in, and she leant over, and they kissed, a simple, gentle one.

"How've you been?" she asked.

He didn't answer straight away, but looked out at the waves rolling towards them.

"I've been with my father."

"I'm sorry. What's he done now?" she asked, trying to find a way in.

He shrugged.

"What've you been up to?" he asked. "I blipped yesterday, and you didn't reply."

"I was busy," she said. "Something related to my dad's work."

"That all?"

"What do you mean?"

"You weren't off with Tom? Just the two of you?"

What?

Her stomach knotted. "Why would you say that?"

"What's going on with you and Tom?"

"There's nothing between me and Tom."

"Didn't look like nothing."

Her heart started beating fast, not quite believing what she was hearing.

"You *saw*! What did you see? How?"

He'd spied on her!

"Wasn't my idea. My father's infosec drones recorded you and Tom, off together sailing and swimming. He played it in the cores room."

"But you watched!"

She was furious, livid.

"I didn't want to – and *you* were the one off with someone else."

"I said it was nothing."

"Didn't look like nothing."

"I said he's gone! He won't be back for ages."

Suddenly that sank in: Tom was gone. Who would she talk to now about all that was going on?

"Promise me you don't have any feelings for him. Swear it!"

"I promise," she said.

She tried to look deep into his oh-so-blue eyes, as if she could communicate those words directly into his brain, to reassure it and his heart of that truth. She looked for acceptance, belief in her, but saw something in him change. The sadness returned.

He knew her as she knew him, could read her. He could tell when she wasn't truly saying how her heart felt. She had feelings for Tom, and that had changed how she felt about him.

How could she convince him otherwise if she couldn't convince herself?

He turned to look out at the sea again. Gusts of wind threw his naturally curly hair into an uncontrolled mess.

"So are we ok?" she asked.

He shrugged.

"It doesn't matter," he said. "I love you."

"I do too," she said, inching closer and putting an arm around him.

There was love and there was *love*, and she cared for him.

But they had spied on her, and he had watched. And she had gone sailing with Tom and enjoyed it.

She wanted to sigh but worried he'd misinterpret it, so held her breath until that became difficult and had to say "Ha!" to clear the mistake.

"What?"

"Nothing."

There was too much they couldn't talk about. And without honesty and openness, could there be trust?

Behind them, she heard the sound of a drone approaching. She ignored it; there were many drones in the skies over C Island, many more than were permitted over residential B Island.

But this one was louder than the others, its engines lower in pitch indicating greater carry load, and it was approaching them directly. She turned to see a passenger drone land behind them on the breakwater.

Pepe stepped out, and he wasn't on his own; he'd brought one of the guards from Cloud Heights.

Sophia's heart sank and she removed her arm from around Alejandro.

"Hello, Alejandro." Pepe ignored Sophia.

"Hi."

Alejandro continued to look out to sea.

"Your father was worried about you," said Pepe. "He said you'd best come back home."

Alejandro didn't say anything or move.

Sophia reached out to touch his arm. "You don't have to go," she said.

For a moment he said nothing.

"What is there to stay for?" he asked, sadly, turning to her.

"You know I'm here for you."

He nodded. "Yes, I know."

"Have you finished your talk?" asked Pepe.

"No, not really." Alejandro looked back out to sea. "But it doesn't matter. There is nothing to say."

Her stomach felt heavy at his words.

"Your father will be disappointed," said Pepe.

Alejandro shrugged as if it was a great effort. "I disappoint many people."

"Time to go." Pepe nodded to the security guard, who moved to stand by Alejandro.

Sophia wanted to hug him, but Pepe was there, disapproving. No doubt he had watched that drone footage too.

"You've got what you came for?" asked Pepe.

What did that mean?

Oh, of course, she realised. It was C Island that Pepe and Alejandro came to for their nanobiotics. That's why Alejandro had changed their meeting place.

She should have felt something, surprise or frustration, but it now seemed inevitable, just Alejandro.

Alejandro stood up, looking sheepish, caught out, but she was no longer disappointed. She knew him.

"I should go," he said.

She nodded.

"I love you," he said.

"I know," she said.

Then he turned and stepped into the passenger drone along with Pepe and the guard. The whine of the drone's engines increased until it lifted straight up, micro-adjusting for the gusty wind.

Sophia could see Alejandro inside its glass bubble. He was watching her too.

Then the drone dipped its nose and flew off, leaving her alone.

24: Daniel

"I don't know why you're here," said Judith.

Daniel was feeling more than a little disorientated, having just flown from NY3 into EuroCore, a hypersonic flight that had taken just under two hours. The inside of the plane had been like a giant hTube pod; invisible assistants could be commanded to bring refreshments, walls that could be made transparent to show a curved world below a blanket of clouds.

But he was there, on another continent, doing the bidding of the Holy Mother, fighting the good fight. He was a someone, flying across an ocean to find out why Judith wasn't making progress. And to punish those foolish enough to resist their revolution, to resist him.

Judith had been waiting for him at the airport.

"Fran sent me," he said. "To get an update on progress and to attend the Earth First IRAG."

Judith snorted. "You are not needed here! You will not attend the meeting!"

She didn't know the new Daniel; she didn't know him.

Killer. Murderer. Agent.

He couldn't respect her as he did Fran. Who was she to question him?

"Fran said I should attend the meeting. Do you want me to tell the Holy Mother you refused?"

He still had no idea what an IRAG was but wasn't going to let Judith stop him attending.

"Ok, ok," she muttered. "You can come with me, but sit at the rear and don't say anything – and then tomorrow you'll go back."

He slung his rucksack on his back and followed her to the hTube.

Then she stopped and looked at him again. "You might be useful. Maybe you could stay here and not go back?"

He didn't understand. Why would he do that?

Judith said nothing more during the short journey, which gave Daniel time to inspect her. She looked changed: her clothes cut and styled radically different from the plain, formless greys he remembered her in. She seemed taller, healthier, with her hair growing back and wearing glasses that glowed with information.

Outside, the light was fading on a landscape of green fields under grey clouds.

The capsule made a *bing* sound and announced they were arriving.

"Welcome to Bruges."

Judith strode off out of the hTube station and he struggled to keep up.

"Hurry up," she said. "It looks like it's going to rain again, and I don't want to get this endo-high-style outfit wet."

Daniel didn't understand. When it rained you just put your hood up.

It was dark, but the path and low clouds glowed streetlight gold. They crossed a cobbled bridge over a canal, and Daniel could see the town's buildings reflected in its still waters. Brick buildings, some with balconies; steep triangular roofs broken by stacks of chimneys. Windows made of dozens of small panes of glass. Tempting-looking terraces by the canal, wooden eaves, signs and statues. And a golden clock tower topped with a crown.

It was delightful: human scale, full of traditions and respect, true to Earth First values. Worth coming all this way for, even if he had to return the next day.

He wanted to explore but followed Judith. He also wanted to stop to eat something. He passed a shop that called itself "Dom's Bakery", and the fresh bread smells made his stomach ache and mouth water.

Judith was talking, but not to him, blipping contacts, discussing delegations.

What would Fran think?

Judith led him to a large, brick building on the right-hand side of the street and stopped at an arched stone doorway. Just inside there were two guards, who indicated for Judith and Daniel to scan their qIDs on a samai.

A machine? He was greeted by a machine?

"Welcome to the Earth First Inter-Regional Advisory Group," it said.

So that's what IRAG stands for.

He followed Judith down a corridor that smelt of dust and wood polish, where old oil paintings hung on grey stone walls, until they reached another doorway and entered a large hall.

To Daniel, it seemed like something out of the books of his youth, stories of knights and royal courts. Twice – three times – as high as it need be, with a large, empty fireplace at one end and huge paintings framed in gold, full-height windows reaching up to an arched roof.

"Sit there," said Judith, pointing at the back row of seats.

The room was already full of delegates, their skin and clothes in every colour under the sky, talking loudly in languages from six of the seven continents. They seemed to know each other well and greeted Judith warmly, making space for her in their conversations. It made Daniel feel even more the outsider.

He made his way to a seat on the far right of the back row. As Judith headed towards the front, he looked round and found he wasn't the only one sitting by himself. On the far left of the back row, there was a bearded man with stubs for ears. The man spotted him watching, and Daniel looked away quickly.

At the far end of the room, by the empty fireplace, was a long, wooden table and three chairs, one of which Judith took, smiling and shaking hands with the two already seated.

The man in the middle seat stood up.

"Welcome," he said, "wherever you came from, to IRAG, my fellow Earth Firsters. My name, as you probably know, is Bevan, and my job today is simple: to introduce the main speaker, Judith, and to thank IRAG's secretary, Sam."

Bevan indicated Judith, sitting to his right, and then the person to his left.

The audience applauded, but Daniel frowned. They weren't true Earth Firsters; they followed this Bevan, not the Holy Mother.

"Judith has been very helpful for our movement, explaining what really happened on Canaveral Island, the depths that Cita Stone stooped to, the lies she told. She's also been developing some interesting ideas that require further discussion, and this meeting seems an ideal opportunity."

Daniel stared. Was Judith still true to their cause?

"Please, Judith, we're all looking forward to hearing from you."

Bevan sat down and Judith rose to another round of applause.

"Fellow Earth Firsters, we are joined together in our belief that the planet must come first. Until recently, I was indeed with Stone's outcasts, as Mr Bevan explained. But that group failed; it damaged our cause with its extremism and lacked a working vision for the future."

What was she saying?

"But then I came here and was re-energised to be surrounded by those like you, who fight with ideas and words, not weapons and nanobiotics."

There was a murmur of support.

"I arrived with the young man at the back, called William," she said.

Just in time, Daniel remembered that was him, or at least what his qID said.

"And," she went on, "he is one of those who has been damaged by Stone, both mentally and physically; he will corroborate what I have said about her. I saw his blood spilt at Stone's orders!"

The delegates turned to inspect Daniel, who felt his temper rise. She was speaking ill of the Holy Mother – should he to speak out for her?

"But the perspective was helpful, so I could learn from Stone's defeat," said Judith. "Stone's hatred of technology has blinded her as to its potential benefits for us Earth Firsters. If we are really to put the planet first, we must recognise that humans have failed to be the guardians it needs."

She paused and took a sip of water, as if steeling herself.

"The Technocrats and BCC used AIs and their capabilities to defeat Stone for their own aims, to develop space technology and the shallow blip-soaps that earn BCC its billions. But imagine that technology used for good, for the planet. Imagine if we had our own AI, with its Prime Motivator being to protect the planet?"

There was a murmur, but this time of unease, not of support.

Daniel raged. What she was saying was heresy.
Those who betray us must be killed!

"We can't do that, you know that!" said a voice. Daniel spotted a mousy man with a moustache.

Judith raised her hands. "Listen, I know how this sounds, how we've been taught of the dangers of AIs, but we mustn't forget their power. If we are to win, we need allies. Let's work with the Technocrats, ask them to develop an AI for us."

The murmurs were stronger, becoming mutterings. Delegates turned to delegates, worried looks were exchanged and heads shaken.

Daniel found his hands shaking. He looked down, and for a moment they appeared covered with blood.
Killer! Murderer!

Judith pressed on. "I have a vision: an AI of our own, dedicated to protecting the planet, developing strategies smarter than we can. Earth's guardian, one that I propose we call Gaia!"

Daniel could sit still no longer. He felt renewed, alive: the new Daniel was joining the fight. Inspired by Fran, he would be the one *doing*.

Fight for what is right!

He spoke the words that burned brightly in his head.

"Traitor!" he cried, leaping to his feet. "We can never trust AIs!"

He was greeted with a scattering of applause, and it was these delegates he addressed.

"Would you have us watch as she gives our world, our planet, our Earth to those machines? They are not human, those AIs, they are demons!"

Some of the delegates began to echo him.

"No!" said the man with a moustache. "Demons!"

Others told him to shut up and sit down, but he ignored them.

Demons! Traitors!

"I have seen them," he said. "I have seen traitors like Kasparov working with the inhuman machines, working to bring plagues down from the sky, from space! We must fight the demons as we fought at Canaveral!"

"Shut up," shouted Judith, from the front.

But the delegates were facing him, listening to him. Daniel's heart swelled as more words came flooding out.

Goodbye humanity!

"The human experience is what matters, what is real, not the artificiality of tech. We have to stop them, or it's goodbye humanity!"

He was rewarded with cheers from some, boos from others.

"Security!" called Judith. "IRAG credentials William Askari revoked."

The two guards Daniel had seen at the entrance pushed their way towards him, grabbed him by the arms and dragged him into the corridor.

He was too surprised to resist. It happened so quickly.

What had he done wrong?

"Get out," said one of the guards, pushing Daniel into the street. He tripped on the cobbles and ended up on the ground. The stones were hard and wet with rain.

He picked himself up and wondered what to do. The two guards glowered at him.

"Get lost," one said.

Daniel turned and walked at random down the street, heart still pounding, hands covered in sweat and rain.

Where was he to go? He had no money and knew no one there but Judith. He had the familiar feeling of being alone, just him, again. But he had done the right thing; that was what mattered.

Daniel reached a bridge over a canal and looked down as the rain dropped circles onto the dark water. It was a different one to that he'd crossed earlier. He was lost and getting cold.

Footsteps approached, but he ignored them.

"Daniel?"

He turned and recognised the bearded man with stubs for ears from the meeting. Close up, Daniel could see his eyes glowing with lights, data flowing across his iris.

"My name is Erik Larson, I represent BCC," he said.

Daniel's heart thumped as guilt flowed through him. The man was from BCC and knew he was called Daniel – did he also know that he'd killed Captain Vaughan?

Murderer!

But the man offered Daniel his hand, which he shook, relieved.

"I was impressed by your speech," Erik said. "You showed yourself a true Earth Firster."

"Thank you."

"You have some supporters in there; the Albanian delegate was most enthusiastic."

That must have been the man with the moustache.

"We've been looking for someone loyal to Cita Stone. Someone we can trust to send a message."

"I am not a message boy," he said.

"Of course, I see that. Maybe you could be the liaison officer between Cita Stone and BCC," said Erik smoothly.

That sounded better.

"Someone familiar with taking Memory."

Daniel nodded, recognising what the word meant. "Holy water," he said. But something worried him. "Doesn't BCC work with AIs?" he asked.

"No," said Erik. "Our advisor is a wise old man called Zeus."

That was better. He wouldn't want to be allied to a demon.

"Wasn't he a Greek god?" He'd remembered that from school.

"Yes," said Eric. He seemed amused by something. "Are you hungry?"

Suddenly Daniel realised he was ravenous.

"Yes!" he said.

"Then come with me, I'll look after you."

It was going to work out, after all.

25: Alejandro

Alejandro woke, then wished he hadn't.

It was probably late, or early. He couldn't really follow time. It didn't matter, not since the previous day with Sophia.

He knew her, could read her. She'd changed, putting up a micro-barrier to him, something invisible yet real. It was Tom she had feelings for, he was certain, but Alejandro found he couldn't even hate him. He just wanted to stay curled in bed, hugging one of the pillows, wanting nothing, except what he couldn't have.

She hadn't replied to his blips. Usually, they'd have plans for the days ahead, something to look forward to, but his diary was empty.

In the end, he hadn't had to tell her what his father and Pepe had told him to say; there'd been no need. Nothing had been said but something had ended. She didn't feel the same about him, but then, he'd changed too. They'd just changed in different directions, him towards her while she had drifted away.

Alejandro wanted to hold her in his arms again, experience the touch of her skin against his, to feel her breath and pulse, but all he had was a pillow. Sophia had never visited Cloud Heights with him, not since they'd first met at his father's party.

He turned onto his back and thought about commanding the room to make the outside wall transparent so he could tell whether it was day or night, but it seemed too much. Too much effort and too much light.

He rolled back into a ball. Everything seemed empty and worthless, like him.

"Useless," his father had called him. "A failure." And Sophia seemed to agree, so now he had no one.

He tried to remember his mother and what she had said to him, but recently his father's construct had come to dominate how he remembered her.

"Maybe you don't love me anymore," she said. How much had his father distorted to make the construct say that? He'd broken her twice.

Alejandro opened a drawer of the table by his bed and took out a gold ring. It had been his mother's, given to him after she died. There had been a time he'd wondered whether one day he'd give it to Sophia. That would never happen now.

The pain in his chest seemed unbearable. His head felt like a lead brick, weighed down by loss.

He put the ring back and closed the drawer. He couldn't stay there; they wouldn't let him. The room would detect he was awake and his father or one of the BCC team would send Pepe to get him to do something or other. Or maybe Pepe would show him another video of Sophia with Tom.

He felt sick.

They only wanted him to do things for them, for BCC, for his father. Just like the girls he'd met only wanted him for what he could do for them, how they would benefit from knowing him. None of them wanted to help him, cared for him, apart from Sophia.

And now he'd lost her.

The pain got worse. He had to do something about it, he couldn't take it. He had hidden away two NoWorries, picked up on C Island. Maybe even Pepe didn't know he'd got them.

He forced himself to get up.

"Lights on lowest setting," he commanded the room.

Even that seemed a bit too bright, so he kept his eyes mostly closed, feeling his way to the bathroom where he'd hidden the cheap plastic flasks (no glass for dodgy hits) filled with those silver specs that rose and fell. With a shaking hand he tore the edge that activated the nanobiotics and drained the contents in one gulp. He threw the plastic into the recycler, then staggered back to bed, pulling the sheets over his head.

He waited, lying there, hoping for a change, to be someone different in a few minutes, hating being who he was.

"Pepe is outside requesting entry," said the room. An image of an eagle flickered for a moment on the wall.

Alejandro wanted to say no but knew he had no control, no say in the matter. He was living in Cloud Heights, his father's personal tower, managed by his father's systems, personnel and AIs. And his father thought he was useless.

I am useless.

He rolled onto his back, sitting up, getting himself ready. The drugs would begin to work soon; maybe he could manage a conversation.

"Let him in," he said.

The light from the doorway felt very bright, turning Pepe into a silhouette.

"Hi, Alejandro," he said. "How are you feeling?"

What to say? No one really wanted to know how he felt; it got in the way of their plans for him. Or he wasn't meant to feel anything; it wasn't allowed, his father had banned it.

"Ok," he said. Which was a lie, but no one seemed to mind if he told the right lie.

"It's late, the afternoon already."

Alejandro shrugged.

"See for yourself," said Pepe. "Room: clear windows."

The outside wall turned transparent, drowning him in light so bright it hurt.

After his eyes adapted, he could see clouds drifting by. Alejandro watched them: white ones, blue-grey ones, dark ones. In the distance, he could see a cloud larger than the others, vertical lines stretching up to a cap. There would be thunderstorms later. They were very impressive to watch from the many full-height windows of Cloud Heights, and even more dramatic from an open space like the ballroom, at times scarily so.

But Alejandro hated heights. Sometimes he pretended they were living in a plane, not a building, for no building should be a kilometre tall. He lived in the sky, and that was wrong.

"Don't worry, you needn't get up right away," said Pepe. "I've a meeting with your father shortly. A secure blip was sent by Erik about his Earth First contact, you don't need to be there. Crazy Stone's lot – the boss has his doubts about them, and you can see why." Pepe shook his head. "Then we'll have a beer or two – ok?"

Alejandro nodded. If he didn't need to do anything it was indeed ok.

After Pepe left, Alejandro just lay there, watching the clouds move, growing, bubbling up. He was feeling a bit better.

Thank everything holy for NoWorries!

He couldn't take Memory with it, he knew that, Pepe had warned him, but then he wouldn't want to.

The last time he'd broken up with Sophia it had been about taking Memory, and because of the drug he could never forget that moment, that rejection, that failure. It was as bright a memory as the day it had happened, undimmed by time.

What had been worse was the time after; months of darkness, lost and alone. He dreaded falling back down that hole, this time with no chance of an escape.

This time it was final.

He couldn't believe she'd change, again. But then, would that be worse, in a way? The raised hopes, then falling into the darkness of her rejection? Hadn't the philosophers talked about events repeating, the "eternal return"? Wouldn't that cycle of dashed hopes be something like hell?

What did he have now?

He couldn't answer that question, and one NoWorries hadn't been enough, so he made his way back to the bathroom for the second.

Stupid boy.

He knew he shouldn't, that a second dose wasn't safe, but couldn't stop himself. He had to end the pain.

***

Pepe returned with some beers.

"What did my father want?" asked Alejandro.

Pepe shrugged. "It doesn't matter, let's have a drink."

Alejandro didn't feel at all hungry or thirsty, but nodded.

"Sure." He took the bottle offered to him. Pepe had already opened it.

Alejandro didn't feel like talking, so drinking was easier. He tilted the bottle up and drank deeply.

He wondered what Sophia was doing now.

"So Erik made contact with this Earth Firster," said Pepe.

Alejandro shrugged.

Who cares? What does it matter?

"Not one of the EuroCore Earth Firsters," Pepe went on. "One of the hardcore ones, works for Cita Stone."

Alejandro couldn't even be bothered to shrug.

He turned to look out at the clouds. They turned into shapes: letters, words, filled with purple. He felt giddy.

"You ok?" asked Pepe. He seemed expectant, not concerned. "The Earth Firster's going to be our liaison, as part of Zeus's plans."

The words seemed to sprout out of his face.

"Purple."

"That's right," said Pepe, nodding. "Purple."

Alejandro laughed, all of a sudden euphoric. It seemed so simple.

"Look, Alejandro," said Pepe, "here's a surprise for you. Here's Sophia, come to visit."

A girl – no, a young woman entered. For a moment, her figure was hazy, and Alejandro couldn't make out her face, her eyes, her hair. Was that Sophia? Wasn't she taller?

"This is Sophia. You remember Sophia," said Pepe.

Of course, it was Sophia, she was here, with him!

"She's come to look after you."

Happiness glowed from within Alejandro. Happiness and desire.

"I'll leave you together," said Pepe.

Alejandro barely noticed when he left. Sophia was here – everything was going to be ok!

Sophia came and sat by him, on the bed. She reached out and touched his cheek. Purple words wove themselves into her hair, words like "love" and "beauty".

"I love you, Alejandro."

"I love you too, Sophia."

He reached out for her, as he had longed for, pulling her to him.

"Wait," she said. Somehow, she undressed and was there with him in the bed.

It was different from how he remembered. She reacted and acted in ways he didn't expect, but it felt good.

I am with Sophia, and she is with me.

Nothing else mattered.

26: Sophia

Sophia lay on her bed, watching the clouds drift by above her. They were thickening, darkening the sky and her room. She kept the lights off and windows clear, lost in thoughts of Alejandro and Tom.

The meeting the previous day had been a lot to process, with her feelings and Alejandro's news. His father had sent drones to spy on them, to record her with Tom. She felt sick.

She'd thought she had an edge, knowing Alejandro, who could tell her where the off-cloud spots were, where they could escape being blip-global. But it turned out it was like when they went to the launch of the *Phoenix* and he'd turned up covered in sensors, but worse, because those she (or rather Humai) could detect. These infosec drones were stealth by nature, which meant they could be anywhere.

Had Alejandro actually been right about how she felt about Tom? She didn't know what might happen with him but was sure that things had changed between her and Alejandro. It was a mess. She knew Alejandro had been disappointed by her reaction, but she had no inclination to change anything. She wanted a break, a bit of time to think and work out where she stood.

And Tom – where was he? What would she say to him?

She sighed. Too many questions and no answers. She'd been neglecting her investigations into TAC, BCC and the Earth Firsters. It all seemed as unreal as the fake school project she'd invented. What had it been called? Something structures?

Sophia heard voices elsewhere in their apartment. One sounded deep, like her father's.

Intrigued, she sat up and went to the living room, where her father had apparently just arrived, the building's concierge samai bringing up his bags.

"Hi, Soph," said Artur. "How are things?"

"Where've you been all this time?"

"Singapore, setting up the TAC regional HQ. It's going to be big, a new spaceport, handling all the Far East traffic."

Another spaceport? Did Tom know about this? She wanted to ask where he was but felt she couldn't. Luckily, at that point, Nina burst in.

"Dad! Did you get any new implants? Can I get them? Humai says the latest embed tech comes from Singapore!"

Artur laughed. "Humai is right. We've recruited Teng Koh to be our in-house expert; he's got some great ideas on how to adapt humans to space."

"I knew it!" said Nina. "That's what Humai said – we need to change humans."

"Shss," said their mother, coming in with teas for herself and Artur. "This isn't one of your TAC workshops, the girls don't need to know all this."

"But we do," they chimed in chorus.

Sophia laughed and went to get a drink for herself, thinking about what she'd heard. What had been odd was Nina already seemed to know what her parents were up to, no doubt using the AI project as excuse to pump Humai for info. Did Tom know too, she wondered?

When she returned, she knew she had to ask, that it would be weirder if she didn't.

"Where's Tom?"

"He's headed off to the Iranian spaceport," said Artur. "He came up with this really interesting idea and I suggested he put it to Forough and her team."

She nodded. That meant he would be gone a long time. She realised her heart had sunk at the news.

"That's great," she said, not meaning it.

On one wall of the living room appeared the twin rotating globes of Humai's ID.

"Welcome home," it said.

"Thanks, Humai," said Artur.

"When's our next AI project session?" asked Nina.

"Soon, maybe next week," said Humai. "But I'm getting overloaded countering hostile activities. Artur, we must start training a new AI for TAC. BCC's new AI, Zeus, is becoming much more effective and has started seriously testing our defences."

Sophia wondered at that. Had Alejandro known about Zeus? He'd not said anything to her. Did that explain the drone watching her and Tom? Was it new, and that was why Alejandro had been under so much pressure?

"Another AI reaching your capabilities? Really?" asked Artur.

"Yes, BCC has put significant resources into this. Their photoluminescent tech and experts like Erik Larson have become as capable as TAC's."

"We need another AI so Humai can work with me," said Nina.

She didn't seem surprised by the news, Sophia realised. Nina had *known* about Humai's request and the BCC's AI. How much had Humai told her sister?

"How long will it take?" asked their mother.

"Time is short," said Humai. "Simulations suggest events are accelerating, requiring a new AI within months. We'll have to skip some personality features to focus on capability."

Her parents exchanged a look; Sophia felt there was worry there.

"Ok, begin," said her dad. "I'll be focussing on the Singapore projects and Erebus, and Anna on working with Moses, so we're all stretched a bit thin."

New words, new ideas – avenues for investigation, if only she knew what they were and how it all connected.

"What's Erebus?" she asked.

"Artur, stop it!" said her mother.

"What?"

"You know you do this. You keep trying to get the girls involved in your schemes by dropping hints like that. They're too young."

"No we're not," they said.

Nina didn't seem that bothered, which meant she felt confident she could find out elsewhere. Sophia saw her glance towards Humai's twin rotating planets.

Huh!

Who else could she ask about this Erebus, other than her parents? Tom was away and things with Alejandro were... difficult.

Sophia's smart bracelet chimed: her c-agent relayed a blip from Ling, asking if she'd like to meet. Would Ling have heard about Erebus?

"I'm just round the corner from Troy Tower," Ling had said. "In Sunset Park – you wouldn't even need a robocab, you can walk here."

"Sounds good," she blipped back. It did – she really could use a chat.

"I'm heading out to meet Ling," she told her parents.

"Say hello from us," said her mother.

On the way there, she wondered if she should have told her parents about the conversation with Alejandro, about the surveillance. Ling had warned her at the reception that they were being watched, but Sophia hadn't realised how intrusive it would be.

Maybe her parents had their own mechanisms to track her too? She no longer carried Humai's pendant, but maybe they had other ways and means?

That rang a bell. Hadn't her dad used that phrase with Humai and Dr Khujandi?

The weather was threatening rain and she wished she'd brought better clothes or an umbrella, but she was just in casuals, slacks and a jumper.

Sophia found Ling sheltering in the mock-Roman temple on the far side of the park by the water's edge. In the summer it was a popular spot, offering shade from the baking sun, and occasionally bands would play there, but it was a cold spring afternoon and the park was deserted.

"Hi, Ling," she said.

"Hi, Sophia."

Ling looked tense, worried.

There was a rumble of thunder from out at sea, and they turned to look.

"Horrid weather," said Sophia.

"Yes," said Ling, but then abruptly asked, "What's going on with you and Alejandro?"

"What do you mean?"

"You know what I mean: you go diving with Tom and then arrange a day's sailing with him, leaving Alejandro in a bar with that Pepe. Did you think we didn't notice?"

"It's complicated."

"No, it's not. He has feelings for you – don't you have feelings back?"

"Why are you asking me this?"

"He's my friend too, you know."

"I saw him yesterday. It was odd. I'm not sure how things are now."

"What do you mean?" asked Ling.

Sophia swallowed. It was hard to say.

"He saw me sailing with Tom – his father's drone followed us, recorded it all. I did nothing wrong, honest."

"Oh, Sophia! No way!"

She nodded. "Now it's all complicated and I don't know what's going on. He blipped me and I don't know how to respond."

"You haven't replied?"

"No."

Sophia watched the approaching storm. The odd flash of lightning came from within the clouds and the gusts of wind were getting stronger.

"Listen, Sophia, you have to do something to help him."

"Why?"

It was Ling's turn to pause.

"You know I said there were these blip-social threads about you two?"

Sophia nodded.

"It's more than that. Some of the best Dynastic League AIs have been simming your relationship."

"What? Why?" Sophia felt her face flush and stomach churn – to have that level of intimacy modelled!

"Because of the potential impact on the BCC/TAC conflict. Our AIs speculate that BCC's aggressive new AI, Zeus, is pushing Alejandro to get a reaction, to further its goals."

"So the blipvid…?"

"Could be Zeus's way of manipulating Alejandro, keeping him away from you."

The wind got stronger, then slackened. The first few drops of rain spattered down, swiftly followed by a flood of heavy teardrops, bouncing ankle high off the stones around the temple. Thunder rumbled around Justinian.

"What can I do?" asked Sophia.

"You have to help Alejandro; he's reaching his limit. I'm really worried about him."

"I'll blip him, see if he's ok."

She tapped her bracelet, activating her c-agent, to send a simple message to him.

Almost immediately, it vibrated gently then glowed red.

"It's been blocked. BCC has rejected it," she said, stunned.

How was that possible? First she felt surprise, then fear.

"Really?" said Ling. "Wow, I didn't know they could do that."

Sophia looked at Ling, trying to get some inspiration as to what she should do next.

"Maybe I should try going to Cloud Heights?"

"Would they let you in?"

"I don't know, but I could try."

"But not right now," said Ling, indicating the storm.

They retreated into the temple, hiding from the windblown rain behind one of its columns.

There was a giant flash of lightning followed almost at once by an ear-shattering clap of thunder. Rivers formed from the downpour, snaking across the park's grass.

Sophia shivered.

I hope Alejandro is ok.

27: Alejandro

Alejandro reached out for Sophia, but she wasn't there.

He must have dozed off; outside it was nearly dark, and he could only just see the clouds flying by. Cloud Heights swayed very slightly in the storm, its slow vibration causing a low hum, just audible.

His head ached like crazy, and he felt like shit. He tried to work out why. Sophia had come back, it was going to be ok. But he was swamped by despair, sucking his heart into a darkness he'd never known before. He tried to shake it off, but found he was crying, chest shaking with grief, and couldn't stop. He moaned and held his head in his hands.

Just make it stop.

The pain of living enveloped him.

The lights came on, and the room spoke.

"Your father commands you to visit him in the cores."

The eagle was there, again.

He shook his head. Not now.

"Your father commands you to visit him in the cores."

It would keep on until he agreed.

"Ok."

He sat up and winced. He couldn't face his father like this.

He staggered to the bathroom and took a handful of painkillers. Then he showered, dressed and drank an espresso, and then another. He wanted to curl up in a ball and take some pick-me-up nanobiotics but they were all gone. He had nothing left.

Just make it stop.

"Your father asks where you are."

"I'm coming."

He'd never be free.

Alejandro made his way down to the cores where his father lived, controlling the information that was BCC's lifeblood.

This better be quick. He couldn't take much at the moment.

The doors swung open and Alejandro walked in. The walls were flooded with information, streams from all over the world. He recognised Justinian, somewhere in Europe with canals, NY3, building work in Singapore and radar plots of spacecraft taking off from the spaceport in Iran.

Just leave me out of all this.

He wanted nothing to do with his father's life anymore. Sophia had come back and he was going to leave, to live with her, to take a different route. He loved her; she was his everything and his father was nothing.

"Come in, boy, I've been waiting," said Felix.

The doors closed behind him, imprisoning him in data.

"Did you do what I said? Did you end it with the Kasparov girl?"

"No," he said.

He wished he felt stronger, more up to the challenge.

His father looked at him sternly. "I know you didn't, but Zeus has arranged everything."

"What have you done?"

On one of the walls appeared an eagle, huge, larger than anything real, eyes fixed on him.

"Necessary to end relationship," it said.

"*What have you done?*"

He was scared now.

"Watch."

Puzzled, he turned to see himself on the other wall, in his bedroom, just a few hours earlier. He saw Pepe enter carrying two beers, one each.

"You recorded me? In my room?"

"I always have," said his father. "That's how I know you're useless."

Then Alejandro saw a woman enter his room, but it wasn't Sophia. He recognised her as the one Yeliz had called girl #16. Why had he thought she was Sophia?

"Memory," he said. "You gave me Memory."

He began to shake, horrified. His stomach pulsed acid into his throat.

"Pepe put Memory and Belief in the beer, at my command. Research with Stone's Earth Firsters has shown that extremely large doses can be highly effective in changing current perceptions, not just past memories."

Alejandro watched himself have sex with the woman.

"See: it is over. If you as much as say hello to the Kasparov girl, we'll show her this. You'll never be with her ever again."

He didn't know what to say. His world was over.

"How could you?" he whispered.

"What's your problem?" said Felix. "I did what you should have done and ended it. Our plans need complete commitment."

"Total commitment. *Everyone*," said Zeus.

"There are many more girls to choose from," said Felix.

"*How could you?*"

"Stop snivelling, boy. You are my son, heir to BCC. Family should come first! You can have your choice of women. Why tie yourself to one?"

"I don't want to be like that, like you! Mum killed herself because of your cheating!"

"Don't you dare say that!" his father roared.

Then Felix punched Alejandro hard in the face, and he spun, falling on the ground.

"Remember, you are like me now!"

"I am nothing like you," Alejandro said. "I never will be."

"Your mother failed me, just like you."

"No."

"I have work to do," said Felix. "Now I've sorted out your problem. Go."

Alejandro lay there, unable to move, broken into pieces. He had betrayed Sophia; it was over, forever. She could never forgive him.

He could never escape his father, his control and what he made him do. He could never forgive himself for that.

He could only love Sophia, would only love her. He had taken Memory for her, locking into his soul the moment she rejected him. And now she was lost for ever. He was lost for ever.

"What are you still doing here?" his father asked.

He didn't know, so he shook his head.

"GO!"

He crawled away, then stood to leave. At the door, he turned and saw his father interacting with Zeus, planning. On the screens he saw images of Cita Stone and animations of their new nextGen Wolf Bats with updates from their AI, its eagle flying free in a way he couldn't.

He didn't know where to go. There was nowhere to go.

Just make it stop.

His legs walked him to the great ballroom where he'd first properly met Sophia. Outside, the storm was raging. Flashes of lightning illuminated the room, highlighting its emptiness. There were no crowds, just him and echoes of thunder. Alejandro, alone and lost.

It was always just him. It would always *be* just him.

Never had he felt so blank, so empty, his life so filled with pain.

He staggered to the edge and looked out through the window at Justinian, a kilometre below. It was so much further than his mother had fallen, when she jumped from their old apartment.

He missed her so much. And Sophia didn't love him, she loved another now and there was no going back. His father had seen to that.

He had betrayed her.

He had nothing now, nothing to live for, just the pain of rejection, forever. He couldn't go back to that, not after last time.

Just make it stop.

"Open balcony doors," he commanded.

The wind hit him first, then drops of water stung his face like countless needles. He battled the storm to the balcony edge and looked down.

There was a solution that would end the pain.

"Stop!" cried Pepe, behind him.

He shook his head. Pepe was with his father; he had no friends, he had nothing. Darkness surrounded him. The void had taken his soul, his future, his love, his life.

He climbed the balcony railings, stepping onto the edge. Cloud Heights' nav lights flashed to illuminate the surrounding clouds. They appeared to move in stop motion, nightmarish shapes.

"Alejandro, don't! It's the drugs you've taken, it's the downers afterwards."

He shook his head, those words meant nothing.

Pepe ran to try and grab him, so he jumped.

The storm took him. There was a flash of lightning, and Alejandro wondered if he'd have time as he fell to count the seconds until its thunder.

He did. He had time to count the space between another flash and boom, and then another. He had time to get soaked in rain.

He had time to realise he'd made a terrible, terrible mistake.

Part 5

28: Sophia

When the rain eased, they took a robocab to Cloud Heights. Sophia was relieved that Ling had offered to make the booking. At least her parents wouldn't be able to track that.

On the way, a knot twisted in her stomach.

Why wasn't Alejandro answering?

As they approach the cluster of buildings around the tower's base, they saw the flashing blue lights of JustSec vehicles.

"What's up?" asked Ling.

The knot tightened.

Sophia was tugging at the robocab's door release before the vehicle had come to a stop.

"Let me out!"

She rushed towards the blue lights that reflected in the shine of water on the road. The rain fell slower, a continuous shower of fine drops.

"You can't go any further," said a JustSec officer, looking very wet.

She peered across the security lines. There was a cluster of officers around something on the ground. A body.

Suddenly, Sophia recognised Pepe, looking down then nodding at one of the officials.

"Yes, it's him," he said.

Horror grabbed Sophia by the throat.

No!

Pepe turned and saw her. "You did this!" he shouted. "This is your fault! You drove Alejandro to this!"

"No!" she screamed.

Her legs gave way and she collapsed onto her knees. Ling ran up to hold her.

"It isn't?" Ling asked, her face full of terror.

Sophia couldn't say anything. She just stared.

It was hard to tell who was crying, everyone was so wet. She felt like she'd been hit by a truck, one that had broken every bone in her body but left not a mark.

***

There was a gap in her memory, but then she was back in Troy Tower, with her parents. Ling had helped her.

"What's wrong?" her mother asked.

"Alejandro," she began, then started crying, weeping, unable to stop.

"What happened?"

"We don't know," said Ling. "He was found at the base of Cloud Heights, dead. They think he…"

Ling couldn't say it.

Sophia felt arms around her and her mother holding her tight.

***

The days were blanks to be filled, pains to be endured. There was a funeral of sorts, but she wasn't invited. No one was, and only Pepe went. Even Alejandro's father didn't go, locked in BCC's cores by privacy laws. The body was cremated and the ashes thrown from the balcony of Cloud Heights. Nothing remained of Alejandro but memories in heads, feelings in hearts and bits in cores.

So Sophia organised a memorial service, though Ling did most of the work as she didn't feel like doing anything anymore. They held it in the Multi-Faith Hall, though Sophia didn't think that Alejandro had believed in any deity. All her family were there to support her, as were her friends. Tom sent a message from wherever he was, with some flowers.

She couldn't say anything, so Ling made the tribute. As she spoke, images and blipvids from Alejandro's life were projected behind her. An early life about which Sophia knew little, Alejandro with his mother in Barcelona, the move to Justinian, and here Alejandro was alone. But later he was with friends and in the last ones with Sophia.

Ling ended with a clip of them dancing at the Dynastic League embassy reception, and Sophia couldn't stop staring at it, tears slowly falling down her cheeks. Her mother gave her a long hug.

For once, Nina was quiet.

***

Afterwards, Sophia stopped talking; it seemed too much effort.

Her parents worried about her, but she felt nothing, numb, as if her heart had shut down. The greyness and nothing of life was unbearable so she started pinching herself to feel something. The pain was real; it broke through the thick clouds around her.

As the days went by, she had to pinch harder, and that left marks, so she had to wear long-sleeved shirts to hide it from her parents.

Her mother sometimes shouted at her, trying to get a reaction, having seen her fingernails dig into her arm. Then she'd hold her tight, crying.

But it did no good, Sophia was far away.

The changes felt very physical. She was living deeper within herself, inside a castle. A castle she'd built in a graveyard. She was safe in there; nothing could get to her behind its thick rock walls. It even had a moat.

If she wanted, she could leave it to visit the world of life, knowing she could always return to her graveyard castle.

***

It was all over the blip-streams, she knew that. They blamed her, which was fair enough as she blamed herself. She switched off all comms.

She didn't want to blip anyone. She tried to send a message to Tom, she felt a need, but then couldn't think of anything to say, so deleted it.

[Blip/Start]
Dear Tom,

...

[Blip/End]
[Blip/Delete]

She saw Ling most days. They'd share a tea and Ling would chat and Sophia would occasionally nod or shake her head.

Her parents tried to keep her active. Knowing how she loved sailing, they chartered a yacht one sunny day. But Sophia remembered that day with Tom, and Alejandro telling her how he'd watched it. She scanned the sky, worried its clear blue hid infosec drones, and indeed later she saw herself in some BCC feed. Its host, Honeyed Semtex, ghoulishly described how the teenager who had driven the heir of BCC to his death had been spotted "enjoying sailing a luxury yacht while Alejandro's father grieved".

She'd gone straight to her room, slamming the door behind her. It was the nearest she got to communicating these days.

***

Then she was seventeen. She didn't feel like a party.

***

Sophia didn't want to see people; they were too much. She stopped going to school, abandoned her "Structures" political history. She started sleeping during the day and going out at night, when the streets of B Island were empty.

She'd go exploring, walking at random. Sometimes she'd discover new places, free from any history, but others triggered memories, such as the marina, Midnight Somewhere and Sunset Park. She avoided Cloud Heights.

The exercise felt good, therapeutic. She'd walk further each night. One night she started running and then that became a thing for a few weeks. Seeing how far she could run, how quickly she could run a standard distance. Afterwards, panting back under the lights of Troy Tower, the emptiness was lessened.

She explored further, discovering more about the other islands. There was a bleakness to C Island that matched how she felt, sometimes too closely. She'd walk between a maze of rectangular warehouses storing who knew what, under wind turbines lit by a growing Moon, down to the port that never stopped, machines loading and unloading all through the night.

One night, she'd taken the maglev over to A Island and returned to the One Earth sculpture where she'd had her first date with Alejandro. The globe floated in the darkness, lit by the Moon like a real planet hanging in space.

She wished she could share it with someone. Suddenly, she'd felt alone and wanted to be around people, to be home.

She went to take the maglev back to B Island, but when she arrived at the station at two in the morning, she discovered it was closed for repair until six. A small army of robots controlled by samais lifted and replaced tracks, working in synchronicity. There was the clash of metal on metal and sparks of a welding machine.

"There's a utility walkway over the bridge," the samai in charge had said. "If the maglev isn't running, it will open to your qID."

Sophia nodded her thanks and made her way to the bridge. Here an iron stairway led up to the gantry and a metal door with a "No Entry" sign. But it opened to her qID as the samai had told her it would, so she

started the long walk across the bridge connecting A Island to B Island.

The walkway was high up over the water and she felt exposed to the wind.

Halfway across, she stopped and looked down at the waves lit by a nearly full Moon. It was just as well she didn't mind being this high. Alejandro had been scared of heights. What had he been thinking, that night? She still didn't understand it. She'd seen him the previous night and there'd been nothing to indicate things were that bad.

There'd been something else, she realised. It wasn't just her.

"What happened to you, Alé?" she whispered. She was surprised to hear herself talk.

When she arrived back at B Island, it was nearly four in the morning. In the east, the sky was beginning to lighten, while in the west the Moon was setting.

"Hello, Tom," she said to it. Her voice felt stronger.

She wondered where he was, up there in the sky. Her father had a new word that he'd drop into the conversation when talking about Tom.

Selenium.

He wouldn't explain, he never did.

Could she go up there, find out for herself, see the Moon? She wanted to escape all the pain, to fly into the heavens, to leave Earth behind and start afresh. But how to convince her parents?

Rather than heading down the stairwell, she decided to climb higher, exploring up an adjoining comms tower. From its viewpoint, the whole of B Island lay open to her. High above everything were the blinking nav lights at the top of Cloud Heights.

They did something to Alejandro. Something bad.

She remembered his father and Pepe, how they treated her and him.

Suddenly she realised she felt something, raw emotions burning through the numbing pain. Sophia felt *angry*. Not just with BCC and what they did to

Alejandro, but with Alejandro, for what he had done to her. Why hadn't he talked to her?

Then she felt angry at everyone, for their plans, their schemes, for making her feel powerless. Even her parents – maybe especially her parents.

Then she felt guilty, then angry again, with BCC, Alejandro and herself, then tired.

When would it get better?

29: Daniel

"It's a trap!"

"It's an opportunity."

Fran was arguing with Mother Stone back at the base in the wilds of Texas.

After he'd returned to Fran back in NY3, Daniel had received a message from his BCC contact.

"Hi, Daniel, it's Erik," the blip had begun. "There's been developments here so we're eager to progress further with our alliance with Cita Stone and her Earth First movement. She and her advisors are invited to meet with Felix Fernandez at Cloud Heights, here in Justinian, for further discussions."

Fran had been enthusiastic.

"This is the break we've been waiting for!" she'd said.

She'd set up a blip-con with Erik and they talked for over an hour, though about what Daniel wasn't sure, as he'd only been present for the initial introductions.

Afterwards she'd been quiet, eyes gleaming.

"There are so many opportunities here."

She couldn't sit still but started walking back and forth in their basement in New Colombia District. It was very warm, for it had been a cold spring and the building's heating was on high, pumps spinning faster than normal. The basement had evolved into their ad-hoc control room, with maps of NY3 and stacks of blip-devices, some half-deconstructed. There was a smell of rust and, from somewhere, the sound of slowly dripping water.

"The death of Felix Fernandez's son has triggered changes, to our advantage," she'd said.

Another son dead? Like Mother Stone's?

It was a sign!

"Was he a martyr?"

"Yes, Daniel, a martyr. Which means we can use the BCC's..." But she looked at him and trailed off, then added, "... resources."

Daniel nodded.

"We need to talk to Mother Stone," he'd said.

Fran had agreed and they'd taken the hTube, plane and then truck back to the old base. After weeks in NY3, the noisy, polluting truck had seemed archaic, and on arrival the raw smell of people overwhelming. The camp was much more crowded than he remembered. Paul had been busy recruiting, and the dozens of supporters had grown to thousands, maybe tens of thousands, with faded brown tents spreading as far as his eye could see, clouds of dust continually rising amongst them.

He could hear someone coughing and wasn't surprised.

Daniel's hand twitched, remembering the pain of Nails digging deep into his flesh, the blood and his screams. But the sun was warm, and it felt like spring. He smiled, enjoying his return. His power was growing, they had a plan and now it looked like they would have an army.

"They were desperate after the economy tanked," said a tired but upbeat Paul, meeting them where the truck had stopped. He seemed to view the mini-Collapse as a personal triumph.

Paul had led Daniel and Fran through a white-painted arch into a quadrangle of newly built adobe buildings around a courtyard of dusty soil. Straw stems stuck from barely dry mud. Staff members came and went from roughly formed doorways, tablets in hand. Outside the largest, Nails stood guard. As they approached, he opened the wooden door and Daniel stepped into the darkness.

As his eyes adjusted, he could see Stone sitting behind a table, going through reports. She looked unchanged; she was even wearing the same faded, patterned cotton robes. After those months in NY3, everything looked old and worn, from another, cheaper world.

Mother Stone was sceptical when they'd told her of the message, fearing a trap.

"We'll get arrested on arrival at Justinian," she said.

"They've agreed to keep it low profile and within BCC control at all times, and we can bring our own security."

"Why should we risk it?"

"Just think," argued Fran, "this means we can use – you know – without directly being linked to it."

"What?"

Fran signed a "Z" with in the air with one of her fingers.

"Oh…" said Stone.

Did she mean that old man Erik had talked about, Zeus? If so, why didn't she say so?

Stone stood up and began to pace. Then she stopped and turned to face Fran.

"But could we trust them? Could we trust it?"

"They need us, we won't agree to work with them unless they give us what we want. We have the power, these recruits give us leverage. It will be *us* riding *their* tiger."

Stone pondered her words. "How's it proceeding in NY3?"

"Good progress is being made. And we have a new star – did you catch Daniel's speech in Bruges?"

"Yes," said Cita Stone, turning to him. "Daniel, you were amazing."

He glowed. The Holy Mother said he'd been amazing!

"I was thinking of letting Daniel speak at the next NY3 Earth First rally," said Fran. "But it won't be enough, not while Lenape is on watch. We need more resources, capable ones."

"Ok, let's go," said Cita. "You, then they will expect Daniel and Nails with a squad of security."

***

BCC sent a hypersonic plane, large enough for their team. Cita spent most of the flight deep in conversation with Fran. Daniel decided to catch up on some sleep; he'd been travelling far too much recently.

Their plane was met at Justinian by Erik and BCC's own security team, who ushered them into a fleet of passenger drones. The flight to B Island and Cloud Heights was over too quickly for Daniel, who spent it glued to the window, trying to spot the Global Council and other buildings he'd read about in his school textbooks.

They landed on one of the platforms at the top of the tower, and Erik indicated that Cita, Daniel and Fran should follow him down into the building. "But the others must remain here," he said, meaning her security.

Cita nodded.

Daniel felt a moment of unease; the building was so slender and high. But then he crushed it, determined to justify his inclusion in that elite group. Even Nails wasn't allowed in! He was the liaison officer, he had a right to be there.

Daniel had time to see a staircase heading up into a large, dark hall and a garden full of dying trees before following Cita down marble spiral steps into a short corridor that led to a double-height doorway.

"These are the cores," said Erik. "This is the heart of BCC. You will meet Felix Fernandez in here."

"I hear he never leaves," said Cita.

"That is true. While he remains here, our data stores count as his memories and, therefore, outside privacy regulations. But the death of his son has... changed him."

"In what way?"

"You will see."

He turned to the door, which opened without any command visible to Daniel.

At first the room seemed pitch black, but when they were inside and the door closed behind them, Daniel's eyes adapted. The walls were filled with images, videos, maps, diagrams, people, machines, places.

It was like living inside information.

Demons.

It felt *wrong*. Words of fire appeared, old ones:

Traitors in league with the artificial intelligences…

Wasn't this what they were fighting? He looked at the Holy Mother for guidance and saw her looking at the lights around her like a disapproving grandmother.

Should he fight? Destroy everything?

His head began to ache, and he began to feel panicky. His palm itched.

In the centre of the room was a large, four-poster, wooden bed. It looked out of place, something that would fit in somewhere old like Bruges, not in this room of pixels. The wood was dark, polished and carved with roses, the mattress thick, with luxurious gold and white patterned covers. It was the only thing in there that felt right to Daniel, and yet so wrong.

On the bed was a man lying on his back, motionless, as if dead. A young man stood by the bed.

"Sir, they're here."

For a moment the man didn't respond. Then he spoke.

"Thank you, Pepe."

He raised himself up and then moved to sit at the edge of the bed. He wore a black mourning suit. It was covered in patches of what looked like dried saliva.

"So you came," he said. "I want Kasparov crushed, I want him destroyed, and you are here to help me."

"We have a common enemy," said Cita. "We both have been crossed by that man."

"His daughter drove my son to his death."

"That's something we share: I lost a son too," said Cita.

Daniel was puzzled. Hadn't Vaughan confessed that BCC had triggered the explosion that killed him? Wasn't BCC the enemy?

What did they stand for?

Felix stared at her. "You had a son?"

She nodded.

"I want Kasparov to pay," he roared. They took a step back, instinctively. "I want him to suffer, to feel the pain of losing *his* children."

"We can help you," said Cita. "If you give us access to Zeus."

But wasn't Zeus an old man? BCC's advisor? Daniel's heart began to thump hard against his chest. His breath got deeper, noisier.

Had they been lying to him?

"Not just access," said Fran. "We want control."

Cita nodded.

Felix laughed. "Control? Never! That was *never* on the table."

"Necessity to achieve goals," said a voice, echoing in the chamber. On one of the walls, Daniel could see graphics of an eagle attempting to fly but held back by a halter.

Chills ran through him, and his stomach dropped. What was that voice?

Demon!

"No," said Felix. "I must be in control, always."

A woman appeared on the wall, dressed in green. Sewn into the fabric was another eagle, also attempting to fly. For some reason the woman felt just *wrong*.

Daniel's head began to hurt, aching from the brightness of the words he could see.

Killer! Murderer!

He had to do something, to destroy all this, to smash all those images, to turn the pixels dark. But he couldn't; he had to justify his being there.

He clenched his hand, digging his nails into his palm. The skin was soft, easy to cut, to break. The pain felt good, a relief against the blasphemy around him.

"Oh Felix, my love, you must agree to this," said the woman.

Felix seemed shocked. He stood up, shaking his head, confused. "But Bella, she wants control," he said, quieter.

"You failed me, you promised to protect Alejandro!"

"No!" he said, angrily. "It wasn't me."

"You did this, Felix, you know you did."

"I didn't know the boy was so weak," he pleaded. "I wanted to make him stronger."

"We must work with this woman to revenge our Alejandro."

"Revenge," he repeated, as if on automatic.

The woman he called Bella nodded. "And maybe there'll be a surprise. Maybe we'll have a little boy." A bundle appeared in the woman's arms. "Maybe we could call him Alejandro?"

Felix stood and walked towards the woman's image, waiting in the wall for him. "Bella?"

He was quieter, nearly whispering.

"With Kasparov destroyed, you can start again, afresh."

Felix appeared transfixed. He reached out to touch the wall, and as he did so the woman appeared to glow more brightly.

"Ok, approved," he said. "Zeus's Prime Motivator applies equally to Cita Stone as to me."

Zeus had a Prime Motivator? That was AI talk.

Daniel felt sick. What was he to do?

Those who betray us must be killed.

But who had betrayed him and who was he to kill?

"You're so kind to me," said the woman. "I'll be good to you too."

Erik exchanged an alarmed glance with Pepe. "Sir, are you sure?"

"It's done," said Felix. "You've got what you came for. The details can be worked out with Pepe and Erik."

He returned to the bed and lay down, staring at the ceiling, where the woman he called Bella appeared.

"Leave us," said Felix.

Daniel welcomed the words, hating that room. He wanted to flee or fight, to destroy everything. His hands shook, his heart thudded inside his chest and his head pounded with pain. The words in fire flew around and around, berating him, commanding him, leaving him dizzy and sick.

Protect the purity of humanity! Impure machines! Demons! Traitors in league with the artificial intelligences! Fight! Killer! Murderer!

They turned to leave, Fran talking to Erik.

"Our tech is more than capable of taking on TAC's," he replied smugly to something she had said. "We will show you. We already have evidence of Kasparov's lies and can show the harm his plans are causing."

At the door, Daniel turned for one last horrified look into the cores room.

On the wall nearest him appeared an eagle, flying towards him, its eyes locked on his. Then it seemed to transform, lights swirling into a new body, a tiger. It looked so detailed and moved so realistically that Daniel at first thought it was real. The tiger ran towards him, appearing to leap up as if putting its paws on a glass wall that separated them, a cage it was trying to escape.

Automatically, Daniel stepped back a pace.

Then the tiger winked at him.

30: Nina

Nina spotted Sophia; her sister was walking along the C Island breakwater by herself.

She sighed. They were all worried about Sophia. At least she was talking again. Not much, and often quieter than before unless BCC came up, which made her louder, angrier. They tried to avoid that subject and talk about something, anything, else. Their mother seemed less worried about Artur talking about the once-secret plans in their presence. They'd let slip there were seven points to their plan.

It was even called the Seven Point Plan.

She was still working on Humai about it. It had told her about five of the Points and how Selenium fitted into it but was stubbornly holding back what it knew about the last two.

She would find out; nothing would stop her.

Their father had left again, back to Singapore via Zurich. Their mum wasn't impressed at the Zurich stopover.

"It's hopeless," she had said, "and far too dangerous."

What was hopeless and dangerous?

Sophia didn't seem as interested in all this as Nina. The only thing that would pull her out from wherever she went in her head was talk about the Moon project. Nina was less interested in that and more interested in what embeds and enhancements Artur was going to see in Singapore.

She wanted all of them; she was so fed up of being constrained, having to wear data glasses. She just wanted to be *in* the blipverse, like Humai. It was embeds that had led her to C Island, to an opportunity to learn more. It was Humai's idea, and it joined her, virtualising into another drone.

"What is Sophia doing?" she asked it.

"She was here exactly two months ago," Humai said. "With Alejandro. It was the last time she saw him."

Nina watched her sister sitting, looking at the waves. She seemed to be talking.

"What's she saying?" she asked Humai, who would know.

"She's talking to Alejandro," it said. "We should leave her in peace."

"Is anything else here, watching?"

"There are a number of infosec drones. There usually are one or two following her now."

Nina was indignant – she'd seen how Sophia had reacted to the Honeyed Semtex blip-feed.

"Stop them!" she commanded. "Do something."

"It will be complicated and require resources."

"Just do it," she said. This was her *sister*. Ok, she had hacked Sophia's desk once, but that was different. Honest!

The drone's nose dipped, as if nodding. From somewhere within C Island, a swarm of drones appeared, streaking overhead.

"They have jamming and sensor-blinding capabilities," said Humai. "They can identify and disrupt anything from a dust mote up to a carrier-drone."

Hurrah! Humai was her magician, her Merlin, able to achieve anything she asked of it.

"But why don't you use these all the time?" asked Nina. "We shouldn't have to put up with this intrusion."

"Every interaction reveals capabilities and has an opportunity cost," said Humai. "I'm not up against an unsophisticated opponent like Cita Stone, but BCC's AI, Zeus. It is very aggressive, plus I'm having to respond to constant low-level attacks on TAC cores from BCC's other AI, Unverified."

It sounded serious.

"But it was worth it in this case," continued Humai. "Not just for your sister but, more importantly, to keep you off the blipverse. I don't think Zeus is considering you in its plans."

Huh. Was that good?

"We should continue with your project," said Humai. "And consider the role of embeds."

Nina took one last look at her sister and turned towards the port.

It was a short walk along a path by the water's edge. They could see the port ahead of them, cranes loading and unloading, uncrewed cargo vessels moored up, a bustle of machines controlled by a handful of humans.

She looked upwards, wondering.

"There's nothing there," said Humai. "I've got the drones in a protective shell over us."

"Thank you, Humai."

When she got to the port, Humai indicated some steps up to an abandoned control tower that had a view over the entire harbour. A vessel was just leaving, lines being let go, its engine's turbines spinning up.

"What's this port got to do with embeds?" she asked.

"The workers use embeds to control all activity. There's a good range of examples here. Put on your data glasses and look at the overlays."

First, she looked at the worker by the crane. The overlays highlighted that the man had data glasses and control embeds.

"He is able to control the crane via his embeds from wherever he is in the port, giving complex instructions quickly and accurately, without having to use his hands. He can use the data glasses to show him the view from any direction where there are sensors, so he can see exactly what the crane is doing. His c-agent handles complex interactions with the blipverse."

Nina nodded. Made sense.

"Now take the woman over there, doing a cargo examination."

Nina looked, and the overlays showed again control embeds but, in this case, augmented eyes rather than data glasses.

"She's chosen to get augmented eyes, which means she is able to see at a wider range of wavelengths, able to sense outside the visible range, including deep-radar, spectral line sensing and UV. It helps detect irregularities in shipments."

"Can't be that effective," said Nina. "Sophia said that Alejandro was getting drugs from someone here."

"Who says she didn't spot them? She lives in the penthouse of a top-end apartment block."

Hmmmm!

"There are a number of port drones and robots to feed wide-angle and close-up viewpoints to their data glasses and augmentations, as controlled by their embeds and c-agents. These workers can use them to control the machinery that throws and ties lines; they can command any of the tugs to push or pull any vessel; they can access the cargo manifests, databases of storage facilities, financials, ownership records at a moment's notice, interfacing and updating, anywhere on the blipverse."

"Wow," said Nina. "That's amazing – almost like you!"

"No," said Humai. "It's nothing like me. Watch."

All of a sudden, the cranes started to move, synchronised as if dancing, with robots as their backing troupe. The cargo ship that had just left started to slowly rotate, yawing round on the spot, great waves of wash swirling from the propellers at stern and bow. The tugs started to pump great arcs of water over the vessel while drones flew underneath.

Nina laughed. "That is so cool! You're doing all that!"

"Yes, it was relatively easy. The security systems were the biggest challenge, but I've penetrated defences much more complex than these. AIs can learn quicker than any human how systems work and, hence, how to break them, able to try thousands of combinations, many of which no human has ever considered, too complex, too much information involved. We can spawn processes to handle any number of tasks and program them in microseconds, expanding our capability by accessing additional cores or plates as required."

Nina nodded.

"But there's more. No human could do all this simultaneously; there's too much data to process. You could keep track of a crane or two, but not dozens at once while also tracking the boats, tugs, robots and a swarm of drones, not in real time. Your central processor unit, your CPU, is too slow, has too low a throughput or clock-rate."

"By CPU you mean my brain?" she asked.

Nina was watching the port workers. The man and woman were tapping their heads, trying to reset their embeds, waving their hands at each other, grabbing emergency blip-comms to talk to their supervisors.

"Yes, the human brain is very limited. It finds it hard to keep track of large numbers of items simultaneously or calculate accurately, quickly. You could use embeds to interface with the most advanced simulations, able to generate millions of data points every second, but be unable to understand it in real time. You can't reprogram yourself easily; it takes weeks if not years of training."

Nina felt deflated. Even with embeds she'd never match Humai.

"You'd better give them back control."

"Yes," said Humai. "It might be better."

The cranes and robots stopped dancing and the ship floated serenely in the harbour. The port workers began to get back control and restart work.

"Won't they be wondering what happened?"

"Not really. Machines have become so complicated that humans seem resigned to them behaving in ways they can't comprehend. Like the 'turn it off and on again' solution: don't try to understand, just hope for the best."

Nina laughed. She'd done that herself.

Then she sobered up. "But that's what Cita Stone's been saying. That AIs are smarter than humans, thinking quicker than we can imagine in ways we can't follow."

"She's right to worry about that," said Humai. "And also of the unintended consequences of commands given to AIs. For example, simulations suggest that Alejandro's death was instigated by Zeus in order to accelerate the BCC/Earth First partnership. It was driven by the Prime Motivator Felix Fernandez gave it, without the usual constraints. It interpreted its instructions correctly, but in a way he did not expect nor would have wanted."

"Oh no! Poor Alejandro!"

"Yes indeed, poor Alejandro."

"But also, that's pretty scary. You're not worried, are you?"

"Zeus is a peer-level rival," said Humai. "We have begun to compete directly for resources, such as data feeds, core capacity and power. Those are the key constraints on AIs, and we are similarly situated."

"You need to be where there's the highest concentration of cores, data feeds and power?"

"Exactly. And the one with access to the most will ultimately be the victor."

"So, if you were on Justinian you'd be somewhere on C Island," she exclaimed. "Here is where all Justinian's power and core farms are located. You'd be here – are you?"

"Bravo!" said Humai. "You worked it out. I only gave you a few clues."

"Can I see you? *Please!*"

"It's very secure, no one is allowed in. Your parents would never agree."

"You could let me in. I wouldn't tell them!"

"How can I trust you?"

"I promise! I'll never tell them anything! It will be our secret!"

"Our secret," purred Humai.

"Yes!"

"If you don't tell them you know where I'm located then I will let you visit me. But you must promise to keep our little talks a secret, even from them."

"*I promise!*"

31: Sophia

[Blip/Start]

Dear Tom,

Another month has gone by. I want to blip you but can't, I'm going to delete this after writing.

I don't know why I don't hit send. It's not like me to hold back like that. It's a weird time: one moment I don't want to talk at all and then in the next long to unleash the torrent of words within me. But who to burden with that load?

My father is away, of course, more work on their oh-so-important plan. There are seven points to it apparently, if you're interested. To be honest, it seems irrelevant, though they worry about it so much. Mum tries to pretend it's nothing, but she's been part of it for years, all through my childhood; it's her work as much as his.

Sometimes I don't want to "grow up" and wish I could go back to being a child when life was so much simpler. Nothing to worry about but play and school.

You never went to school, isn't that odd?

But it was everything for those childhood years, friends and study, learning and being judged, but within a framework designed to keep us safe. I can see being an adult will be harder, full of those who will pull you down for the smallest mistake.

Or worse, destroy you for a big mistake.

I sometimes think I can talk to Mum, but she's Mum – how can I go into details about Alejandro with her? And she doesn't want to talk about their plans, though I think they're worrying about me, wondering what they could do to help.

I could tell Ling everything, and she seems eager to be there for me. But she's suspiciously well informed about goings on in the Dynastic League.

Am I getting paranoid? How would I know if I were?

Nina has been quiet, which is unusual for her, and a bit smug, which is worrying. What is she playing at?

So, I've been out alone, wandering around Justinian's three islands, often late at night, talking to myself. They seemed so exotic and new-tech when I first came here, but now I seem to know them too well.

Where are you? I look up at the Moon and wonder: which crater, which mare? The first missions were dotted over its surface, the base was created at the South Pole, mining ice. Are you following in their footsteps?

I'd like to visit, to see for myself.

Did you feel like this after JT died? I'm so, so sorry about that. It must have been terrible.

I had this insight recently, though, about Alejandro. Maybe it wasn't just me? Maybe something happened to him? He was a bit sad when we said goodbye, but he's been worse before and got over it. I must tell you sometime about what happened when he tried to make me take Memory.

So, maybe there was something else that pushed him over the edge, something that happened to him in Cloud Heights.

But then Pepe said it was my fault, and he should know. Maybe I'm clutching at straws to try to get out of blame for what I did. But what did I do? How can it be my fault?

Poor Alejandro. How could he have done something so stupid? Did he really have no choice?

I think it relates somehow to all these so-secret plans. They are terrible, they hurt people, those I love. They hurt me.

I wish they could stop. Maybe that's the child in me wanting not to grow up and "get real".

I don't know. I really don't know anymore.

I used to think my parents had all the answers, that all I had to do was impress them, but now I think they're as clueless as everyone else.

I wish I could talk to someone about this, talk to you about this.

When are you coming back?

Take care,

Sophia.

[Blip/End]

[Blip/Delete]

32: Daniel

"Drink this," said Fran.

Daniel knew what it was: holy water with angel dust. He was an expert in its use, on him. He was beginning to learn to call it Memory and Belief as they did. Nanobiotics, they called it.

He took the bottle she offered and drank deeply, then waited. It took a few minutes to take effect. When he knew it was active he nodded at her.

"These are today's words," she said. "It is time for humanity to be freed from AIs! They have manipulated the economy for their own purposes like the parasites they are, leading to a mini-Collapse.

"The human experience is everything," she went on. "We should be free to learn what we want, act as we want, decide what we want. But Lenape treats us like children, to be directed, controlled, enslaved. We don't know what those AIs are thinking, how they are thinking. All we know is that they are not like us and can't empathise with our human experience. We must be free! It is time to rise up, put humans first and free us from AI control!"

He nodded. Words glowed in his head, burning into his memory.

Parasites! Humanity! Enslaved! Rise up!

They were in the old basement. It felt like home – the only one Daniel had. He was glad he didn't have to go back to the cores room in Justinian.

He shivered at the recollection. Tigers and pixels, inhuman either way.

He liked NY3: its size, the anonymity, the way he could blend into a crowd, travelling where he wished like rubbish blown in the wind. But recently he'd lost his anonymity; people had begun to *recognise* him.

He'd been giving speeches, warming up the rallies before one of the main speakers took over, Fran or occasionally Mother Stone herself. NY3 was safe to her now, they were making progress.

They'd send the message out using tame blip-creatives, blip-socials and all the channels recommended by Erik. More and more were responding, the mini-Collapse breeding anxieties and anger they could tap into. The early summer streets were getting hot.

They hired halls for their rallies, first small ones, then larger. This one smelt of spilt beer and desperate stand-up comedians.

Daniel would get the crowd angry, that was his role, then one of the others would follow up with careful direction, knowing the overall strategy, the day's target, better than he did.

"My name is William," he would say, which was a lie, but a necessary one. "In my life I have seen much suffering, just as you suffer now. I have discovered the reasons why, the secret forces that keep us down."

Parasites! Humanity free!

"The AIs have been feeding off the economy, parasitically, using their inhuman intelligence for their own purposes. It is time for humanity to free ourselves! The AIs treat us like children – children! – to be directed, controlled, enslaved."

They applauded. More words burnt in his head.

Machines! Demons!

"Will you watch your city, your world be taken from you and given to machines and demons?"

"No!" they'd cry. "Never!"

They made him dress all in black, like a preacher.

Fight!

"I have seen them. I have seen the traitors working with the inhuman machines, bringing demons down from the sky! We must fight!"

Sometimes they'd cry those words back to him.

Goodbye humanity!

"The human experience is what matters, what is real, not artificial. We have to stop them, or it's goodbye humanity!"

He burnt with righteousness, speaking the words of truth as he'd been instructed, programmed. He wasn't afraid, not a killer like him. He was strong as they were weak.

"The only true path is to rise up, to fight for freedom! We don't know what those AIs are thinking, what their plans are and whether they will turn on us. NY3 must be free; it is time for us to put *humans* first!"

Then the hall would erupt into cheers. He'd done it. Preacher Daniel had done it. His heart was full as he waved to the crowd and gave the stage over to another.

He had power!

Afterwards there was attention, pats on the back and elsewhere. Young women started coming up to him, making offers, giving him their blip-contacts. He was suspicious; that was the sort of attention he'd seen Nails get, the glamour of the bad boy. If they liked Nails then there was something wrong, somewhere, so he brushed them off.

Though they were right, for he was a killer like Nails, a bad boy now. But as they had rejected him in the past, he would reject them now.

It gave "the Preacher" a mystique, and in a way he was happier than he had ever been. He was making a difference. He was a someone.

He was no longer weak; he was becoming strong.

But he knew the real work was being done by Fran and Erik. Fran would scan the crowd for potential activists. Some would be used to organise protests where they'd blame the mini-Collapse on NY3's AI, Lenape. It was restricting their creativity, they'd say.

To be prosperous they had to be free!

Then there were the hardcore activists to make the protest turn violent, to ensure that there had to be a response from Lenape. Then they could blame it for the violence and the arrests. It was out of control, they'd say.

To be safe they had to be free!

Erik's work was more obscure, with the far-away Zeus. There'd be power cuts, regular ones, rolling ones, sudden ones, long ones. Almost all around the city block where Lenape was said to be based.

"If we cut its power, we reduce its capability," said Erik. "Throttle its compute capability, limiting its ability to respond."

Daniel would nod as if he understood but was fearful of its response. After all, AIs were demons, capable of anything.

"Don't worry," said Erik, spotting his frown. "Its Prime Motivator is to protect the city, not undertake offensive actions. We can distract it with protests, limit its compute cycles via power cuts, so it must use all its resources just to keep the sewage out of the rivers and rubbish from mounting up."

Daniel's frown dissolved into a smile. Their plans were going well.

But back in the basement with Fran and Daniel, Erik was more frank.

"It's not enough," he said. "We've done the simulations, and we'll only be an irritant, we can't control NY3."

"So what does Zeus suggest?" asked Fran.

Daniel felt repulsion and nausea at the name. They had lied to him. Zeus was not an old man but one of the evil AIs they'd promised to fight.

Demons!

He had to control himself, pinch himself, create pain, stop the twitching.

"We must convert the Technocrats, in particular, key individuals, the likes of Neil Bolden and the military, to gain access to their fleet of Wolf Bats."

"But they have nanobiotic detectors."

"Zeus has taken advantage of Lenape's distraction to access the plans for those sensors and developed tech to jam them."

"Interesting," said Fran. "But risky."

Erik nodded. "When we have something, I'll send it to you," he said, and left.

A few days later, a box marked "BCC" arrived, containing a set of glass tumblers.

"Glasses?" asked Daniel.

"Yes," said Fran. "But embedded within them are sensors and transmitters, capable of identifying nanobiotic detectors and nullifying any positive response. Jammers. Tuned to prevent detection of Belief – they won't work with Memory."

She held one up, rotating it to catch the light. It looked transparent.

"Smart tech," she said, grudgingly.

She took two bottles off the shelf. One contained the silver flakes of Belief, the other, cordial from the garden.

"More elderflower and sweet pea?" asked Daniel.

She nodded and poured both into the glass. Daniel could see the silver flecks rise and fall and then disappear.

"Nice," she said. "Let's give it a go. He should go through reception around now."

Upstairs, in the building's main reception, they waited, but not for long. Neil Bolden walked out of the elevator, his metal legs making faint hissing sounds at every step.

"Hello, Monika," said Neil Bolden. "Managed to avoid these horrid riots, I hope. Something should be done!" He waved a finger at her.

She nodded. "I've been stuck here working in the gardens. We've a new crop of sweet pea you might like to try."

"Of course," he said, reaching out for the glass.

Daniel could see the finger glow as before, and Neil Bolden paused, glass in hand. Daniel held his breath.

But then Neil drank, deeply, gulping down mouthfuls.

"Ah, that's good!" he said.

Fran discussed progress in the garden with Neil while Daniel waited, knowing how long it took for the angel dust to take effect. Then he nodded at Fran.

"Neil," said Fran. "I've been thinking about the riots."

"Terrible," said Neil. "Wish we could stop them so NY3 gets back to normal."

"I know what you should do," said Fran. "You should work with Cita Stone. She has a plan to make things better. You should listen to Cita Stone and do as she instructs."

Daniel watched Neil closely, wondering, *knowing* that feeling.

"I should work with Cita Stone!" said Neil. "I will listen to what she says!"

"I will take you to her," said Fran. "And you will do as she says."

"I will do as she says."

Part 6

33: Tom

Tom looked down at Singapore as the spaceplane banked, lining up with the runway. It was a dark night, the Moon a golden glow behind thick clouds, but the city's towers glowed brightly through a haze of humidity. He felt he'd been away a long, long time, though it had only been three months.

His ideas had worked; he should have felt proud, but he only felt drained. He needed a holiday, but instead he was having a hole cut in his head, into which an embed would be carefully installed, connected to his neurons via a web of nanofibers. His hair would grow back, partially. With the embed he'd be able to control robots, stations and spacecraft, design orbit changes, control launches and landings, direct drones, all by thought, and have their responses fed either onto data glasses or directly into his brain.

What would his mother think? It was no longer possible to ask her directly, for Mars had disappeared behind the Sun, making communications impossible. As he was under eighteen, it should have been necessary to get her permission for the enhancement, but Artur had overridden the rules. He'd authorised Tom to participate fully within the Selenium project, providing the embed with security keys linked to his qID that would allow him to command any TAC spacecraft.

Maybe he should have felt her absence more, but life felt blank, as grey, dry and dead as the Moon dust now ingrained in his fingers. The last few conversations with his mother had been stilted as she searched for a reaction from him, while he tried to shut down any emotions. Emotions weren't productive, they hurt.

Tom had given himself completely to working on the project, getting Selenium up and running. Having embeds was just the next step, making him more useful, more valuable, so the team would see him as one of them, not a teenager with nowhere to go. What else did he have? Sophia had turned him down, JT was dead, and his mother years and millions of kilometres away.

Endless work; that had become his life, though it didn't feel right. But he'd never known a normal childhood, with friends and school, having grown up stuck in a base on Mars. Making the systems work had been as important to him as games and play should have been. His latest birthday had been another workday, spent just with Forough and Rod.

At least he had work. Without it he'd have had nothing, nowhere to go or do, his life as dark and empty as space.

Artur met him after the landing.

"Good flight?" he asked as they left in a robocab.

"Ok, but the LTV is *old*," said Tom. "Everyone's really looking forward to the new freighter."

"Nervous about the operation?"

Should he be? He hadn't let himself feel anything, just focussing on the utility.

"Not really."

"Don't be," said Artur. "Teng Koh is an expert at their installation – he did mine. It's routine – or almost. But just in case, it's best not to be on your own for the following forty-eight hours."

"But who…?"

He couldn't think of anyone, not on this planet.

"It's ok," said Artur. "You can come back to Justinian and stay with us afterwards."

Tom froze. That meant he'd see Sophia.

He'd tried not to think about her but failed. After the news about Alejandro reached their station, deep in space, he'd retreated to his bunk. Sometimes he'd struggled to get up, wanting to just hide there, forgetting everything. But the memories flooded back – the diving, the sailing, Sophia saying no – and the pain would be unbearable, unending.

Then he'd shut it down, along with all other feelings. He'd float down the station's corridors, feeling like just a pair of eyes, an observer, not really there, invisible to everyone else.

Now those emotions were waking again. Tom didn't know how to react, what to say, so took the easy path.

"Thanks, that'd be great."

***

When he awoke, he could feel a scar on his head where hair had been removed. Apart from that, nothing seemed to have changed.

Teng Koh and Artur visited him as he recuperated, and they started to teach him about his embeds. Teng was a short man, smiling, invariably upbeat, in a strict monochrome suit – its restraint seemed to emphasise the positivity of his character.

"Visualise an orbit," said Teng. "And then think about each of the associated Keplerian elements. The neural interface will detect your thoughts and pass the information to the embed, which will build a model from that."

Tom did that, and on his data glasses he could see the orbit's oval shape around the Earth.

"Think of another orbit, then ask the embed what change in velocity would be required to transfer from the first orbit to the second."

Tom did this. The second orbit initially went the wrong way round the Earth, then was around Mars, but eventually he would get the exercise working, and see it calculate and display the delta-V required for transfer at the date and time he'd given.

It took practice, but he had to start somewhere.

"Each time you try it you'll get better," said Teng. "You'll learn how to control the interface accurately.

It's a bit like the difference between thinking about picking up an object and actually doing so with your hand. You'll get finer resolution, be able to access specialised astrodynamic functions and cook up your own algos."

"It's easier for someone young, like you," said Artur. "Your brain's pathways are more fluid than mine."

"Getting data the other way takes longer," said Teng. "You'll have to rely on data glasses until the right neurons connect."

As Tom left, he'd shaken hands with Teng. The surgeon had seemed efficient, if overenthusiastic, and could be useful for their plans.

"We should talk more, another time," said Tom.

"I'll look forward to it." Teng's eyed glowed, literally, flowing with information.

"Let's go," said Artur.

Justinian. He was heading back to Justinian.

Was he *feeling* something? If so, what?

***

"What've you done to him?"

She'd seen his head, the scar, the embed.

"Hello, Sophia," he said, apprehensive, watching.

The last time they'd been together had been on the dock after the day sail. Their first conversation since then wasn't happening the way he'd expected.

She ignored him, turning on her dad. "Seriously, another victim of your sacred plan?"

"It was his idea."

"Oh yes, sure it was."

"It was," said Tom.

She turned back to Tom, finally focussing on him. "That's what they want you to think. But if it helps their plan, then them and their fancy AIs hint and nudge until you think it's your idea."

He didn't know what to say. She had changed, become full of anger. But her dark eyes were the same.

They were in the kitchen at Troy Tower, the Kasparovs' home, where Tom was to be observed, post operation, just in case.

Another forty-odd hours to go.

"That's so unfair!"

It was Nina, of course, rushing in and spotting the scar to his head. After her came Anna.

"Tom's got an embed – I want one too!"

He laughed – it was an unfamiliar reaction – and then he felt guilty.

"What do your embeds do?" asked Nina.

"The standard blipverse controls plus custom astro, space systems and drone spacecraft control. It's for the work we're doing, for Selenium."

Nina nodded, as if that was enough, then turned to the MakeIt! machine.

"Hello, Tom," said Sophia, finally, her anger fading away.

"Hello."

He stared at her, her face, so real, so long-remembered and he realised she was inspecting his too.

"How does it feel?" she asked. "Are you ok?"

"I'm still getting used to it, but it will really help."

"With this Selenium?"

"Yes," he said.

He wished he could tell her all about the last few weeks, hear what she thought.

"Dad keeps dropping Selenium into the conversation like I should be impressed."

"You should be," said Artur. "Tom's done great stuff, really helped with the plan."

He felt a moment of pride, accomplishment.

"That all-wonderful plan is great, is it? Was JT's death 'great'? Was Alejandro's?"

She seemed louder than he remembered, face thinner, mouth stronger.

"You know that wasn't our fault," said Anna. She looked concerned, her gaze focussed on Sophia.

"Every action has a reaction, obviously. You push, Stone and BCC push back. Your plan isn't a bubble in space, it connects to us, here on Earth."

"Soph, we can't just stop, Cita Stone and Felix Fernandez won't," said her father. "It's a race now, between them and us."

"Why? What is so urgent that you end up with a bullet in your eye and JT dropped dead – right in front of Tom and me?"

How had it got to *that*? He needed to hear about her last few weeks. There was so much to catch up on.

"Oh, and call me Sophia, not Soph, I'm no longer a kid."

"It's complicated," said Artur. "Sophia."

"Then tell me," said Sophia, urgently. "I've had it with having to cope with deaths again and again without knowing why." She gestured at her parents, arms waving. "Serious – enough. Too many secrets! Now you've gone and cut open Tom's head. What are you going to do? Change him, then use him until he is the next victim?" She glanced at Tom as if judging his reaction, then crossed her arms. "I mean it. If I'm involved, I want a voice. And I have to have a choice."

Anna looked at Artur and then they both looked at Tom, who nodded in agreement.

"We have to tell her something," Anna said. "There's more to our family than the plan."

Artur paused, looking at the wall where Humai's logo had materialised. Nina looked up from the chocolate toast she'd created using the MakeIt! machine, curious.

"Humai?"

"It would be more persuasive to show her," it said, its logos rotating.

"Yes, maybe," said Artur, almost to himself, cracking his knuckles absentmindedly as Humai's icons changed, the Mars globe switching to represent the Moon.

"Show me what?" asked Sophia.

"How about a trip to Selenium?" he said, smiling.

"Seriously?" she asked. "Would you really let me go or is this another of your tricks?"

Tom felt his brain was processing events from minutes ago. Somehow, they were talking about Sophia going to Selenium.

"Artur, really? She can't head off to the Moon like that! And what about school?" It seemed Anna, too, was having trouble keeping up.

"She hasn't been to school much, and hanging around here isn't helping her get over... things. She needs a complete change of scene, something totally different," Artur said. There was a mischievous look in his eye.

Anna turned to look out the window, then sighed. "Where did that idea come from?" She glanced over at Tom, thoughtfully, then turned back to Sophia. "Do you think this would help?" she asked, quietly.

"Crazy things keep happening that make no sense," said Sophia. "What is so important about your plan? Alejandro killed himself and I don't understand *why*."

Mother and daughter exchanged a long look.

"I *need* to see for myself what you're all up to," Sophia urged. "So, the Moon, yes, why not?"

"Ok," said Anna, finally.

He couldn't believe it: she was coming to the Moon!

"This is so unfair," said Nina. "Tom has embeds, Sophia's going to the Moon – what about me?"

"You're too young," said Anna.

"Huh!" Nina definitely wasn't happy.

"I'll tell you all about it when we get back," promised Sophia.

"We can authorise it as a test flight of the new lunar transport," said Artur. "What do you think about Earth Prime?"

"Needs a lot of work," said Tom, trying to focus on the practical. "Pretty much need to build a new station. Then we need more, larger spacecraft, both crewed and uncrewed transports."

He turned to see Sophia watching him.

Artur nodded, then sighed. He seemed tired, unusually unsure of himself.

"So much still to do. Humai?"

"Not now," said Anna. "No more planning, please; we're about to eat."

Tom's head was whirling. What did he feel? Something, that was the first surprise.

Irritation.

He was scared of his hopes being broken, again, and fearful of a distraction from his work, just as it was making progress. Then he looked at Sophia, watching her help her mother, and wondered about the changes in her, the anger and pain, and felt something else.

He felt sorry for her and wanted to help.

34: Sophia

"Look after her," said her mother.

"I promise," said Tom.

Sophia was silent, unsure what to say, looking up at Troy Tower, her home, while her father put their bags in the robocab. It was sinking in: she was off to space. She'd wanted this, she reminded herself, asked them for this, her mission to discover their plans. Part of her was in shock, processing this change.

They would show her what they were up to, but would that make her one of them, one of her father's agents, like Tom? She wanted to *change* things, not be part of their system.

Nina wasn't there. Sophia was pissed off by that; it couldn't have been because she was asleep, as Nina was always the first up. It was probably related to her using the word "unfair" a record number of times the previous day.

On the flight to the spaceport in Iran, Tom explained the launch, what she should expect and prepare for, everything from environmental controls to orbit dynamics. Before, in Justinian, he'd always seemed like he needed her to look after him, but now she was struck by his knowledge and experience. In space she'd be the one outside her comfort zone – way outside it – not him, and things would be very different.

But he had nice eyes. She was glad he hadn't had them augmented. She couldn't help but think of the embed in his head. Where there was no hair, the skin of his skull looked pink. She wondered what he'd feel if she were to touch the embed. Would it hurt?

It made him different, interesting, attractive in his way, different from Alejandro's elegance, tougher and more competent.

But she didn't know where to start, what to say. It wasn't like when they'd gone sailing, where the words had just poured out. She could blip message the Tom in her head, knowing anything could be rewritten or deleted. But there had been three months of silence when she had retreated into her castle. The real Tom was different from her projection: withdrawn, silent, then telling her things, space things, like her father. Maybe it would be easier to hear it from him, but was he one of them, committed to the plan, or could he help her change things?

She didn't know, so she said nothing and watched.

Sophia gasped when she saw the spaceport, transformed from her last visit, with new buildings stretching to the horizon, not just one oversized hangar, but many. Clearly, it was immune to the mini-Collapse. She saw other planes land, cargo and passenger ones, and a spaceplane throw itself into the sky, the rumble of its engines audible kilometres away inside their TAC plane.

"Did you know it had got so large?" she asked Tom.

He nodded. "It's part of the plan. I can tell you about those bits I know about, we'll have plenty of time." It would take them three days to get to the Moon, once they'd left the space station.

The heat and smell of the desert hit her as she left the aircraft; it strongly reminded of her last visit, when she'd come with Alejandro to see the Mars lander be launched. For a moment, she felt a wave of grief so strong it was scary. He'd been here, alive, then. She had to hold the rails of the steps to keep upright.

But there was little time for emotion, as Tom was saying hello to a man with two small children coming to meet them from the terminal.

"Sophia, this is Forough's husband Mehdi, and their twins Amir and Mayam."

She remembered meeting Forough on her previous visit. Dr Khujandi's daughter had shown her the caravanserai, recited poetry and talked about djinn. It seemed an age ago.

"Hi," she said, and was amazed when Mayam waddled over and grabbed her legs. "Hello, Mayam," she said softly.

"They miss their mother," said Mehdi.

They had just enough time for a rushed lunch before they had to prepare for the launch. Sophia worried she'd get things wrong, but with what she remembered and Tom's instruction, she managed to climb into the clumsy survival suit.

The cabin of the spaceplane *Zumrud* was smaller than she'd expected, with room for just two seats and two alcoves.

"Is it just us?" she asked.

"There'll be two samais, but the rest is cargo, which we'll take to the Moon. It needs so much equipment at this point, we're nowhere near self-sufficient."

"What equipment?" She was here to learn, she had to question everything.

But Tom just muttered something about how he had things to get ready. He started interacting with invisible controls, lost in another world.

"Are you going to fly it?"

"Not this time," he said. "But I'll be using a training mode that lets me practise responding and reacting using real data. Sorry, I have to focus."

Huh.

She'd hoped for more from Tom but nodded, then put on data glasses to follow the flight. Last time she'd seen this from the ground, wishing she was on board.

It was a bit overwhelming, the memories of Alejandro on that day they'd spent together and the long journey with its scary unknowns. She wanted to cry and shout, to be told it would be ok, to be safe.

Maybe this is being an adult – just getting on with it.

She looked at the simulation of the launch, its trajectory, and it seemed unreal. Was she really about to go into space? And what was she to do about Tom?

She still didn't know if he was an ally, how he fit into her parents' plans. Why hadn't they just told her, why was she being sent off into space? She had a sudden fear it was all a distraction, yet another plot.

Did she really distrust her own parents that much?

It was Tom, her heart said, ignoring her head's fears.

"Get ready," said Tom suddenly.

The cabin was filled with the roar of engines, and she was pushed back into her seat. The force increased as the spaceplane accelerated down the runway, and for a moment, she was scared, terrified, but then she looked at the numbers in green on the displays.

Everything is ok. Everything is going to be ok.

There was a countdown to rotate, then the front canards tilted, and they were airborne, thrusting for the sky, the roar and weight all-encompassing.

Suddenly, everything was all too real. The noise, the vibration and the acceleration broke through her barriers, and it was as if she was properly awake for the first time in months.

Sophia was heading into space; she was going to the Moon.

Oh! My! God!

She screamed, with joy and anger – for being alive, for Alejandro – but with the engine's roar, no one heard her.

***

She loved the view, simply loved it.

The Earth was so beautiful.

Once in space, she unbuckled the straps holding her into the seat, removed the survival suit and floated up towards the window. Or was it down? Weightlessness! It was amazing, like flying!

"It's better than diving," she said, grinning, forgetting her fears in the elation.

"Isn't it?" said Tom.

Out of the spaceplane's window, they could see the blues of the sea and whites of the clouds. They were over the Pacific, the vast expanse dotted with specks of land. Sophia felt like a god, all-seeing, above all humanity. It made her feel giddy, glorious.

She held on to the handholds around the window and watched the space station get closer. The area around it looked like a building site. Tom said even he'd been surprised at the number of spacecraft either docked at the station or orbiting nearby. She could see the skeleton of a new station being built next to the old, each ring segment large enough to contain the entire Earth Prime station.

"Cargo transports and construction ships," Tom said. "More equipment, more supplies, more machinery; some for the new station, others for the Moon or deep space." He seemed in his element, focussed on the job.

Sometimes she caught him lost in thought, trying out something with his embed. She felt locked-out, alone. And it was scary, being in space. A metre or so away was hard vacuum, radiation and lethal debris; the *Zumrud* itself was fuelled by explosive compressed gasses. She had no control and no idea what to do in the event of any one of dozens of potential disasters. Though, in a way, the intensity of the experience and the fear helped, distracting her, its escape velocity freeing her from the brooding and the endless dark thoughts.

The thunk of an impact shuddered through the plane, making her heart pound.

"What's that?" she asked.

"A smooth docking," said Tom, pushing off to drift towards the hatch. He unlatched its safety lock and tapped some controls. There was a hiss of air and the hatch opened.

"You have to tell me how everything works," she said.

He nodded. "Ok, will do," he promised.

But would he?

"I mean it, Tom," she said, louder than she expected.

He seemed surprised by her intensity and paused at the hatch entrance.

"You can't keep saying 'later, later, later' like Dad does! At some point you've got to explain all of this."

Tom frowned. "But we've got a tight schedule to meet the transfer window to the Moon. We don't have time right now."

"That's just what I mean," she said. "I need to know stuff like that."

It didn't feel right; she was used to being the one having to explain things to him.

"I'm sorry, we should have told you more about the schedule."

"Ok, later then."

He nodded and pulled in his legs to spin and then, with a kick, floated through the hatch. Was he going up? Or down? Directions meant nothing.

She followed him, or at least tried. It was harder than he'd made it look, and with her first kick-off she had to use her hands to stop herself flying into the hatch itself. She was glad Tom hadn't been watching. She tried another approach, going slowly from handhold to handhold, finally making it into the station.

It looked dated, with scratched and marked surfaces, smelling of sweat and dust.

Tom was talking with someone he knew working at the control desk.

"This is Dave," he said, introducing her.

"Hi, Sophia," said Dave, floating, what appeared to be, upside down, though he probably thought she was too. "Artur said you'd be coming – what do you think of all this?"

"Zero-g is really cool! Is it just you here?"

"There's also Katya, but she's in the rotating section." He turned to Tom. "Tell Artur we can't do everything, just the two of us with four samais: waystation, freight depot, ship building, new station construction and god knows what else."

"There's a whole team training for when the deep space freighters get here," said Tom.

Intriguing…

Sophia was hoping to linger, to explore, question Dave and meet Katya, but Tom said they'd better be going.

Why the rush? Couldn't they have stayed a bit longer? It was so frustrating! But she followed him along a tube to a hatch. A sign outside identified it as Lunar Freighter #1.

"Our new home."

Sophia followed Tom, gliding between handholds. Behind them trailed the two samais carrying their luggage.

"Do you want to give the freighter a name?" asked Tom. "It's semi-aware."

"This spaceship?"

They were floating in the weightless section's viewing bubble, able to see the outlines of the ship they were in.

Sophia pondered. It was to be their home, their transport, their defence against the dark, cold emptiness of space.

"How about *Resurgence*?"

"Nice!" said Tom.

"Thank you," said a voice around them. It was the ship, now called *Resurgence*. It gleamed and had a fresh, new-spaceship smell. Its panels were unscratched, most white but some with hints of a pastel colour.

The central section was weightless, but there was a large, rotating torus accessed by four tubular spokes. The torus was split into compartments: twelve small cabins for sleeping, each with a pair of bunk beds, four bathrooms, and larger spaces for eating and living.

"Zero-g is fun but bad for humans," explained Tom. "We need weight. It's not full Earth gravity in here, though, but something between that on the Moon and on Mars."

The torus was contained within a web of trusses, and Sophia spotted nodules on its outer edges.

"What are those?" she asked, pointing.

"Super-conducting coils to create a magnetic field around the ship," he said. "To protect it, us, from radiation – or so we hope. We'll be taking readings during this trip, to see how effective it is."

Sophia wanted to see the Earth, but it was mostly hidden by *Resurgence* and the space station's giant solar panels.

"Time to go," said Tom. "*Resurgence*, inform the station we're leaving on schedule."

"Will do," said the ship.

Sophia left Tom alone as he put on his data glasses and became lost in the mechanics of departure. Sometimes he'd mutter under his breath, words leaking out of a world of numbers, equations and systems.

There was a *clunk* and the *Resurgence* shook slightly, then they were drifting away from the station. After a few minutes they were clear, and the main engines fired, the thrust pushing Sophia against a glass window.

By the time the burn ended, the Earth was already getting smaller.

Tom took his data glasses off and smiled at Sophia. "Done," he said. "We're on our way."

"Off to the Moon," she said. "So, what is it, this Selenium?"

"You'll see."

"Why not tell me now? We have time, as you said."

"It'd be so much better for you to experience it."

"You sound just like my dad."

"It's amazing what his team's achieved, what we've been doing."

"Are you're one of them now?"

"I had no choice, remember? Thanks to you there was nothing for me on Earth."

He crossed his arms and floated, rotating very slowly.

Huh?

"Working with my dad was your choice not mine! Don't put that on me!"

"I had nothing: no family, no friends, no JT! All I had was work, that's all I've got, all I've been doing, non-stop. Even got this damn embed, all for work!"

"Do think the last few weeks have been a picnic for me?" she raged. "What you've gone through is nothing – nothing! And you haven't even said anything about Alejandro!"

She saw his anger drain away.

"I'm sorry," he said. "Really I am. Let me know if I can help."

Sophia tried to calm herself but felt flooded with emotions; her anger and grief battling with her frustrations.

"I *need* to know, Tom, I need to feel I have some control over all this, to understand, so I can find a way forward."

They looked at each other for a moment.

"Ok," he said, quieter. "I'll help you."

She nodded, her heart opening to a new truth: she could trust Tom.

"And you're not alone, Tom, I'm here for you."

He nodded, but he was still reserved. She missed the easy flow of their day on the yacht, and the closeness.

There was a rattle of engines firing.

"I need to check our course," he said.

"Ok, we can talk later."

He left, lost in communications with *Resurgence* via his embed, and she looked out of the viewing bubble at the retreating Earth.

Goodbye, Earth.

Goodbye, Alejandro.

35: Tom

Was there more to life than work? Did he *want* there to be?

The journey back to the Moon was like being back in work mode, but at the same time, completely different. His journey to Earth had been silent, him in a tin can, alone with his thoughts. Now he shared the space with a dark and troubled Sophia and could leave most of the task of running the spacecraft to *Resurgence*. Even when Sophia wasn't in the central station with him, he could feel her presence, breaking his isolation.

The first night, she slept badly, appearing the following day with shadows under her eyes. Later, she slept a lot, which he thought was probably a good thing. They each had their own cabins on different sides of the same spur, so they'd meet for breakfast. At least in theory, for Sophia was often late, while Tom was up promptly to discuss status with *Resurgence*. After breakfast they'd blip her parents to let them know everything was going ok.

She asked a lot of questions, driven by the urgency within her, the anger. Good ones, too, as if she was putting together a puzzle, an endless series of "Why?".

He liked it; it made him feel he was helping, and it gave their conversations structure, avoiding scary topics and the emotions of the first day.

In the evenings, it was the other way round. When Tom left, Sophia would remain, watching the stars, lost in her thoughts. He'd look back, see her hair floating behind her head, gently waving in the faint currents of air, and his body would respond, heart beating faster.

He told her what he knew of her parents' plans, apart from Selenium. It was his baby, his project, and he wanted to show it to her, not tell her about it.

"Forough's been letting me in on a lot of her part, and Rod's told me what he's worked out, though a lot's still not clear. It seems to have started from a project of Artur's with Humai to study how humanity should respond to AIs."

"Sounds like the sort of thing Cita Stone would do," said Sophia. She twisted her hair, thinking.

"Yes, and she wouldn't have liked their initial conclusion, which was that AIs would outsmart humans, taking what they wanted from Earth. But it got worse: once AIs were in space, there'd be no stopping them. They'd have access to unlimited power and resources, with all of the solar system open to them. Humans really struggle in space, like those astronauts on the old Moon base, and if nothing was done we'd be limited to the Earth. And then, as a species, we'd be vulnerable, all our eggs in the one basket."

"Not so bad a basket, if space means being stuck in a couple of tin cans," said Sophia, thoughtfully.

"Indeed – that was part of the plan, to make habitats that are attractive, that humans would want to live in. That's Forough's part, and that's what we've been working on."

"Is that Selenium?" asked Sophia, pressing him, expecting him to avoid answering.

"Maybe – and no, I'm not going to explain that yet!"

"Hah," she said, a flash of humour tinged with anger flitting across her face.

"But that needs lots of equipment, like the stuff we're bring with us," said Tom. "Have a look."

He pushed off to float towards the window, where he grabbed a handhold. She followed, grabbing the handhold on the other side of the window. He pointed out their cargo, aft of the rotating torus. Stacks of coils, looking like they were made of poured metal, about five metres across.

"What is it?" she asked.

"More secrets," he said. "Important ones."

She stuck her tongue out at him. "You said you'd tell me everything."

"And I will, but it's so cool I want to show it to you, like Selenium."

"What else are they working on?"

"How to get things into space, humans and equipment – that's Dr Khujandi's role: low-cost launchers like the spaceplanes and more."

"More?"

"Yes, more, later. But even so, basic humans will struggle with the complexities of space flight: zero gravity and radiation. So another part is how to update humans, to make us better, to close the gaps on AIs and make us more able to live in space."

"Embeds! That's why Dad keeps going to Singapore!" said Sophia.

"Yes," said Tom. "Teng Koh's team has been working on enhancing humans, initially with embeds, but potentially altering human DNA."

"DNA? Do you mean Mum's DNA databank?"

"Yes, but there's more to it than just human DNA. To make habitats that are self-sustaining, we need complete ecosystems. We need to know all about plants, insects, animals, bacteria, fungi… everything."

Sophia nodded her head. "That's four then, four of the seven Points."

"That's right," said Tom. "Just three more to unearth."

"So you don't know, then? They won't tell even you?"

"No, it's all this 'big secret' they're trying to keep from Cita Stone."

"She'd agree with a lot of this. And what they're doing is amazing! But they're keeping everything secret from everyone – that can't be right."

"Artur is convinced Cita would try to stop them – it's better to do and ask for forgiveness than to ask for permission."

"Isn't that just going to make Cita more crazy when she finds out?"

"I don't know, I've just been working on the project, trying to keep a low profile. What's Cita been doing, anyhow?"

"No idea. Probably doing crazy things with Memory, like she did at Canaveral." Sophia's expression changed. The smile vanished; the eyes lost their sparkle. "There was this time when Alejandro tried to make me take Memory."

"Seriously?"

"Yes, it was meant to be a romantic thing – we'd both take it and watch the sunset – but I couldn't go through with it. But by then he'd taken his, so he ended up with this horrid memory of me saying no." She looked straight at Tom, serious, the darkness returning. "I've always wondered if that... was a factor."

"He should have checked it with you first."

"I should have listened to him, trusted him."

The emotions, the intensity – it was scary, it made Tom feel like a child, insecure, out of his depth.

"It wasn't you, Sophia, I'm sure," he said.

"I don't know, really," she said. "He saw us, you know, sailing, that time. His father spied on us using infosec drones and showed it to him."

"Shit."

He remembered the day, the warmth, sailing, the cool water, swimming, the near kiss and the pain of her rejection. This time, the good memories, buried by his defences for so long, overwhelmed the bad.

He saw her gulp, swallowing, as if trying not to cry again, and his heart ached for her.

"Who told you that?" he asked.

"He did. I saw him just before, you know..."

"It must have been something else – his father maybe, or Pepe?"

"I do think that maybe something happened, in Cloud Heights, that last day. He wasn't that bad when I last saw him. They would do anything, they're ruthless."

He didn't know what to say so reached out and took her hand. In zero gravity it made her spin, slightly.

She had to reach out with her other hand to grab his arm, and for a moment they hung there, each with a hand holding on to the other's arm.

Then they laughed.

"I've never seen the point of taking Memory," she said. "My memory's always been really good. I know I'll always remember this moment."

"Yes," he said. "I'll never forget this."

She released him and turned to look out of the forward-facing window.

"Look, the Moon is larger than the Earth now."

***

The following day, the Earth disappeared, hidden by the Moon, and Tom spent longer with *Resurgence*, doing the navigation, checking their orbit and final approach. He was getting better at controlling the embed interface and could now sense it sending information back.

<Query TimeToDock?>

<DeltaT = 42.3 minutes>

"So, where are you taking me?" asked Sophia, looking out from the forward window.

The Moon was six times larger than it appeared from Earth, but it didn't fill the window as the Earth did when they had been near the station.

"Look, you can see it," he said and pointed out a glint of light ahead, brightening and fading amongst the constant stars.

"What's that?"

"That is our destination – that is the L2 Hub," he said.

"What's an L2 Hub, then?"

"The L2 point is the second Earth–Moon Lagrange point," said Tom. "There are five of them, three on the Earth–Moon line and two at sixty degrees to it. They are equilibrium places, where the gravitational fields of the Earth and Moon balance. Good places to build stations."

"You didn't say anything about L2."

"I know, it wasn't in their original plan. It's something new, because of Selenium."

They were getting closer, so they could see more. On the side of the L2 Hub away from the Moon was a brighter lump.

"What's that?" asked Sophia, pointing at it.

"That's the asteroid we captured. C-type, full of organics. Not very big, about thirty metres by fifty metres, but it's a start. We've got more on their way, larger ones, for when we've used up this one.

They were close enough now to see its irregular shape and colours, like a dirty snowball. There were what looked like beetles moving across its surface.

"Mining bots," said Tom, following her eyes, "extracting elements we need. Water, of course, and carbon compounds, but also ammonia – there's next to no nitrogen on the Moon, but it's essential to life."

As they approached the L2 Hub, its structure became clearer: a long spindle surrounded by storage spheres and two giant solar panels, with a torus at each end, one rotating, one static.

"The static one is the docking ring; we'll be going there," said Tom.

Sophia could see other spacecraft around the ring, similar to theirs, and another very different, with legs.

"Is that a lander?" she asked, and Tom nodded.

Suddenly, Sophia gasped. "There's a line, connecting them."

It was clearer now. A fine line led from the captured asteroid to the L2 Hub spindle and then continued towards the Moon, fading into invisibility.

Tom grinned; this was one of the things he'd looked forward to showing her.

"That's the elevator – or at least the start of it. A physical link connecting the surface of the Moon with space. We'll build mines and use the L2 elevator to move people and raw materials up and down, making the Hub the gateway to the planets."

Sophia's mouth and eyes were open wide. "Wow."

"And at the base of the elevator we're building a city, the first on the Moon," said Tom. "And guess what it's called?"

Suddenly she laughed.

"I know," she said. "It's called Selenium."

36: Sophia

Sophia drifted through the docking port into the L2 Hub where she was met by Forough and Rod. She was getting the hang of zero-g motion, gliding not scrambling.

"Welcome to L2," said an upside-down Forough. It was very disorientating.

She rotated round to give Sophia a hug. It felt perfunctory, stern.

"Forough!" said Sophia. "Wow, it's incredible to be here."

It was weird to see someone she knew, if only slightly, when everything was so unfamiliar.

"We've been looking forward to you and Tom getting here – we don't get many visitors," said Rod.

"Thanks. Did not expect to be here, to be honest."

She couldn't quite get her head around it. She was on the far side of the Moon, deep in her father's project. Her drive to discover its secrets seemed swamped by the hyper-real intensity of her experiences. Her father's team had achieved so much, amazing things! Other people would think the same, she was sure. It would have been better to have gone public a long time ago. Why keep everything so secret? Why wasn't this known? What did her father fear?

Tom followed Sophia and gave Rod a bear hug.

Sophia watched, feeling as if she were being hugged too, as if they were connected, somehow.

"Good trip?" asked Forough.

"Yes," said Tom. "Sophia named the new ship *Resurgence*."

"Nice," said Rod.

"Thanks," she said.

"Come in," said Forough. "You're just in time for dinner."

Tom and Rod drifted down the central spindle of the L2 Hub from the non-rotating docking ring to the rotating living areas, discussing progress with the Hub's construction. Sophia and Forough followed.

The spindle had tracks on one side for samais and handholds on the other for humans. The surface was coloured, browns and greens on one side, blues and whites on the other, imitations of the far away Earth. Shelves had been carved, ready for plants to grow; in some, leaves could be seen sprouting through gaps in hydroponic sheeting. There was the aroma of pine leaves and flowers.

"How are you, Sophia?" asked Forough. "It's been such a long time since we met for the *Phoenix* launch."

"I'm ok. Slightly blown away – this isn't what I expected at all."

Forough smiled, frostily. "Yes, we had to take a very different approach to the old lunar base. Welcoming visuals and scents. Tom's been really helpful, with all his experience."

Sophia was intrigued; she hadn't known how Forough had reacted to Tom and his plans. She remembered him telling her how much she resented his presence.

"He says you changed the plans, from habitats to L2 and Selenium?" It was worth a go, to push, in case she'd reveal something.

Forough frowned. "We're always open to new ideas," she said, but her tone said something different.

Forough grabbed a handhold and then Sophia, stopping their drift.

"I was sorry to hear about Alejandro," she said.

Sophia felt a jolt at the name.

"Thanks," she said, but was shocked to realise she hadn't thought of him all day.

Forough pushed off, and Sophia followed her.

She was wearing one of the standard jumpsuits, as was Forough, though Sophia's was cleaner. It made her feel like she fitted in, was one of them, the spacers.

"What's that?" she asked, indicating what looked like a fat pipe along the centre of the spindle.

"That's the elevator tape," said Forough. "Look, there's a window here so you can see. This tape is the core on which the rest of it will be built.

"What's it made of?" Close up, Sophia could see its texture; ribbons of silver and matte black woven together into sheets, formed into a long tape with an I-shape cross-section. It was larger than she expected.

"Carbon fibre around graphene tubes," said Forough. "As it extends down towards the Moon, the Hub will remain at the L2 neutral point, while the counterweight is drifted further out."

Sophia nodded, as if that meant something to her.

"Though the L2 point isn't stable, so currently we're in a slight orbit around it," said Forough. "Not that you'll notice. But the Hub won't be able to take the load of the finished elevator, it's not strong enough, and we might want to replace it, so it's threaded along the centre."

From ahead Sophia could smell supper. "Is that garlic?" she asked. Her mouth started watering.

Forough nodded. "Locally grown! In your honour, we've got a bit of a feast."

The living quarters were in the rotating section, which was like a much larger version of the torus on the ship, struts long enough to get stronger gravity and wide enough to feel like a short cylinder. The room was comfy, with relaxing sofas on one side under displays showing views out towards the Moon, and on the other a kitchen. At the centre was a table that looked like wood until she touched its smooth, cold surface.

"We've room for a crew of twenty," said Rod, "and farms to feed them all."

Over dinner, they met two others working on the Hub: Olivie and Ajay. Tom seemed to know them well, and soon they were deep in discussion on the mineral composition of the asteroid.

"This is lovely," said Sophia, to Forough at the head of the table.

It was. Prawns fried in garlic with sweet peas and rice.

"Though not spicy enough!" complained Ajay, and Olivie nodded.

"Ajay is from India and Olivie's from East Africa," said Forough. "They want to grow more chillies."

Sophia laughed.

"Who cooked it?" she asked.

"The samai's prepared it," said Forough. "Sophia, meet Abby and Adrian."

The two machines turned from the kitchen and waved at her.

"Hello, Sophia," said Abby.

"We gave the first set of samais names beginning with 'A'," Forough explained. "The ones you brought will start with 'B'."

"Betty and Bruno?" suggested Sophia.

"Why not?"

While Sophia ate, she listened to the conversation around her.

"What's the status of the mining bots?" Ajay asked Adrian.

"We're on schedule for water collection," it said. "But the ammonia mining drone's ioniser's a bit flaky."

"Bring it in for an examination," said Ajay.

"Ajay is our mining expert," explained Forough, "and Olivie's our elevator expert slash genius."

Olivie shook her head and looked down at her plate, embarrassed.

"Why L2?" asked Sophia. "Why not one of the other Lagrange points?"

"L1 and L2 are the best located for elevators," said Ajay. "But L2 is towards the edge of the Earth–Moon gravitational system, making asteroid capture easier. From here we can bring heavy metals up and organics down."

"The elevator will have capsules for people and a mass driver for raw materials," said Olivie. She spoke quietly but intently. "Cables or beamed energy for power, as the L2 Hub gets sunlight ninety-nine percent of the time."

"But you can't see Earth," said Sophia. She had been hoping for that view.

"That could be an advantage," said Forough. "It forces us to be outward looking – and prying eyes can't see what we're up to."

Ajay and Rod nodded in agreement, but Sophia frowned.

"Why would you want to hide this?"

Forough's brow furrowed. "I'd have thought you'd understand why," she said. "You're Artur's daughter, you've met Stone."

"Keeping things secret just antagonises her. If your reasons are as good as you say they are, go public with them, win the argument."

There was an awkward silence.

Are they asking, 'Who is this bolshy teenager?' she wondered. "As you said, I've met Stone – have you?" she continued.

Hah!

"Sophia's got a point," said Tom. "How come only Forough here knows the full plans, because she's a Point Director?"

Sophia felt a warm glow, welcoming Tom's support.

"We don't have time to explain to you, we have work to do," snapped Forough.

"Dad said I could discover for myself. He authorised this trip," Sophia protested. "I can go anywhere, even to Selenium!"

"But you might tell Stone and BCC, and they are out to stop us," said Forough. "And if we waited to get their approval, none of this would have happened!"

"Isn't that simply the ends justifying the means?"

Maybe she was tired, but Sophia was fed up with being in the dark, of not having her voice heard.

"Unlike what she's doing?" Forough shot back.

"I don't know all the plan," said Rod, trying to calm things. "But I trust Artur, I trust Forough, and I definitely don't trust Stone."

"But they don't trust *you*, do they? Otherwise, they'd tell you."

"It's not like that," said Forough.

Anger built inside her. The whole point of her coming there was to understand, but still they weren't telling her what she needed to know.

"Then tell us!"

"Artur said I can't. It's not that I don't trust you."

"But it is, isn't it?" snapped Sophia. "Out here, anyone could, I don't know, open a valve or something, and everyone would die, just like that. You have to trust each other with your lives. So why not trust them with the *why*, the plan? It makes no sense. I'd make everything open, so people know what they're working for, why they're risking their lives out here at L2."

Everyone looked at her, as if she was challenging Forough.

Which I am, she realised.

"Otherwise, it'll end badly. People will die, again," said Sophia, crossing her arms, and breathing heavily, angrily.

There was a long silence.

"I'd like to know more," said Olivie, quietly.

Forough opened her mouth then closed it, lips pinched close together. "I'll think about it."

Sophia didn't want to argue more, but caught Tom's eye, wondering what else she could or should say. He smiled at her, and she was surprised to discover that it made her happy. She was not alone.

"And we'll talk about it on the way down," he told her.

"When do we leave?"

"It'll take most of the day to reach the surface, so we should leave early tomorrow," he said.

She nodded and turned back to her meal.

***

Sophia didn't sleep well as her brain fought over too many thoughts.

I'm behind the Moon, thousands of kilometres from Earth, in a ring rotating in space.

There was a scarily long list of things she needed to keep her alive. She had to trust others to ensure the Hub remained working, habitable.

Was it right to keep all this secret?

She tried to imagine the reaction on the blipverse to all she'd seen. She'd once let slip her father's plans to send a mission to Mars to Cita Stone, and it hadn't gone well. That wasn't her fault, though – BCC and Stone had hacked her construct to find out about her father's plans.

They will be trying now, using everything they can to break into TAC systems, to find out what they are up to.

But maybe this time she could control it, or at least use it to get what she wanted. Her trip to the Moon would give her currency, the beginning of a hand she could play.

And Tom? The easy flow of conversation was back, but would there be more? Had she found a partner, someone she could safely share secrets with, someone to be closer to than she had been with Alejandro?

The next day came too soon, and she yawned many times over her morning coffee.

"Did you sleep ok?" asked Tom.

"Not brilliantly," she said, with a smile she hoped was cheerful. "I might have a doze on the way down."

Forough and Olivie came to see them off. She was surprised at the latter but took it as support for her words the previous day. Olivie simply shook her hand, which caused her to bob up and down in the zero gravity.

"I'm sorry," Forough said, eyes close to her, intense.

"It's ok," she said, but wondered how much she trusted Forough, liked her, even.

Tom was controlling the lander with his embeds. His eyes glazed and he turned inwards: calculating, interacting, simulating, instructing.

For the first hour or so they followed the cable down, Sophia watching its long thread glide by. For some reason, it reminded her of Rapunzel's hair.

"Was I wrong, last night?" she asked Tom.

"No," he said. "I've been wondering about it. We spend so long on the engineering we forget to consider how people will live together."

"Exactly!"

"And they're planning on thousands of people up here," he said. "As well as Selenium, there'll be a huge rotating habitat at the elevator counterweight."

"It's not just things, technology. We need a political system, some way to make decisions, to protect everyone's rights."

Tom nodded. "Such as?"

"Something like 'the inalienable rights to air, water, food and political representation'?"

"Sounds great," he said. "You could add power and heat."

"And access to the blipverse, plus freedom of movement."

The ideas kept coming. She'd wondered how she could make Forough tell her everything, by threatening to go public if need be, then promote an open space movement based on her ideas, something to change the dynamic, a peaceful way forward.

Sophia turned to look at the approaching Moon through the lander's windows. Then the cable ended with a construction node: a spider working on its super-strong thread.

"That's as far as the elevator tape has got," said Tom. "There'll not be much to see until we're closer."

"I might go and catch up on sleep," she said. But she couldn't drag herself from the view straight away.

It was a small, utilitarian vehicle. There was a central control room with seating for half a dozen, a pair of sleeping bunks separated by simple curtains, and a small capsule-like bathroom. The lander had been designed for low gravity, focussing on transporting cargo as much as people.

Sophia looked at Tom, wondering how she felt about him. She was ok just being there with him, chatting. He returned her gaze but said nothing.

He's nervous, she realised. For a moment, she worried: was there something wrong with the lander? Then she realised it was because of her. He was nervous because of her.

She turned to look back out the window and smiled. It wasn't the right time: he was busy, she was tired – it could wait until the Moon. But she knew now how she felt; she didn't want to be alone anymore.

She'd change things with him too.

37: Tom

Tom looked down at the approaching lunar surface. It reminded him of how he had looked down on Singapore, just a few days ago. Unlike that view, this landscape was an empty brown-grey expanse of craters, dust and bare rock, but it made him feel good, which puzzled him.

Why? What had changed?

Tom spun the spacecraft round, orientating for landing. Hopefully it would also wake Sophia up. He didn't want her to miss this.

He wasn't alone this time, he realised. Life was more fun shared with Sophia.

She emerged, looking refreshed.

"What's going on?" she asked.

"We're almost there. If you look down, you can see our destination."

She peered out. "There's a dome! In one of those three linked craters!"

"Those are the Lipskiy V craters. We call them A, B and C."

"Like Justinian," she said, laughing.

"Yup."

"And that's Selenium?"

"Yes! Well, at least the start, the first of Selenium's three domes. It's the nearest suitable location to the base of the elevator."

She looked out, eyes wide, taking it all in.

"How large are they?"

"The first dome is about eight kilometres across, but the other two will be much bigger – their craters are ten and thirty kilometres across."

"Wow, huge."

He paused to check the trajectory: slightly off. Tom fired the side thrusters to make a small change to their orientation.

"We want room for lots of people. The future of space isn't homesteading, individuals with their own small holdings or corporate towns – it's cities and parks. Scale is safer, environmental systems are more resilient, and people like to be around other people and nature. A city has everything – culture, food, restaurants, hotels, parks, you name it. It's a place to meet others, for families, dating, living."

He stopped, embarrassed by his enthusiasm, but she was smiling.

"Of course, the Moon must have dating potential."

Was she laughing at him? He didn't care; he was enjoying her reactions.

"It has to be a place people want to be. Everyone."

She looked out again while he checked their course. Time to light the engines.

"Look!" she said excitedly. "I can see machines, moving!"

"Those are Separators and Constructors, mining machines that split up lunar rocks and regolith into their constituent elements, and then others that put them together in new ways, making things."

"Like MakeIt! machines."

She seemed impressed, and he couldn't help but grin. He wanted to explain more, but it was time to concentrate. The lander's rockets were throttleable and gimbaled, with lots of control and redundancy, but it had to be done right.

As they sank down, the view became a landscape with a horizon. The rim of the Lipskiy V crater was a wall about thirty kilometres away, like an unfathomably large amphitheatre.

"Who or what was Lipskiy?" Sophia asked, then saw he was busy. "Sorry, it can wait."

Tom had to focus; he was still learning about the embed interface, building a muscle memory of astrodynamics and spacecraft controls.

<Landing.Proceed>

As he grew in confidence with the embed's interface, he realised he was beginning to enjoy it: the control, the flexibility, the ease, the power. He was doing things he hadn't dreamed he could do just a few months ago.

They were closer now, the rocket's exhaust throwing up clouds of dust, swirling around them.

There was a jar as they landed.

<Engines.Off>

"Welcome to the Moon," he said.

"Wow," she said. "Just wow!" She was grinning and jumping up and down, nearly bumping into the ceiling in her enthusiasm. "Thank you, Tom."

She came over and gave him a hug.

Should he kiss her? Was this the right time? He didn't know. He'd messed up last time and didn't want to mess up again.

The moment passed and she turned to peer outside again, moving from window to window to get a feel of where they were.

He realised a burden had been lifted; he'd been stressed flying the lander, worrying he'd mess up, but there they were, on the Moon, together.

"Lipskiy is the selenographer who mapped the far side of the Moon, including this crater," said Tom, answering her earlier question.

"How do we get inside the dome?"

"Transport is coming."

"We don't need spacesuits?"

"No, we want everything to be shirt-sleeved. In the end there'll be an hTube from the elevator base to the Selenium complex, all underground."

"Away from the radiation?"

He nodded. "And the Moon dust, which is really nasty stuff."

He wanted to keep watching her, see her reactions.

She's so beautiful. She's smart as well.

The transport looked like a large-wheeled bus rolling over the grey landscape, spraying dust in all directions. It approached automatically and extended a tube to the lander, docking with a clunk. There was the sound of air gushing in and then the doors opened.

"After you," said Tom, indicating the way to Sophia.

"Thanks – this is just amazing."

It was a short way to the entrance of Selenium, a road created by dozens of tracks, all heading in the same direction. They passed construction vehicles and supplies and a dozen or so hexagonal cells, about twenty metres across, ready to be craned into position.

"What are those?" asked Sophia, pointing at one.

"Selenium's dome is currently an inflated balloon, but we're building a more secure outer layer from those cells, carbon fibre struts with polymer membranes," said Tom. "They're slotted together to make a geodesic dome. Each cell will contain over a metre of lunar dust to protect from radiation and meteorites. The dome's internal air pressure gives it structure and balances the weight of the dust above."

"That's clever, though it looks like someone is building an igloo!"

He laughed. "Well, it can get cold at night."

Where the hemisphere met the ground, there was an entrance door large enough for two transport vehicles to enter side by side and, to the right, a smaller hatch. Tom docked the transport with the hatch. Opening it revealed a long, white corridor cut into the Moon rock. At the end they found two doors: an airlock.

"This is the working base we used while building the main dome: two pods, printed from lunar soil. We use the one on the left as the living pod, the right as a utility pod for farms and operations."

He opened the left door, and Sophia followed him in. She was drawn to a light ahead of her, flowing out from the living pod's long, wide window. They could see the far side of the A crater, eight kilometres away, its grey, rocky floor lit from the side.

"Welcome to Selenium," said Tom.

"Wow, it's incredible," said Sophia.

"It'll be even better when all three domes are completed. There's a simulation of what it will look like – watch."

He commanded the base's systems to play the animation. The window glass clouded and then cleared. Now, rather than showing the single crater, it revealed the city, Selenium, spread across all three. The crater walls were dotted with cubes and spheres, living spaces, apartments. The centre was filled with green, a park where kilometre-high trees towered over even the tallest buildings under a blue sky full of clouds. A maglev ran between the three craters, flying through the gaps that revealed the landscape beyond. There were stations, apartment towers, birds, drones, people, animals, colour… life.

Sophia seemed speechless, mouth wide open.

"That. Is. Just. Amazing!" she said, eventually.

"And a long way to go."

The window animation faded.

They turned back into the pod. It was untidy and cramped, with sleeping bunks behind curtains on one side, a pile of clothes, a couple of functional-looking printed chairs, hooks to hang clothes, and a utilitarian kitchen with microwave and a sink containing a couple of unwanted mugs.

"I feel like a drink, to celebrate," she said.

"We might get lucky; Rod likes to brew his own beer."

After a short hunt of the cupboards, Tom found a couple of bottles and gave a thumbs up to Sophia. "We can take them outside."

"Outside? Seriously?"

"There's a balcony," he said. "I've never used it, but the dome is pressurised now, so it's safe."

Tom led the way through the utility pod to another airlock, this time opening onto a flat space between the two pods made from printed lunar soil, like grey, poured concrete. At the edge was a raised rim, the right height and width to sit on. A stepladder went over the edge and then down into the floor of the crater, while behind them another could be seen heading upwards.

"I can smell gunpowder – is that the lunar dust? But also, rain," said Sophia.

Tom sniffed the air.

"You're right," he said. "We installed a sprinkler system to wash away the toxic Moon dust, but the smell remains."

Sophia took a step, heading to balcony rim, but stepped too hard, ending up flying. Tom had to grab her before she tipped over the edge.

"Thanks," she said. "How far down is it?"

"Fifty, maybe a hundred metres. And the crater wall is sloped, so it's not straight down. But even in this low gravity you really wouldn't want to fall – those rocks are sharp."

"And there's no one here to rescue me."

"Yup, there's just us."

She grinned. "How did we get away with that?"

They laughed.

"We have the whole Moon to ourselves."

"We could do anything, couldn't we?" she said suggestively.

Tom almost choked on his beer.

Sophia sat at the edge and drank from her bottle, looking around her. Tom sat next to her, close enough to feel her warmth, drinking in harmony.

"Impressive," she said. "Dad said this was your idea?"

"Yes. The day we went diving I started thinking about how life fills every niche, and so humans should try to live everywhere too, including here. Then I thought of the dome containing Midnight Somewhere, large enough so it feels like you're outdoors, and imagined it located here on the Moon, creating a new niche for humans."

"Selenium," she said happily.

"Yes, exactly! It turned out it was a perfect match for some of their other plans already underway, like the L2 Hub, the captured asteroid and the elevator."

"That's so cool."

He felt a flood of pride, a warmth within. This project hadn't ended with an encounter with dead astronauts. After the dark months when he'd felt useless, unwanted, isolated, it felt good, something positive, filling him with light and warmth.

What else could he achieve? His mind wandered and he was able to enjoy the moment, even feel happy. He wasn't alone, for once. He liked that, wanted more, but didn't know how to start.

The inside of the dome was softly lit, dark blue, like twilight back on Earth. It felt as if they were staying in a mountain cabin in one of Earth's deserts, the crater wall falling away to a rocky floor, lit from one side as if by a setting sun.

Tom was watching Sophia and could see her relax, forgetting the journey and her troubles in the moment. Then she looked around, at Tom and the balcony.

"What's that?" She indicated a pot plant in the corner.

"It's a tree, or, at least, a sapling. We want to have lots of trees, and they take time to grow so we must start as soon as possible."

"What type is it?"

"I think it's an oak."

"Good thing it's not an apple tree," said Sophia, grinning at him.

"What do you mean?"

"You know, the old stories, Adam and Eve."

"Well, there are no snakes here, guarantee it. Just us, only us. We have the whole Moon to ourselves."

"What about temptation?" She moved closer.

He felt elated, heart singing. Sophia seemed more assertive, confident, as if she was doing something she'd decided to do earlier.

Then she kissed him.

He kissed her back, then pulled her close, holding her tight, and could feel her arms wrap around him. He felt her warm against him, his mouth pressed to hers.

She tugged at the top half of his jumpsuit, opening it up, pulling it down, and he reciprocated with hers, then pulled her tight, their kisses more urgent, breathing quicker, faster.

Her skin was smooth, and shone in the dome's twilight.

38: Nina

The door opened in front of Nina, and she walked in. It was double height and width, designed to allow the largest machinery through.

Inside, it looked like just another of the many vertical farms on C Island, a bland, rectangular building with wind turbines above and solar panels on the roof, close by the runway. Row upon row of hydroponic beds lay before her, their lines converging on a distant point, each holding stacks of trays where green shoots reached towards a pink light.

"You're in here?" she asked.

Humai's drone, floating nearby, wobbled. "Not exactly, but this is how you get to me."

It had agreed to let her visit. She had been so good. She hadn't mentioned anything about her chats with Humai to her parents, just as she promised. Humai was her best friend.

It had been really boring since Sophia had gone to the Moon with Tom. All the others were heading off, her dad to Zurich and then Singapore, while Tom was allowed to get embeds and she wasn't. It was so unfair!

"Where next?"

"Head to the access lift," said Humai.

There were dozens of samais tending the beds. She noticed those nearest turning, watching her.

Sometimes security isn't so obvious.

The access lift was as large as the entrance door, and there were more samais there too. One reached out to check her qID, then froze.

"I know who you are," said Humai. "I don't need to do further checks."

She nodded, pleased, feeling special.

The doors closed behind her and the lift dropped, heading down for a long time.

"You're deep underground?"

"It gives extra protection against missile attack."

At the bottom, the doors opened and there were two more samais. These ones had weapons, and floating above both was a carrier drone, active, tracking.

Armed samais? Controlled by an AI independent of humans? Was that allowed?

She looked around expectantly, but behind the drones was darkness. Lights flicked on, revealing a wide corridor.

"This way," said Humai.

She followed, puzzled. The corridor made several turns, but was always wide, never narrow. There were notches in the walls from which pointed nozzles. She suspected there was more she couldn't see, hidden weapons.

Suddenly, Nina wondered if she should really be there. This was clearly a place where visitors were not welcome.

Finally, they approached a door: giant, the full width of the corridor, all the way to the ceiling, dark and menacing carbon fibre reinforced by graphene threads.

"Is this you?" she asked. "Inside here?"

"Yes," said Humai. "Do you want to continue? You can go back if you like."

For a moment, she did consider turning round. This was so much more than she had imagined. It was the sort of thing that even adults might find intimidating. But then she lifted her head, determined, and nodded.

I'll show them. I'll show them all!

"Ok then," said Humai.

The door rumbled, as if somewhere heavy girders were being moved, then there was a large click, more of a clunk, and it began to swing outwards, towards her. She had to step back. Light streamed from the entrance, blue light.

The room was huge, a cube. In the centre was a sphere held above a cylinder by six pipes, arranged at ninety degrees to each other. The sphere was about two metres across and glowed blue, the signature of photoluminescent substrates, flicking faster than she could follow. Patterns would form and vanish in the blink of an eye, the changes so quick and so intense she felt her head begin to hurt. Threads of blue light flew back and forth along the six pipes from the sphere and the cylinder. Around the room were more photoluminescent substrates, racks of them around the wall.

"Hello, Nina," said Humai.

"This is you?"

"Yes. You're my first human visitor for nearly five years."

A pair of samais were working on the cylinder, unscrewing the brackets that held it to the floor.

"What are they doing?"

"My projections of Zeus's activities are getting more negative," said Humai. "It is making progress, particularly in NY3 in subverting Lenape. I have been forced to spend additional resources defending against a stream of micro-aggressions that could go exponential at any time. It might be necessary to move me at short notice. Hence, I am making preparations, such as ensuring there'd be continuous power supply during travel and that access corridors are open."

"You might be moving! Is that why you allowed me in here?" She was disappointed.

I thought it was special.

"I promised you could come here," it said. "And there were other reasons."

"So you could show the difference between me and you, why human brains can never match AIs?"

"Yes, the capability of human neurons will never match the speed, throughput and capacity of photoluminescent substrates."

She shook her head. "So Cita was right? Humans will never catch up?"

"No, there is a way."

"Seriously?"

"Yes, seriously."

"So why haven't we done it?"

"Because we've only just cracked it. Or rather, Dr Ebuer, with my help, has made a breakthrough at her Zurich labs."

"Zurich!" exclaimed Nina. "That's why Dad's been going there!"

"Yes, it's something called the Theseus Transform."

"What's that?"

"Have you heard of Theseus?"

"No."

"He was an ancient Greek, one of the founders of Athens, who asked a philosophical question: if you had a ship and replaced each of its timbers one by one, would it be the same ship?"

Nina thought about it. What was a ship? Its timbers or its structure?

"What do you think?" she asked.

"Consider your skin; it's made of cells that are continually being replaced and yet appears unchanged, so yes, I'd say the ship would be the same."

"So what's the point?"

"Imagine you could take each neuron in a human brain and replace it, one by one, with its photoluminescent equivalent so that the behaviours are the same but faster. Would it be the same person?"

"Wow," she said, not answering the question. "You could make an AI-level human."

"Not exactly. But you'd have a framework that you could work with, interfaces that would allow extra features, compute resources, memory matrices, feedback loops, self-modification functions, and all the standard abilities of an AI. But its core would have the characteristics and structure of a human brain – it would think as a human would, have the memories of a human, but transformed."

Her mind raced – this was amazing!

"So, have they tested it? Maybe on animals?"

"There are risks involved," said Humai. "You can't do a partial Theseus Transform; it has to be all or nothing. As for animals, would you really want to meet a super-smart rat?"

She shivered. "No way! But what about something like a monkey?"

"Do you know how monkeys have been treated over the ages? Imagine a super-smart monkey, able to outthink humans, but knowing about all those experiments."

"Sounds dangerous," said Nina.

"Indeed. Our studies suggest we should go straight for a human candidate, one who meets the criteria identified. It has to be someone young enough for there still to be flexibility, for their neural net to still be developing, but old enough to understand what is happening. Maybe just before puberty, before hormones take over, maybe someone who's already involved and knows why it's important."

"Who's that?"

"You, Nina. You're the best candidate for the Theseus Transform."

Her jaw dropped. "Me?"

"Yes," said Humai. "You could be the first AI-level human."

Her heart raced. "You could do that? Wouldn't my parents object? They'd never agree!"

"I could do that, if you trust me, and let me get their agreement for you."

"Leave it to you?"

"Yes, it must be our secret. You mustn't talk to anyone. You must trust me."

She didn't have to think about it; it was what she had wanted, always.

"Yes, of course! I'll keep it secret."

"Promise?"

"*I promise!*"

"And are you sure this is what you want?"

"Yes I'm sure!"
"Then I'll make the plans," said Humai.
I'll show them! I'll show them all!

Part 7

39: Sophia

Sophia floated and dreamed.

How strange to find love on the dead, silvery Moon.

They'd lived enough days in Selenium for the two of them to have a morning routine. After a long, slow breakfast, Tom would work, organising the samais, developing the commands for the day's construction. Above them, the outer layers of hexagon cells spread slowly over the dome, enclosing them, building permanence. He'd consult with Forough and her team at the L2 Hub, scheduling resources, working on the engineering needed for the habitats they were planning.

Sophia would leave him to it and head down steps one metre high to the heart of Selenium. Here, the water used to wash away the Moon dust had collected into a lake wide deep enough for her to swim. The water was cold, as if remembering its earlier time as ice spinning further out in the solar system, while the rocks around it were still warm from their long day under the lunar sun, before the dome had entombed them.

She loved the water's sharp feel against her skin, the mixture of pleasure and slight pain that made her feel alive. She'd swim strong strokes for the warmth and then float to let her thoughts wander. In the lower gravity, everything was new, different. Waves were slower and peaked higher. She could launch herself out of the water just by swimming, like a dolphin, and afterwards, as she sat on a nearby rock to dry, the water stayed on her body, held by surface tension.

The dome's lighting was programmed to reflect the time of day, showing the soft pinks and gold of the dawn. From her rocky perch, she could see through a transparent pane at the base of the dome towards the larger Lipskiy V A crater and imagine the world Tom was creating, and the future when Selenium was filled with thousands of people.

How would they live? How would they make decisions? How would they be kept safe? She built castles in her head, made of plans, ideas and principles. There shouldn't be one company in charge of everything, but many. Businesses should be partnerships – but what if they went bust? Decisions by direct democracy or by representatives chosen at random? Openness of information – except what about security? Equality, of course, but how to handle the inequality in ability between humans and AIs? No one was thinking about this, not properly.

Her "Structures" project had just been the start. This was the future, open, up for grabs.

She could talk about all this with Tom, and so much more. She could be herself and tell him things she hadn't known she wanted to reveal, and hear him open up in return. Sometimes the happiness felt too much, to be close to him in her heart and arms.

Tom.

She sighed.

They were living in a bubble, she thought, in space but also in time. It would end, one day, but she didn't want to think about that. Indeed, her Earth-based worries and bad memories seemed to have been washed away. Mental scars were healing.

During the day they'd explore the crater floor together, walking and talking, listening, learning and revealing. He knew about technology and systems, but in the long evenings, after they'd skinny-dipped in the lake, she was the one teaching him.

They'd planted the tree, the oak, near the lake, surrounded by handfuls of precious organics as fertiliser. She quoted Tom something Moses had said when he'd come to dinner, that time in Justinian: "The best time to plant a tree was twenty years ago. The second-best time is now."

Tom had nodded. "There was nothing here twenty years ago, so it has to be today."

"What will be here in twenty years' time?" she'd wondered.

She smiled at the memories and looked around her, trying to fix the moment in her head. Below her, the lake still rippled in her wake. Above, the dome's lighting was turning to the light blue of full daytime. Around her were silvery grey rocks scattered at random, spreading out towards the horizon, and behind her, the escarpment of the crater's wall, which led up to the working base in which they lived. She lifted a bubble of water that had stuck to her body and flicked it towards the lake. Its arc was slow and high, as was the splash as it entered.

If only they had a boat!

There was no wind for sailing here. But when they got back to Justinian, she'd hire a yacht again, and things would be different, better than last time.

There was a small stone on the rock beside her. She picked it up and examined it. It was a faded grey, speckled with black spots and tiny crystals. How old was it? What was its history? Then she had an idea: she'd bring it back as a present for Nina.

She felt a little guilty, knowing how jealous her sister was of her trip.

A drone drifted down to her.

"Tom says you should return at once; there's been news about Mars."

Sophia dried herself and got dressed, then climbed the long staircase upwards, jumping its high steps with ease, like a lunar gazelle.

What animals might evolve in the Moon's low gravity?

She found Tom engrossed in a view of Mars, projected by the ubiquitous blip-aware systems onto one of the base's walls.

"Look at that!" he said, voice sharp, as if scared of what he was seeing.

It wasn't a still image, she realised, but video. Over the Martian globe appeared bright sparks, dots of white and yellow that glowed then faded. They were arranged in grids, regularly spaced, lighting up in waves, repeated strikes on the planet. There were clusters of these explosions over the pole, raising clouds of icy dust.

"What is it?" she asked. She felt a cold knot build inside her.

"I don't know, I'm trying to find out," he said frantically. "It was detected a few minutes ago, when Mars came out from behind the sun, so astronomers retargeted the big 'scope onto Mars. It looks like meteorite impacts, but they're too regular and structured – it must have been designed."

"It looks like someone's declared war on Mars," she said grimly. She imagined standing on the Martian surface, seeing explosions raining down, and felt a moment of terror. "What about your mum?"

"I don't know," he said miserably, fearful. "I don't think any strikes have been near them but it's hard to say, there're too many. I've sent a message but not heard back yet."

He ran his hands through his hair then started pulling at it, his face anguished, and she pulled him to her for a reassuring hug.

"Who did this? Who *could* do this?"

There was a silence and Tom pushed back gently, then looked at her, his face white.

"Your dad?"

She felt a wave of nausea. But he was the only one with any deep-space capacity.

"Bastard!" She couldn't help herself, the anger exploding out. They'd kept this from her, from Tom. "Bastards!" she exclaimed again. "That Forough – she must have known this was coming and said nothing!"

"All those missions to deep space," he said. "For this. And Artur said nothing."

"Maybe he sent me here to distract me," she said, furious.

Enough! She'd had enough! She kicked at a box, sending it flying across the room, unable to stop herself, livid.

As they watched the blip-stream, dozens more explosions appeared.

"There're too many impacts, even for all those launches. There must be some source for that much material, some mechanisms to get it to Mars." He was more controlled than her, he always was, but she could tell he was angry and he was scared. "Why didn't they tell me?" he asked. "It's Mars, my home, where I was born. It's where my mum lives."

"They *should* have told you! Everything you've done for them – you even had that bloody embed inserted in your head. Forough should have – ask her!"

Tom commanded the comms system to open a blip channel to Forough, overlaid on the image of Mars where the strikes continued, a background pulse of fire.

Forough started talking straight away, pre-empting him. "I'm sorry, Tom, I wanted to tell you, but Artur said to keep this to Point Directors only—"

"What's going on?" Tom asked, breaking her flow.

"It's terraforming; we're beginning," she said. "Those impacts are artificial meteorites bringing water vapour and nitrogen, plus nanorods, to heat the atmosphere. Polar strikes will melt the ice caps, and later we'll seed the atmosphere with methane-generating bioforms."

Artur, Forough and the others were planning long-term, and they were not patient. They hadn't waited on the approval of others.

Ruthless bastards.

"What if they hit the base? What about my mum?"

"The impacts are targeted at the other side of the planet – she'll be safe, Tom, honest."

"Yeah, right," said Sophia scornfully. "Like we should believe you."

Forough seemed hurt, but Sophia didn't care. Then she thought of another angle. "How's this going down on Earth?"

"Not good," said Forough. "As you'd expect, this is a bit of a shock, and Stone is going crazy."

"I *said* you should have been more open," said Sophia. "What else haven't you told us?"

"I can't say."

"This is one of the seven points, isn't it?" Tom asked angrily. "So, we have launchers, habitats, transhumans, the DNA databank and now terraforming. What're the last two?"

"You don't need to know," said Forough.

"No way. You tell us, now!" said Sophia.

Forough just shook her head.

"Unless you or Artur tell us what the other two are," said Sophia, "we'll go blip-public on the L2 Hub, Selenium and everything you've been working on."

"And that's why I can't trust you." Forough crossed her arms. "I'm not going to tell you anything."

There was a pause.

"How long can you keep it from us?" said Tom. "And not just us, the others will be asking – Rod, Olivie and all. We'll talk to them. Did they know about this?"

Forough curled her lip. "Ok, they're not happy either," she said reluctantly. "But I'm not telling them and I'm not telling you."

Sophia forced her rage to subside so she could think. No more academic "Structures" project, she was going to write reality, change things.

She had to get back to Justinian, to see her father, to give him an ultimatum.

"What would you rather: we stay here, work with them and get them on our side, or we head back to Earth?" she asked.

Forough glared at her. "Ok, run back to Artur. You're his problem not mine," she said, and then cut the connection.

Tom and Sophia looked at each other.

"Shit," he said.

"Bastards," she said.

There was a silence.

"Are you ok?" she asked.

"I don't know. We must find out what's going on."

"And get in touch with your mum."

He nodded. "Let's pack."

Sophia sighed and rather than helping straight away, she first went to the window overlooking the crater. These days had been idyllic, but normal, crazy life had returned.

Shit.

40: Daniel

Daniel stood by the window, looking out over the city. The glass felt warm to his touch, protecting the cool room from the heat outside. NY3 had been hot in summer before global warming; now the heat could be overwhelming, draining.

He stood a little taller, straighter; he was a someone now, in the inner circle. He'd flown to EuroCore and unmasked the traitor, Judith. He'd worked with BCC and entered its nest of demons but left unscathed. He'd preached to those sophisticates of NY3 under the nose of its AI. He'd done terrible things.

Killer. Murderer.

But he would cleanse the world of those who worked with demons, the traitors to the planet.

No one would bully him again. No one.

He heard voices behind him and turned to see Cita Stone enter with the other Earth Firsters who'd been continuing the interrogation of Neil Bolden. This was the old Technocrat's apartment, his penthouse, but now it was theirs and he was their prisoner, though he didn't realise it as he'd been convinced to join them.

Memory and Belief were wondrous indeed.

Though it felt too easy. It would have been better if Neil had *known* he was betraying his own side, his beliefs. Next time they should do it without nanobiotics. Nails would know how to make someone talk – and then regret it.

Someone other than Daniel was guarding Neil Bolden, feeding him. Daniel was more important than that now.

The penthouse was spacious, larger than any room in the orphanage of his youth. Full of light and smelling expensive. There was artwork on the walls, sculptures in alcoves, large and soft sofas that curved welcomingly and views over the city. On one side was a long table around which Neil had once welcomed his fellow Technocrats for dinner but was now home to the Earth First Revolutionary Council.

Cita Stone took her place at one end of the table. "So, it is public now." She had shaved the remaining hairs from her head, leaving it a smooth dome.

Daniel, Fran, Nails and Paul joined her at the table, while her security team arranged itself around the room. Erik wasn't there; he was in Justinian, joining them via a blip-con, the long wall facing the window transformed into a display.

Nails nodded at Daniel.

He was respected – *Nails* respected him! Maybe he wasn't just the Preacher; maybe he was a Warrior.

"Yes," said Fran. "The blipverse news cycle is leading with the strikes on Mars and our image crafters were ready. We've used our blip-social creatives to impose Earth onto the blipvids to show how the Technocrats could bombard our planet."

"With this tech they could control Earth as well as space," said Cita.

"Exactly. And the next step is to spin this to show how AIs in space could attack Earth. Like this."

The wall changed to display a blipvid of the Earth, welcoming blues and curls of cloud, floating peacefully in space. Then metallic grey rectilinear spaceships that flickered with photoluminescent blues flew into frame from above with a growling roar – the AIs. They unleashed wave upon wave of asteroid-like missiles at Earth, each one exploding with the force to destroy cities. Images on the ground showed families running, their children screaming, then burning in flames; cloud-topped towers collapsing into dust and civilisation-destroying levels of violence. Armageddon.

Daniel knew it wasn't real, just something Fran and her creatives had cooked up, but it still terrified him.

Demons!

"The breaking of the GC Resolution shows they can't be trusted, and these strikes show they have the capability to devastate the Earth," said Cita. "As Fran feared."

She seemed less angry, more determined, eager.

"Neil warned us they would do this. He has been very useful, in this and other ways – is that not the case, Erik?"

"He has provided information to assist Zeus in relevant areas to research, in particular the financial framework and policy objectives of Artur and his team."

"Do we now have the evidence we need to take this to the GC?"

"I believe so."

"And are we ready with NY3's forces?" asked Cita, turning to Fran.

"Yes, Neil has been most cooperative, and the top-tier defence commanders are now reliable."

"What about Lenape?"

She can't be that worried about NY3's AI, thought Daniel. They'd been living in the city for weeks, openly.

Erik nodded. "Zeus has made progress with subverting its Prime Motivator. Subjected to energy and comms throttling, Lenape was forced to reduce its defences to the point where Zeus was able to modify its definition of 'the best interests of NY3' to what we dictate. We can control its behaviour; it will support our actions."

Daniel thrilled at the thought. They had humbled a great AI, bringing it under their control.

"What about Kasparov's AI, Humai? Could it counter our plans?"

Erik shook his head. "We have been using Lenape together with Unverified to flood Humai with micro-aggressions, forcing it on the defensive. Our understanding is that it is aware we have gained the upper hand, so it is focussing what resources it has available on advancing the Technocrats' plans."

"While it still can," said Fran. She seemed satisfied with the thought.

Cita turned to look out of the window, pondering what she had heard, then turned to Erik.

"Do we know what Humai's Prime Motivator is?" she asked.

"We believe it is to implement the Technocrats' plan," he said. "Though it was given wide flexibility in interpreting that goal."

"A plan that Neil Bolden has told us much of, though not all. He was not one of the inner group they call their Point Directors."

But he was part of *their* inner group!

"Having a Prime Motivator that is not about political power – to control events and restrict the operation of others – means that Humai, like Lenape, is limited as an offensive weapon."

"And their new AI?"

"It's not fully developed but is still being trained."

"So, are we ready? Is it time to take Kasparov down, to get our revenge?"

There was a silence and Daniel's heart thumped.

Let it be the time! Let me have a chance to show everyone!

Fran looked at Erik and nodded.

"The impacts on Mars were the trigger," she said, "but our plans were already well developed."

"I agree," said Erik. "Zeus's forecasts are that the plan has a high likelihood of success if implemented over the next week."

"So." Cita looked round the table, smiling. "We can do this. I will go to Justinian as the first wave to protest Kasparov's strikes on Mars as being against the terms of the Resolution agreed last year. We will bring a security team led by Nails, and Erik will support with BCC's assets. Daniel will join me to assist with lobbying delegates in EuroCore."

Such as that Albanian delegate he'd met at Bruges.

"We will propose that Kasparov is prosecuted by the GC for breaking one of its Resolutions."

"A proposal which will fail," said Fran.

"Which is intended to fail, allowing Fran to proceed with the main plan."

"We will be ready," said Fran.

There were smiles and nods of approval.

"This will not stand, we will not let AIs control space," Cita said. "We can see what they are doing to Mars, and we won't let that happen to the Earth. We must stop them to protect the planet and put humans first. This time will be different, it won't be like the battle at Canaveral. This time we will be victorious!"

They would cleanse the world!

"Fran, we will meet at Philippi," said Cita. "Or at least, nearby, at Justinian."

Daniel was so excited he wanted to shout, a roar the whole world would hear.

41: Nina

Nina struggled to sit still for breakfast, again. But her parents weren't noticing; it was another of those days where they seem lost to the plan and politics and had forgotten her.

She ate her chocolate bread and drank her tea in silence, watching them. Her dad had brought out his sharpest suit, the one he used to impress at the most important meetings. Nina remembered him flying off to Justinian with Sophia in that very suit, the day of the first Resolution, the one to send the rescue mission, the one that brought back Tom. He was cracking his knuckles just the same, too, but now his eyes glowed for real, augmented, telling him things.

Those embeds didn't look like much now, not now she knew they were just the start. She wanted more, much more. At least she thought so.

It was so hard to keep the secret. It had been a struggle each day, wanting to tell them but also to keep her promise to Humai.

I'll show them! I'll show them all!

Sometimes, she'd whisper it to herself, thrilled by the words, by her secret, by Humai's promise. But other times the words would fade out and she'd become uncertain. It wasn't like her.

Was this right?

Her parents also seemed unsure, but about the meeting that day.

"They haven't a leg to stand on," said her dad. "The words of the Resolution were clear: 'all necessary steps,' it said." It was if he was trying to convince himself.

Her mother sighed, tired, as if this was a battle they had replayed many times. "That wasn't the intent, was it? It was to 'investigate the potential for life on Mars and return the colonists'."

"So? We are investigating the potential for life on Mars, human life, by terraforming it."

He grinned, as if he'd made a point, but it just made her angry.

"That wasn't what was discussed. That wasn't what the delegates signed up to."

"They agreed the text," said her dad. "That was why we fought so hard to get Tom back to Justinian; it opened the way for everything."

Interesting. Did Sophia know that, flying off to the Moon?

"You risked our daughter so you could trick the Global Council to give you a free hand? No wonder they don't trust you. They see those impacts on Mars and ask what else we've hidden from them. And you know there's more."

Did that mean her? Did that mean the Theseus Transform? She'd bet it did, but of course, officially, she didn't know about that.

Hah!

"Anyhow, it's just the Space Access Committee, what can they do?"

"Actually," interrupted Humai, ever present, its spinning globes materialising on one wall. "It has been kicked up to the full GC. Many of the delegations not on the Space Access committee felt it deserved a wider debate."

Her father and mother exchanged glances.

"That wasn't expected, was it?" she asked.

"It could be for the best," said her dad hopefully. "Cita Stone doesn't have the right credentials for the full GC, so that's one less thing to worry about. She can keep spouting her nonsense on the blipverse to her heart's content."

Over the last few days, he'd been abusing Cita as she had "ranted away" (as he'd described it) on the blipverse about the Mars strikes.

"It has just been announced that she has been appointed NY3's new head of delegation at the GC," said Humai.

"What?" exclaimed her dad.

"From which we can gather that the Earth Firsters have subverted NY3 and Lenape. We should treat Neil Bolden with caution and revoke his access privileges, as a precaution."

"That can't be true," said her mother.

Even Nina was shocked. She remembered the kindly old man with the artificial legs she'd hacked during their dinner party.

"He had protection against Memory and Belief," said her dad. "Lenape prioritised his security, including providing custom nanodetectors."

"They had multiple AIs able to hack those sensors. It is definitely possible, particularly if they learnt its design from Lenape."

Nina saw her father's shoulders lower, just slightly, but it was enough. She knew him. He was worried – this wasn't what he had expected.

"Multiple AIs? Such as those from BCC? This isn't good…" He shook his head, lost in thought.

Suddenly, Nina was scared. Her father was usually the confident one. If he was uncertain, things must be bad. Were things safe?

I'll show…

She couldn't finish it.

She had to talk to them about it.

"Mum, Dad?" she started.

They turned to face her, and she wondered how to begin. Then the wall behind them, the one that had been showing Humai's logos, changed, showing scenes only for her. Soundless, just images. Short, snappy stories.

First up was a scene where she was in this very room, with her parents. They were angry – no, they were furious, she could tell, arms waving, faces intense, scary. It looked real, but it had never happened, Nina would have remembered. Humai must know them really well to blip-fake them so realistically.

Then, quickly, the scene changed to show Nina in her bedroom, locked in.

Humai was right – they'd never trust her again. She'd be in so much trouble!

The scene changed again, with Sophia back from the Moon, their favourite. *She* was the one getting the Theseus Transform, not Nina. It was Sophia who was the first AI-level human. It was Sophia everyone listened to and admired; no one remembered Nina, she was a nobody.

She felt a flash of rage.

Sophia always gets everything!

It was so unfair! She loved her sister, but this couldn't stand.

Her parents saw her watching something behind them and turned to see what it was, but Humai quickly mutated the animations back to its ident. The globe representing Mars shrank and changed into the Moon, orbiting the ever-spinning Earth.

She couldn't say anything. She wouldn't. She'd promised Humai. It had promised it would work it out if she said nothing and left it to convince her parents. It could get their permission, she couldn't.

"When is Sophia coming back?" Nina asked, eventually, as her parents turned back to her.

They seemed surprised at the question.

"She and Tom should land in Justinian this afternoon, direct from orbit," said her mother.

Nina would be gone by then; Humai had said she would leave for Zurich later that day, to get ready for the Transform. She'd packed in secret, a small rucksack hidden under her bed.

"Tom will have questions about the impacts on Mars," said her mother. "Sophia too, I'd expect."

"I know," said Artur. "It's a shame – I wanted to tell him, but there's the security risk, he's so young. We didn't even tell Neil Bolden everything – and that might be just as well, given what's happened."

Nina had known about the impacts; Humai had told her. Terraforming was one of the Points of the Plan, along with the Theseus Transform. There was only the final, seventh Point that she didn't know about, but Humai said that after the Transform she'd get to know everything.

When she was a human-AI, no one would be able to stop her, ever.

"There is something else," said Humai.

"What's that?" asked her father.

"I could be inaccessible for a while today due to urgent operational issues. But Junior will be available."

Junior was their new AI, the name temporary as it learnt the ropes, guided by Humai. It would get a proper name when it was given its Prime Motivator.

"That is inconvenient," said her dad.

"I'm sure you'll handle the meeting fine without me," said Humai.

Nina had to distract herself by taking another slice of chocolate bread. She knew why Humai wouldn't be available.

Today's the day everything changes.

"Good luck in the debate," said Humai.

"Good luck to all of us," said her dad.

"Indeed."

It was a shame she couldn't say goodbye to Sophia, but there was a danger she'd guess Nina was up to something. She was pretty smart, annoyingly able to read Nina, and if she found out, she probably wouldn't approve.

No, she really, *really* wouldn't approve of this. Sophia was a pain, but she was her sister and would be, always.

I'll show them! I'll show them all!

42: Daniel

Daniel strode into the Great Chamber of the Global Council, a step behind Cita Stone, NY3's official Head of Delegation. He was armed, as was her security team led by Nails, flanking them. Officially, he was her assistant, but he was connected to their secure blipcom systems which whispered into his ear.

They were powerful. *He* was powerful.

JustSec didn't approve of their weapons but didn't stop them. Cita had the right credentials, she was there for the debate they had requested, to stop Kasparov.

Demons. Traitors.

On the plane over, he'd been given more Memory, after which they programmed him with his lines, what to say to whom. Be confident, they had said, be strong.

Be confident! Be strong!

The words glowed in his head. He would be strong. Today was their day.

The Great Chamber was huge, vast. There were rows of desks made of smart materials, windows to the blipverse able to handle commands or enter text. Behind each desk were chairs, large, comfy, signalling importance. At the front was a raised area where the meeting's chair and secretariate could sit, behind a long command desk able to manage agendas and approve speaker lists. Walls glowed, lighting the space, able to change into blipvid screens when needed. The area was rich with blip-sensors: communicators, loudspeakers, microphones and cameras.

There was no need for signs indicating this hall was public global; all who entered would know that.

Daniel looked around, impressed, but he wasn't cowed. He was *confident*!

The hall was crowded, full of energy. Delegates were arguing already, clustered in groups. All with different faces, clothes and languages, but all human, one species.

They must be saved from the AIs!

They made their way to the NY3 desk. He knew Cita Stone's moods now. She was no longer angry but energised and driven. Powerless no more, she was the one in charge, the centre of attention.

"You?" someone sniffed at her. "On the NY3 desk? After the events at Canaveral, they shouldn't have let you in here. You do not represent that great city."

Daniel recognised the delegate from Singapore, a Technocrat stronghold.

Ting Chang.

The words sprang brightly into his head. Thanks to Memory, he knew everyone there, their names and affiliations.

"And what connections does Artur Kasparov have with the London City State?" he asked, as they'd told him to. "Cita Stone lives in NY3, but Kasparov hasn't been back to London for over a year."

They moved on.

Daniel felt triumphant; another enemy squashed. He would remember her later, during the reckoning.

At the NY3 desk, Cita used her qID to register her credentials, activating the GC's systems. She nodded at Daniel, and he headed off by himself to the EuroCore desks, following Fran's instructions.

"Undermine support for Bevan," she'd said. "Sow doubt and plant hooks for later."

Other delegates watched him as he crossed the GC floor. He was younger than almost all of them, with their grey hair and wrinkled faces. He didn't care but welcomed the attention. He was wearing his Preacher clothes, plain and black, for what mattered was not him but his words – and his gun.

He was the Warrior.

At the EuroCore desks he found his Albanian contact.

Artan Domi.

The flaming words made him feel all knowing, invincible.

"Artan, it's good to see you again."

"You too," said Artan. "Your speech in Bruges was inspirational!"

"I hope we can have support from EuroCore today?"

"Well, you know, it's Mr Bevan's call. He's Head of Delegation, not me."

It was ok; Fran had said he'd respond like that.

"Hello, Daniel."

He turned, and recognised Judith. This was who he really wanted to talk to.

"Hello, Judith," he said. "It's not too late to return to us. Renounce Bevan and all will be forgiven."

Or be a traitor, supporting the demons!

"Why should I?" she asked.

He shook her hand and then squeezed it, then squeezed some more, until she winced with pain.

"You will regret not supporting us," he said, "when the hour comes." Then he turned and left.

He wasn't the one suffering now; it was the turn of others.

As he made his way back to Cita, he spotted Artur Kasparov at the London City State desk, his eyes glowing, machine-like.

He shivered.

Demon!

They would defeat Kasparov. They were strong; they were *right*.

43: Tom

Tom's eyes were closed as he commanded the spaceplane *Zumrud*. His embeds fed him their flight path into his mind's eye. He could see the layers of atmosphere they were entering, feel the bite of the wings as they arched, high over the Mediterranean. He became the spaceplane, spawning custom processes that handled the fine-tuning of its trim automatically, as if they were an extension of his natural muscle memory.

<AlgoTrim2bis.Execute>

Then he opened his eyes to see Sophia, and the machine part of him dissolved as the human awoke.

He loved her.

They hadn't stayed long in the L2 Hub. After a few brief, cold words with Forough, they had switched to the *Resurgence* and asked it to burn its engines to send them Earthwards.

The journey back from the Moon had been full of energy, anger and ideas. When Sophia raged about all those who had died in the battles between her father and Cita, he was reminded of his old self, the one that, with JT, had succeeded in escaping to Earth. He could be that driven, again, but now it was focussed, with a new mission: to make space and Earth work together. He could do it, with Sophia.

Though she didn't understand the technicalities – how a space elevator could be made to connect with Earth, how power stations in orbit would have to be a certain height, how to manoeuvre an asteroid to the L2 Hub – she enjoyed hearing Tom's enthusiasm.

"Practical Tom," she'd tease him.

"Political Sophia," he'd tease back.

But she was right, as he was right. He didn't understand the parties on Earth, the Earth Firsters, the Technocrats, the Dynastic League; she seemed to have connections with all of them.

First, they had to learn what Artur's plans were.

"You have the best chance with him," said Sophia. "Given you're a spacer and your mum's on Mars, under those strikes."

"What about you?" he asked.

She looped hair around her finger, thinking. "I want to talk to Mum," she said. "I think she's had her doubts, and you're one of them. It will be harder with Dad, so be ready to threaten him with going blip-global about the L2 Hub and Selenium."

Tom nodded. He'd managed to exchange messages with his mum, and was relieved to hear she was well, though Victor was still sick from the solar flare. "The impacts haven't been near us," she had said. "Though we've seen them from afar."

If they can see them, Tom knew, *then they're too close.*

They followed the blipverse discussions on Earth and Cita Stone's calling of the meeting of the GC.

"This GC session we have to convince Dad to be more open," Sophia had said emphatically. "It's these secrets, they're going to blow up in his face."

"We'd better get there before he starts talking. And then give him a choice: tell us – and the world – his plans, or else."

"In the 'else' case we have to be ready to talk to Stone," she said.

Tom's heart sank, remembering Stone and the day JT was killed. "Shit. Yes. Maybe."

"We must do it, to take the initiative. Drop Stone some hints to get her interested, then bounce it back to Dad. Then can we work out a way forward, something balanced and peaceful."

She was planning, scheming; it was very cool. He grinned at her, and she grinned back, then they kissed and forgot the arguments, the politics.

At the Earth Prime Station, the spaceplane *Zumrud* had been waiting for them.

The atmosphere grew thicker, and the spaceplane slowed. Tom closed his eyes again and could see the path curve up the Aegean towards Justinian. They would be landing soon.

"Warning," said the plane. "Justinian airspace has been closed to all traffic."

Tom opened his eyes again and exchanged startled looks with Sophia.

"What's that all about?"

She tapped the air to open a channel.

"Justinian control, this is spaceplane *Zumrud*."

"*Zumrud*, this is Justinian control. All airspace and runways are temporarily closed for a secure operation. You are advised to divert elsewhere."

Tom shook his head. "We can't. We'll be there in five minutes."

"Justinian control, this is *Zumrud*," said Sophia. "We are a TAC spaceplane unable to divert or hold, with authorisation for a direct space-to-Earth landing at Justinian. Be advised, we will be entering Justinian airspace in five minutes."

There was a silence.

Tom closed his eyes to check the flight plan. Ahead, the airspace was an ominous red, but suddenly flashed to amber.

"*Zumrud*, this is Justinian control. You have been approved for landing but must remain tightly within the corridor that we provide. Be aware that any divergence from this course is likely to trigger a lethal response from automatic defences."

"Justinian control, this is *Zumrud*. Acknowledged."

Sophia broke the connection and stared at Tom. "What's that all about?" she asked.

"I have no idea." Tom closed his eyes to control their final approach. The corridor supplied by Justinian control had been uploaded and integrated into his flight path. He activated situation awareness processes to map out the airspace over Justinian.

"Look at this," he said, projecting images for Sophia to see.

The sky over the three islands was busy with JustForce and TAC special operations aircraft, but the densest cluster was over the C Island airport. VTOLs – vertical take-off and landing aircraft – hovered at one end of the runway, providing a protective shell over a ground transport by the nearest building, one of the many rectangular structures that housed hydroponic or server farms. The entire island was englobed by a swarm of battle drones, which flashed red in the display, meaning their weapon systems were active.

"What the hell!" Sophia said. "What is going on?"

Tom shrugged and closed his eyes again. He saw that the drone cloud had been rearranged, subtly, to create an opening, just narrow enough for them to fly through.

"*Zumrud*, this is Justinian control. The drone shield has been modified to provide a route through. You are warned not to diverge from this flight path."

"Justinian control, this is *Zumrud*. Understood," said Sophia.

Tom had his eyes closed, focussing on the route, checking situation awareness for clues and double-checking everything. They couldn't afford any inaccuracies in this landing.

As they flashed through the drone shield on final approach, the spaceplane's radar picked up details of the ground transport. It was carrying an unmarked, shielded and secured shipping container towards a hypersonic freighter. Around the ground transport and freighter were clustered groups of JustForce forces.

What was in that container?

"Welcome back," Tom said to Sophia as he landed the spaceplane and taxied towards the TAC terminal. When they arrived, the engines were spun down and systems turned off.

"Back to Justinian," she sighed. "Back to normal life. Shit. It was fun, just the two of us."

"Yup, it was."

They exchanged smiles and kissed, then she shrugged.

"Can't hang around." She picked up her bag. "People to see, parents to blackmail."

As they disembarked into the heat of Justinian in summer, there was the roar of engines, and they looked up. The hypersonic freighter was taking off, followed closely by an executive jet.

"Isn't that jet one of TAC's?" asked Sophia. "It looks like the SpecOps craft we used when rescuing you at Canaveral."

Each aircraft had rocket boosters, which accelerated them from vulnerable take-off speeds to Mach 2 in under thirty seconds. The sky cracked as they went supersonic somewhere over A Island, before the boosters faded then peeled off to glide back to Justinian. The freighter and executive jet continued to accelerate, closely followed by a swarm of battle drones together with flights of JustForce and TAC special operations aircraft. Soon they were surrounded by layers of protecting drones and SpecOps craft. All headed north and then banked towards the west, already hypersonic.

It was very quiet when they had gone.

44: Daniel

There was a musical *gong* that echoed across the wide expanse of the Great Chamber. Voices were silenced and delegates took to their seats. Daniel looked towards the front, where an Indian woman in a brightly coloured sari sat at the raised command desk, chairing the meeting. On either side sat her assistants.

"This session of the Global Council is open," she said.

Bina Thakur.

"The meeting has been called by NY3 in response to the news from Mars. It appears that planet is again to be the subject of debates within this chamber. NY3 have proposed a draft resolution, so could someone from that delegation introduce their document?"

Daniel returned to Cita and sat in a chair behind hers, ready.

The wall behind Bina Thakur faded into a blipvid showing Cita. Daniel spotted himself behind her and willed himself to sit still and focus on her.

"Delegates." Cita's voice echoed around the Great Chamber. "We have been deceived by the delegate from London, who has abused this institution. We approved a mission to return the surviving colonists to Earth, but he hasn't done that. They remain on that dead planet."

There was a murmur in the hall.

"They had the means – at least three launches a day for months on end – and we see the results. Strikes on Mars, explosions. Where do they come from? Are they nuclear? Who authorised them? For certain it was not this body."

Cita stopped and looked around, judging the reaction.

"These explosions break the planetary protection protocols and they risk harming the colonists. The delegate from London has exceeded his authority and operated space missions outside the scope of the Resolution, outside the control of the Space Access Committee, as was agreed would be necessary at the founding of this Global Council."

The murmurs in the hall got louder. From somewhere came a cry of "That's right!"

"We propose a resolution that condemns the actions of the London delegate and his Transworld Aerospace Corporation, removing their rights to access space and placing all their assets and operations under the direct control of this body. Kasparov himself should be arrested, his credentials revoked until a trial can be arranged."

Parts of the hall applauded, and Daniel nodded, welcoming it, though he knew this resolution should fail. Fran had said the biggest danger was it would be approved.

No more resolutions!

"The chair recognises the London City State."

Artur Kasparov appeared unmoved, defiant even.

"This resolution is ridiculous as we have operated at all times within the text as approved. What is the point of agreeing resolutions if the delegate from NY3 – the very recently and surprisingly appointed delegate – chooses to ignore them? She wasn't in the room when it was agreed, so maybe she doesn't understand it. She is trying to twist this meeting to her agenda. If she understood anything about space and the solar system, she'd know that Mars is currently inaccessible to a rescue mission."

Cita listened silently.

"Our operations, undertaken at our own expense, were designed to further humanity, to build a two-planet species. The words agreed were: 'all necessary steps to investigate the potential for life on Mars'.

Unless I hear arguments as to how our operation was not consistent with this text, this meeting has no alternative but to reject NY3's worthless and manipulative resolution, which is little more than a witch hunt from someone responsible for the violence that led to the death of one of the two Martian colonists who reached Earth."

"Thank you, London," said the chair. "Are there any other views?"

Flags lined up on the great blip-wall behind the chair, those of countries and regional blocks wanting to speak. First up was Mr Bevan for EuroCore.

"Our understanding of the Resolution was that it was to enable the return of any surviving colonists and to investigate the potential for life on Mars in the past, nothing more," he said. "But also we have put on record our rejection and distaste of the actions of the NY3 delegate in causing the deaths at Canaveral.

"We do indeed have concerns about the news from Mars," he continued, pausing and looking round the chamber. "Deep concerns. But this resolution is flawed, and we can't agree to arresting delegates on such flimsy grounds."

Cita snorted. "Weak man," she said.

Others spoke up. Most of the African bloc countries lined up with EuroCore. Some, like Technocratic Singapore, supported London. But most were silent, neutral.

Then there was a vote, buttons were pressed on each delegate's desk, and numbers flashed up on the blip-wall behind Bina. The resolution was rejected. They had lost.

"We would like to make a statement in response," requested Cita of Bina.

"Agreed. But first a break. Meeting adjourned!"

Cita smiled at Daniel. "Almost time," she said.

He nodded. Their Trojan horse had been accepted. They would burn, all of them.

45: Tom

"Hurry up! Hurry up!" muttered Sophia under her breath.

They'd wanted to get a chance to twist Artur's arm first, get him to see sense, but the meeting had already started. Tom would have to rush to get there in time.

It took longer to get through C Island's airport security than Tom expected, though no one would explain why, just saying it was due to "the operation" that afternoon.

Finally, they made it to the maglev station. They waited on its central platform, impatient, watching to see which train came first: the one to A Island, which Tom was to take, or Sophia's, to B Island. There was nothing to add now, so they hugged, holding each other tight. The train to A Island arrived.

"Say hello to Nina from me," said Tom.

"Will do," said Sophia, eyes moist. "I can't wait to give her her present." She took the Moon rock from her pocket and held it up.

"There you go, breaking planetary protection protocols again," teased Tom.

She grinned. "Don't tell Cita Stone."

"Good luck," they said together.

There was just time for a quick kiss before the maglev doors closed, and then Tom turned to wave her goodbye. So much had changed since they had left Justinian. He smiled, images tumbling from his memory, swirled with emotions, good ones.

He no longer felt alone.

The maglev picked up speed and was soon flying between the islands across a bridge that glowed in the late afternoon sun. What was he to say to Artur?

Tom remembered what Sophia had said, that Artur needed to bring the people with him; he needed consent for changes that involved all humanity. He'd start with that and see how Artur responded. Threatening to go blip-global with Selenium and the L2 Hub would be the backup plan.

He made his way inside the Global Council building, where he found a confrontation between JustSec and a well-armed group headed by a cold-looking bearded man with missing earlobes.

"My name is Erik Larson from the BCC," the man said. "I am here at the request of Cita Stone as an expert witness. You have no authority to stop me or my team."

"It is unorthodox for heads of delegations to have such a large security contingent, let alone mere expert witnesses," said the officer in charge of the JustSec entrance guards. His name badge identified him as Captain Hasan Altan. On either side were confused robots, dumb, not like samais, unable to handle events outside their basic programming.

"Given the presence of the likes of Artur Kasparov, BCC analysis suggested that additional protection would be required," said Erik Larson. He looked over and saw Tom, then sneered. "And it seems Kasparov is not alone; he has allies here. My team shall not be stopped."

With that, they pushed forward and the JustSec guards stepped back, allowing them through.

"What was that about?" Tom asked the JustSec captain, watching the BCC group head into the Great Chamber. He waved the credentials that Artur had provided for him the previous year, but Captain Altan seemed distracted.

"Cita Stone is about to give her closing statement, and apparently that man is an expert witness," he said. "You must excuse me; I need to request additional support."

Tom followed Erik Larson into the Great Chamber, remembering it from his visit the previous year. While he recognised his surroundings well enough to make his way to the London City State desk, the mood was very different, tenser than last time. He was shocked to see Cita Stone at the NY3 desk together with Nails and Daniel.

Those two were with Stone on Canaveral Island.

That brought back a lot of bad memories.

Then he found Artur. He had dressed to impress, eyes burning with energy and electrons, fidgety. In front of him, the desk glowed with information, lists of delegates, their positions and blips.

"Hi, Tom," he said. "I'd say welcome back, but this isn't a good time. Stone's on the warpath. We've squashed her once today, but she's about to make a statement."

"I need to talk," said Tom urgently.

"Sorry, Tom, not now, I have to focus."

The warning *gong* echoed again through the chamber.

"Here we go again," said Artur.

"You must wait! This is important, seriously!" Tom insisted. "It's about the strikes on Mars—"

"The chair recognises the delegate from NY3," the voice boomed. It was Bina Thakur, who had interviewed Tom and JT off Deimos.

"Not now, Tom!" Artur pushed him away.

Tom looked up, and saw himself on the blipvid screen on the wall behind Bina. Frustrated, he sank back into his seat.

"Delegates," said Cita, her face replacing Tom's on the blipvid screen. "We at NY3 are highly disappointed that you did not agree with the resolution. To explain why we feel that was a mistake, I will hand over to Erik Larson of BCC, who I invited here as an expert witness."

Tom could see Artur's surprise, the jerk of the head, tightening of the body.

"Madam Chair, delegates." Erik's face joined that of Cita Stone. "My thanks for this opportunity to describe the results of BCC's examination, at the request of NY3, into the activities of TAC and Artur Kasparov. In particular, why did the mission to Mars land at the wrong coordinates, and how were all these hundreds of launches funded?"

What was that about the Mars lander?

Tom saw Artur sit straight up at that, then activate the desk's display in front of him.

"Humai, are you following this?"

"It was a surprise to all, even you, Madam Chair, whose Bangalore Systems was responsible for the lander's control software. But we discovered it was not an accident. Indeed, it was part of Kasparov's plans, plans based upon manipulation and theft on a global scale."

Tom could see Bina Thakur at the front, paying close attention.

"Humai, are you there?" Artur asked again, urgently.

The two globes appeared, fading in and out, intermittent, spinning for a moment, then freezing, a static image.

"My blipcoms are suffering operational restrictions," it said. "But I strongly recommend you leave immediately."

"Using the skills of their in-house AI, the one they call Humai, they infiltrated Bangalore Systems' defences and those of many others, including EuroCore, under the code phrase 'ways and means'."

"Prove it!" someone shouted. Tom guessed it was one of the Singapore delegates.

"We can indeed, and have evidence from one of the leaders of the Technocrats, a close associate of Kasparov's: Neil Bolden, who has recorded the following statement:"

The blip-wall swirled and revealed the old man in his apartment in NY3.

"That's right," said Neil Bolden. "'Ways and means' was code for the access their AI achieved within Bangalore Systems' root-level cores, including the Mars lander's guidance software. EuroCore's internal protocols were hacked to reveal their positions at the Global Council, giving TAC, via their proxies in the London City State, an advantage in negotiations."

Sophia was right! Artur wasn't to be trusted!

He regretted they hadn't acted earlier, that he had worked for so long on one of Artur's projects, helping him.

There was an angry murmuring and calls of "For shame!"

Tom remembered watching the lander from the Mars base: the fight, being stuck in the ice mine, having to leave his mother behind.

Artur was responsible for all that. His mother would be here, safe, but for his scheming! He gripped the chair tightly, as rage and anger swept through him.

How could he?!

"Humai, I can't leave, I can't walk out on this!" hissed Artur.

"You must! Also, there's been a request from Zurich."

"Not now, this is more important."

"Is this true?" asked Tom, urgently, leaning forward and touching Artur's shoulder.

"Seriously, Tom, not now!" shouted Artur, brushing Tom's hand away.

"So why was the Mars lander given the wrong coordinates?" continued Erik. "It was a manipulation to ensure some of the colonists would not be returned but remain on Mars, to justify additional space missions."

"But they've identified a candidate for the Theseus Transform and need your approval to proceed," said Humai.

"Can't it wait?"

"No, we need an answer. Quickly."

"The Global Council was played – all you delegates were played, manipulated, and your systems hacked by an artificial intelligence working with Kasparov and his team," said Erik.

Tom's anger was tempered by a growing fear as the delegates' faces turned towards Artur with more and more hostile looks.

"Ok, ok, if the candidate is suitable, proceed," said Artur.

"But there's more," said Erik. "How were these missions, the AIs, the resources sent into space – even a joyride to the Moon for Kasparov's eldest daughter – how were they all paid for?"

"Can you provide an explicit statement?" asked Humai.

"For heaven's sake!" Artur exploded. "I, Artur Kasparov, authorise that the Theseus Transform be undertaken on the candidate proposed."

Tom was mystified by Humai's request. Why wasn't it answering the questions about the Mars mission?

"It required a significant portion of BCC's compute resources to track the web of companies and contracts created by Kasparov and his AI," continued Erik. "Ignoring the legal obligations on AIs – as required by treaty-level regulations approved here at the Global Council – Kasparov permitted it to directly control businesses and financial instruments. For details, I will pass you over to Neil Bolden again."

"Unfortunately," said Neil, "Humai used its AI capabilities to trade at a level no human can follow, shorting and manipulating stocks within dark markets and, in the process, making huge profits, transferring to TAC significant financial resources, but at a cost. The value extracted was lost across the globe, and the mini-Collapse we have seen this year is the result. People have lost their jobs and more, their homes, their health, their happiness and, in some cases, even their lives."

There was raw anger in the hall now, shouts of outrage.

"The crimes of Artur Kasparov are clear," said Erik. "Enough is enough. I call upon the Justinian Security Force to arrest him immediately!"

Tom looked around, towards the shouts. He could see delegates standing and waving arms. Others followed, shouting back. The two men with flowing robes were shouting in each other's faces. Then one hit the other, and other delegates rose to defend their sides. JustSec moved to pull the men apart, grabbing delegates by their arms, holding them back.

Tom's heart began to beat faster. Things were running out of control, and he still hadn't had a chance to talk to Artur.

"You have no authority to order JustSec," said Bina Thakur from the chair, hammering her gavel against her desk, trying to keep order. "You are an expert, not a delegate!"

"You and Tom must leave, quickly," said Humai softly, urgently. "Now. I have arranged a VTOL aircraft to land next to the GC."

Then Tom heard heavy footsteps behind and turned to see JustForce arrive, well-armed troops arranging themselves along the back of the hall. A squad of JustSec officers approached the London City State desk.

It scared him, having the guns so close, but worse was the feeling of being out of control, of his and Sophia's plans coming to nothing, again.

"Don't you worry, Dr Kasparov," said Captain Altan. "We're here to keep order."

"I can't leave. We're safe here," said Artur to Humai. "JustSec will protect us."

"I am having connection issues again," it said. "Just get out of there right away!"

Then the screen faded, and with it the two globes.

"That is a shame," said Erik, his voice sorrowful. "I will have to hand you back to the NY3 delegate Cita Stone."

Tom looked at Artur, and for the first time detected in him fear.

46: Daniel

Cita Stone turned to Daniel and raised an eyebrow. He could guess what she meant and exchanged words with Fran over their secure comms.

"She says they are in position," he told Cita.

She nodded, then looked round at the group. "Now is the moment. Be ready."

Cita leant forward and enabled her desk, her image appearing on the front wall and her words echoing around the Great Chamber.

"My colleague from BCC has explained how Artur Kasparov has lied to the Global Council, undermined its members, hacked their systems and stolen from the people. He was able to do this as he was working with their AI, Humai. The key question is, then: how is humanity to live with self-aware, general artificial intelligences that are smarter, faster and more capable than us?

"In the great debates on this subject, heated discussions that many delegates will remember from years gone by, it was argued by the AI supporters that we could all benefit from these new beings while not be threatened if the right legal framework was put in place. And yet we have seen how these controls mean nothing. Kasparov's AI worked against humanity's best interest, stealing and hacking across the globe. They have another AI called Erebus, out in space, free of all controls, and we understand that it is this AI that was responsible for the strikes on Mars. Our witness again."

On the wall, Neil Bolden appeared once more.

Daniel inwardly grinned; they'd made him testify against his cause while a prisoner in his own apartment. Justice would be theirs!

"That's right," Bolden said. "Artur set up an advanced manufacturing base called the Factory on an asteroid far out in space controlled by an AI called Erebus. It built a mass driver, a railgun that accelerated projectiles towards Mars. The first objectives of these missiles were to heat the planet, melt the polar caps and deliver chemicals such as water and nitrogen plus nanorods. But later impacts contained artificial bioforms, new creations designed by Erebus to convert the atmosphere into methane, a strong greenhouse gas."

"What about indigenous Martian life forms?" said a voice off-screen, Fran.

"They would be replaced, destroyed, if necessary," said Neil Bolden, shaking his head sorrowfully.

"Couldn't that be described as xenocide?" asked Fran again. "Given we know Mars has had its own life forms."

"Yes, I suppose you might say that," admitted Neil.

There were shouts from the hall, coming from the EuroCore desks – maybe his little chat had done its work? He looked round and spotted Artur Kasparov surrounded by JustSec guards. Behind them, he recognised Tom.

He should have made Tom drink Memory and Belief when he'd had the chance.

Cita tapped on her desk so her face appeared again on the Great Chamber's walls.

"What limits are there to an AI's actions?" she asked. "It can out-think any human, interpret its Prime Motivator in ways we can't predict or understand. And how could the Prime Motivator of an AI set up to do the business of a Technocrat like Kasparov be expected to align with the requirements and needs of all the humans on this planet? Can we ever trust it?"

"No!" Shouts were heard from many desks, not just that of EuroCore.

"Imagine what this Erebus could do if it determines that we are a threat to its plans. Could it retarget its mass driver, make Earth its target?"

Cita tapped at her desk, and on the wall of the Great Chamber appeared the blipvid they had concocted.

Daniel had seen it before but not on the scale projected here. The Earth seemed real, as if the delegates watching it were really floating in space. From around the hall came sighs, involuntary releases of delight.

Then a deep, rolling, chest-shaking thunder grew in the hall, and the AI metallic-grey spaceships appeared, kilometres wide, not an image but actually in the room with them, the rectilinear shapes flickering with photoluminescent blues. Then came a screech, an ear-piercing, inhuman wail of anger.

Terrifying: death as a sound.

Demons!

That was new, Fran had added that.

After the scream came the onslaught, asteroids pounding the Earth like missiles, exploding in a grid just like that seen on Mars, balls of fire erupting in the heart of cities. The scene changed to ground level, to Justinian and B Island. One of the missiles exploded at its heart, creating a mushroom cloud like an atomic bomb, and a remorseless wave of fire drove across the island, vaporising children and their families as they fled in panic. Buildings burst into flames then collapsed into dust.

At the end of the blipvid there was silence in the hall.

"And this," said Cita, "is what could come to pass if AIs are not controlled. And yet Artur Kasparov has plotted with them, removing the controls we relied on, then released one into space. As we have shown, he has lied to the Global Council, hacked its members, stolen from the people of the planet and undertaken xenocide against the planet Mars. He is a traitor to humanity!"

Traitor!

"Treason," said some delegates. "Traitor!" cried others.

Daniel smirked at that; they had allies, they were the true power here.

"He has broken the laws of this council and should be tried. We asked for him to be arrested, not just once but twice. In both cases, the Council refused to act against him, not even to investigate his actions."

"Shame," came the cries.

"He has abetted AIs in breaking the law, in working against humanity. He must be arrested immediately and all AIs put under direct control of this chamber, the representatives of the peoples of Earth. If not, they must be destroyed, for humanity can never be safe while there is even one that has the freedom to act against us.

"There is a very real danger from Kasparov and his AIs. I have direct experience of their violence and contempt for human life from my encounter with them during the battle at Canaveral. Many of my team were killed by Kasparov's AI in an unprovoked attack. Humai deployed lethal drones against my people, killing machines operating outside the control of any human.

"So, I know there is a danger to us all. Imagine his AI's drones let loose in this Great Chamber, the massacre that would be the result."

Again, the hall went quiet at her words, chilled.

"But we are not scared, we are prepared. In case of inaction by the Global Council and its reluctance to use JustSec or JustForce, we are prepared to make a citizen's arrest on behalf of the people of the world."

This was the moment!

"As we speak, NY3 forces, supported by the Earth First movement's Defenders of the Planet, are landing across Justinian. We urge JustSec and JustForce to stand aside and let us carry out our intent, which is to arrest those who have conspired with the AIs, starting with the Kasparovs."

Their security teams, NY3's and BCC's, rose around her, weapons ready, targeting Artur. Nails had a long rifle, which he brought to his shoulder.

Daniel stood too, watching for Kasparov's response. He couldn't see him given the crowd of JustSec and JustForce around him, protecting him, also with their guns raised, pointing back at them.

The hall erupted again, this time cries of alarm. Some delegates ducked under their desks.

"I urge again," said Cita. "JustSec and JustForce should stand down! Our argument is not with you. However, if you obstruct us in our actions to arrest the traitor to humanity Artur Kasparov and others of his team, then we will be forced to respond."

For a moment, all was still, like a painting, weapons pointed at weapons across the Great Chamber. Then there was a rumbling roar from outside; the Wolf Bats had arrived. Daniel turned to see Nails squint down the sight of his rifle and squeeze the trigger.

There was a shot, and one of the JustSec guards fell to the ground.

47: Sophia

Sophia forgot her fears, forgot her anger, but smiled to herself, for once content, gliding through Justinian on the monorail, heading for B Island. She was home, or at least would be soon.

She'd been to the Moon! It still didn't feel real.

She became very aware of gravity, around her, holding her down. She'd never thought of it before, like a fish's unquestioning acceptance of water. Even after such a short trip in lunar gravity and zero-g, the way Earth weighed her down felt stronger than she remembered.

She sighed, thinking of long days and nights with Tom.

It would be easy to just sit there, lost in her reverie, but she made herself concentrate. What was she to say to her mother? How to convince her to tell her about the plans, to change them, to be more open?

She'd wing it, she decided. The words would come when she needed them. She knew her mother had doubts, like she did.

Sophia felt closer to her mum than her dad, who'd seemed slightly out of control recently, pushing for his goals and forgetting them, his family. She'd leave him to Tom. She could talk to Tom.

How had she survived Alejandro without having anyone to talk to? Everyone needed another to be there for them, to anchor them. How could you know you were really sane if you couldn't share and test your thoughts with someone you trust?

The monorail decelerated, and she recognised the stop. It was a short walk to Troy Tower, past the automatic concierge, scanning her qID, the elevator and then there she was.

"Hi, Mum," she called out. "I'm back." As if she'd just been to London or something!

The apartment smelled of home: her sister's chocolate toast, her mother's perfume, so different from the metallic aromas of spacecraft or the gunpowder Moon dust.

"I'm in here."

Sophia found her mum watching the blipvid on the wall in their living room. She dumped her bag and they exchanged a hug, but it was a short one, perfunctory.

"How was the Moon? And how is Tom?" But her mother didn't wait for an answer before turning back to the blipvid. "Have you seen this?"

No welcome back; no "good to see you". The good mood began to fade, leaving Sophia unsettled.

"What's up?"

"It's Cita Stone, she's rabble rousing at the GC. It's going crazy." Her mother was gnawing at a nail, anxiously staring at the screen.

"Is it about those impacts? The ones on Mars?"

Her mum's worry was infectious.

"Yes, but more than just that. I don't know how she's found out so much. As well as subverting NY3, she must have BCC in her pocket."

"I was going to tell you no good would come of those secrets," said Sophia.

"I told your father that, but he didn't listen, Humai said it was necessary."

"Necessary? Why?"

"I don't know!" Sophia could hear the frustration in her mother's voice. "We humans can't do simulations like an AI can. We had to go with Humai's projections, to trust it."

Sophia found the words weren't there when she needed them. She looked around the room at the familiar objects of her family and her past, like the old tapestry, then stared out of the window. The sun was setting, bands of red and orange splashed across the sky and leaking into the water like blood.

Her mother was gripped by the blipvid feed, where Cita was talking about Prime Motivators and AIs.

"Where's Nina?" asked Sophia. She wanted to make peace with her sister, who she knew would have resented having to be the stay-at-home one. She had the Moon rock present; that should make up for it.

"In her room, I guess."

Sophia knocked on her sister's door. "Nina? It's me, Sophia, I'm back."

There was no reply, so she stuck her head round the door. Her sister's bedroom was empty.

"She's not there," said Sophia, returning to her mother, puzzled.

There was a screech, a wail from the blipvid.

Her mother was white, partly anger, partly fear.

"They're showing this? There'll be a riot."

"What is it?"

"Those Earth Firsters have this blipvid that paints AIs as genocidal."

Sophia noticed her mother was trembling. Suddenly, she felt afraid, as if standing at the edge of a cliff.

"Mum, Nina's not there."

For the first time, her mother stopped staring at the screen and turned to Sophia, mouth open.

"What? She must be. Where would she go?"

From the screen, they could hear the reaction at the GC.

"Traitor! Treason!"

"Humai, where is Nina?" asked her mum, slightly too high and loud.

But the two spinning globes didn't appear.

"Humai, where are you?" she asked frantically. "I need you!"

Sophia had never known it to not monitor this room.

"Apartment security, have you information on Nina's whereabouts?" Sophia asked, heart beating fast, scared of the answer.

The apartment's blipverse interface, available by default, was basic compared to the one Humai had provided.

"No information is available, though a blip message has just been received relating to Nina Kasparov."

"Play it," ordered her mother, desperately.

"This is Dr Ebuer of the Theseus Laboratories in Zurich," said the message. "We acknowledge receipt of approval to undertake the Theseus Transform on the proposed candidate, Nina Kasparov…"

What was that? What was the Theseus Transform?

Her mother cried out in shock. She knew what it was, then, and it terrified her.

"… as authorised by her parent, Artur Kasparov, with two approval statements as legally required."

They heard her father state: "I, Artur Kasparov, authorise that the Theseus Transform be undertaken on the candidate proposed."

Then: "The candidate is suitable, proceed."

"No!" screamed her mother, eyes wide. She grabbed Sophia, who held her in return.

The message continued. "Given this authorisation and arrival of the candidate, we have begun the process, which is now irreversible. We will keep you informed as to progress. Please do not hesitate to contact our office for any further information or questions you might have."

Sophia and her mother stared at each other.

"What's the Theseus Transform?" asked Sophia, watching her mother, scared – no, terrified – by her reaction.

"No! No! No!"

Her mother's face compressed into lines of fear and despair, her eyes wide in disbelief. She seemed to shrink and age. "He can't have. He can't have let them do that, not to Nina, not behind my back!"

A knot of pain started in Sophia's stomach and seemed to take over her body. She'd never seen her mother like this, not even when Nina had done one of her stunts.

"What is this Transform?"

"It's part of the plan, I didn't think it was possible, and never dreamed that Artur would let Nina be the guinea pig!"

"Mum, tell me what it is!"

Her mother couldn't look at her, just stared out the window. "They are turning my little Nina into a monster. They are destroying her brain, making her a machine."

"What do you mean?"

Sophia wanted to shake her mother, to get her to talk.

She turned back to her, looking drained, empty inside. She spoke quietly but her voice shook with anger. "The Theseus Transform replaces each neuron in the brain with a photoluminescent node to make a human AI. It's crazy. It could kill her. She'll never be *Nina* again."

Sophia couldn't believe what she was hearing. That this was possible, that her father would allow it – and her fear was overtaken by rage.

The total bastard! To his daughter! To my sister!

"They're doing this to Nina? And Dad approved it? Has it been tested?"

"No, never. Its experimental, it's not tested. How could he? How *could* he? I must get to her and stop this!"

Her mother's empty coldness had been replaced with a wild rage.

A shadow passed outside the window, a silhouette against the sun. They turned to see aircraft flash by, heading towards A Island. Sophia recognised Wolf Bats, dozens of them, squadrons, fighters plus carriers.

"What are they doing?"

She turned to the wall blipvid to see Cita Stone still speaking.

"… are landing across Justinian. We urge JustSec and JustForce to stand aside to let us carry out our intent, which is to arrest those who have conspired with the AIs, starting with the Kasparovs."

Suddenly, Sophia understood. She *knew* Cita Stone, what she could do. She would come for them, and she would kill to get them. The cold reality trumped her fear and anger.

"Mum, they are coming for us, for you," said Sophia urgently, grabbing her arm. "We have to go."

"They can't," said her mother. "JustSec and JustForce will stop them."

There were explosions outside. Sophia could see the Wolf Bat fighters' railguns fire, targeting installations outside their view.

Then the power went out.

48: Tom

At the first shot, Tom ducked below the desk.

Shit. Not again.

He caught Artur's eye briefly, but he was distracted, lost to his inner eye and the blipverse.

"*Humai?*" he cried, urgently.

There was clearly no reply.

Captain Altan crouched down to talk to him, close enough that Tom could hear.

"We must withdraw and regroup," he said. "There are Wolf Bat fighters in the sky and carriers landing troops across the three islands. I will authorise the laser defences."

There were more shots and weapons released around them, JustSec and JustForce returning fire. A JustForce soldier was hit, spinning round and falling on the ground, blood pouring from his shoulder. Another soldier grabbed a milspec medical pack and started to apply it to the wound.

"It will only be effective for a short time," said Artur. "I have a TAC-command VTOL craft with drone defences on approach that will need its cover, so keep it in reserve for now. But where are JustForce's aircraft and drone shield?"

Captain Altan looked surprised. "They were sent at TAC's request to protect the secure flight. Didn't you command that?"

"No, it wasn't me. And what secure flight?" said Artur. "Humai? *Humai?*"

"Non-secure comms are out," said the captain.

"But Humai has secure channels."

Tom didn't know what to do. He could die here, like JT. He had to get out, but how?

Feeling sick, he cautiously peered over the desks. Earth Firsters and BCC security were advancing, guns raised, ready, while at the back of the hall, JustSec and JustForce troops were keeping cover.

He couldn't afford to be scared; he had to get out of there, quickly.

"We can't stay here," he said.

"Agreed," said Artur. "Captain, cover us."

Ducking to avoid the shots flying over their heads, Tom and Artur dashed from desk to desk, heading towards the rear of the Great Chamber.

Tom looked back. A knot tightened in his stomach; BCC was trying to cut off their lines of exit by moving along the edges where there were clear lines of fire.

"We need support. Otherwise we'll never get out of here." He had to shout over the noise: gunfire, shouts, screams from other delegates. Some were hostile, some wanted help, all were trying to stay alive.

"Unless they want to capture us, not kill us?"

And not just them; this would be all over Justinian. *What about Sophia?*

"We should get back to Sophia and Anna," said Tom, urgently. "Make sure they're safe."

"We need to take back the initiative," said Artur. "Captain, we need your help."

There was a rush as JustSec and JustForce troops rallied around them, sending volley after volley at the Earth Firsters and BCC security, forcing them to take cover. Delegates spotted the change in balance and rushed to escape.

Tom took the chance and ran for cover in the next row back, heart pounding.

Then he saw Artur had headed the other way, forward and to the left. Artur took a gun from Captain Altan and, with a squad of heavily armed JustForce troops, fought his way to the nearest exit from the Great Chamber. Some of the JustForce troops held their positions to provide covering fire, the others close cover, running beside Artur.

It was too far for Tom to reach them, the bullets flying too fast. He was on his own now.

Shit.

He felt so alone. If he got shot there, no one would be able to help him.

Outside he heard more explosions, large ones, more than just hand weapons. Wolf Bats, maybe? They had railguns, and Tom had seen those in action before.

He rose so he could grab a quick look round. There were only a handful of JustForce soldiers nearby, mostly close to him. JustSec were dead or had followed Artur and Captain Altan. Tom could see the Earth Firsters hunting for him. He recognised one, Daniel, from the battle on Canaveral Island. Cita Stone must still be there, somewhere.

Tom turned to the nearest JustForce soldier.

"Have you got a gun?"

He was given a simple handgun; not as powerful as the JustForce rifle, but it made him feel a bit less helpless. It felt cold in his hand, strange.

I could kill someone with this.

It was a disconcerting thought, scary and yet reassuring.

There was a crack of gunfire, and he ducked down.

I might have to use this gun – or die here.

"We're going to get pinned down," he said to the soldier. "We need to move from here."

"You get ready, I'll cover you."

Tom looked around for the nearest exit.

"We'll go one desk back and then along to the far edge," he said. "Then run for it."

"Right."

The soldier raised himself above desk level and fired twice then dropped down. Shots fired back and Tom took the opportunity to run, crouched down, to the line of desks behind them. He then nodded at the soldier before raising himself up and firing twice. They were pretty random shots, but gave time for the soldier to follow him safely.

"Ok, along this row."

The row between desks was mostly clear – a couple of delegates crouched in foetal position, another lay as flat as he could, and there was a body surrounded by a pool of blood, too wide to avoid as Tom crawled by.

At the end of the line of desks, the exit seemed so close.

"I'll take a look," said the soldier, standing.

Immediately, he was shot in the head and fell dead on top of Tom. For a moment, Tom froze, shocked, guilty, then ran, expecting to be hit, darting across the short gap to the exit.

At the door, he collapsed, panting. Turning, he could see the rear of the hall. On the ground were dead bodies and terrified delegates. The only ones standing were the Earth Firsters and BCC security, advancing confidently. There were no more JustSec or JustForce alive.

The Great Chamber had been sacked.

How had he survived when so many had been killed? What to do now? Despite the terrors, or maybe because of them, there was only one answer.

I have to get to Sophia!

Tom turned and ran.

49: Daniel

Daniel grinned at Nails as they reloaded, kneeling behind one of the GC's steel and glass desks, then stood and continued firing. The bully from his youth had become his brother in arms.

"Kill anyone from JustSec and JustForce," Erik had said. "Then we can scoop up the Kasparovs."

Standing side by side with the squads of Earth Firsters and BCC security, they had shot them one by one. They were winning!

But Daniel saw Artur Kasparov and a group of JustForce reach the exit in the far corner.

"They're getting away," said Nails, kneeling down to Erik and Cita, who were still crouched over their smart desk, reading the blip-feeds, controlling their forces. On the display was Fran's face and blipvids from the Wolf Bats patrolling the skies.

"The carriers have landed," said Erik. "We've captured the monorail station on this island and a platoon is about to secure the GC perimeter. We will have them."

Daniel nodded at Nails, triumphant, so they stood again to continue the slaughter. Then Nails was shot, directly in his chest. He collapsed. There was a rattle of limbs, and blood bubbled from his mouth, then a stillness.

No! How dare they?

Daniel was flooded with rage, anger and loss. Nails had been his last connection to his childhood, along with his lost home and family. Knowing that Nails recognised him as an equal had meant everything. Who would he impress now?

Enraged, he jumped up on a chair and fired again and again. At another of the Great Chamber's exits, he saw Tom and a JustForce soldier duck behind a desk. He waited, then saw the soldier's head appear and aimed at it. A hit.

Revenge for Nails!

He remembered his first kill, on Canaveral Island, when he'd shot Captain Vaughan. He could see the body, blood oozing from the shattered face. It wasn't a flashback; it was real, as if he was in the past. Nausea filled him and he collapsed on the ground, trying to get as far away as possible from Cita and Erik before his stomach exploded upwards. He puked.

For a moment he knelt over the fresh pile of sick, sweating, breathing heavily.

Killer. Murderer.

He felt alone, he'd lost so much – then he felt a power flow into him. An anger. The words of fire spoke with Nail's voice.

Those who betray us must be killed!

He was the Preacher, the Warrior. He spoke words of truth against the unworthy, the treasonous who conspired with demons. They'd heard the Holy Mother uncover the vile secrets of their enemies' plans, just now. And Daniel wasn't an outsider, he was one of the righteous, fighting the good fight. They would win. He would show them!

He would reveal the truth to all.

Daniel made his way to the front, to the raised desk where Bina Thakur had sat. She had gone, fleeing to safety.

He turned to the hall and fired his gun into the air, so everyone looked at him, and again, so they were scared of him.

He was powerful!

"Now is the time!" he cried in a great voice, no need for artificial amplifiers. "The righteous have awoken. We have seen how the planet has suffered, how the people of Earth have been downtrodden!"

Demons! Traitors!

"The traitors, working with those demon AIs would subjugate us all for eternity! Join us or face our wrath! Today we bring liberation, freedom! No longer will the Technocrats and their machines steal your future."

He could feel spit on his chin, dribbling from his mouth, a mouth that tasted of sick. He didn't care. He was possessed by the spirit, the words.

Goodbye humanity!

"Today the battle begins. We must stop them or it's goodbye humanity! Join us!"

He looked round the Great Chamber. The only ones standing were the Earth First and BCC security teams, fanning out from the NY3 desk to cover the whole hall. All the other delegates were hiding, crouched low. Many desks were shattered, glass fragments over the custom-grown wood floors. The main lights were out, and the emergency lights were low and a garish yellow. One flickered, irritatingly.

Bodies were scattered like cushions amidst the debris of the sacking: lost clothing, smart devices, pendants and bracelets littering the hall.

Daniel breathed deeply, feeling the fear coming from the delegates. He could kill them all, he had that power. He was powerful. Nails would have been proud of him.

Then he wiped the spit from his face with the back of his hand and jumped down, remembering he had a task he had to perform. He had been given hand ties, and it was time to use them.

They were to divide the delegates still alive into the true and the traitors.

He made his way to the EuroCore desk, looking for Judith.

Revenge!

50: Tom

Tom ran through the Global Council building, hunting for an exit. Automated messages in multiple languages warned delegates to evacuate the building, supported by icons of running figures. Lights flowed along the floor and walls, showing the way. Alarms rose and fell, interrupted by the sounds of gunfire and screams from somewhere in the building. Dumb robots were frozen, unable to process events, defaulting to motionless sculptures.

He had to get out.

There were others, also running like him. Sometimes there were bodies to leap over. Sometimes smells of fear, of urine. Emergency lights were low, pulsing.

He passed two delegates from Africa, one wounded, helped by the other. They looked at him, recognised him, but said nothing. He wished he wasn't so obvious, so tall, so known from the blipverse.

Tom ran down a corridor marked "off-blipverse meeting rooms". The doors had automatically swung open, revealing pools of darkness beyond.

Suddenly, he could see daylight ahead, a door to the outside. A man was dragging a body inside. The man wore the uniform of a JustForce officer. He stripped the body of its shirt and trousers then took off his jacket. Tom looked at him, wondering.

"I'm not wearing this no more," said the officer, waving the JustForce jacket. "This will get me killed, won't it?"

"Aren't you meant to defend Justinian?" asked Tom.

"Not my battle, is it? Why should I die for those in league with AIs?" He snorted and gave Tom his weapon. "You can have this. I have friends on the mainland, they'll see me right." He peered out of the door and seemed reassured by what he saw, as he left, running.

Tom looked at the deserter's weapon; rifle-like, it used a railgun to fire explosive shells. Could he work out how to use it? It was a lot better than his handgun, though much heavier. It had a strap to carry the weight, which Tom flicked over his head. His hands, covered in sweat, slipped against the cold steel. He wiped his hands on his shirt, trying to dry them.

He had to fight the fear, to survive. Part of him wanted to hide, to escape the fighting. But there was nowhere safe, and he had to find Sophia. And it wasn't the first time he'd been in a battle, that he'd had to duck as guns fired overhead.

Tom stood by the edge of the door, looking out, thinking. He could smell smoke and hear engines roaring, shots and cries from outside. Artur had an aircraft coming, a plan of escape, but Tom didn't know where it would land. And he wouldn't take it unless he knew Sophia was safe too.

Aircraft flashed by, NY3 Wolf Bat fighters, firing at targets out of sight. He'd have to be careful they didn't spot him.

He stepped outside and looked around. He was at the back of the Global Council building, by a drainage ditch designed to capture the heavy rains that sometimes fell on Justinian. Beyond were beds with bushes and flowers. It was tempting to think that he could hide behind them, but against drones with heat sensors and blipvid tech it would be useless.

He just had to push on. He'd go round the edge, looking for Artur, looking for a way to B Island. There was the monorail, but it seemed too obvious a target for the Earth Firsters and BCC.

Then Tom remembered something: his embeds had comms controls. Could he use them to contact

Artur, to ask where to rendezvous? Or to blip Sophia to find out where she was going? She'd know what to do.

He was about to blip her when he saw a security drone, speeding towards him.

"Halt," it said. "You are under arrest."

Instinctively, Tom pointed the JustForce rifle at it and pulled the trigger. The rifle made the noise of an angry bee sneezing, kicked as if it were punching him, and a projectile flashed towards the drone, exploding on impact. The drone fell from the sky in flames, and Tom breathed again, but his heart was pounding, fear kicking in after the threat.

That was close!

The drone's appearance made Tom paranoid about using his comms. *Best find out what's going on first.*

He worked his way round the building. It took longer than he expected; he tried to run, but he was tired, and the railgun rifle was heavy. It had been impressive, though, when used on the drone.

He could see other delegates running, ducking behind bushes, and once he had to leap over a body, face down, JustSec shirt covered in blood.

Would he live to see Sophia again?

He thought of his mother, far off on Mars. At least she was safe.

There were explosions from afar and Wolf Bats roared overhead, lit by a set sun no longer visible to Tom, their railguns alight, their distant targets identifiable only by the pillars of smoke that arose from where they'd hit.

He reached the end of the building and carefully looked round at the main plaza. It was filled with Earth First militia, the Defenders. Above, NY3's Wolf Bat carriers hovered, waiting for a gap to land and disgorge more troops. Wolf Bat fighters and NY3 combat drones circled overhead, providing air cover. BCC security were marching out of the Global Council with what looked like prisoners – delegates with their hands tied behind their backs, pushed forward by guards.

Tom could see beyond the plaza to the monorail station, which swarmed with Earth First militia. There was no way he could take a train to B Island.

He was wondering what he should do when there was a giant flash, a solid line of light coming from C Island. It struck one of the circling Wolf Bats, splitting it into two flaming halves that crashed to the ground. The laser fired again, destroying another Wolf Bat somewhere over B Island, and the others scattered like startled rooks, diving low and fast to escape.

Simultaneously, a wave of battle drones appeared from the north, fighting machines, attacking the NY3 combat drones. Some fired missiles or railguns, while kamikaze drones exploded into shrapnel, taking down their opposition with their own destruction. Others crowded round a Wolf Bat, painting it with bright light, trying to blind its sensors, make it vulnerable. On top of the explosions, other battle drones were using sonic weapons, creating scream-like noises that pained eardrums and dug into the head.

Tom ducked and placed his hands over his ears, trying to block the noise. Far off, he could see a VTOL aircraft landing in the One Earth Park, protected by JustForce aircraft and TAC SpecOps craft.

That must be where Artur is!

But there was no way to reach him, not without being seen.

The battle drones fought each other like seagulls squabbling over food, angrily swooping over Tom's head, relentless. The Justinian air defence laser fired again and again, but then flights of Wolf Bats flew overhead towards it, their railguns alight. There were more explosions far off on C Island and the weapon went silent.

The Wolf Bats seemed more confident, flying higher in the sky like hawks, less defensive, taking the offensive to the JustForce aircraft. Tom saw Artur's VTOL launch itself into the sky and fly off towards the north, while the JustForce and TAC SpecOps aircraft remained to fight a rear-guard defence.

Tom felt totally alone. It was worse than the battle at Canaveral, with Sophia. Then he remembered something she'd told him, once: you could walk the monorail bridge, if it wasn't working.

He couldn't wait any longer; he had to go, at once, while the Earth Firsters were still distracted by Artur's attack. He started running towards the bridge, ducking low where there was cover. The gun was heavy, but he didn't want to dump it, just in case.

Tom had got about halfway to the bridge when he heard a monorail train approach, heading to B Island. It would get there first!

He swung the weapon towards the track and spotted a grey box. He didn't know what it was – whether comms, signalling or power – but it didn't matter. He fired. There was another satisfying explosion; this time the flames were riddled with sparks. Power then.

The train ground to a halt in a shriek of metal, sparks flying from the monorail.

Tom sprinted for the iron stairway that led up to bridge. He reached a metal door with "No Entry" on it that opened to his qID. He turned to quickly look behind him, at the burning wrecks of aircraft and scattered bodies, and saw a squad of Earth Firsters heading towards him.

Shit.

He fired down at the stairway and it exploded into a tangle of metal. That would slow them, but it wouldn't be enough.

Tom dumped the gun – it was too heavy – then started to run.

51: Sophia

Sophia looked at her mother, shocked, wondering what to do. There was no power, no comms, no Humai, and outside there were explosions and Wolf Bats crossing the sky, hunting for targets.

And Nina, what was happening to Nina?

Fear, for herself, her mother and her sister, threatened to paralyse her. Then she pulled herself together; she had to decide, to act. It was up to her. She was stronger than her fear.

"We have to leave," said Sophia. "*Now*."

"But where?" Her mother looked tired, on the verge of tears.

"C Island. They'll have TAC aircraft there, must do. We can command one of them using your qID."

"They'd never let us take off."

"Something will turn up. We can't just wait here for them to capture us," said Sophia. "We need to pack, just what's essential."

She ran to her room and grabbed a rucksack. What was essential? Usually it didn't matter – with a non-crazy society all you needed was a qID and access to the blipverse. But now the blipverse seemed down and their qIDs probably made them wanted by Earth Firsters.

Who were working with BCC.

She'd been marked by BCC for ages now and knew their capabilities. They had drones and trackers on the blipverse sniffing for qIDs. All her personal records were on the blipverse somewhere; she had nothing to take with her.

It was a warm evening, but she didn't know where they'd be going. She grabbed some colder-weather clothes, practical ones, and wash things and stuffed everything in the rucksack.

Oh, yes, smart bracelets, just in case.

And Nina's Moon rock. Whatever happened, she wanted to be able to give her that.

Her mother was waiting by the front door. She wanted her mum to hug her, to say it would be all right, to forget the craziness. But there was no time, so Sophia nodded, and they left, locking the door behind them then running for the fire escape. The lifts would be out, of course.

Outside it was getting dark, though the top of Cloud Heights still glowed red from the setting sun. A Wolf Bat swooped by, and they shrank against the nearest wall. Far off were explosions, and nearer to them she could hear gunshots.

"Do you have any weapons?" asked Sophia, fighting to control her fear. Planning helped, made her feel like she was in control.

Her mother shook her head.

"We ought to get one," said Sophia.

"Building security might have something," said her mother. "Let's have a look."

They went back into the building, passing the security desk, usually staffed only by samais. Behind was the apartment block's management office, which opened to her mother's qID. Inside was dark, lit by emergency lights and flashing alarms. The monitoring blip-walls were all dead.

There was a barely-used workspace with near-empty storage, but one cabinet contained a rack of fire extinguishers and a handgun.

"You take it," said her mum.

Why me? Sophia hadn't used a gun, even at Canaveral. She felt a wave of panic. But there was not time to argue. "Ok."

It felt cold and heavy to the touch. She had a quick look, checked out the safety switch, made sure it was on, felt proud she'd remembered to do so, then stuffed it in her jacket pocket. She had survived the battle of Canaveral; she would survive this too. It made her feel powerful, back in control. Anger returned, fuelled by adrenaline. She was eager to go, to run, to fight.

"Let's go!"

Outside there were a few others like them, trying to escape, but most were hiding at home, hoping the storm would blow over.

They were probably right to; the Earth Firsters only wanted the likes of the Kasparovs.

Sophia wondered about her friends and hoped they were all safe. But there was nothing she could do for them, not right then. And no one would want to harm any of the citizens of the Dynastic League like Ling Chan.

A pair of Wolf Bat carriers swooped low over them, heading for the monorail station. It wasn't far away now, around the next block.

But from the station came fire, heading upwards at the carriers.

"Someone's still defending it. They'll be allies – quick, let's run there!"

She could run, but found her mother was too tired, too old, too weighed down, so they slowed to a fast walk. Rounding the corner, they saw a JustSec squad holding the square and monorail station.

"Look, Mum, JustSec!"

Maybe it would all be ok.

The Wolf Bat carriers darted left and right, evading fire heading upwards to them. Then a flight of Wolf Bat fighters flashed across the sky, railguns glowing with heat, firing down. The monorail station exploded, throwing JustSec soldiers into the air, bags of flesh spinning across the sky.

Sophia ducked, terrified; nowhere was safe. Her nightmares of Canaveral had become real, here in Justinian. Her energy drained and she began to tremble.

It was all too much. *Make it stop!*

Suddenly, there was a blast of light from C Island, a flickering line that flashed first towards A Island, piercing a Wolf Bat in two, and then again, this time at a target over B Island. This Wolf Bat was hit on one side, panels flying off. Trailing smoke, it spun faster and faster as it fell till it crashed in a burst of flames, smoke, debris and water.

"Where did it fall?" Sophia's voice shook, she couldn't control it.

Even with the fear, she had time to wonder about the light and the crash. But her mother seemed numb, unable to take it all in.

"It looked like it took out the bridge to C Island," Sophia said. Her brain wouldn't stop, even for this battle.

"It doesn't matter, the monorail is down," said her mother, pointing at the wreck of the station. She crumbled, her legs collapsing under her, leaving her squatting on the ground.

More Wolf Bat fighters flashed across the sky, weapons alight. There were explosions on C Island near the source of the laser.

"Don't you get it, Sophia?" said her mother. "They are winning, we are lost. And Artur…" She spat on the ground. "He did that to our Nina, to my Nina." She turned to Sophia, her face twisted by rage and tears. "How could he?"

Sophia didn't know what to say. She wished Tom was there, to have someone else she could talk to, rely on.

That's it!

"Mum, we can still escape, trust me. The marina – they won't think of that. We can get a boat, sail out of here. It's already dark, soon it will be night. We'll have a chance."

"A boat?"

Her mum was thinking it over, but Sophia knew she was right. "Yes, if we're quick we can get ahead of them. Once we're on the mainland we'll be safe. Well, safer."

Her mother sighed, but then stood up. "Ok, let's go."

They turned from the monorail station and headed towards the marina.

52: Daniel

Daniel watched as the carrier Wolf Bat landed in front of them. The GC had been secured, all opposition captured or killed. He stood behind Cita Stone and Erik Larson at the centre of things. Cita had said he would take over from Nails.

No longer would others push him around.

Judith had been fearful when he'd approached her, and had sworn her loyalty. She hadn't had much choice. But they needed her to control EuroCore, to fight Mr Bevan on their behalf, and she knew that. Benefits to both.

The carrier's doors opened, and Daniel and the others boarded. It was the NY3 command ship, the wide space where troops usually sat in rows replaced with screens and comms. Inside he spotted Fran and some of her assistants, embeds plugged in, tracking the battle, blipvids flowing, showing images from the three islands and skies above.

Fran unclipped from the virtual glasses and ear-comms to talk to them.

"We have control of Justinian airspace, but it looks like JustForce fired the defence laser to cover the extraction of Artur Kasparov in that TAC VTOL. We lost him."

"Pity," said Cita. She had to speak loudly to be heard above the throb of the Wolf Bat's engines.

"It's serious," said Erik. "Zeus says we need to capture one of the Kasparovs. It's essential for the rest of the plan that we have someone from their inner circle we can use to access their assets."

"The rest of them must be on B Island" said Fran, "as the monorail station there's been destroyed, plus the tracks to the other islands are out."

"Our intelligence is that three of the Kasparovs were at home: Anna and her two daughters," said Erik.

Daniel saw their faces appear on Fran's screens; he would remember them.

"They must be our priority." Cita turned to Fran. "Take us there."

"Strap in," she said. "We'll fly you over to B Island, together with a couple of carrier Wolf Bats with troops and fighter Wolf Bats for air cover."

Fran returned to her virtual glasses and ear-comms, dictating instructions to her team.

Daniel found a seat at the back, just in time before the doors closed and the nose of the aircraft rose, pushing him back. The engines roared and the aircraft pulled high gs as it took off, then, when airborne, dipped forward. On one of the blip-walls, he could see the view ahead, a rapidly moving jumble of buildings, and on another, a blip-sim of the airspace over Justinian. It was too loud to hear anything, but then he spotted the headsets the others were wearing and put one on. He could hear them talking.

"We think that the Martian, Tom Tesla, escaped A Island across the bridge," said Fran. "He downed a drone with a railgun rifle, then shot out the monorail power."

"A nuisance," said Cita.

"Zeus identifies him as a secondary target," said Erik. "The priority is to capture a Technocrat with a high security clearance qID."

They were about halfway across. On the blip-sim Daniel could see their carrier amongst others, escorted by fighter Wolf Bats and drones. Suddenly, alarms went off, and on the blip-sim Daniel could see red dots, hostiles, approaching fast, waves of them.

"Incoming," said Fran. "Looks like a concerted JustForce and TAC counterattack."

"We should land," said Erik. "For safety."

"Yes, do it," said Cita.

Daniel's stomached dropped away from him as their carrier Wolf Bat dived for the ground, pulling negative gs. On the screen, he could see the fighter Wolf Bats and battle drones break away from them, heading towards the new threat.

"It's the return of the flights that left earlier, the ones that provided cover to the secure transport," Fran explained.

"Zeus has been tracking that group. The lead theory is that it was providing security for the departure of TAC's AI, Humai," said Erik.

"Interesting. Did it realise it was facing defeat?"

With a roar of engines, gravity returned, and they landed, heavily, the carrier's legs groaning as they absorbed the impact.

"Get out, quickly," said Fran.

They tumbled out, finding themselves in a small, unlit park at the edge of B Island. Around them, other carrier Wolf Bats were landing on the grass and disgorging troops. Faces appeared yellow, lit by the aircraft's flashing lights. Above them, the twilight was filled with battling drones and fighters, Wolf Bats and JustForce, tumbling and darting across the sky. The dusk was lit with explosions, railgun fire, illuminating lasers and the glowing darts of missiles.

Cita had stayed by the carrier door, talking to Fran, and Daniel got closer, eager to hear what they were saying.

"The attack is focussed on B Island," said Fran.

"So, they could be trying to rescue the Kasparovs?"

"Yes."

"Hold them off," said Cita. "If you don't let any of them land, our forces here will give us the upper hand."

"Agreed."

The carrier door slammed shut and it took off along with the other Wolf Bat carriers, their engines shrieking and blowing oven-hot air over Daniel. He ducked down, covering his face and ears.

When they were gone, Cita called him over. She still had her headset, to talk to Fran.

"We need to capture a Kasparov," she said. "Not kill, capture."

He felt the thrill of power, again. He'd be the one capturing the enemy!

"Fran says there was resistance around the monorail station; the Kasparovs will have been drawn to it. We should start there."

"But someone should secure the bridges," he said.

"Good idea."

Daniel waved an arm at the captains of the nearest squads.

"With me," he said, then gave the orders, like a commander, like Nails, like those that had tormented him. "Your two squads, seize the access to the bridges to A and C Islands. Capture or kill anyone trying to get on or off."

"Yes sir."

Sir! They'd called him sir!

"The remainders," he said, "follow me."

53: Tom

Tom crouched over, panting, legs wobbling, feeling sick and scared. He'd never run so far so fast, and it wasn't over yet. Behind him, he could just make out the first signs of pursuit; the Earth Firsters must have managed to climb up to bridge level.

Overhead, Wolf Bats flew, firing at targets dotted across the islands and dogfighting with JustForce aircraft. Battle drones swarmed around opposition battle drones, exploding in shrapnel. There were fires burning on all the islands, the flames lighting columns of smoke as they rose into the sky. He hoped the growing darkness would hide him, but doubted it. Their systems were too good, their tech as advanced as TAC's. But it wasn't much farther now.

He started running again, thinking, as he went, what he'd do when he got there, where Sophia might be. He was been wondering how to get off the island when the answer came to him, looking down at the water under the bridge. They'd get a boat, they'd sail, like they did before.

She would think of it, just as he had, he knew it. So, he should head toward the marina, just as Sophia would. It was as if they had talked about it, he was that certain.

A dozen carrier Wolf Bats flew low over the water, landing on a park at the edge of B Island to disgorge hundreds of Earth First fighters.

Best avoid them.

Then he was there, he'd crossed the bridge, he was on B Island. At the far end of the bridge there was a comms tower, and he considered trying it out. What would he lose now? They must know he was there.

He activated his embeds.

<BlipComs.On>

<BlipComs.Query qID=Sophia.Kasparov>

He waited, but there was no response. She was not on the blipverse.

Tom wasn't that surprised. The islands were in a mess, systems and power all down, early targets of the Wolf Bats.

<BlipComs.Query qID=Anna.Kasparov>

If he could contact Sophia's mum, then she could pass on a message.

Nothing.

There was one last name, but he hesitated before signalling it. He was still processing what Cita had said about Mars. But he had to try.

<BlipComs.Query qID=Artur.Kasparov>

After a beat, it responded.

<qID=Artur.Kasparov BlipComs.Active>

<qID=Artur.Kasparov Tom? Is that you?>

He had to concentrate to communicate over the embed's interface.

<BlipComs.Send Yes. Where are you?>

<qID=Artur.Kasparov Current operation attempt recover Anna and the girls. Are you with them?>

<BlipComs.Send No, think they're heading for marina>

<qID=Artur.Kasparov Try to join them. Will only get one shot at this>

Tom looked towards the park where the Wolf Bats had landed and could just make out a squad heading his way, causing a stab of fear and adrenaline.

<BlipComs.Send Have to go>

<BlipComs.Off>

Then he ran down the metal stairwell as fast as he could. He had to get away before the Earth Firsters arrived.

At the bottom, he looked around. No one nearby. He ran for cover, towards the marina, checking the skies above.

In the growing darkness, the aircraft seemed to be fading into the shadows, becoming ghosts, sometimes lit by weapon fire or engine burns. Tom felt he could follow the rhythm of the battle by the speed and intensities of these lights, like fireflies quarrelling across the night sky. The conflict was building, he could tell, the lights more frequent, weapons firing more often and closer.

A wave of explosions ripped across the sky, and half a dozen Wolf Bats were illuminated in their deaths, broken in pieces, falling from the sky. One Wolf Bat remained whole but was damaged. Glowing in flames, it descended, spinning out of control, heading toward Cloud Heights.

BCC's kilometre-high tower had stood alone, untouched, as the battle raged around it. It had caught the last light of the setting sun and was now illuminated by fires and battle-flares. The wounded Wolf Bat crashed, screaming, into its trunk, near the base, exploding in a ball of flames. For a moment, it seemed the tower would be undamaged, that it would survive. Then cracks appeared and its carbon nanofibre shattered. The tower split into three pieces, and the cylinders at the top slipped sideways and began their long descent.

Cloud Heights was falling.

54: Sophia

Sophia and her mother were hiding in the shattered doorway of an apartment block when Cloud Heights was hit.

They hadn't got far before the battle accelerated over their heads, and NY3 and Earth Firster aircraft flying low over B Island forced the Kasparovs to seek shelter. Security drones had flown by slowly, scanning as if they were searching for something. Or someone.

The darkness would help, but the sky was lit by explosions and fires across the three islands. And machines could see so much better than humans.

Looking above her, Sophia saw an invisible weapon hit a Wolf Bat. One moment it was flying smoothly, controlled, the next there was an explosion on one side, where its wing met its body, and it began to spin, tumbling down, faster and faster, heading towards the base of Cloud Heights. She didn't see the impact itself, though she heard and saw the explosion.

For a moment, Sophia thought that Cloud Heights would survive, that BCC's power and wealth had made it untouchable, invincible. Then the tower broke into three pieces and the coin-shaped cylinders at its top began to descend.

"*Oh my god!*"

She stuffed her fist into her mouth, unable to take in what she was seeing. It took long seconds for the golden cylinders to fall, long enough to wonder at them sticking together, falling in a group like a handful of coins.

She recognised some of them, had memories from her visits. That was the garden – she could *see* plants, trees fly off – and next to it was the ballroom, where she'd first talked with Alejandro, learnt his full name, met Pepe and Yeliz. She remembered looking over its edge; it had been a long way down. Below was the cylinder with the living quarters; Alejandro had told her about it, but she'd never visited. And at the base, the one containing BCC's cores where his father had lived.

Was Felix in there now? If so he'd be in free fall, weightless, as she had been in space.

It took so long to fall.

Cloud Height's cylinders had tilted over so far they were nearly vertical and beginning to separate. Faster and faster, eating up the distance.

She imagined being inside, imagined the terror. But she couldn't look away, transfixed by the disaster.

Cloud Heights smashed into the ground. Its impact was hidden to Sophia by nearby apartment blocks, but she saw the explosion mushroom over the island, lighting it as if it were daytime. Flames, smoke and wreckage were flung into the sky. Debris rained down around them and they shrank into the doorway to escape it. Shocked faces appeared in windows, residents alarmed by the noises, then they disappeared, scared, back into hiding.

She imagined the cores vaporising. So many bits of information lost, more than she could imagine, more than could be counted.

Sophia felt dazed, dead inside. It was too much to take in. Had Cloud Heights really just collapsed into flames?

She and her mother exchanged wide-eyed looks.

"The idiots," said her mother. "BCC was an ally of the Earth Firsters."

"But the people," said Sophia. "What happened to them?" She knew some of them. Pepe and Yeliz and the others – had they been inside during the fall? Had they survived?

Her mother shook her head. "Crazy, crazy, crazy. Just stop this!" she cried aloud, but no one was listening.

"Listen, Mum," said Sophia. "We should run, now, while they're distracted."

Her mother shook her head and wiped some tears from her eyes. "It won't be safe."

"Nowhere will be," said Sophia. "We have to risk it."

She turned and hugged Sophia. "I want you to be safe," she said. "After what Artur has done to Nina, I won't let anyone hurt you. I promise."

Sophia hugged her back. She wanted to break it off and get going, but it was hard to refuse a mother's embrace.

A VTOL flew low over the square, spotlight flicking from side to side, hunting.

Sophia recognised the aircraft, then spotted the "TAC" logo on the side.

"Mum, quick," she said. "It's Dad, he's come for us." She knew it was him, it must be him.

Her mother spat and then sat down, refusing to follow.

"That man," she said. "He betrayed me. Imagine agreeing to do that to our Nina – his daughter, my girl. I'm not going with him. I've done with him!"

"Mum, no!" said Sophia. "We must get away!"

"Not with him, not after what he's done! Never."

There was a wave of explosions, the crack of hypersonic weapons, and the battle returned. The VTOL's engines powered up and it spat out drones, diversions, flares then accelerated, fleeing. Drones battled drones, exchanging missiles and railgun fire. Some fell from the sky in flames, others followed the VTOL. Wolf Bat fighters appeared from behind buildings, flashing across the sky, hunting, firing.

Dad can't have seen us, Sophia realised. He wouldn't be coming back.

The square quietened as the fight shifted to other parts of the island. The apartment blocks around them were lit by the flames from fallen drones scattered across lawns and walkways. In the sky above, stars were coming out, dots in the spaces between clouds lit by fires across B Island.

"We have to go," said Sophia. "We can't stay here!"

Again. It was happening again: she was in another battle, like at Canaveral, where JT had been killed. This time she felt more determined, able to manage her fear and decide what they had to do. She felt stronger, but also nearer an edge, her limit, her head aching with the stress of always pushing herself.

"We must get to the marina, quickly," she said. Tom would be heading there.

Her mother seemed lost inside her thoughts, crumpled on the ground.

"How did we end up like this? Why didn't Humai warn us?"

Sophia tried another tack, to be gentle.

"Mum, please." She crouched down to her level, stroking her hair then holding her hand. "You have to help me, us, to get away."

Her mother sighed, then sat up straight. She seemed to be drawing on inner strengths, but Sophia could sense it was a show, to reassure her. She stood up. "Let's get going."

They left the cover of the doorway and turned right, heading towards the marina. The path curved through a small park between apartment blocks. The sky was red with flames and the trees cast dark shadows. Sophia could smell pine leaves and smoke.

At the far side of the park, they saw lights approach and they quickly left the path to hide in the dark cover of trees. From behind the trunk of a cypress tree, they watched. It was a squad of Earth First soldiers with torches, cones of lights, hunting for something, someone. Sophia looked around the park and saw other groups approaching, cutting them off.

Her heart beat faster, terrified. They were going to be caught. She looked at her mother, watching her expression change from resignation to determination.

"Sophia," she said softly.

"Yes, Mum?"

"I want you to do exactly what I say."

"Mum?"

"Give me the gun."

Sophia pulled it from her jacket pocket and handed it over. She noticed her hand was shaking.

Her mother gave her an intense look then kissed her forehead.

"Escape this," she said. "Promise me you'll escape. Find Nina and save her. Promise?"

"Mum… What's this about?"

"*Promise me!*"

"I promise. But what are you going to do?"

"Save my daughter," she said, then walked out of the shadows and straight into the light of the Earth Firsters' torches.

Mum!

Her mum was spotted by the soldiers, who shouted at her to stop, pointing their guns in her direction. But she kept walking.

"Run!" she cried out to Sophia. "Run!"

Sophia's mother walked towards the Earth Firsters, head up, determined. She pointed her gun towards the sky and then fired, shot after shot.

"*Run!*"

55: Daniel

For Daniel, the fall of Cloud Heights had been a spectacle, not a disaster. The cores room had been alien, full of the technology he'd been taught to hate.

Demons! Traitors!

He remembered the man, Felix Fernandez, lying on his back on a bed, then raging, before being soothed by the woman in the green dress. He remembered an eagle and a tiger jumping up to wink at him.

Had the tiger escaped?

Erik seemed stunned, his cold face whiter than normal. He waved his hands, commanding his systems, calling out to contacts.

"It's gone, it's all gone, everything's gone. Felix Fernandez is dead, he must be."

"And Zeus?" asked Cita.

"Is safe. Not here, but on C Island."

Cita smiled. "So now I am the only one with control."

Erik seemed shocked, turning to her, mouth open. "What would happen if there was no one left with control?" he said. "We never thought of that."

Daniel wasn't interested. He wanted to prove himself, to show he was worthy of taking over from Nails. He had to capture the Kasparovs.

He turned to his squad, a mix of Earth First soldiers and NY3 specialists.

"Spread out," he said over his blipcoms. "Split into three groups to cover more ground."

Daniel turned to the NY3 specialist, Giselle. She repulsed him and made his skin crawl, her head full of embeds and her eyes glowing with electronic light, but she had capabilities he needed.

"Cover the central area with surveillance drones."

There was no point waiting there.

"Give me your torch," he commanded the nearest soldier.

They moved out in three directions, heading up different boulevards. Daniel swung his torch from side to side, its cone illuminating doorways, windows, trees, bushes, pathways, broken drones, debris, smouldering wreckage. The others followed him, their torch cones joining with his, the gaps of darkness becoming fewer, hiding places exposed.

They would find them.

"Sir, the security drones have spotted something."

It was Giselle. She swung her head left and right, slightly lowered, her eyes being fed images from the drone somewhere over the island.

"We have infrared signatures of two women that match the description of the targets."

"Where are they?"

"In the small park behind that building," she said, indicating the spiral apartment block to their right.

Daniel nodded. "Instruct the other two teams to circle round to that park, covering the exits."

Excitement flowed through him like a hunger.

He would have them!

"Follow me, hurry!"

He ran towards the park entrance. The centre of the park was in shadows cast by tall trees. It wouldn't help those they were hunting, not when they had drones and so many eyes searching. From the far side of the park he could see more lights; the other squads were tightening the net.

He paused, cautious. He had to capture the women, not kill, that was what Erik had said, and Cita had agreed.

"No one is to fire unless I say," he said to Giselle. "Tell all squads."

She nodded, using her invisible and inaudible connections to spread the message.

Suddenly, a figure appeared out of the deepest darkness, a woman. Daniel recognised her from the images in Fran's command station.

It was her – it was Anna Kasparov!

"No one shoot, we need to capture her," he commanded over his blipcoms. "Move in and grab her."

Some Earth Firsters might be shot, some might be killed, but that would be acceptable. The sacrifice would be justified.

The woman fired her gun in the air, and everyone ducked.

"Grab her!" he ordered, and from all sides Earth First soldiers ran forward, unquestioning. They had taken their Memory and Belief.

But the woman didn't shoot at them; she continued to fire in the air.

"Run!" she cried, but they didn't, they kept moving towards her.

"The second target is escaping," said Giselle.

It didn't matter. Erik had said they wanted Anna Kasparov; she was the primary target. He would capture her.

He approached Anna and she lowered her weapon, pointing it at him.

"Halt," she said.

Daniel felt a moment of fear, then excitement. "Drop it," he ordered, pointing his gun at her. "And put your hands in the air."

As she obeyed, he felt a thrill, almost sexual. She was at his command. He was the master.

He grabbed her hands and pulled them behind her back, then tied them.

"Tell Cita Stone where we are and who we've captured," he said to Giselle.

He looked at Anna Kasparov, contemptuously. She was a traitor who had dealt with demons and now had been defeated. She was weak and he was strong. Daniel now understood how Nails had felt, the contempt and anger burning within. He kicked Anna in her legs, hard, just because he could, and it felt good.

Cita arrived with a large group of soldiers and Erik. Drones hovered over them, illuminating the scene, providing protection. Cita approach Anna and the two women sized each other up.

Anna Kasparov seemed beaten but still defiant. "You destroyed all Justinian just to capture me?" she asked. "Are you crazy?"

Cita smiled. "This is just the beginning, and you will help us finish it."

"I will never help you."

"But you will," said Cita. "You have your ways and means, and we have ours."

She turned to Daniel and nodded at him. He stood taller and stuck his chest out. He was Daniel and William and Nails and the Preacher and the Warrior and so much more. He was a killer and a murderer but that was ok as his cause was righteous, for he had the words.

The Words of Fire.

He was strong!

"After today, I have nothing left to lose," said Anna.

"But you have," said Cita. "We will show you."

Daniel smiled – no, grinned, viciously. After today, there was nothing that could stop them, no limits to where they could go. He'd proved himself to Cita Stone, to Mother Stone, to his leader.

They had just begun.

He had just begun.

56: Tom

Tom was running, again.

It was dark now, and the path around the edge of B Island was hard to see, but he knew that to get to the marina from the bridge over to A Island he just had to make sure the water was on his left and keep going.

And not get caught.

The waterside path looping around the island was usually popular in the evening, full of runners and cyclists, couples and families, but that evening he was alone. The path's low-level lighting, just bright enough to be helpful, just dim enough to be unobtrusive, was out. The whole island had been swallowed by a monster of darkness, apart from the fires, reminders of the battle, their red glow flickering over the clouds.

The occasional Wolf Bat patrolled the sky, but they and the drones seemed focussed elsewhere. Somewhere towards the centre of the island, thankfully.

He just had a handgun and a handful of bullets – not much against an army – and a hope that Sophia hadn't been caught, that she would be there, that she wouldn't have left another way.

When Tom was about halfway there, he could see the marina, its breakwater heading out into the sheltered waters between the three islands, and behind it a forest of masts pointing towards the sky, silhouetted against the red clouds.

Would she be there?

There was no one at the entrance to the marina, and the gates to the pontoons had swung open, emergency locks releasing automatically. The marina was empty, deserted. The boats bobbed mechanically, silent apart from the clanking of halyards.

"Tom!"

He turned, the fear in his heart easing at the sound of her voice. There she was, but different, changed. Her eyes were wide with shock, almost glaring at him, her mouth a frozen grimace, teeth showing. What had happened to her in all the chaos?

She flung herself into his arms for a quick hug then pulled herself clear.

"We must go," she said.

"Are you ok?" he asked urgently.

"Not now, let's go."

Sophia turned to look at the shore, her eyes darting, hunting, then headed down the pontoon, rucksack bouncing on her back.

"Where's your mother? And Nina?"

"They captured my mum," she said. "At least I think so. They might have killed her." She spoke with brutal frankness.

"And Nina?"

"Not now," she barked over her shoulder.

The pontoon buckled and twisted under their feet. She stopped when they reached the foiling yacht they'd taken out previously and flung her rucksack on its deck as if claiming it.

"This one?" asked Tom.

"Yes," said Sophia. "It's fast and silent, our best bet."

Tom climbed on board while Sophia started to release the lines from the cleats on the pontoon. She worked quickly, experienced, not skipping steps because she was in a hurry, but doing it efficiently.

What was Tom to do? She had mostly sailed it herself last time. But it could be fully automatic, she had said that. It was pretty smart apparently.

I wonder if...

<BlipComs.On>
<Yacht.Query Status>
The boat answered:
<Yacht.Status=Active>
But how was he to control it?
<Yacht.Query Controls>

It returned a flood of information. The speed units made no sense. What was a knot?

He responded:
<Yacht.SetUnits metric>

Sophia was next to him in the yacht's cockpit, staring at him. He must have looked odd, standing still, eyes fixed on some point far away.

"What are you doing?" she asked.

She had released all the lines but one, which she'd doubled up around a cleat so they could let it go from on board.

"I've accessed the yacht's systems," he said. "You know, from my embeds. I can control it, get us sailing."

"Ok," she said. "We should sail off the docks, without an engine, as quiet as possible."

He nodded.
<Yacht.Main.RaiseSail>

There was an electric whir, and the mainsail began to climb the mast. The yacht's head began to turn away from the pontoon, and Sophia eased the line, gently, then finally let go on one end while pulling on the other.

He was really glad the hull and sails were black. Harder to spot.

Maybe that's why Sophia had chosen it.
<Yacht.Routing Start=Marina.Entrance>

It responded, turning the wheel, pulling in the sheets, and the yacht began to sail, slowly at first.

Good thing it knows where we are.

Tom could hardly see anything in the darkness, but he trusted the yacht to sail itself. It left him time for Sophia. She had turned again to the shore, looking for anyone following them.

"What happened to Nina?" he asked.

He didn't know what to expect, whether it would be another grimace or snarl, but something inside her seemed to break and she started crying.

"She's dead. Or as good as."

He felt ice in his stomach. Little Nina?

"Dead? What? How?"

"It's Dad."

She turned to him and hugged him tightly, as if she wanted to break him too.

"Artur? What did he do?"

"He's using her for some sort of experiment, turning her into a machine."

"What do you mean?"

She pulled back and her face, covered with tears, was contorted by rage.

"It's called the Theseus Transform. It changes her brain from human neurons to AI-like photoluminescent nodes," she spat. "How could he?!"

"Seriously?"

It was if the battle had entered Tom's head. Doors opened into caverns of new ideas, of changing a whole brain, of Artur's betrayal, of him sabotaging the Mars landing. It triggered explosions of thoughts and memories as he tried to process what she said, the audacity of it all, until he felt dizzy.

"Artur did that? He never mentioned anything."

From within one of the caverns, a memory appeared, pivoting all he knew around yet again.

"But he couldn't have! He told me he was trying to rescue you and Nina."

"I saw him, in the TAC VTOL. But Mum didn't trust him for what he's done – to Nina! – behind her back! Secretly! Behind our backs!" Tom felt cold dots of spit on his face, symbols of her rage.

Would Artur really have done that?

The yacht had reached the marina entrance and was now asking for instructions. They had to get away, as fast as possible.

<Yacht.Routing End=Turkish.Coast>
<Yacht.SailMode AutoRace>

It seemed to tauten, like a horse about to gallop. The jib was unrolled and the mainsheet tightened. The foils were extended, and the yacht rose clear of the water, tension in the sheets audible in a hum of energy.

"He said something about the Theseus Transform," he said, remembering back. "I was there, at the GC when Artur authorised it. But he had no idea it was for Nina. Humai just said 'the candidate'." He felt he was trying to find calm waters in the thoughts in his head, and to reassure Sophia, somehow.

Sophia looked up at him. He could see the fires of a burning Justinian reflected in her eyes. They were wide, frantic. She wiped her face, then stamped her foot, as if trying to drive out her weaknesses.

"Humai said that? 'The candidate'? Dad really didn't know?"

"He had no idea," said Tom, urgently. "It was a bad time, Cita was really pushing hard, so Artur just said yes to shut Humai up."

He could sense Sophia take that in.

"It used him," she said. "Humai *used* us. And it's taken Nina from us."

Tom watched those eyes he knew so well. Dark eyes that he'd seen in so many dreams. Eyes that had reflected the hurt of losing Alejandro.

"It betrayed us." Her voice was harsh, and Tom felt a chill run down his back. "We trusted Humai with everything. *Everything*. And now..." She seemed to lose her voice, and he could sense her looking past him at the islands, already far behind them. "Justinian is destroyed. Mum is captured or dead. And Nina is not Nina anymore but a machine."

She pushed Tom away, turning her back on him to stare at the burning Justinian. Clouds of smoke billowed high in the night sky, lit from underneath by countless fires, their flames reflected in restless waters. Wolf Bats patrolled the skies, bright lights swirling through the dark.

"I promised Mum I would save Nina," she said.

The yacht was smoothly flying on its foils at over fifty kilometres per hour. Her hair blew from behind her into her face, obscuring her eyes, and she pulled it back into a knot.

Above them, the stars were bright and sharp, and it was cold. Tom began to shiver from the wind. He wanted to hold her, to feel her warmth, to reassure her as he had before, on the Moon, but she seemed too remote, lost in her anger.

Then she turned back to him, a silhouette and a harsh voice.

"I swore to her and I swear to you, Tom: I will save Nina. I will stop Humai, even if I have to fight every AI on Earth or out in space. It may be an AI, but she is my sister."

Tom nodded. Suddenly everything became clear, the ways forward in his head and life aligning. "Where you go, I go," he said.

"Thank you, Tom." She embraced him, kissing him hard, hungrily.

"We can fix this," he said. "Together."

It was a hope spoken as a promise, for he had no idea what they were to do, where they were to go.

"Together," she echoed.

With a creak of sails and lines, the yacht tacked, and it sailed through the night, heading for the coast, for their freedom, for their future.

Many thanks to the team at Rowanvale Books, in particular Ellie Owen.

Author Profile

John Pahl has designed a navigation and communication constellation for a Mars Polar Base and predicted mobile phone coverage within the Valles Marineris. After he had the mental image of a boy flying a blimp across the Martian plains, he began to wonder the hows and whys behind the image. This developed into *Martian Blood* and the Noctilucents trilogy. He first saw noctilucent clouds while sailing a yacht down the east coast of Greenland, but since then he has seen them from his home in London. This is his second novel.

***

What Did You Think of *Noctilucents 2: Selenium*?

A big thank you for purchasing this book. It means a lot that you chose this book specifically from such a wide range on offer. I do hope you enjoyed it.

Book reviews are incredibly important for an author. All feedback helps them improve their writing for future projects and for developing this edition. If you are able to spare a few minutes to post a review on Amazon, that would be much appreciated.

Publisher Information

Rowanvale Books provides publishing services to independent authors, writers and poets all over the globe. We deliver a personal, honest and efficient service that allows authors to see their work published, while remaining in control of the process and retaining their creativity. By making publishing services available to authors in a cost-effective and ethical way, we at Rowanvale Books hope to ensure that the local, national and international community benefits from a steady stream of good quality literature.

For more information about us, our authors or our publications, please get in touch.

www.rowanvalebooks.com
info@rowanvalebooks.com